Under a Starlit Sky

Also from EM Castellan

In the Shadow of the Sun

Under a
Starlit Sky

EM Castellan

Feiwel and Friends
New York

A Feiwel and Friends Book
An imprint of Macmillan Publishing Group, LLC
120 Broadway, New York, NY 10271

Our books may be purchased in bulk for promotional, educational, or business
use. Please contact your local bookseller or the Macmillan Corporate and Premium
Sales Department at (800) 221-7945 ext. 5442 or by email at
MacmillanSpecialMarkets@macmillan.com.

Library of Congress Cataloging-in-Publication Data is available.

ISBN 978-1-250-22606-8 (hardcover) / ISBN 978-1-250-22607-5 (ebook)

Book design by Mallory Grigg

Feiwel and Friends logo designed by Filomena Tuosto
First edition, 2021

10 9 8 7 6 5 4 3 2 1

For my parents

1662

King Louis XIV is twenty-three.

He rules France alone.

A year ago, he decided to make his father's hunting lodge at Versailles the seat of his power.

A safe haven away from Paris.

A dream palace for his court.

A gilded cage for the nobles.

The legacy

    of a

        Sun King.

SPRING

CHAPTER I

The enchanted clock in the salon chimed three o'clock in a bright outburst of colored paper and glitter, signaling the end of the party.

Yet the revelry had been winding down for some time already, and general indifference met the disbanding of the string orchestra. As the musicians stretched and exchanged tired nods, the scraping of their chairs on the parquet floor echoed in the unnaturally quiet gilded rooms of the *château*'s ground floor. Like a flower closing up for the night, Versailles gently drifted into sleep.

The train of my shimmering gown clutched in one hand, and one of my silk shoes in the other, I stepped gingerly across the cluttered floor. The king had decreed the party's theme should be "Nature, Nymphs, and Fauns," and the *magicien* in charge of the court entertainment, the Comte de Saint-Aignan, had made it so. Hours ago, a select group of Louis's relatives and friends had gathered in the newly renovated small castle, wearing all manner of magically enhanced costumes. Ignoring the April chill, they'd strolled in the manicured gardens, danced to Lully's latest compositions in the salons, eaten pastries off silver plates by the open windows, and drunk gold-dusted wines under sparkling chandeliers. For a while, music and chatter and laughter had filled the king's *château*, like a rehearsal of the grander entertainment he hoped to provide here soon for his entire court.

Now, however, the revelers scattered, some wandering off outside, others retiring to their chambers. A few still dotted the salons as I made my way to my own apartments: snoring figures collapsed on settees like puppets with their strings cut, giggling people shuffling along with their arms linked in an attempt at balance, flirting lovers still whispering in corners under the illusion of privacy.

And as the party slowly dissolved into the night, so did the magic conjured by the count. All around me the temporary scenery meant to turn the salons into hubs of lush greenery faded before my eyes. The ivy on the walls shrunk and crumbled, the flower garlands withered and fell to the floor, the feathers and glitter in the air vanished, and the candlelight dulled, casting long shadows onto the gilded ceilings. Fauns and nymphs turned human again, their glittering costumes now garish, the stains or rips sustained in the course of the evening like many faults in a formerly perfect painting. The cool night air coming in through the open windows billowed the sheer curtains like sails and dissipated the sweet smell of magic in the rooms.

My stockinged feet snagged on a thorny branch, and I released a sharp breath, my musing interrupted. With a wince, I stepped away from the already crumpling rosebush.

"Madame! Are you all right?"

A well-meaning gentleman appeared at my side with a respectful bow, his hands extended should I need rescuing. Dark-haired and dressed in a bottle-green outfit with lace fashioned in the shape of leaves, he sported a thin mustache and a familiar face, and I blamed the late hour and the excitement of the night for the moment it took me to recognize him.

"Charles Perrault, Your Highness." He bowed again. "In charge of literary and artistic matters at court for the benefit of His Majesty. Monsieur Colbert introduced us . . . ?"

He shot me a hopeful glance, and I hid my mortification at having failed to recognize him behind a grin.

"Of course, Monsieur Perrault, do forgive me. I'm afraid I'm very tired."

As if on cue, the draught from the open windows reached my fragile lungs, and I had to turn to cough into my handkerchief. Monsieur Perrault tactfully looked away. My illness was well-known around court, and he was gracious enough to not gawk until the fit passed. At last my breathing eased, and I put away my handkerchief with a reassuring smile. Concern was still etched on his features, however.

"May I be of any assistance, Your Highness?"

His gaze traveled to the shoe in my hand, down to my stockinged feet. Another wave of embarrassment shot through me, which I brushed away with a self-deprecating roll of my eyes.

"You're very kind. And I'm afraid you've caught me in quite a discomfiting position. As you can see, I have lost a shoe *and* my retinue, and even making my way to my apartments appears an endeavor fraught with danger."

I gave a pointed look at the disappearing rosebush and let out a theatrical sigh. Although I was playing my part and dismissing the whole situation with a laugh, I couldn't help but wish no one had noticed it. But this was the Sun King's court, where every step one took was scrutinized and gossiped about. However, as far as nosy courtiers were concerned, I could have had worse luck than running into Monsieur Perrault. Eager to please yet more discreet than many, he took the hint and held out his arm.

"May I offer you my company on your way to your chambers?"

I thanked him and linked arms with him, hopping over the remains of the rosebush to show him I wasn't at death's door nor above making fun of myself. It did the trick, and his eyes twinkled with amusement.

"Have you been working on any more of your fairy tales?" I asked to avoid an awkward silence as we ambled through the salons. I had enjoyed the story in verse, "Donkeyskin," that he'd published the previous year, about a princess with magical dresses who refused the marriage arranged for her. Hopefully the writer had more tales of this sort to entertain the court next winter.

"I have, Your Highness, thank you for your interest." A slight blush crept over his cheeks under my encouraging smile. "I've been writing a new tale, about a merchant's daughter whose wicked stepmother and stepsisters make her life miserable, until she marries a prince."

I widened my eyes, my curiosity piqued. "How does she manage that?"

"Thanks to a spell she goes to a ball in disguise, and the prince falls in love with her."

"Magic, a prince, and a romance?" I said. "People are going to love that!"

Despite my encouraging words, my enthusiasm was already waning. Unlike his previous tale, this new story sounded less daring in its content. A girl whose life was made perfect by magic and a marriage to a prince—this was pure fantasy.

In real life, the girl's magic was the cause of half her problems, and her husband the source of the other half. I shook my head to chase away my sudden bitterness, likely brought on by my weariness after a long night. Being a Source—the vessel for magic that a *magicien* could wield to perform a spell—had allowed me to serve my king, to defeat a dark *magicien*, and to save the life of the people closest to me. And being married to the king's brother had given me safety and love. None of it was perfect—magic had also brought danger into my life, and my relationship with Philippe was complicated by many standards—but it was real.

Oblivious to my train of thought, Monsieur Perrault blushed deeper at my compliment and shook his head.

"I do hope so, but I must admit it is still very much a work in progress. For instance, I can't fathom how the prince will recognize the girl once she's robbed of her magical disguise. I'm thinking of having her pass a test, but what, I don't know."

"I'm certain you will find the answer very soon," I replied in a confident tone. "You are a very talented man, and I, for one, am pleased you're among us at court." This last compliment undid him, and he muttered something incomprehensible as we reached the doors to my apartments. I dismissed him with a gentle wave. "Thank you very much for this lovely walk, Monsieur Perrault. I wish you a good night."

He bowed, thanking me in return, as a guard opened the gilded door for me.

"Oh," I added as an afterthought, one stockinged foot over the threshold. "And if you come across a lone silk shoe somewhere in the *château*, you will know it's mine."

He smiled with a nod, and the door closed behind me before I could hear his reply.

With a relieved sigh, I pulled out the pins holding up my long hair while I crossed the candlelit antechamber. My train trailed after me, its gems thudding against the parquet floor with each step. On any other night, at least three of my ladies would have been fussing over me at this moment, eager to help me with my gown, my hair, and the shoe in my hand. Since Athénaïs had left court to marry and Louise had started devoting all her time to her secret affair with the king, the Queen Mother had appointed new ladies-in-waiting to join my household. But they were all young and far more interested in finding their one true love or a wealthy husband than in waiting on me, especially on a night like this. As the party had unfolded tonight, they'd drifted off one by one, no doubt assuming the others would remain by my side and cover for their absence. And so by the time Monsieur Perrault had come upon me in the salons, I had been left to my own devices for long enough to have the time to be bored and annoyed with the world—and to lose a shoe in the gardens' *parterres*.

It was in those moments that I missed Moreau, the *magicien* in charge of the king's security whom the dark sorcerer Fouquet had murdered last summer at Vaux. Whenever I had found myself alone or feeling vulnerable at court after my arrival a year ago, he'd materialized at my side, always with a kind word and a helping hand. No one now filled his role, and tonight I felt his absence even more keenly than usual.

Excited barking inside my bedchamber distracted me from my thoughts and teased a smile out of me as I crossed my private salon. I pushed open the decorated wooden panel and dropped my lone surviving shoe to the floor, but the clunking noise it made as it hit the carpet was covered by my dog Mimi's welcome. I greeted her by scratching her belly and cooing at her, and called for a maid without looking up from her adoring eyes.

"I swear you love this dog more than me."

I gave such a start Mimi let out an alarmed yelp and tore out of my embrace. My heartbeat thumping against my corset, I stood up and took in my surroundings for the first time since entering my bedchamber. The heavy velvet curtains were drawn over the windows, lending a cozy darkness to the room lit by soft candlelight. My nightgown lay on a silk-upholstered armchair, and a *chocolatière* sat with porcelain cups and silver spoons on an ornate tray on my desk. And on my canopy bed, spread out in a lazy pose with his dark hair pooling on the embroidered bed-cover, rested my husband in nothing but his nightshirt.

"Philippe," I managed once my heart had somewhat settled.

"Henriette." He mimicked my tone with his eyebrows raised in irony.

"I . . . didn't realize you were here."

He propped himself up on one elbow. "So I gathered from the shock on your face and that small frightened noise you just made."

I coughed, the last of my body's reaction to the fright he'd just given me. A frown pulled his eyebrows together as I covered my mouth with my handkerchief, and he pushed himself off the bed.

While Mimi orbited around us in anxious circles, he steered me toward an empty armchair and poured some hot chocolate into a cup. The warm liquid soothed my throat a little, and I recovered enough to put my handkerchief aside.

"I really didn't mean to frighten you, my love," Philippe said, sheepish. He knelt in front of me, both his hands on my knees in the absentminded way he had of touching me. "I just didn't think my grand gesture would be upstaged by your tiny dog."

I suppressed a laugh to avoid sparking another coughing fit, then set aside the cup to give Mimi a reassuring pat on the head. She settled on the carpet, her tail wagging. Still acutely aware of the warmth of Philippe's hands seeping through the fabric of my dress, I met his gaze. Since he wasn't a *magicien*, his eyes weren't tinged with gold but were a reassuring shade of brown. Unlike his brother or any other *magicien*, he would only ever see me as his wife, never a Source. Knowing this meant I had trusted him even before I had learned to understand him.

"I'm all right, really," I replied at last. "I just wasn't expecting you here. I haven't seen you all night. Someone said you and Armand had absconded with ten bottles of wine and hidden in the gardens with all your friends."

He grimaced in false disbelief. "I have no idea what you're talking about, and I resent anyone who's been spreading such slander. Rest assured I attended my brother's tasteful party with all the expected decorum, and it is mere chance that we didn't cross paths."

This time I did laugh. Philippe's relationship with Louis was complex at best—he having been raised by their mother Anne d'Autriche in the shadow of his older brother so that he would never be tempted to challenge his right to the throne—but since the birth of Louis's son last November, the pressure of being his brother's sole heir had lifted off Philippe's shoulders, easing his interactions with Louis.

"See," Philippe said in a soft voice. "I made you smile."

Pushing thoughts of the royal family aside and echoing his earlier act, I tilted my head and pretended at naivete. "And what did you mean to do, if not frighten me?"

"Well." His expression turned mischievous. "I heard there was this beautiful princess who attended some very dull party in this castle in the middle of nowhere, and I thought, as a handsome prince with singularly good taste in clothes and unparalleled charms, I would seek her out and steal her away."

I rolled my eyes and shook my head at his antics, rising from my seat to hide my warming cheeks. This was how Philippe went through life: by jesting and pretending nothing was ever serious. It had taken months after our wedding for him to show me the real Philippe—a far braver, cleverer, and more able man than anyone took him for. A man I had fallen in love with.

"I fear you've been misled," I replied, choosing to play along so the mischief in his eyes would linger. "The princess you're thinking of is already married, and she doesn't need rescuing."

He gasped and stood back up. "No! What's her husband like?"

"Tall. Strong. You don't want to be here when he arrives."

He gathered me into his arms and began unlacing my corset. "I think I'll take my chances. The princess is very pretty."

I silenced him with a kiss, our lips meeting in gentle collision as his fingers deftly finished freeing me from my gown. It pooled around my feet, and Philippe lifted me up to take me to the bed without breaking our kiss. When my back landed on the bed-cover, I slid my hands along his neck down to his chest, opening his nightshirt. The familiar scent of his perfume mixed with the smell of hot chocolate in the closed air of the bedroom. I removed the fabric from his shoulder, but he pulled back to catch my gaze.

"It's very late. We don't have to if you don't want—"

I traced the side of his face with my fingertips, my earlier weariness and my coughing fit forgotten, all thoughts attuned to his presence in my arms.

"I want to."

A grin lit up his face. He leaned forward to resume our kiss, and the rest of the world vanished.

Afterward, we lay in the tangled bedsheets in the soft glow of the candles. One arm around my waist, Philippe played with a strand of my blond hair, the thudding of his heart back to an even rhythm under my hand on his chest.

"We ought to get some sleep," he said with a yawn. "Louis wants to return to the Louvre in the afternoon."

And so it went. The Sun King threw a party in his private castle, and we followed. He returned to Paris, and so did we. For as much as Louis wished for Versailles to be a *château* important enough to hold his entire court and to be the center of his power, it still was only large enough to welcome a small number of people, and it was too far from the French capital to lead the country from. His court, his ministers, his archives, his palace . . . everything was in Paris—much to his mounting frustration.

As the king's Source, I had helped turn the old hunting lodge in Versailles into the beautiful small castle it now was, but I knew it wouldn't be long before Louis asked for my help in making it even grander and bigger. The palace fit for the absolute monarch he wanted to be. I only hoped I would be up to the task.

Philippe coiled a strand of my hair around his finger, as much lost in thought as I was.

"Our return will please your mother," I replied.

Much to everyone's growing dismay, it had recently become clear Anne d'Autriche wasn't well. Called to her bedside, *magiciens* had shaken their heads in helplessness. As my own condition proved, magic didn't cure illnesses or stop death. Doctors had replaced the *magiciens* to attend to the Queen Mother, without any more success so far.

"She'll be pleased to see Louis, at least," Philippe said, a hint of bitterness in his voice.

It was rare for him to acknowledge the tensions within his family, and I kept silent in case he wished to say more on the topic. Instead, he released a sigh and kept toying with my hair.

My mind wandered, and the thought of Anne d'Autriche's illness reminded me of my encounter with Paris's best fortune-teller and her prophecy, a year ago now. At the time, the *magicienne* had frightened me with talk of four maidens coming to court to meet terrible fates: a broken heart, a fall from grace, a betrayal, and a death. The Queen Mother had been a maiden coming to court, once, and now her health was failing. Although I doubted she was the object of the seer's prediction, it prompted me to wonder again who the maidens were.

As time went by, maybe I ought to find out, before further

calamity struck the king's court. I liked to see magic as a gift, and such a prophecy, far from being a prediction of doom to come, could also be used to fight future dangers and change those maidens' fates. If there was anything I could do to stop disaster from happening, I had to act—the events of last summer had proven as much.

Philippe shifted under me, drawing me out of my thoughts. I had assumed he was falling asleep, but he appeared more alert than I had suspected.

"I have to ask you something."

A glance at his face showed sternness mixed with uncertainty on his features, so remote from the happiness he'd displayed until moments ago that my pulse quickened. I held his gaze. "Anything."

"You know the Duchesse de Valentinois," he started. "Catherine?"

I nodded, surprise at hearing the name at this hour and in this context likely plain on my face. Armand had nicknamed the woman the "diabolical duchess" on account of the fact she had made no secret of flirting with Philippe at a time when my husband struggled with his relationship with both his former lover and me. But as far as I knew, the duchess had now left court after her husband had become prince of Monaco in January. The now princess lived a thousand leagues from Paris, and I had to admit I had not spared her a thought since her departure.

"She said something," Philippe explained, "before she left. And I didn't think much of it at the time, but tonight Armand said something else, and he's always joking about these things, and I suppose it made me wonder—"

I stopped him with a slight pressure on his chest, my trepidation worsening. What on earth was he talking about?

"Philippe, I don't understand a word of what you're saying."

He dropped my strand of hair and pulled himself upright against the pillows to face me, all traces of earlier mischief gone. "She said Armand's in love with you."

My jaw went slack. My thoughts sluggish all of a sudden, I tried to come up with an answer, and found nothing to say. Armand and Philippe had been together since they were teenagers. It was only Philippe's marriage to me that had prompted my husband to choose between us, and he had chosen me, with the understanding that Armand would remain at court and I wouldn't object to their friendship. With time, I had grown fond of Armand myself, and I had hoped that the three of us were now past any awkwardness. I had obviously failed to account for the Duchesse of Valentinois's interference.

Finding my voice at last, I said the first thing that came to my mind. "But . . . Armand likes men."

Philippe snorted. "Maybe he's like me after all. Maybe he likes people. And he's always going on about how pretty and perfect you are."

My temper rose. The duchess's snide remark had upset Philippe, and I wouldn't have it.

"He says these things because he thinks that's what you want to hear. Because he thinks teasing us will amuse you. Because we're all friends, not because he's in love with me!"

But Philippe's gaze was unflinching. "He said it again tonight. And when I asked him about it, he just . . . took off."

"He was probably drunk!" I struggled not to lose my patience and to sound reasonable, when all I wanted was a chance to growl in the duchess's face. "And likely as flabbergasted as I am to hear you entertaining such ridiculous ideas."

He crossed his arms over his chest. "So he's never said anything to you? Never suggested anything when I wasn't around?"

I took a deep breath to calm down, and realized I now knelt on the bed without remembering when I had moved. I folded my hands over my heart, in the most sincere pose I could devise.

"He hasn't. I promise you. Armand is your friend, and I'm your wife, and he would never do that to you. As much as I would like to say otherwise, he loves you, and he likely always will, just like I do. So *please* forget the duchess's gossip and stop accusing Armand of such nonsense."

Philippe's stance relaxed a fraction, and uncertainty returned to his features. He knew I didn't make a habit of lying, and it seemed enough to reassure him for now. Still, as I nestled next to him again to try to get some sleep before dawn, I couldn't help but ponder how easily he'd believed the duchess's lie and how jealous his reaction had been. I had thought such dark feelings were the preserve of his brother.

I had evidently been wrong.

CHAPTER II

An early summons from the king rendered void my hopes of a lie-in.

"What does he want?" Philippe groaned from under a pillow as I read the short note brought in on a small salver by a servant.

"He just asks for me." I nodded my assent to the attendant, who retired with a bow.

A maid opened the curtains under Mimi's supervision, and I squinted in the daylight from my seat on the bed. Gray clouds filled the sky above Versailles, a drizzle dampening the atmosphere. Although I was a morning person, wool now seemed to fill my head and I yawned, all my moves sluggish. The maid offered me a glass of water, which I drank gratefully. The combination of the journey to the castle and the subsequent party had taken its toll on me, and I longed to be back home in Paris, where I would have more opportunities to rest with the king busy with affairs of state.

"Tell him you're not going," Philippe grumbled. "Tell him you're busy."

He crawled across the bed to grab my waist and rest his head in my lap. Memories of the previous night warmed my limbs, and his half-hearted protestations prompted me to caress his face in an automatic gesture of affection. With his eyes closed and his features still rumpled from sleep, his expression was so unguarded that it washed away any annoyance his earlier question about Armand might have brought on.

If I had come to understand anything about him in the past twelve months, it was that his insecurities didn't make him like his brother—arrogant and domineering—they set him apart from him. His life was so little his own that he was terrified to lose what he came to cherish. That included me, and, unfortunately, Madame de Valentinois had known exactly what to say before her departure to make him doubt himself.

I deposited a gentle kiss on his forehead and slid from under his weight. He let out another groan and caught my hand before I could slip away.

"What can he possibly want? Isn't the whole point of us being here for him to be with his mistress and leave the rest of us alone?"

He was right on that account. The reason Louis favored these small gatherings at Versailles—his love for the place notwithstanding—was that they allowed him to spend time with Louise away from court. Whether to spare his wife, Marie-Thérèse, or to avoid the disapproval of his mother, he was careful not to flaunt his affair in front of everyone. Instead, he left the queen with his mother in Paris to visit the renovated *château*, even if, I suspected, most courtiers were aware of the situation.

I kissed Philippe's hand to extricate myself from his grasp. Mimi followed me as I hurried to the service rooms behind my main chamber, where I splashed my face with water in an effort to gather my wits. I shivered in the morning cold, my bare feet unhappy with the chill seeping in through the wooden floor.

"Tell him he can only have you for half an hour." Philippe's voice filtered through the open doorway. "Then you need to come back here and eat breakfast."

I shook my head at his attempt at setting terms. We both knew Louis wasn't used to hearing the word *no*. And despite my weariness, I was intrigued by his request for a meeting. When I had married his brother a year ago, everyone had expected my duties to be the ones of an English princess at French court. But when I had been compelled to reveal I was a Source to save the king, my position had changed from one day to the next. All of a sudden the magic inside me made me valuable to Louis the *magicien* and not just Louis the king: his plans for an absolute monarchy and a dazzling seat of power required a potent Source at his side, and it wasn't long before events involving his former Crown *Magicien* Fouquet prompted me to accept this new position.

The fact that Louis wanted to see me now, while we were at Versailles, drove me to think he was calling upon me as his Source, not as his sister-in-law. In an effort to accede to his request promptly, I hastily washed and got dressed with the maid's help and hurried out of my apartments with no more than a quick parting word with Philippe. He grunted from the bed, and my dog jumped on the bedcover to keep him company while I was gone.

Louis waited for me in his antechamber, and he dismissed guards and servants as soon as I stepped inside his apartments, my breath wheezing after the short walk. He stood before two gilded stand mirrors, and for a heartbeat the thought crossed my mind he'd summoned me to ask my opinion on his outfit. The blue silk ensemble was trimmed with gold galloon and buttons, which glittered magically in the bright light of the many candles lit around the room. His long blond hair framed his face in the same way his brother's dark hair outlined his.

I muffled a cough into my handkerchief before giving him a smile along with my curtsy. "Good morning, Your Majesty. You asked for me?"

He surveyed me for an instant, his golden gaze seemingly taking in every detail of my rose gown, whose bodice and skirts were lined with tiny silk flowers and gems. His impassive expression softened, and he gestured for me to join him.

"Good morning, Henriette. Did you enjoy the party last night?"

The question was perfunctory, as his attention had already drifted to the mirrors before us. I gave an equally polite reply, my curiosity piqued despite my persistent weariness. The situation reminded me of the last time we'd found ourselves together in another antechamber with a mirror: at the time, we'd performed a spell to unveil Fouquet's plotting.

Following the same train of thought, Louis asked, "Do you recall our spell at Fontainebleau?" I opened my mouth to reply, but he went on without waiting for me to acquiesce. "Today I would like us to enchant these mirrors so one will allow me to see what's reflected in the other."

A slight frown tightened my brow. This was complex magic, which we'd never attempted before. The spell in itself was complicated, and it sounded like Louis wanted it to last for as long as possible. Magic was by definition ephemeral: spells lasted for a few minutes, a few hours, a few days at most. Few *magiciens* in history had had the power to cast long-lasting spells, Fouquet being the only one I had ever met. It turned out the price for his gift had been terrible. Many Sources had died by his hand before we'd defeated him in Nantes last September. As everyone doing magic knew, the more intricate the spell, the greater its dangers.

"It's an expansion of the spell we used last time," Louis explained, focused on his goal. "Instead of seeing what one mirror has seen, I'll be able to see what *this* mirror reflects in *that* mirror."

He pointed at each mirror in turn, and I nodded. I understood the principle of the spell: We had to make the mirrors both reveal what they witnessed and link them together, so one would be the gateway to the other. However, an uncomfortable thought crossed my mind: the memory of another linking spell, one Fouquet had forced me to perform to tie Philippe to Louis and murder them both. I swallowed, my throat still tingling from my earlier coughing fit.

Louis's confident gaze landed on me, oblivious to my misgivings. He offered me his hand. "Shall we?"

Calming my uneven breath, I slid my fingers into his. "What's the wording of the spell?"

As the Source, I was to speak the spell and to lend my magic to Louis so he could shape it into reality. I practiced saying the word a few times under my breath, getting used to its sound and weight until I could sense the power in it. Then I squeezed Louis's hand, schooling my expression into one of calm and confidence. Louis and I had worked well together on ambitious spells before. This was just another one of those.

We faced the mirrors.

"*Raccorde.*"

With self-assured practice, Louis drew my magic to him: the golden flecks floated toward the mirror on the right in a bright swirl. I held on to one with my mind and closed my eyes to follow it inside the first looking glass. There the enchantment scattered into multiple glittering particles, like stars in a clear night sky. They danced before my eyes, dazzlingly distracting. Hesitation gripped me for a heartbeat—which one to follow? Then an odd instinct whispered to me it didn't matter: I could just stay here and admire this wonderful spectacle for a while. Stargazing into infinity, a calm settled over me. Breathing was easy, or maybe I wasn't breathing at all. Time became suspended, my mind disembodied, and I couldn't have said who or where I was.

No matter, the night whispered again. *Stay and rest and watch. Reste et relaxe et regarde.*

I floated under the starlit sky, and let peace swathe me in a warm embrace.

Reste.

An icy draught crashed over me. Cold encased me, wrenching me away from the infinite firmament. *No!* I struggled against the ties bringing me back to earth, against the terrifying cold seeping through every pore of my skin, against the threads of my dream that threatened to turn into a nightmare. Noise filled my ears, and pain engulfed my lungs, and cold gripped my limbs. I screamed.

A shout echoed mine. "Henriette!"

I flailed, water splashing around me, light blinding me. More indistinct shouting deafened me. My breathing was ragged.

"Henriette!"

Something lifted me out of the water, and my limbs shook uncontrollably. My eyes fluttered open at last, and a gilded ceiling swayed above me. The pattern was familiar.

Versailles's gilded ceiling.

I was at Versailles, and I was drenched, and I was shivering, and I was weightless. The wall paintings moved past me, and all of a sudden I was wrapped in warmth again. Several silhouettes shifted at the periphery of my vision. I listened to my breathing until sounds resolved into conversations around me. Then one voice cut through the fog.

"Henriette, my love, look at me."

I blinked. My eyesight sharpened, and the silhouettes became people. Servants buzzing around a copper bathtub. Doctors in black robes gesticulating. My ladies clutching each other by the window. The bright figure of the king standing nearby.

"My love, just look at me."

Heaviness weighed down my body, and turning my head toward the familiar voice took more effort than I ever thought possible. As I moved, my listless mind kept inventorying its surroundings, like a traveler returning home after a long journey and taking stock of what had changed in their city. The pillow under my wet hair was soft, and the bed under me sturdy and motionless. The room was more heavily decorated than my own bedchamber, with golden patterns on every surface. The canopy above me was a midnight blue that reminded me of a night sky, without stars.

My gaze landed on the person at my bedside. Philippe's face was a mask of anxiousness, and tears ran freely down his cheeks.

"What—?" My voice a raspy whisper, I couldn't finish my question, unsure of what I meant to ask.

Philippe let out an incredulous gasp of relief and planted a fierce kiss on my cheek. "Oh, my love, you scared me half to death!"

He gripped my hand like a lifeline as the doctors and my ladies flocked around him, their voices overlapping in their eagerness. My mind still clouded by confusion, I focused on Philippe, whose gaze raked over my face as if trying to memorize every detail.

"Enough." The voice of the king slashed through the babblings of the gathered crowd. "She's awake. You may all leave now."

Philippe bristled. "I'm not going anywhere."

His gaze left mine to hold his brother's, and for a suspended moment, no one moved in the warm bedroom. My sluggish thoughts registered the sudden tension in the air, Louis's tense jaw and Philippe's defiant pout. I tried to form a sentence to stop them from arguing, but before I could speak, Louis waved the matter away.

"My brother will stay. The rest of you go."

The servants and my ladies were the first to shuffle outside, but the doctors hesitated.

"You too," the king said, his tone turning harsher with impatience. "We'll call you back when we need you."

Dismissed, the men left. As quiet settled over the room, so did the tumbling thoughts in my head. My mind clearer every second, memories of the morning flooded back: Louis, the mirrors, the spell.

The spell.

My pulse quickened. The spell had gone wrong, and I had become lost, and—

"Did I faint?" I asked, my voice already stronger.

Silence greeted my question, and my gaze went from Philippe's colorless features to Louis's stern expression.

"Henriette," Philippe said, his tone gentle, "you were unconscious for over an hour."

I blinked at him, then looked at Louis for a sign that I'd misheard him. "What?"

"We couldn't wake you up," Philippe went on, his tone still patient. "Until the doctors suggested we plunge you into a cold bath, but then you stopped breathing—" His voice broke, and he wiped more tears off his cheeks with his shirtsleeve.

It struck me then that his shirt was soaked, his coat discarded on the floor. Horror at what had happened and guilt at having scared him engulfed me. My breath caught in my throat, and I coughed, my eyes watering. With soothing words, Philippe lifted me and rearranged the pillows until I sat upright in the bed. My breathing eased, my lungs shuddering with each breath.

"I'm sorry," I said, unable to find anything else to say. "I'm sorry."

Not only had the spell failed because of me, but I had also

let myself be caught in it like a neophyte stumbling through their first enchantment, causing everyone a fright and sending Philippe—whom I had sworn never to hurt—into a frenzy of worry.

My apology felt inadequate, but it was sincere, and I turned to Louis to ensure he knew it was so. His face unreadable, he didn't acknowledge my words.

"We're just glad you're alive," he said instead.

"I'm sorry about the spell—"

But Philippe cut me off with a growl. "No one cares about the bloody spell."

"Actually, I do," Louis snapped back, his tone cold.

Both brothers stiffened on opposite sides of the bed. All of a sudden the tension in the room was palpable, and I raised a weak hand in an attempt to stop them from arguing.

"Please—"

My plea went utterly ignored, as Philippe stood up.

"This ends now."

A hint of disbelief crossed Louis's inscrutable features. "I beg your pardon?"

"You heard me," Philippe replied, anger swiftly replacing distress in his expression. "I'm putting a stop to this nonsense. From now on, you will not use Henriette for her magic anymore. You can find another Source for your self-aggrandizing plans."

Louis snorted. "This has nothing to do with you, and you don't get a say in these matters. Or shall I remind you who's king here?"

"Shall I remind you who's her husband?"

He was shouting now, and my temper rose alongside his. The

two of them were talking about me as if I weren't even there. As if they were still boys and I was a doll they were arguing over the ownership of.

"Stop it," I said.

But Louis raised his voice to answer his brother, and my command was lost in the noise.

"Henriette being a Source has nothing to do with you! Her duties to me have nothing to do with her duties to you. You do not get to decide anything on this matter."

"She nearly died!" Philippe shouted back. "Are you so arrogant that you can't see that? When does it stop, if not now?"

I had enough. Anger warmed my skin and tightened my lungs. How dare they behave that way in front of me? I was a princess. I shoved aside the blankets wrapped around me and pushed myself off the bed. My unsteady feet landed on the floor and I wobbled, but I followed my momentum and my irritation, gripping the bedcover for support. My breath came out in wheezing gasps.

"Stop it!" I barked. "Stop it, the both of you!"

My lungs hurt. My limbs hurt. Dark spots danced across my vision, and the room oscillated like a pendulum.

"Stop it," I repeated.

But the weak sound that came out of my mouth didn't match the indignation lacing my veins. The gilded room tunneled into a dark corridor, and the bedcovers slipped between my fingers like eels. The world became silent again, and then dark.

* * *

Light filtered across my vision, like golden filigree across a black fabric. I squinted against the brightness but forced my eyes to open. The blue canopy of the king's bed greeted me again, and silence surrounded me. Candles had been lit to chase away the shadows of the gloomy day. Embroidered bedclothes covered me, and the sweet smell of magic permeated the air.

"Louis and Prince Aniaba performed that spell on the air so you'd breathe better."

Turning my head was easier this time, and I met Philippe's gaze. He sat in an armchair by the bed, alone in the bedchamber.

"How long was I . . . ?"

"Not long." He chewed on his lower lip, guilt and concern warring on his face. "And this time it was our fault, anyway. I'm sorry."

I nodded, grateful for the apology. He made a vague gesture at my lying form.

"How are you feeling?"

I breathed in the crisp scent of the room, filled with the smell of fresh-cut grass and sweet-blooming flowers. The magically altered air coated my lungs with ease and soothed my breathing. My mind clearer, I straightened against the pillows.

"Better, I think."

Philippe surveyed me for a moment, and I waited for him to speak.

"Louis is going back to Paris," he said at last. "With everybody. We'll follow when you've rested."

He paused, and I let him take his time, sensing he had more to say.

"I'm sorry about earlier," he added after a while, his voice low and calm. "It wasn't right to speak for you, but I still mean what I said. I think when it comes to magic, both Louis and you struggle to know when to stop. I'm not interfering because I'm your husband and I get to decide what you do. I'm interfering because you both seem to have lost sight of what should come first here. Your health. Your well-being."

He stood up and circled the canopy bed with slow steps.

"I don't pretend I know what it feels like to do magic. I'm not a *magicien*. I'm certainly not a Source. I don't know what happens when you cast a spell and reshape the world to your liking. What I know, however, is what it does to you."

He stopped his pacing to meet my gaze.

"And it's killing you, Henriette."

I opened my mouth to protest, then found it hard to argue. I *was* lying in a bed, my limbs weak as a newborn foal, with no recollection of how long I had been there. I bit my lip and remained silent.

"I can't stop you," Philippe added when I didn't reply. "If you want to be Louis's Source, I can't stop you. But I'm asking you— No, I'm begging you to stop. I don't want you to get hurt, and I certainly don't want you to die. So please. Get some rest. Get your strength back. Let Louis find another Source for now."

He knelt by the bed and grabbed my hand in his. "Believe me, his world won't stop turning if you're not in it. But mine will."

I held his gaze, thoughts of duty and magic and love tumbling through my mind. He was giving me a choice, yet of course it was no choice at all.

He was asking if I loved him more than his brother.

And the answer was yes.

CHAPTER III

───────────

Sparrows fluttered amid the buds in the chestnut tree branches above me, their chirping loud in the quiet afternoon. Removed from the Parisian bustle behind the brick walls of the Tuileries Palace gardens, I lounged in my reclining chair, the fragrant flowerbeds of the geometric *parterres* swathing me with a sweet smell.

Five days had passed since my return from Versailles, and it was my first time outside. Modern medicine argued that the crisp atmosphere of the outdoors would cause me more harm than good, but I chose to ignore the physicians' dire warnings in order to escape into my favorite place in the world: my garden. While Mimi investigated every scent under the trimmed bushes, I breathed in the fresh April air, relief at being freed from the suffocating confines of my apartments loosening my chest.

"Are you certain you're warm enough?"

Athénaïs tucked my blankets more firmly around me, fussing like an overbearing nurse. Her brow furrowed in suspicion, she surveyed the blooming flowers and clipped topiaries as if looking for signs of an imminent attack from Mother Nature.

"I'm perfectly all right," I replied, an amused smile tugging at the corners of my mouth. "Now stop worrying and tell me everything."

I grabbed her gloved hand so she'd stop fidgeting, and she settled in the wooden chair next to me at last. Her presence was my second treat of the day: Freshly returned to court, it was the first time we met after months apart. The last time I had seen her was at Versailles in November, when she was about to leave for Gascony to get married. She now returned as the Marquise de Montespan, dressed in a fashionable ruby-red gown that highlighted her dark hair and round figure.

"What would you like to talk about?" she asked. "Your doctors gave me such stern admonitions against getting you flustered that I scarcely dare broach any subject aside from maybe the weather."

My smile turned into a giggle. "Don't tell me you've started listening to advice from old men."

Her eyes widened in mock horror. "Never! Which is why I'm asking: What piece of gossip do you want to talk about first?" She gave me a conniving grin.

I squeezed her fingers, more solicitous than playful. "Tell me about you, first."

Last summer had seen her in love with Prince Aniaba, whom her parents had refused to consider as a possible match for her. She'd been distraught at the news of her arranged marriage with a provincial nobleman, and for a while I had feared her to be the brokenhearted maiden from the seer's prophecy. I had to know where her feelings stood now.

She waved the request away. "What's there to say? I'm back, which is the most important piece of news about me."

"What about the *marquis*?" I insisted.

She was my friend, and I refused to let her hide behind a mask of cynicism with me. Listening to her was the least I could do for her.

She rolled her eyes with a sigh. "My husband is exactly as you might imagine a twenty-two-year-old marquess from the southern confines of France who finds himself at the Sun King's court for the first time: embarrassingly eager and hopelessly unsophisticated. But we seem to get along for now."

Half-reassured, I was about to ask for details when she went on without prompting.

"And I saw Jean yesterday. I wouldn't say it was a delightful conversation, but it wasn't an ordeal either. Water under the bridge and all that, I suppose. He's busy with his work, nowadays, and I've moved on too, I suppose."

Jean Aniaba was a Source as well, and I knew the king had called upon him to assist with the artist *magiciens* he was gathering at court in preparation for the second phase of renovations at Versailles. The prince's magical gift was especially impressive when used for artistic spells, as his partnership with the Comte de Saint-Aignan had shown the previous year.

"In any case," Athénaïs concluded her own train of thought. "I hope now he and I can be friends."

"I'm sure you will."

"Speaking of friends," she added, her eyes bright again. "I

heard the most ridiculous rumor at the Louvre yesterday. I'm glad you're sitting down, because I nearly fell off my own chair when I heard it, I laughed so much."

I gave her an incredulous look, wonder at what nonsense was currently going around court pulling up my brows.

"They're saying that Armand is in love with you." She let out a laugh and shook her head. "Of all the absurd tales to spread! As if *anyone* is going to believe this foolishness for a moment!"

Cold that had nothing to do with the weather spread through my limbs. Was this why Philippe had broached the subject at Versailles? Because he'd known the story was going around court? My anger at the Duchesse de Valentinois rose in my chest anew, promptly replaced by disquiet.

Rumor was the poison of the French court. People loved nothing more than a scandalous piece of gossip to whisper behind fans at the gaming tables or over a glass of wine at dinner. The more shocking the tale, and the higher ranking its object, the better. Sometimes the rumor died out on its own, but other times . . . reputations could be tarnished in a few days, marriages ruined in a few weeks. I couldn't afford my hard-earned safety and place at court to be jeopardized by a malicious word from a spiteful courtier.

My alarm must have shown in my features, for Athénaïs's laugh died on her lips.

"Oh, Henriette, don't let it upset you! It's so outlandish no one believes it for an instant! I just told you because I thought it would entertain you."

I threw her a doubtful look, and she squeezed my hand.

"I promise you everyone I've heard mentioning it was doing

so to dismiss it and to share a good laugh with a friend. No one takes it seriously."

But someone had taken it seriously, to the point that he'd felt compelled to ask me about it. And for that reason alone, I needed this rumor to end now.

"But this isn't funny," I said. "And this has to stop. I don't want Philippe to have to deal with this."

"All right." Athénaïs's expression turned serious. "Then if I hear it again, I'll tell people off for spreading lies. You have nothing to worry about."

The hint of fierceness that underlined her words was a stark reminder that she had never been one to be underestimated at court. I had once been among those who dreaded her venomous tongue, and I was glad she was now on my side.

"It's already old news anyway," she added in an obvious effort to reassure me even further. "You know how courtiers are: give them a new shiny plaything to focus on and they'll forget the old one."

"So what's the new shiny one?" I asked, warmth returning to my body as my worry deflated. The French court *was* fickle, and if a more exciting piece of gossip landed at their feet, they would flock to it like scavenger birds.

"A newcomer, of course," Athénaïs replied. "They already call him the Angel, he's that handsome."

"A man, then?" I raised a skeptical eyebrow, my tone turning sarcastic. "More interesting than *me*?"

"Oh, yes," she said. "He's the younger son of the Comte d'Armagnac. Nineteen years old. Very clever and charming. Not the best catch pedigree-wise, but no one seems to care, and everyone's already under his spell."

How interesting. How long would it be before Louis took umbrage at this attractive charismatic nobleman? I wondered.

"I'll have to meet him, then," I said.

"You shall," Athénaïs agreed. "He's at every party. As soon as you rejoin us, I bet it won't be half a day before you two run into each other. The *Gazette* will headline: 'Madame and the Chevalier de Lorraine: The two most exciting people at court meet at last.'"

I acknowledged the compliment with a smile, even if her comment brought the topic of my health back to the forefront of my mind. Despite my eagerness to be active and part of the court's daily life again, my body still protested too much for me to do more than sit in a garden for an hour every day.

"Speaking of which," I said, "I think I'd better go back inside now."

Clouds had gathered above us while we chatted, and getting caught in a shower was the last thing I needed. At once Athénaïs stood up and her fussing resumed as she helped me out of the blankets and up from the chair. I called for Mimi, who bounded ahead of us with her tail wagging, and disappeared into the building.

Arms linked, Athénaïs and I made our way back inside, our feet crunching on the gravel path. The afternoon lull meant the corridors of the small palace were quiet, but as we reached the ornate entrance hall, a flurry of sudden activity greeted us: servants running down the grand staircase and erupting out of hidden passageways, all converging to the main door and babbling excitedly.

I stopped the first maid that ran past me. "What's happening?"

"Your Highness." She curtsied, breathless and flushed. "Has no one told you? The king is here."

Indeed the double doors now stood open onto the paved courtyard, where a gilded carriage surrounded by musketeers in blue-and-red uniforms was pulling up. A gust of wind blew through the vestibule, and the first raindrops hit the ground just as Louis made his entrance into my home.

A hush fell over the stuccoed hall at once, my whole household bending into deep bows and curtsies.

"Henriette, my dear, such a pleasure to see you well again."

Louis's hand rested on my forearm, and he landed a light perfunctory kiss on my cheek, which allowed me to rise from my own curtsy.

"Your Majesty." My mind spun with questions about the purpose of this unannounced visit, but I plastered the most gracious smile on my face to hide my surprise. "Welcome. Please, do come into the salon and leave behind this dreadful weather."

Footmen had already closed the main door to keep out the growing storm, though the wind rattled against the windows. I gestured toward the receiving rooms on the ground floor, confident the kitchens were already preparing an appropriate *collation* that would soon materialize before the French sovereign. But instead of following my lead, Louis's attention strayed to Athénaïs, still frozen in her curtsy. Now that he'd acknowledged her presence, I had to make the proper introductions.

"Your Majesty, I'm certain you remember the Marquise de Montespan, who's recently returned to court."

His intense gaze fixed on Athénaïs, Louis bowed. "And the French court is a brighter place for it."

The silence of the gathered servants in the hall was so thick that the rustling of Athénaïs's ruby-red skirts appeared to echo under the painted ceiling when she deepened her curtsy. A collective breath was held, as everyone waited for her to reply to the king's compliment. Other ladies might have blushed, stuttered, or played coy, but Athénaïs raised her bold dark eyes to meet Louis's stare.

"Brightening up a room is always my intention when I enter it, Your Majesty."

The hint of a smile played on Louis's lips, lightening his usually inscrutable expression. "Then I look forward to our next encounter."

Such talk would have elicited gasps at court, but here in my home, only the servants' stunned silence greeted the flirtatious exchange, as I stood to the side like an awkward supporting actor in a play without a script.

Before Louise, and despite his marriage to Marie-Thérèse, Louis had been a well-known womanizer. Handsome and powerful, his charms were often irresistible to beautiful women. Even I had briefly mistaken his interest in me for something more meaningful, and although the sting of that error had long faded, it made me aware of how easily my friends could fall prey to it too. Louise was still besotted with the king, and I refused to see her heartbroken. Athénaïs herself was still recovering from her breakup with Prince Aniaba, and I didn't wish to see her hurt any further. As previously proven, the French court could be such a nest of intriguing vipers that I would do my utmost to protect my friends from their bites.

Dismissed by the king's comment, Athénaïs curtsied again

and turned to thank me for my hospitality. Our exchange stifled by the king's presence, I returned her thanks and promised to see her soon, with a nod and a squeeze of her arm. Soon she was ushered out to her carriage in the rain, and Louis entered my receiving salon at last.

Maids and footmen buzzed in and out of the room for a moment, bringing in refreshments and various *pâtisseries* on silver plates. Taking off his gloves, Louis munched his way through several little cakes while I made small talk and pretended to drink coffee. His presence unnerved me, and the urge to fidget was strong, but I stamped it down.

The last time Louis and I had been in the same room, I had just failed to perform a spell with him and he was shouting at my husband. I had already apologized for the unsuccessful enchantment, but Louis's surprise visit renewed my guilt and worry. He counted on me to help him realize his dreams, yet Philippe was right: I had to acknowledge my limitations. The wheezing in my lungs, the dizziness that struck me when I walked longer than a few minutes, the sleepless nights and near-constant fever made it impossible for me to rejoin court, let alone do magic. But how did one break such news to the king of France?

Louis ate another *macaron*, and my anxiety rose further. Maybe his visit hadn't been prompted by his concern for my health or our failed spell. Had he heard the rumor about Armand? If he had, the situation couldn't have made him happy. If there was one thing the French royal family didn't need, it was a scandal. Good behavior wasn't required, but discretion was mandatory.

At last the servants' ballet ended and we were left alone. My throat dry with trepidation, I waited for Louis to speak first. Wiping his fingers on a lace handkerchief, he surveyed me with his inscrutable gaze, silence growing heavy between us until he spoke.

"You look pale, Henriette. And the doctors tell me you aren't fit to leave your house."

Shocked by the bluntness of his words, I forced a smile on my face. "They're always so pessimistic. I'll be all right in a handful of days."

He sighed and stood up, his jeweled hand resting on the back of his upholstered armchair.

"Your health isn't my only concern, I'm afraid."

He fixed his attention on the rain dripping down the panes of the nearest window, and the fact he avoided my gaze chilled my limbs. I put down my coffee cup to prevent it from rattling in my hands.

"When we performed the spell," he said, "something went wrong for me too."

I had already opened my mouth to renew my apology, but I gaped mutely at his last words. The spell had gone wrong for both of us? I thought I was the one who'd lost control—was he telling me the spell itself had been doomed from the start?

"When I tugged at your magic," he went on, his attention still on the storm outside, "I immediately felt something wasn't right."

A frown now pulled at my brows, as I tried to recall the order of events. I had spoken the spell, then he'd taken my magic, which I had followed before losing myself in the enchantment.

"You see," Louis added, "I drew your magic, and it was so, so weak. Almost . . . insubstantial. I could barely grasp it, and then I lost it, and you collapsed."

My frown deepened, and my heart beat faster. What was he saying? Of course my magic had been there. Golden flecks floating toward the mirror in a bright swirl. Glittering particles, like stars in a clear night sky. If anything, my magic had been so strong I had been unable to let it go so he could perform the spell with it.

I bit my lip, too many thoughts swirling in my mind for me to express in words. He resumed his seating position and grasped my hand in his, as if comforting me after delivering terrible news. Except his news made no sense.

"Henriette," he said, his patient tone belied by the coldness in his eyes. "I think that the weaker you become, the more your magic . . . wanes. It's barely there anymore, and I can't access it to perform spells."

I opened my mouth to protest, then stopped. His stern expression made it obvious he believed what he was saying with absolute certainty. For some reason, he had been unable to use my magic for his mirror spell, and he blamed me for it. Contradicting him was impossible, because it would mean laying the blame on us both, or even on him. But he was the king: He didn't make mistakes, and he was always right.

And maybe he *was* right. Maybe the magic I knew to be present in my body was weakening along with it. Louis gave me a sad smile that felt more automatic than true.

"I'm sorry, Henriette. I know you hope this is only temporary. But I want you to focus on your health now. I've decided to take on a new Source, someone strong enough to carry out the spells I've planned and to help me with my ideas."

I blinked, the weight of his words—and all his unspoken ones—settling on my chest. So he'd arrived to the same conclusion as Philippe after all. And, more important, he'd found a replacement for me.

Louis kept talking, but the conversation barely registered after this. The succession of announcements was catching up with me, and tiredness made my shoulders sag. My attention drifted to the untouched cakes on the low table, their shine and colors dulled in the declining light. They were all Philippe's favorite—hopefully he would enjoy them when he returned home from court tonight.

"I see I've exhausted you." Louis's voice cut through my wandering thoughts. "I'll take my leave now."

Despite my weak protestations, he stood up and forbade me from seeing him out. Too drained to argue, I let him leave and stood by the window as servants came in to light the candles around the salon. Rain still streamed down the glass panes, and the blurry silhouette of the king's carriage rattled out of the courtyard among the puddles, his guards already soaked.

A sigh escaped me, and I wrapped my arms around my chest to fight the rising chill.

"Shall I fetch you a shawl, Madame?" a young maid with bright eyes asked. "The fire will be lit in just a moment."

Whether on Philippe's instructions or not, all the staff in the house showed a concern for me that I didn't feel I always deserved. I made a point of treating them well and of making certain everyone else did, yet looking after an ailing English princess couldn't have been the most exciting position in Paris.

The girl's gentle question brought a smile to my lips. "I think

I'll just retire to my chambers for now, thank you. But would you bring me ink and paper? I need to write a letter."

For if I wasn't the king's Source anymore, I needed to ensure I didn't lose my place at court in the process.

* * *

To my relief, the Comte de Saint-Aignan accepted my invitation the next day as if he'd never had any plans to begin with.

"My dear Madame!" he gushed as I welcomed him in one of the smaller receiving rooms.

Yesterday's rain hadn't abated, and I shivered in the bigger salons. Both of us sat in comfortable armchairs in front of the fireplace, with Mimi sprawled on the carpet at our feet, and we chatted for a while in a relaxed manner. The count had been the one who'd saved Philippe's life with Prince Aniaba after Fouquet's plot last summer, and he remained one of my closest allies at the French court. He was also a *magicien*, which suited my purpose well for the day.

After Louis's visit the previous day, I had spent my evening replaying our conversation in my head. And despite his proclaimed concern for my health and his announcement about a new Source, a doubt nagged at me. He'd used my waning magic as the motivation for his decision to let me go, yet I stood unconvinced of its veracity.

And the only way to know for certain whether my magic was weakening was to perform a spell with another *magicien*. Someone who couldn't refuse me anything.

Slight guilt needled me at the thought of using the ever-kind Comte de Saint-Aignan for my own purposes, but I was out of options: There were only a handful of *magiciens* at court, and the count was the only one who could be convinced to help me.

Performing a spell in my condition was likely a bad idea as well, but Philippe hadn't returned home last night, preventing me from running my idea by him and therefore being talked out of it. Pushing aside thoughts of where my husband might have spent the night—in all probability, making up with Armand after their fight at Versailles—I focused my charm on the count.

"I hear you're putting together another wonderful entertainment for His Majesty," I said. "What clever spells have you thought of this time?"

The count chuckled, folding his hands over his prominent stomach.

"So you've heard? His Majesty wants the most wondrous entertainment yet. It will be the court's first time at Versailles, and he wants everything to be perfect. He's handling the majority of the artistic decisions and spells, of course, but I'm helping in my small capacity." Sweat dampened his forehead in the firelight as he leaned toward me conspiratorially. "I have a few new ideas for fireworks, but shhh . . ."

He winked, excitement shining in his eyes. If anything, Louis's increasing interest for magic meant pressure off the count's shoulders. As an aging man, I could see how he didn't mind it in the slightest. He remained at court, liked by all, yet with more time to enjoy his stay here.

"Any games?" I asked, memories of the magical hide-and-seek

he'd organized at Fontainebleau coming back to me. Although it had ended in chaos, with Fouquet attacking Prince Aniaba and getting shot by Moreau, it had been a remarkable enchantment. "I did love that *jeu de cache-cache* last summer."

He waved the memory away. "Of course, of course. But I'm thinking of ways to amuse His Majesty's guests with magic as well."

"Yes, I meant the magic you used for the hide-and-seek game."

Confusion crossed his features, and I paused. Was he thinking of another game? For he had definitely performed a portal spell that evening at Fontainebleau, allowing guests to move at random between rooms in the *château*.

A deep frown now linking his bushy brows, the count hesitated. "I apologize, Your Highness, but I don't recall using magic for the game you mention."

His gaze on me was concerned, as if I were the one confused. Impatience rising in me, I insisted, "You used a portal spell, to connect the rooms. It was an impressive enchantment."

The count burst out laughing. "Oh my dear Madame, you're always so entertaining!" To my dismay, he patted my hand, his deep laugh echoing under the ceiling. "What a wonderful sense of humor you have! A portal spell! As if such things existed. You should give this idea to Monsieur Perrault for his fairy tales!"

He kept laughing, as my annoyance rose to replace my surprise. Was the man mad? Or playing a joke on me? He wiped his eyes with a large embroidered handkerchief, mirth still all over his features, and not a hint of malice there. Suspicion tugged at me. The count was many things, but he wasn't a good liar, nor a cruel man. He clearly couldn't remember casting the portal spell. Something was wrong.

I made myself smile. "I couldn't resist a little jest. I know you'll forgive me. Although I did enjoy that game at Fontainebleau, despite its lack of magic."

"That's the secret," the count said, his breaths easing as calm returned to his expression. "Mixing the mundane with the magic. Keeping people guessing."

His face kind and serious, he patted my hand again. "Young people like you and His Majesty always dream of casting incredible spells. But if I've learned anything in all my years, it's that simple ideas and simple enchantments are often the most effective. Who needs to open portals onto other places when one can simply turn a pretty clock into a magical one?" He pointed at the enchanted clock on the mantelpiece and grinned.

I forced myself to return his smile, but anxiety now gnawed at me. How could the *magicien* believe a spell he'd cast himself didn't exist? And was he the only one to have forgotten it? I did my best to behave like a lady for the remainder of the conversation, but I ached to bolt out of the room and discover the truth.

Philippe hadn't been there for the game, but Athénaïs had. I could write to her and find out what she remembered. And if something were amiss, I would need to tell Louis as quickly as possible.

At long last the count bid me farewell, with many compliments and good wishes for the future. I let him go, hoping he would blame my curt manners on my poor health. Then I half ran upstairs in my haste to ensure that I wasn't indeed the one going mad.

In the bookcase in my apartments sat an old *grimoire*, which Louis and I had used to find the ancient binding spell that had defeated Fouquet. If there was a book that contained the portal spell the Comte de Saint-Aignan had performed at Fontainebleau, this would be it. I dumped the heavy volume on my desk in a cloud of dust and leafed through the yellowed pages at a frantic pace. Ancient spells were organized in alphabetical order, which made it easy to locate them once one knew their names. I reached the page of the portal spell—*Ouvre*—and let out a small dismayed sound. On the left-hand side, the spell to give someone an order they couldn't refuse to obey was scribbled in a near-faded handwriting. And on the right, the page was blank.

The portal spell was gone.

CHAPTER IV

The Louvre Palace had already been one of the royal residences for a few centuries when Louis became king, and its complex layout stood as the result of various architectural endeavors layered atop—and mounted beside—each other over the years. A more recent addition to the general pile of pale stones was an extended western wing that housed Louis's apartments and a chapel where he attended mass every morning.

Following my discovery of the missing spell the previous day, I had spent a restless night, troubled even further by Philippe's continued absence. When a gray dawn grazed the Paris slate rooftops, finding me already awake in my large bed, I resolved to no longer postpone what appeared as my duty: if a plot involving the disappearance of spells was afoot, the king ought to be told without delay.

Dismissing my maids' polite protests, I dressed for a court appearance in a yellow silk gown and ordered a carriage to be brought around. The vehicle rattled on the cobblestones along the palace's tall facades, jolting me as it hit potholes and navigated the busy street by the Seine to the entrance of the royal residence's main pavilion. Thick clouds hung above the capital, and a draught caught my heavy cloak as a guard helped me out of the carriage. A shiver ran along my body, and cold air stung my lungs. I coughed into my handkerchief, holding on to the guard's arm longer than appropriate. A look of alarm crossed the soldier's youthful face.

"Madame, shall I fetch someone?"

By now the palace's guards and footmen also had their attention on us, and I shook my head as heat spread to my cheeks. I put away my handkerchief.

"No, thank you. I'm only going to attend the service. Please be here when I return."

Attending mass was my excuse for coming to the palace without my ladies and for contriving an opportunity to speak with Louis in an informal manner. My intention was to make my presence at court as discreet as possible, but I should have known better than to plan for a stealthy visit: I was too recognizable. I wasn't halfway up the large stone staircase leading to the chapel on the first floor of the ornate building when Louise, my lady-in-waiting turned king's secret mistress, caught up with me.

"Your Highness! What a pleasure to see you here. I heard you were unwell."

Another princess might have pointed out that, as one of my ladies, she ought to have done much more than just hear about my illness. But the love of a king made her face glow with such undiluted happiness that I had long ago given up on reminding her of her supposed duty to me. She was my lady only in name, to offer her the safety of an official position at court when she in fact devoted all her time to Louis. I didn't resent her for it—glad that at least one young woman at court enjoyed a love story worthy of a fairy tale, even if it was a clandestine one.

"I'm feeling better now," I replied with a reassuring smile.

My breath was short after climbing the stairs, and sweat gathered along my temples, but Louise, oblivious to those symptoms, linked arms with me.

"We've missed you here! The French court just isn't the same without you."

A gaggle of early-rising courtiers gathered at the chapel doors, and I acknowledged their bows, curtsies, and murmured greetings with polite nods. Their whispers trailed after me as I passed the oak double doors. Inside, we dipped the tip of our fingers in the stoup and crossed ourselves before sitting in the front pew reserved for the royal family. We were a few minutes early, and while the small chapel filled, Louise chatted about the court entertainment I had missed. My replies to her were short and perfunctory, my focus divided between my efforts to keep my breathing even and my rehearsed speech to Louis.

At last the bells rang and the assembly rose to greet the king and queen with the appropriate show of respect. Louis and Marie-Thérèse made their way to the front—his face an impenetrable mask and hers a pouting expression of annoyance with the world in general and the courtiers in particular. They both acknowledged me with a nod but remained quite indifferent as Marie-Thérèse sat next to me and Louis took his position in a gilded seat to the side.

Mass was uneventful, and Bishop Bossuet's sermon was

blessedly short for once. At the end of the service the assembly rose, some making a swift exit while others mingled and waited for a chance to get the king's attention. I was already trying to think of a strategy to catch Louis's gaze when Marie-Thérèse moved to speak with the bishop and her husband made a beeline for me and offered me his arm.

"Henriette, such a pleasure to see you back among us," he said loudly enough for others to hear.

"A brief spell," I replied in the same tone, "thankfully all over now."

I cast a quick glance around to check that our exchange was enough to satisfy curious courtiers and to spread reassuring gossip. Acknowledging that the king's attention was now set on his beloved sister-in-law, the remaining courtiers gave us space, allowing Louis and me to slowly make our way out of the chapel and whisper the rest of our discussion.

"You're pale as a ghost," Louis said, reproach in his eyes. "I praise you for wanting to attend mass, but I can send Bossuet to you at the Tuileries if you wish to have a private service."

I waved his reprimand away. "I'm afraid I needed to see you urgently."

His stern expression turned even darker. "I thought I made myself quite clear. It's better if you're not my Source anymore. My decision is final, and I wish you'd understand it."

His censoring tone stung—I always strived to *not* be difficult, and he made it sound as if I were being a demanding child—but I ignored it to focus on the more important matter at hand.

"Something happened," I said. "I had to speak with you. It's about magic."

He let out an annoyed sigh. "All right. I have a few minutes before the council. We can go to my apartments." A look back let him see Marie-Thérèse still deep in conversation with the bishop and Louise busy with a couple of young ladies. His grip on my arm tightened. "Let's go now."

He whispered a few orders to the nearest musketeer, who dashed away. Louis led me down the large marble staircase and steered around the courtiers lingering in the corridors leading to his apartments. On our way we walked by the Queen Mother's set of rooms, and the oddity of her absence at mass struck me then.

"Is your mother all right?" I asked. "She wasn't at the service."

Louis's expression remained inscrutable. "She hasn't been feeling well. She receives Communion in her chambers now, except on Sundays."

I cast him an alarmed look at the news. Philippe hadn't mentioned anything to me, but I hadn't seen him in a couple of days, now. I would have to ask him for details, as Louis's severe face clearly meant to prevent further questioning on the matter, and we were arriving at his apartments.

Beside the usual guards standing at attention by the gilded doors, a young man waited in an impressive red-and-green outfit with intricate gold embroidery. His blond hair fell around his shoulders in waves when he bowed to the king.

"Your Majesty sent for me?"

His accent was suave and sophisticated, and as he straightened, he gazed at me with dramatically blue eyes. He was the most handsome man I had ever seen, which was probably a sacrilegious thought to have when standing at the Sun King's side.

"Madame," he bowed again.

Louis gestured irritably. "Yes, thank you for coming. Have you two been introduced?"

The man flashed an amused smile, as if privy to some information I ignored. "I'm afraid I haven't had the pleasure yet, Your Majesty, as Her Highness has been unwell."

"So," Louis said most informally as he ushered us inside his antechamber with renewed impatience, "Henriette, this is the Chevalier de Lorraine. Lorraine, may I present to you my sister-in-law, Henriette d'Angleterre, Duchesse d'Orléans."

"Delighted," I said as an automatic reply while my mind raced to remember where I had heard that name before. Then it struck me: he was the newcomer Athénaïs had mentioned the other day, the one with the face of an angel whom everyone thought clever and charming. What was he doing here?

Louis ordered the doors closed as Lorraine's gaze remained on me, a brazen smile still floating on his lips, now verging toward impertinence. I remained composed to hide my confusion and waited for Louis to give me leave to sit down on one of the silk sofas in the parqueted small room. But the king, either oblivious to my weak state or eager to get this conversation over with as promptly as possible, clasped his hands together in front of him and raised an inquisitive eyebrow at me.

"What was it you wanted to say?"

This time, I couldn't help but shoot a puzzled look toward Lorraine.

"I'm sorry, but I assumed we would have a chance to talk in private . . . ?"

Louis dismissed my concern with a wave of his hand.

"Lorraine is my new Source. You said you wanted to talk about magic. Whatever you have to say, he needs to hear it too."

It was only my deeply embedded good manners that prevented me from gaping then. Of course, Louis had mentioned he'd already found a new Source. It had simply never occurred to me that I would find myself introduced to this person in such an offhand manner, as if everything Louis and I had shared over the past few months amounted to nothing.

Magiciens *don't care about their Sources. They just use them.*

My mother's warning tugged at my mind, a timely reminder of Louis's attitude. He was a king, and he was a *magicien.* Someone such as him couldn't let their feelings get in the way of their grand plans. I had been useful to him once, but I wasn't anymore. He had no qualms replacing me and no interest in sparing my feelings when doing so.

So I swallowed my surprise and my pride, and addressed both young men as if talking about magic in front of a stranger was the most normal thing to do.

"Something happened yesterday. I mentioned to the Comte de Saint-Aignan the portal spell he used at Fontainebleau last summer for the game of hide-and-seek, and he had no recollection of it. Then I looked up the spell in the *grimoire*, and the page for the spell is blank. As if the spell has . . . disappeared."

Silence greeted my words. Louis's brows pulled into a slight frown, his features stern, while Lorraine's smile widened. At last the latter burst into a hearty laughter.

"What an extraordinary story!"

He shook his head in mirthful disbelief and turned to the

king, who appraised me with a mix of concern and gravity. He released a sigh.

"Henriette, what on earth are you talking about?"

Both their reactions stopped me short. When I had rehearsed this conversation in my mind, Louis and I had been alone, and he had been ready to trust my judgment. It occurred to me only now how fantastic my revelation might sound to one unprepared for it.

"I think someone somehow made the spell disappear," I explained. "Maybe to prevent others from using it, or maybe—"

"But, Your Highness, portal spells don't exist," Lorraine interrupted.

Flabbergasted by both his audacity and his claim, I turned to Louis for support as heat rushed to my face.

"Of course they do," I insisted. "The count used one last summer at Fontainebleau. And Fouquet used one—"

Louis's look of utter incredulity stopped me from saying another word. He hadn't been present for the game of hide-and-seek, and neither had he been here at the Vaux-le-Vicomte grotto when Fouquet had created portals to move around the place. We'd never cast a portal spell together, and from his expression, he did believe no such enchantment existed. My resolve faltered. What was happening? Why was I the only person who seemed to recall this spell?

"So you think there was a spell," Louis said, his tone reasonable. "And the count can't remember it and it's gone from that spell book you say you have?"

His patient reply gave me heart. He *wanted* to believe me.

"Yes," I said. "That's why I thought you ought to know about it. If someone is making—"

He held up his hand to stop me. "That spell book, where is it? Did you bring it with you?"

My chest deflated. Of course I should have expected him to ask for proof to support my claim. But between my trepidation and my silly arrogance, I hadn't thought to bring it.

"It's at home," I said. "At the Tuileries."

He nodded at Lorraine, who had remained quiet but still looked at me as if I were the most entertaining creature he'd ever encountered. Dislike rose in me, a vague instinct that I seldom felt in anyone's presence. A protective feeling that whispered warnings in my ear.

"I'll send someone to retrieve the book," Louis announced, "and I'll study it with Lorraine."

His confident reply distracted me from my suspicious train of thought. Louis would see the blank page and understand something was wrong. He would investigate, and the threat would be dealt with in the efficient manner that was his trademark. My heart rate settled, making me aware of how rapid my pulse had been until now.

Louis took my arm and led me toward the door. "Now, I want you to go home and rest, Henriette. You're obviously exhausted, and it's not helpful for you to come to court and get yourself into such a state."

For a heartbeat his concern for my health warmed my chest, then a thought occurred to me that doused this feeling with cold.

"You . . . you do believe me, don't you?"

To my dismay, he avoided my gaze. "I think you believe what you're saying, and I don't want you to worry about it. As I said before, you don't need to think about magic anymore. You need to focus on getting well."

I pulled my arm out of his grasp to face him, consternation tightening my throat as I replayed his last sentences in my head. "I'm telling the truth. You'll see for yourself the page is blank."

Again, he let out a resigned sigh. "Henriette, I'm asking you to go home. You're unwell, and you're upset, I understand. Whatever your feverish mind has made you think is real, you'll soon see it's not true and nothing to worry about."

This time, I gaped. Not only did he not believe me, but he also thought me unbalanced. He grabbed both my hands in his and held them to his chest in a display of emotion he seldom resorted to.

"I care about you deeply; you know that. But you've gone through more than enough these past few months, some of it my fault. Fouquet, Versailles . . . I've asked too much from you, and you couldn't manage. There's no shame in that. You have your limits, like any woman. I should have seen it sooner."

My limits? Like any woman? Blood rushed to my cheeks again, as my temper rose at last. He thought me hysterical. Delusional. Just like the count, he didn't remember the portal spell, and he thought I was telling this story either to earn back his favor or because I was ill and weak.

I opened my mouth to protest, but my body chose this moment to betray me and confirm his suspicion. A coughing fit tore through me, so violent Louis had to let me sit down this time, and servants were called in with water and linens. My lungs on fire, it wasn't long before tears streamed down my face unchecked, and my whizzing breaths vibrated under the gilded ceilings like a whistle.

More people crowded the antechamber, and a couple of my ladies were brought in to help take me home. As Louis gave orders and undefined silhouettes moved around me like puppets on a strange stage, the golden head of Lorraine appeared stark against the light of the window. His features cast in shadows, his striking blue eyes stared at me, two burning lights in the chaos that held in them a mix of delight and contempt.

The Angel, the courtiers called him, as if as a praise. But angels were righteous, vengeful, and uncompromising creatures. And this one seemed to quite enjoy my fall from grace.

* * *

In a scene that was becoming distressingly familiar, Philippe found me dozing in bed when he came home that afternoon. Rushing to my bedside, he sent away my lady and the maid who'd been looking after me and surveyed me with an anxious expression.

"They said you went to mass and fainted afterward when you were talking to Louis. Is that what happened?"

Remorse squeezed my weakened chest. I had promised him to be reasonable and to look after myself, yet we still found ourselves in a situation that caused him anxiety and guilt.

"I thought I was well enough," I said in a low voice, so that I wouldn't spark another coughing fit. "And I wanted to speak with Louis."

His lips tightened in worry, and he pressed my fingers between his. When he spoke, his voice was very gentle.

"But you had a fever and you weren't making much sense, were you?"

Louis had spoken with him, then. Yet it wasn't embarrassment that turned my cheeks a deeper red, but the renewed anger at how quickly Louis had dismissed my claims as nonsense and swept under the carpet months of shared trust.

"It was just a misunderstanding," I said. "When Louis has the *grimoire*, he'll see what I said was true."

A shadow of hesitation crossed Philippe's face, making me pause. By now Louis should have the spell book in his possession, and I expected a letter from him before tonight. But Philippe's tone was still soft as he replied.

"My love, the servants searched the bookcase in your salon from top to bottom. There was no *grimoire*. In fact, they searched your entire apartments. I even lent my help, although everyone knows how useless I am at anything. We couldn't find it."

This time, I remained speechless. I had left the *grimoire* on its shelf last night, I was certain of it. Someone had removed it. Just like someone had made the portal spell vanish. They knew I knew, and they were erasing all traces of their deeds, using the fact I was ill and alone to make my claims easier to dismiss.

And I could have borne it, if Philippe had not kissed me on the forehead then and tugged my hair behind my ear with a caress.

"Forget about it," he said. "Just get better, all right?"

Of all people, he was the one whose opinion mattered. And even if I could still read love in his eyes, I also saw pity and concern there, and it was what brought tears to my eyes. They welled up and fell so quickly that within seconds I was sobbing, and Philippe climbed onto the canopy bed to lie at my side and wrap me in his arms.

"No, no, no, my love, don't cry," he begged. "Please don't cry. You'll get better, and you'll do magic if you want, and you'll go swimming and horse riding and all those things you like even though I don't know why. It'll all be all right again, you'll see."

My chest heaving with sobs, I hid my face in my hands, but he pulled them away and wiped my cheeks with a silk handkerchief that smelled of his perfume. He kissed my temple and repeated soothing words, until at last my breathing slowed and the tears stopped.

Maybe he was right. As today's events had proven, I was in no state to deal with any of this yet. So maybe I ought to forget about it all for now, until I was better.

"There," Philippe said with another kiss as my fit subsided. "Let's ask the maid to bring in that horrid dog of yours, and I'll stay so you can go to sleep and not worry about anything."

His effort at teasing made me smile, and soon enough a maid opened the door for Mimi. Philippe lifted her onto the bed, and her tail wagged in delight as I petted her and encouraged her to lie at my side. Philippe resumed his position atop the bedcovers next to me, his arm firmly tugged around my shoulders.

"Now rest," he said, his tone still teasing. "As your husband, I command you."

I nestled against him, my body relaxing at last in that safe embrace.

"I missed you," I whispered against his chest as my eyelids closed, already heavy with sleep.

If he replied, I drifted off before I could hear it.

* * *

I couldn't have said what woke me up. A floorboard creaking, Mimi jumping off the bed, or the opening door letting in a sudden draught. Or simply an emptiness at my side where Philippe's reassuring form had lain moments before.

I blinked drowsiness away and stretched, my foggy mind slowly registering my husband's absence, my dog's alertness, and my bedroom's darkness. The door stood ajar, faint light coming in through the gap as the soft sound of receding footsteps resonated from my antechamber. Whether because of the fever or the exhaustion, it didn't occur to me to call out. Amid my twirling thoughts, only one jumped out at me.

Philippe was leaving. I had to stop him.

Throwing my blankets aside, I staggered out of bed. Dizziness struck me for a heartbeat, but I gritted my teeth and pushed through the mist clogging my thoughts and slowing my gestures. Barefoot and in my nightgown, Mimi trailing after me with her tail wagging, I tiptoed through my salon, where a single candle burned on the windowsill and a maid on duty sat slumped in an armchair, fast asleep. The urgency of my quest made me overlook the situation, and I hurried through the rest of my apartments like a ghost in the obscurity.

Once in the corridor outside my rooms, the cold marble floor under my feet startled me for only an instant before voices and light ahead caught my attention. People were talking in the main hall, their presence drawing me like a moth to a flame. My legs still unsteady, I used the stuccoed wall for support as I made my way along the hanging paintings of Louis and Philippe's ancestors.

I was halfway along when light-headedness forced me to a stop by the portrait of a sour-looking *gentilhomme* in military uniform. Ahead in the entrance hall, the flickering candlelight illuminated two figures: Philippe's familiar silhouette and a blond man in a hard-to-forget red-and-green outfit.

Lorraine. What was he doing here in the middle of the night?

My knuckles white against the wall in my effort to remain steady and standing, I forced my feet to move closer. A couple of steps forward allowed for the two men's conversation to reach my ears.

"I had to wait until she was asleep." Philippe's soft tone, apologetic and slightly muffled as he put on his coat. "She's terribly unwell. I couldn't just leave her like this."

"You're too kind." Lorraine's reply, drenched with sarcasm. "What are servants for, if not to look after tiresome wives?"

My heart hammered against my ribs, almost drowning the sound of their voices. The familiarity of the exchange triggered a sense of foreboding in me.

"Well, are you ready to go?" Lorraine, impatient now as Philippe arranged his long hair around his shoulders. "Will you stop fussing? It's three o'clock in the morning, no one is going to see you, let alone judge your appearance, I promise you."

"*You* are going to see me." Philippe, teasing and with a smile in his voice.

My heart sank into my stomach. He only ever used this tone with Armand, or me. For a brief moment I closed my eyes, frozen in the corridor, just out of sight and out of reach. It all made sense, of course. Philippe's absences. Lorraine's smug expression when Louis had introduced us. Not only was the man the court's new darling and the king's new Source, but he was also my husband's new lover.

As if to confirm my suspicions, he grabbed Philippe's arm, whispered into his ear something that made him chuckle, and silenced him with a kiss. Then they left the palace in a rush of clacking heels and rustling fabric.

Everyone is already under his spell, Athénaïs had said. I should have known better than to expect Philippe wouldn't be one of them.

CHAPTER V

———————————

"I heard the reason we're all invited for seven days is because the party itself will last seven days. Think of the extravagance!"

I nodded and sipped my hot chocolate, impressed by Louis's ambition despite myself. Following my discovery of the true extent of Lorraine's interference in my life the other night, I had spent a few exhausting hours replaying the last days in my mind and casting a bitter eye on every moment. Then, sometime around dawn, sleep had claimed me, and when I had woken up that afternoon, I had made at last the decision everyone pleaded me to make: I resolved to put myself and my health first. By this point, it was obvious my body demanded my attention far more than my personal woes. I had to get better before I could investigate spells' disappearances or Lorraine's suspicious aura.

So for the past few days, I had remained at home, looked after by everyone in my household except my husband, and as soon as my fever had abated, I had hatched a plan. In a court obsessed with Louis's approval and enthralled by Lorraine's charisma, my isolation was my worst enemy. I would never find out who made magic spells vanish or how to retrieve my lost position alone. I needed allies, and if I couldn't go to them, I would invite them to come to me.

And thus I lounged in my salon on a sunny afternoon, dressed in a gown of pastel satin and sipping hot chocolate with Mimi asleep in my lap, while Olympe de Soissons soliloquized about the court's latest gossip.

"I'm not certain I even want to spend seven days at Versailles with half the court," she added. "People are saying there aren't rooms for everyone and accommodation will be provided elsewhere. Can you imagine?"

I made an approving noise, which again was enough to prompt another tirade. As the Comte de Saint-Aignan had hinted at the previous week, Louis had announced his most impressive court entertainment to date would be held at Versailles in a fortnight. Invitations had been sent out the previous day, and all the courtiers were in a fever—the ones invited getting ready for the event while those left off the list tried to bribe their way onto it.

"And it's all for *her*." Olympe sneered at the word. "Everyone knows it. Dedicating the party to the queens—his mother and his wife, you see—is fooling absolutely no one."

Last year, Olympe had been Fouquet's ally in his attempt at overthrowing Louis and seizing power for himself. After the Crown *Magicien*'s fall, however, she had used her old friendship with Louis to obtain a pardon and remain at court as if nothing had happened. Her visit had surprised me at first—after all, she had threatened and scared me during her alliance with Fouquet. But if Louis could find it in himself to forgive her, so could I, and I wasn't in a position now to refuse her extended hand of friendship.

Although it was becoming clear her presence in my home was far from a selfless deed but rather the calculated move of a countess in need of allies herself.

"I'm not sure what you mean," I replied tactfully to her veiled diatribe against Louise.

It was rumored Louis had once loved Olympe enough to consider marrying her, before his political alliance with Spain had made him wed Marie-Thérèse. But it was obvious Olympe still harbored feelings for him and a definite grudge against his new mistress, whose identity wasn't the secret he hoped.

"Oh, don't play coy," she snapped. "This whole entertainment is in her honor, you can't deny it."

I suspected it was also a chance for Louis to show off his *magicien* skills for the first time in public and to establish his magical partnership with Lorraine. Which meant it was imperative I was well enough to attend the event in two weeks and to use it as an opportunity to keep an eye on Lorraine and to find out what was really happening with magic at court. In short, I had two weeks to get better and to surround myself with people I could trust.

"Molière is writing a play, of course," Olympe carried on. "And there's a rumor about a menagerie."

"The Comte de Saint-Aignan mentioned fireworks," I said to contribute to the conversation. "He visited the other day."

"That's nice of him." Olympe set her teacup down on a pedestal table by her chair and held my gaze in that unnerving way of hers. "The poor man is getting old. But he still knows how to cast a good artistic spell, I'll give him that."

A *magicienne* herself, Olympe rarely used her gift in a court where women weren't encouraged to practice magic. She'd sided with Fouquet in a bid for more power despite the fact that, as the superintendent of Anne d'Autriche's household, she was already one of the highest-ranking ladies at court.

"How is the Queen Mother?" I asked to distract her from her vindictive train of thought.

Sadness slackened her features. She wasn't all hard edges after all. "Still unwell. The doctors are doing what they can, but she's very ill, and at her age—" She shrugged, her sudden silence squeezing my heart with its implications.

I knew Anne d'Autriche had been thirty-seven when Louis was born, which meant she now was a venerable lady, even when her formidable strength of character made everyone forget it. And I knew all too well no one was immortal, especially not royals.

"Please pass on my good wishes to her," I said, for lack of a more comforting reply. "I do miss her wisdom."

Olympe flashed me one of her rare genuine smiles. "I will."

Conversation unraveled after that, and soon Olympe was up, saying her goodbyes.

"I almost forgot," she said as a maid helped her into her light silk cloak and Mimi jumped off my lap to circle her with interest. "Athénaïs sends her best regards. She's been awfully busy, but she promises to come and see you soon."

All of a sudden Olympe's surprise call made more sense: she and Athénaïs were close friends, and it occurred to me this whole reunion might have been engineered by my former lady to make up for her lack of visits.

"Busy?" I asked, fearing she was involved in some nefarious activity. Athénaïs was nothing if not bold in her endeavors.

Olympe let out an exasperated sigh. "As I predicted, that husband of hers is useless. Riddled with debts, for one, and far too boring for her."

Her comment caught me off guard. Athénaïs had complained about her husband when I had seen her, but she hadn't mentioned any money problems, and her red gown had been the height of fashion and elegance. Likely Olympe was exaggerating that piece of gossip, as usual.

"But," she added while she tugged on her gloves, "she's quite the social butterfly, as always. Attending every *salon* in Paris and discussing poetry and philosophy with sophisticated people. I'm sure she'll tell you all about it next time she visits."

A faint pang of envy shot through me at the thought of all these courtiers gathering across Paris to hold entertaining discussions in my absence. These days, I counted myself lucky if I managed to rise before noon and to stay up until dinnertime without being brought down by a fit. I dismissed my sullenness with a shake of my head and stood up to walk Olympe to the door, when an idea struck me.

"May I ask for a favor?" I said, sparking interest in Olympe's golden gaze. "Will you pass on my regards to Prince Aniaba as well when you see him? I'd love for him to visit."

The prince was a Source and definitely someone I trusted at court. He would be the perfect person to speak to of my theory about vanishing spells. I could send him a letter, but Olympe's intercession might be more effective—and more discreet.

"I will if I see him," Olympe replied, curiosity already gone from her eyes. "But I must warn you, the man is always at Versailles these days, working with Le Vau, Le Brun, and Le Nôtre when the king isn't there himself."

My shoulders sagged. It sounded like I would have to find someone else to help with my investigation. Much like the Comte de Saint-Aignan, Louis's favorite architect, painter, and gardener must have realized how talented the prince was, and I couldn't blame him for spending his time working with them.

Olympe left, and I was ready to retire to my bedroom when another carriage rattled into the courtyard below my windows. A maid came rushing into my apartments, a hint of panic in her eyes as she announced:

"Madame, it's the queen!"

For a heartbeat I thought she meant the Queen Mother, since Olympe and I had just been discussing her moments ago. Then realization dawned on me.

For the first time in her life, Marie-Thérèse was calling on me. Swathed in rich embroidered fabric and as pale as usual, her short frame seemed to drown in her dress despite her plump figure. Her presence in the palace sent my household into a frenzy, and soon we both sat in my salon surrounded by piles of cakes, swarms of servants and ladies-in-waiting, and a pack of Bolognese dogs. The smells of sweet food and sweaty bodies filled the air and rendered me nauseous, and I made a discreet gesture for a window to be open while Marie-Thérèse ate several *pâtisseries* and her dogs yapped after Mimi across the thick carpet.

I made polite conversation, which she mostly ignored. Breathing in the saturated air was becoming difficult when she snapped an order and the room emptied, leaving only her four dogs behind. She called them to heel as well, and in the sudden quiet she focused her attention on me at last. Her expression was anything but pleasant.

"I'm here because I know," she said, her Spanish accent lending a lovely lilt to her words that belied the sternness of her tone.

"I'm sorry?" I replied, my puzzlement genuine.

"I know you're Louis's mistress," she went on, spatting the last word. "I'm not stupid."

My first instinct was to gape. My second was to laugh. Somehow I stopped myself before doing either and kept my composure in the face of Marie-Thérèse's obvious upset.

"My queen," I said, making a point of being formal to avoid angering her further. "It's not my place to assume anything about the king. I must, however, strongly deny your allegations. I assure you I am not, nor have I ever been, his lover."

Tears welled in Marie-Thérèse's blue eyes, and she replied in a strained voice, "They say you don't lie. Then why are you lying to me? I know he has a mistress, and I know he has always doted on you! You pretend to be ill so he can visit you here at his convenience, while your husband is off with that man everyone likes."

It was my turn to feel tears brimming in my eyes. To hear her say such horrid things was like a slap in my face. As if I could be that deceitful, that wicked? Heat spread to my cheeks, and all thoughts of whom I was addressing fled my mind.

"I do not pretend to be ill. I do not have an affair with the king. I am *not* lying. I am, however, a princess of the blood, and I will not be insulted, even by you!"

This time Marie-Thérèse burst into tears. Her dogs gathered around her, whining and wagging their tails in anxiety. Heaving sobs shook her corseted chest, and she fished a large lacy handkerchief out of her pocket to blow her nose, in the most unroyal display of emotions I had ever witnessed. My own mother would have been appalled. I bit my lip, my temper forgotten, replaced by guilt at having prompted such a torrent.

"Your Majesty," I said in a more controlled tone, "please forgive me. I've been very unwell, and I'm still very tired. It's no excuse, but it does make me irrationally irritable."

"And I'm pregnant!" Marie-Thérèse replied.

My eyes widened at the sudden announcement, but I recovered quickly. "That's wonderful news. Congratulations!"

She wiped her round cheeks with her handkerchief and sniffed. "Only my ladies and Louis know. Not that it makes a difference to him! I never see him." Bitterness laced every word, and she grabbed my hand, her face intent all of a sudden. "Do you know who it is? The woman he's in love with?"

My shoulders slumped. Louis and Louise's secret wasn't mine to share, yet I didn't want to lie to my sister-in-law. She led her life surrounded by her own crowd of devoted courtiers, most of whom were from Spain. Who knew what news reached her and what was kept from her by her well-meaning entourage.

"I think maybe you already know?" I said, my voice gentle.

She sniffed again and rubbed her reddened nose in her handkerchief. Her discomfited expression was a reminder of how young she still was. "Do I? I really thought it was you. You're the prettiest. If it's not you, then I don't know."

She released a heavy defeated sigh, which prompted my reply.

"Maybe it's better if you don't know. The reason you don't is that the king has tried to be discreet to spare your feelings."

"Well, he hasn't done a very good job of that, has he?"

I pressed my lips together, running out of ideas to comfort her. It was true Louis's behavior was a terrible insult to her, and I really wished he would deal with his own problems rather than leaving me to sort out his messes.

"Why don't you talk to him, then?" I said.

Marie-Thérèse's eyes widened. "Confront him? Oh, I could never! Too unseemly."

"Not confront him, but talk to him. About your feelings, about how you miss him and wish to spend more time with him."

I knew for a fact Louis thought his wife boring, but maybe there was a way to bring them closer regardless. The irony of me attempting to fix Louis's marriage when my own was collapsing wasn't lost on me, but the thought of helping my family when I felt so helpless otherwise warmed my chest a little. Marie-Thérèse's weeping had ceased, which was already a victory.

"You do have a few things in common with Louis," I said, emboldened by her hopeful gaze. "Why don't you think of a few conversation topics for when you're next together?"

She waved my suggestion away with her handkerchief. "It's easy for you. You always know what to tell people, how to make them laugh and love you. People look at me and—" She rolled her eyes and threw her hands up.

"You don't give yourself enough credit," I insisted before I could think about her praise and squirm. "You fulfill every duty required of you. Louis sees that, and I'm certain it wouldn't take a lot of effort to remind him of everything you bring to him."

Marie-Thérèse nodded and put away her handkerchief, some serene confidence returning to her features. I had found the right words, and the result was pleasing. I just couldn't dwell on the fact that, unlike Marie-Thérèse, it was my inability to fulfill my duties—whether magical or marital—that could be blamed for Louis's and Philippe's absences from my life.

But as the light dimmed outside my windows, Marie-Thérèse kept chatting in a relaxed manner, distracting me from my gloomy thoughts. At some point she resumed her eating and introduced me to her beloved dogs.

It was the longest time I had spent alone with her and—I'm ashamed to admit it—the first time I had deigned to see past her pouting and her lack of conversational skills to try to get to know her. As sisters-in-law, we had far more in common with each other than with any other women at court, and I wished it hadn't taken the rest of my life to unravel for me to see it. Allies could come from unexpected places, and I supposed the royal palace was a good place for me to start.

* * *

A few days later, the tailor came to the Tuileries, and he didn't call empty-handed.

He brought heaps of fabric rolls, countless chests of accessories, and Armand, the Comte de Guiche.

"Surely you didn't think I was going to let you choose a dozen outfits alone?" he said as the tailor—a *magicien* renowned at the French court for his fantastical skills—displayed shimmering fabrics around my salon and pulled magically enhanced shoes, fans, and gloves out of silk-covered boxes.

"A dozen outfits?" I asked, slight alarm pitching my voice higher.

It was another clear afternoon, and sunshine filtered through the closed indoor shutters, layering the room with slanted shafts of light. The weather had warmed up significantly as April ended, awakening gardens and ushering us into what promised to be a lovely spring. Fragrant flower arrangements decorated the room, their wonderful smell permeating the air.

"Of course!" Armand replied. He slouched in an armchair, a glass of wine in his hand and a critical eye on the tailor's exhibit. "This is a seven-day affair, remember? You need at least one outfit per day and one per evening."

My chest caved a little. Following Olympe's and Marie-Thérèse's visits, the last few days had been quieter, which had allowed me to recover some of my former vitality. The king's entertainment was now ten days away, and I felt more confident I would be able to attend. Yet the thought of having to manage a whole week of parties and courtiers' scrutiny felt a bit too ambitious after my bout of illness. Still, the court entertainment would be an opportunity for me to seek answers to the questions left in suspense by my forced inactivity.

"I say pastels for the day, bright colors for the night," Armand went on. "Lots of lace and ribbons, *definitely* magically enhanced jewels, and accessories, accessories, accessories."

He stood up, gestured at various brocades and velvets, and asked the tailor pointed questions. The *magicien* rushed around the room to show him more damasks while his assistant fluttered about, riffling through tissue papers in boxes in an effort to help.

My feet up on the sofa and Mimi in my lap, I relaxed in my seat, watching them move about the room like actors stepping around costumes backstage.

When he had appeared on my doorstep, my first instinct had been to turn Armand away. Given the growing rift between Philippe and me, I didn't want to fuel my husband's concerns regarding my relationship with his former lover. But aside from a few hastily written notes sent to the palace to ask after my health, Philippe had disappeared again, and his continued absence made me less eager every day to follow his advice. It also encouraged me further to turn to people I could trust, and Armand was among them. He knew about my magic, he had played a key part in our fight against Fouquet, and he was always the first one to concoct conspiracy theories. And he was *here*.

"HATS!" Armand's shout startled me out of my musing. "You'll need to wear hats in the afternoon. With feathers. And jewels. And ribbons."

I sat up. "Why don't we give everyone here a short break while you and I make a list of all the items we need?"

Armand paused mid-stride, vague incomprehension slackening his expression. I gave the tailor, his assistant, and my servants a pointed look. Understanding dawned on him, and he clapped his hands once.

"Right. Everyone out for a moment! Her Highness and I need to confer in private about such important matters."

The room emptied at once, leaving us alone amid a chaos of glittering fabric and sparkling accessories. Armand dropped next to me on the sofa, rested his hand on my ankle, and settled his green gaze on me with an eyebrow raised.

"I'm sensing mischief."

I swatted his hand away. "No mischief. We just need to talk."

His face darkened, and he crossed his arms over his chest. "I'm not talking about *him*. It's not good for my complexion, and all the crying makes my eyes puffy."

Underneath the bravado, real bitterness steeped his words, prompting me to grab his hand. If the past year had taught me anything, it was that Armand cared about Philippe as much as I did, and seeing him with Lorraine was likely as hurtful to him as it was to me.

"You know Philippe," I replied, saying aloud to him the words I had been repeating to myself these last few days. "He can't resist charismatic people and shiny new things. But soon he'll tire of having to share Lorraine with his brother, or he'll get bored of Lorraine himself. And when that happens, we'll still be here."

"Stop saying his name." Armand wrinkled his nose. "It makes me want to stab things."

"Shall I call him the Angel?" I teased.

"Eww. As if he's more handsome than me. And he's just the second son of a count. Practically a plebeian!"

I laughed. "Now you're being snobby."

"I'm a French courtier, of course I'm snobby." His tone was still gruff, but his features softened.

A lull in the conversation allowed us to exchange a tentative smile.

"So what was it you wanted to talk to me about?" Armand

asked after a minute. "Whatever the problem is, I blame Lorraine."

I opened my mouth to reply, then paused. Up until now, I had treated my problems with magic as a separate issue from Lorraine's arrival wreaking havoc in my personal life. It only now occurred to me that both had happened at the same time, and Armand might be right: Lorraine might be the link between everything.

CHAPTER VI

―――――――――

"So let me make sure I understand," Armand said.

He had draped a square of red velvet around his shoulders in an absentminded gesture, and he paced my salon with a feathered hat on his head like a general on a battlefield.

"You've been ill, and we're not sure what's happening with your magic." He ticked off his fingers as he spoke. "You think spells are disappearing from books and from people's memory. Lorraine has taken your place as the king's new Source. And he's convinced Philippe he's not the worthless peacock we can all see he is. Have I got this right?"

He stopped in his tracks to turn to me.

"I don't *think* the portal spell has disappeared," I replied. "I know it has, and I don't understand why I seem to be the only one aware of it."

"Maybe because you can't prove it?"

"Well," I said, "there was the *grimoire*, except it has vanished as well, and now no one believes me."

He brought his index finger to his lips in an exaggerated thoughtful pose. "I mean, it's quite obvious Lorraine is behind it all. He has access to this place and could have taken the *grimoire*. He has the most to gain from you being unwell and unable to do magic or leave your home."

"Lorraine isn't the one who made me ill," I protested.

Armand held out his index finger toward me. "Isn't he though?"

I conceded that point. No one knew for certain why I had been feeling so wretched these past three weeks. "Then why would he make spells disappear? And how? He's only a Source: He would need a *magicien* to perform the spell."

"You're right." Armand threw his hat down and resumed his seat by my side. "I say this is where we start. The fiend must have accomplices. To find out what his treacherous plans are, we need to know who his people are."

A warm, reassuring feeling spread through my chest. Whether he realized it or not, Armand was offering me what I had longed for these past few weeks: a sympathetic partner who didn't look at me with pity or concern but believed what I said and wanted to act on it. I hadn't realized how very much alone I had felt until this moment, when he laced his fingers through mine and announced:

"Darling, let's bring down the villain."

* * *

It took us three days to devise a strategy.

The king's entertainment at Versailles was only a week away now, and uncovering Lorraine's secrets was becoming a more pressing matter with each passing day. Armand visited every afternoon, each time with some impossible scheme on his mind to find out the evil designs of our designated foe. Each of his ideas was more outlandish than the last, but since I struggled to formulate a good approach myself—why, oh why did magic have to be so restrictive and complicated when I needed it to solve all my problems?—in the end I gave into one of his less eccentric plans.

The *auberge* was called *la Couronne d'Argent*. Situated on a wide street between the Bastille fortress and the Seine river, it was a better establishment than the many taverns of ill-repute scattered across Paris, but not as renowned as the inns in the *rue* Saint-Honoré or *rue* Montmartre. Still, apprehension tightened my chest as I followed Armand into the dimly lit dining room where patrons filled every table for the midday meal. The smoke from their pipes blackened the low ceiling and hung in the air, mixing with the strong smell of bodies and the undefined odors of hot food.

"Twenty *sous* for the meal," a tall innkeeper in a dirty apron announced as we walked in. "Best bean soup on the street, partridge fresh from the market, bread and beer as much as you want."

My gaze lowered, I kept half my face hidden behind the cowl of my plain borrowed cloak, but Armand greeted the man with a cheerful smile and warm thanks. We were led to an empty table by the fireplace, where we sat on creaking chairs and were provided with the aforementioned food in pewter dishes. I held the fabric of the cloak against my face to prevent a coughing fit triggered by the patrons' smoke, but Armand misread my gesture. He leaned toward me when the serving girl withdrew to the kitchen.

"No one can recognize you here," he whispered. "So stop looking like a frightened rabbit. People will start to notice, and they'll think you've been kidnapped by a handsome ruffian."

"Don't flatter yourself," I replied in a low tone.

The noise of the nearby conversations drowned out our own words and no one gave us more than a passing glance, so I took in a few controlled breaths. The pungent smells of the place tingled my nostrils and teased my lungs, and I focused on calming my breathing to prevent a coughing fit. Meanwhile, Armand was taking to his role as a commoner like a duck to water. He ate his soup with approving slurping noises and dropped bread crumbs all over his borrowed servant livery. My own maid outfit too large for me, I sat as still as possible to avoid attracting attention.

"Darling," Armand said between two mouthfuls of soup, "you sitting there unmoving as a Roman statue isn't really helping us blend in."

I gave him a pointed look. Speaking to one of Lorraine's domestics had been my idea, but this whole plan—borrowing my servants' clothes to disguise ourselves as commoners and meet with one of his footmen in a Parisian inn—was *not* what I'd had in mind when I had suggested it. Obviously I had no desire to put us in jeopardy, but, as my stint at the fortune-teller's lodgings last year had proven, blending in with the Parisian crowd wasn't my strong suit. The danger of being recognized as aristocrats was slight, but the possibility of the situation going wrong weighed heavy on my thoughts.

"I'm not eating, if that's what you're suggesting," I replied.

Armand's mischievous expression softened. "I'm just saying there's no need to fret. Your household thinks we're visiting

Athénaïs. No one in this part of Paris can even begin to suspect who we are. That footman employed by you-know-who is going to meet us here like he promised, and he is going to tell us everything we need."

His words made sense, and I forced my shoulders to relax. After all, I had come here by choice, seeking answers. We weren't in any immediate danger. And Armand had proven last summer he could hold his own in a precarious situation.

"In the meantime, you get to admire how dashing I look in a green livery," he added. This time I bit my lip to prevent a smile. Armand grinned. "There it is. That lovely spark in your eyes. I'm not saying you make a convincing maid, but you definitely make a very pretty one."

I rested my arms on the rough wooden table to show him I could play my role if I wanted to. "You're fishing for compliments now. Just eat your food and pray we haven't come all this way for nothing."

Armand let out a theatrical sigh. "So coldhearted. Unrequited love is the worst."

A cold pang of anxiety reverberated through my chest at his joke.

"You need to stop saying things like that," I said, my brief moment of calm forgotten.

He paused, his spoon halfway between his plate and his mouth. "Things like what?"

"Things about how you love me."

Puzzlement pulled his brows together. "Why?"

"Because people are starting to believe it! Because Philippe listens to those people. And I can't afford—"

Frustration at his lack of understanding cut me short in my speech. Armand still regarded me with a confused frown, and I struggled to explain myself without hurting his feelings.

"But I do love you," he said, his tone matter-of-fact and serious now. "Why can't I say it?"

"Because people don't really know you, and they don't understand that when you say these things, it's not—"

Again, words failed me, and Armand's frown deepened. "I don't understand—"

A shadow fell over both of us, and a low voice interrupted, "Are you the chap who sent this note?"

We both startled so much that Armand dropped his spoon and I knocked over my empty cup. A lean red-haired man held out a folded piece of paper to Armand, an inquisitive look on his rugged face. He wore a coat over his expensive blue livery—to appear less conspicuous, I assumed—and sweat moistened his forehead in the warm atmosphere of the inn.

Armand stood up to shake his hand. "I did! Thank you so very much for coming. Please take a seat and have some of this wonderful soup."

The man appraised him with a disdainful look as he resumed his seat.

"What is this?" the footman asked without sitting down. He didn't spare a glance for me, which suited me fine. "I got a note promising a reward for information. Is it a joke?"

"My dear fellow," Armand replied, and one had to admire his composure. "It is most assuredly not a joke. I just felt our encounter required the right amount of discretion, for both our sakes. Hence the note. But it was definitely meant for you, and everything it contained is true."

I had my doubts using a series of people to send an obscurely worded note was the best way to approach a man one wanted secret information from, but Armand's ploy appeared to have worked. Word on the street was that this particular footman had gambling debts, and we hoped the promise of money would entice him to tell us what we needed to know about Lorraine. However, the man still stared at him, as if debating whether Armand was mocking him.

"You're a strange one," he said at last, and it almost sounded like a question.

Armand smiled. "Thank you. Now please share a drink with us, at least."

He pulled a coin out of his pocket and laid it on the table. His fingers covered it, but the man's eyes widened at the sum. He sat down at last and accepted both the coin and the proffered drink.

"There's a lot more where that came from," Armand said while the man drained his pewter tankard. It wasn't clear whether he was talking about the money or the beer.

The footman set down his empty mug and turned his dark gaze to me. "And who's the girl?"

His expression could have been described as chilling, but, as I held his gaze, I found my earlier anxieties were forgotten. I'd come all this way for answers, and this man had them. Despite his shady nature and vaguely threatening manners, there wasn't much he could do to us, two perfect strangers in a crowded tavern in the middle of the day. So I gave him my trademark gentle smile.

"Well, I'm the one asking questions."

The man blinked at me, as if it had never occurred to him that girls could speak. Then, after silence had stretched for so long that Armand had begun fidgeting, the footman chuckled. "Go ahead, then."

It turned out that Armand had been right. The man did have gambling debts and a low opinion of his employer, both facts combined enticing him to speak to us. He was also as eager as we were for our encounter to remain a secret, which prompted him to answer my questions with efficiency.

"The *chevalier* performs spells with the king," he confirmed, speaking of Lorraine. "He's a Source, a powerful one, from what I've heard. And he knows a lot about magic. *A lot*. He's got a library full of books about it, and he keeps a journal of sorts, where he records things."

Both Armand and I leaned forward at this information.

"A record of what?" I asked. "Spells?"

The man shrugged. "I don't know. I've never read it, have I? But he always keeps it about his person, and he takes notes in it after discussing magic with people."

I exchanged a conniving look with Armand. We needed to know what was in that journal.

"But I can tell you he knows spells about everything," the footman went on without prompting. "I've heard him brag he can perform any type of magic. Illusions, divination, you name it. I've seen him change the weather, turn objects into other things, heal people . . ."

He trailed off, but his last words drove Armand to speak.

"Have you seen him do darker spells? Like make someone ill, or—"

"Oh, for sure," the man interrupted, before catching himself. "Well, I've never seen him do anything, obviously, but he's definitely the sort of man who's ready for anything, including curses and such."

The revelation sent a chill down my spine. What if Armand was right and Lorraine had made me more ill with a spell? But our informant, now that he'd started talking, was warming to his subject.

"The king isn't the only *magicien* he's in business with, you know," he added. "He's always worked with more than one at the same time, and right now he deals with at least two other *magiciens* in Paris and who knows how many at court."

"Would you be able to give us names?" I asked, eager to get concrete evidence.

"No." The man shook his head. "I work at his house in Paris, I don't go with him anywhere. And he's a private man. He doesn't like to get visitors at home, he sees them at court or at their houses. The only one he brings home is, you know . . ."

He raised his eyebrows in a suggestive manner, and both Armand and I froze. We could guess fairly well who Lorraine liked to open his private house to, but this stranger didn't have to know we did. His eyes glimmered with malice. This was obviously the biggest piece of gossip about his employer, the one he thought we were after. So I cut off any further attempts at covering such grounds.

"We're only interested in the magic he does," I said, and the malicious light went out of the man's eyes. "Have you ever heard him talk about special spells he might have performed recently? Something unusual?"

I was hoping for a clue about the vanishing spells. The man thought for a moment, his long fingers absentmindedly playing with his empty tankard.

"No," he replied after a while. "He's talked to his . . . friend about the magic he's done with the king at Versailles, if that's what you're asking. Creating things in the castle and the gardens, from what I gather. And preparing for that party everyone's excited about. But mostly they talk about the people at court they don't like or about what they've got planned for the evening, you know?"

"So he hasn't bragged about cursing someone?" I insisted. "Or about performing a rare spell?"

Again, the man shook his head. "Listen, I want to help you, *chérie*, but I'd be lying if I said he did. He brags a lot, don't get me wrong, but it's all about the fancy magic that those people at court like him to do."

Too disappointed by this lack of revelations to get upset about his familiar tone, I gave Armand a dispirited look. He was pursing his lips, thoughtful.

"That journal of his you spoke about," he said. "Is there any way someone might have access to it?"

For the first time since the beginning of our conversation, the man shuffled his feet and cast an anxious look around the inn.

"Look," he said, "I don't mind spilling a few things for a bit of money. But stealing things and such? I'd lose my place for sure, or worse, if I got caught. I'm sorry, but whatever you two are thinking of, you're on your own. I can't help you."

Armand opened his mouth to reply, but I caught his arm to stop him.

"I think we have everything we came for."

I gave him a pointed look, and Armand took the hint. We would find a way to get our hands on that journal by other means. He handed the man another few coins, and we parted ways before this encounter could last any longer and attract attention.

When we emerged back onto the thoroughfare, rain fell heavily from the cloudy sky. We hurried in the April shower, water gushing down gutters and drains onto the pavement in large rivulets. The rain had emptied the streets, and the few passersby were too busy attempting to get themselves or their goods out of the downpour to notice us as we made our way back to my carriage, waiting for us a few streets away.

"We need to get that journal," Armand said as I clung to his arm to circumnavigate a large puddle. "All the proof we need has to be in there. And we need to find out who else he's been performing magic with."

I nodded my assent, too out of breath to give a full reply. Despite my best effort, my borrowed clothes were drenched and my leather boots heavy with water by the time we reached the carriage. Armand slammed the door against the deluge, and the vehicle took off, its wheels and the horses' hooves splashing their way along the near-empty street.

"There must be a way to find out which *magiciens* he's been working with," Armand said, following his train of thought.

"I can make a list of the court *magiciens*," I replied, my teeth rattling. Violent shivers shook me in the enclosed space. I pulled a blanket over my legs, determined to fight off a fit while the carriage carried on through the muddy lanes at a slow pace.

"It's the Paris ones I'm interested in." Armand bit his lip, oblivious to my condition. "He wouldn't cast curses and dark spells at court. He's too clever for that."

"We don't know if he's doing any of that," I said. "We only have the word of a disgruntled footman to support our theories. And there are dozens of *magiciens* in Paris."

My voice had weakened, and my breaths came out with a wheezing sound that alerted Armand at last.

"You're all wet and pale! Are you all right?" He wrapped one arm around my shoulders and took my hand. His skin warmed my icy fingers, but a cough rattled through my chest. "Oh, darling, it's all my fault! I shouldn't have dragged you to that awful inn."

The cold air still seared my lungs, but my coughing abated long enough for me to reply with a weak smile. "You give yourself way too much credit. Nothing is your fault. I wanted to interview that footman, and you didn't drag me anywhere. So stop fretting."

But there was no calming him, and he wouldn't rest until he'd wrapped me whole in the blanket, and, once the carriage pulled into the stables at the back of the palace, it was all I could do to stop him from carrying me into my home. Thankfully, it was midafternoon, when most servants rested in their quarters and left the kitchens empty, and the few lingering in the downstairs rooms and courts only saw two silhouettes in soaked uniforms hurrying through the servants' corridors.

"I'm all right." I tried to disentangle myself from his grip and the blanket. "You can let go." My protests would have been more convincing if another cough hadn't interrupted me.

"You can't even speak," Armand replied. "I'm putting you to bed and that's that."

My blanket half hanging behind us, he kicked a door open with his knee and we spilled into the main hall, where Athénaïs stood speaking with my majordomo.

Athénaïs's mouth dropped open. Armand stopped in his tracks. To his credit, he didn't freeze but rather loosened his hold on me enough to allow me to pretend at some semblance of composure. Such efforts were in vain, however, because Athénaïs swooped on Armand like a hawk.

"What on earth have you been *doing*? Where have you been?"

She shrieked in his face with such uncharacteristic indignation and alarm that it occurred to me our little scheme might have impacted the people we cared about after all.

"I came here to visit Her Highness!" she went on before Armand or I could say a word. "And I'm told she's supposed to be at my house! So I'm confused, because everyone knows Her Highness isn't well enough to visit her friends at home or at court. But then"—she punctuated her tirade by slamming her pointed finger into Armand's chest—"I'm told about *you* visiting her, about *you* spending all your time here, and now *you're* here, soaked to the bone in some ridiculous disguise, and I can't believe you'd be so stupid!"

She stopped, out of breath and tearful, and I couldn't bring myself to be angry with her for her words or her absolute disregard for my presence in the hall. It was obvious her outburst was born of love and frenzy, and the only reason she was ignoring me was out of respect for my station, which prevented her from directing her outpour of feelings at me.

"Listen," Armand started, "it's not—"

"It's not what I think it is?" she exploded again. "Is that what you're going to say? You tell me you haven't been spending all your time here, you haven't been putting on disguises, and you haven't been scheming?"

Armand shot me a helpless look. My legs still unsteady and my body wracked with shivers, I held on to him for support. Athénaïs's reaction was warranted in many ways. We had been reckless, and it was lucky no catastrophe had occurred while we were out and no one else had caught us in the act. But my investigation into Lorraine's actions and the vanishing spells was my priority, and Armand had proven to be the only one I could rely upon to carry it out. I considered Athénaïs a friend, yet I had spent very little time in her company these past few weeks, when she had been busy at court and in the Parisian *salons*, places that were now Lorraine's dominion. I didn't know if I could share my doubts and beliefs about him with her.

"Do you even realize how guilty you two look?" she added when none of us replied. "I understand having an affair, believe me, I do. But you must be clever about it. She's a princess! She's the king's sister-in-law! Everybody adores her. Everybody's constantly talking about her. You can't behave that way and expect no one will notice!"

Again, she was shouting at Armand when it was clear all she wanted to do was scream at *me*. Armand opened his mouth to protest at the word *affair*, but I squeezed his arm to stop him. Better Athénaïs think we were in love than investigating

Lorraine. It pained me not to trust her, but until I was sure she wasn't under Lorraine's thumb like everyone else, I would let her believe the most obvious reason for my behavior.

"Promise me you won't say anything," I said.

She turned to me for the first time, her gaze fierce and her hands on her hips. "Of course I won't. I'm your friend, even if both of you seem to have taken leave of your senses." She gazed at Armand. "But don't ever make me part of your lies again!"

And on that last warning, she gave an angry curtsy and marched out of the palace. The majordomo, who'd spent the last few minutes uncomfortably looking into the distance, closed the door behind her and left, presumably to fetch more servants.

Armand stared at the closed door. When he spoke, disbelief tainted his words. "So everyone really does think we're having an affair."

I let out a sigh. "Well, if it keeps them from finding out we're spying on Lorraine . . ."

I didn't finish my sentence, exhaustion catching up with me at last. "Help me walk to my rooms," I said instead. "I need to take off this dress before my maids arrive."

He obeyed, and an unusual silence, punctuated by the dripping of our clothes onto the marble floor and my labored breathing, settled between us as we walked along the dim corridors. At last we reached the door to my antechamber. No guard stood there, as security in my own home was considered achieved with a few guards patrolling the palace and grounds.

"You should go now," I said. "Let's both think about how we can gain access to Lorraine's journal and find out which *magiciens* he works with. Then we can make a new plan."

Armand nodded, still distracted. When he finally looked at me, concern clouded his features. "Will you be all right?"

I gave him a reassuring smile. "I will. I always am."

He considered me for a heartbeat, his head tilted to the side in a more thoughtful manner than I was used to seeing in him. Then he kissed my hand. "Indeed you are, Madame."

The clacking of his heels resonated under the high painted ceilings as he walked off, and his last reply resounded in my head. It was the first time he had called me by my title, and it had sounded as if he was trying to remind himself of who I was.

How peculiar.

CHAPTER VII

———————————

Overflowing trunks and boxes clogged my apartments like the scattered gems of a broken necklace. Filled with shimmering dresses and shining accessories, they glittered in the afternoon sunshine that poured in through the open windows. Fair weather had replaced the showers of the previous days, as if nature itself was getting ready for the king's entertainment due to start the next day at Versailles.

My carriage was meant to leave the Tuileries Palace in a couple of hours, but most of my luggage still sat open in my rooms, with maids and footmen dashing about like worker bees in a hive. Sat at my dressing table with Mimi at my feet, I supervised the packing of my toiletries while one of the maids finished lacing up the corset of my satin afternoon dress.

All of a sudden the servants' murmurs next door rose to words of greetings I could recognize, and I turned toward the open door as Philippe entered my bedchamber for the first time in two weeks.

"Henriette!" He pointed behind him. "Please tell me the chaos

I just walked through is about to disappear and you're ready to go." He closed the distance between us in a couple of long strides and kissed me on the cheek like I were some distant cousin.

I frowned at him and dismissed my maid with a nod. She slipped away with my box of toiletries under one arm and Mimi under the other. The door closed behind her, leaving us alone.

Oblivious to her exit, Philippe grabbed an abandoned ribbon off my dressing table and stood in front of the open window, the shimmer of his magically enhanced yellow-and-green out-fit reflecting the sunlight. For a moment he twirled the ribbon around his fingers, his stance relaxed and his gaze on the gardens below. I didn't speak, waiting to see how—and if—he would acknowledge the fact he had deserted me for a fortnight to spend his time with a courtier.

"Your doctors assured me you were better," he said at last, his attention still outside. "I was glad to hear it, because you know Louis, he has planned a hundred and one ways to keep us busy at his party, and he'll make a fuss if you're not there."

I rested my elbows on the dressing table and my chin in my hands, and didn't reply. If he wanted to pretend nothing was wrong between us, I wouldn't enable him. I deserved better than being treated like a mere acquaintance he could afford to ignore then run back to whenever the whim took him.

"I heard there'll be a parade tomorrow," he went on, as if unperturbed by my silence. "Or something equally ridiculous. And a banquet, of course. Then I think there are races scheduled, and all sorts of magical nonsense. Poor Molière has to perform no fewer than four plays in a week. And I'm guessing a ballet is planned as well, Louis simply can't resist dancing in front of an audience. But being the center of attention is the whole point of these shenanigans, isn't it?"

A hint of bitterness tinted his words, and I caught a glimpse of the husband who had confided in me and allowed me into his life last summer. The thought would have brought a smile to my lips if it hadn't been marred by the fact Philippe had withdrawn from me again since then.

At last he turned to meet my gaze. "You're quiet."

I bit back a sarcastic reply. I didn't want us to argue, and antagonizing him would lead us nowhere. So instead, I released a sigh.

"Why are you here, Philippe?"

Several emotions crossed his features in quick succession. Confusion, amusement, and then something like embarrassment.

"Why do you think I'm here?" he said in a gentle tone. "I'm here to take you to Versailles for my brother's party. I'm here to make sure you're ready and you have everything you need. I'm here to check you're actually well enough to attend said party."

I held his gaze, so he carried on, his tone turning mocking.

"Are these good enough reasons for you? What do you want me to tell you?"

The fact that he chose to hide behind sarcasm when we were alone, with nothing to prevent an honest conversation, awakened my temper.

"The truth would be a good place to start," I replied, my tone colder than I intended.

He raised an ironic eyebrow. "The truth?"

His casual attitude turned my temper to ice. "Yes, the truth. You're here because the Chevalier de Lorraine has already departed for Versailles with the king. You're here because you know you're supposed to attend the party with me and people will notice if you don't. You're here because Louis or your mother or both spoke to you, and you gave in to their demand."

I hadn't meant to say all this. I wasn't even certain the last part was true. But once I started talking, all the loneliness and sadness of the past two weeks bubbled up inside me like water coming to a boil and spilled out in a torrent of unkind words I couldn't seem to stop.

Philippe gasped. He moved toward me, but I stood up and slipped out of his reach before his outstretched hand could make contact with my arm.

"Henriette, whatever you've heard—"

"Please don't lie to me," I interrupted. "Months ago you promised me honesty. You owe me that much today."

He closed his mouth and hesitated. It was that pause, that moment of uncertainty when his reply should have been clear and resonant, that drove me to keep speaking.

"I've been really unwell, Philippe. And you just *left me*. You promised to love me, to look after me, and when I needed you the most, you simply disappeared. And I'm supposed to pretend everything is fine when you decide to return?"

I didn't raise my voice, but my words hit their mark nonetheless. Philippe paled and tightened his jaw. His posture grew rigid, and just like anytime he was hurt, he bit back.

"Jealousy doesn't become you, you know."

"Of course, I'm jealous," I said, keeping my tone as even as I could in my resolve to handle this like an adult. "We've been through a lot together, and I obviously don't enjoy seeing you attracted to a complete stranger. But I'm not talking about him. I'm talking about you and me. I'm talking about how you expect me to always be there for you, when you're too selfish to be there for me when I need you the most."

"Selfish," he spat, anger and pain flashing through his features at last. "Is that what I am to you too, then? I thought you knew me better than that!"

I took a step back, my certainty wavering in the face of his reaction. I knew he was good at playing a part, at pretending to be a narcissistic, superficial, and cynic man no one should feel threatened by. He had acted that part for four months at the beginning of our marriage to shield himself from heartache and to protect me in the process. But we had moved past this, or so I had thought.

"What are you saying?" I snapped back.

"You want the truth?" he said, closing the gap between us to loom over me. "You think I'm selfish? I'm worse than that, my love. I'm a coward. I see you ill, I see you bedridden, and I can't stand it. I know I'm supposed to protect you, I'm supposed to help you, and I can't, so I just *run away*." He threw his arms up and gave a mirthless smile. "I leave you to your fate, and I run to the first person willing to give me a little bit of affection, and I seek as much distraction as I can to try to forget the fact that the person I love the most in this world has an incurable sickness and that I'll eventually lose her."

I blinked, too shocked to reply. Hot tears ran down my cheeks, and I made no motion to wipe them, instead staring at Philippe as he carried on, seemingly unable to stop from talking now either.

"And guess the worst part. When I hear you've recovered, I come back, hoping I can placate you with a few lies and you'll forgive me for abandoning you. And because I'm a rascal, I get angry when you don't!"

So much self-loathing and hurt laced his words, I couldn't stand it. I pressed my hands to my ears, tears still streaming down my face. Sobs built up in my chest, strangling my breaths so that my voice came out hoarse.

"Stop it! Stop shouting, and stop saying such horrid things!"

"Why?" he retorted. "You wanted the truth. Maybe it's time you face the fact that I'm not a good person. Armand figured it out a while ago. I don't deserve either of you, and you need to stop pretending otherwise."

His eyes brimmed with tears, too, and I knew exactly what he was doing. He was pushing me away, waiting for me to lash out at him and confirm his self-destructive notions. The mere thought crushed my chest under a heavy weight. We'd made so much progress in the last few months, and for a moment, I had deluded myself into believing we were happy. But it was all coming crashing down, and it struck me that I had a choice to make.

A cough shook my entire frame, a reminder of how fragile my health was. I loved Philippe, but maybe it was time to be the selfish one in our relationship. It was now clear I couldn't fight for him, my health, my magic, and my status at the same time. I had thought that unmasking Lorraine's dark intents would bring Philippe back to me. But today's scene was proof our marriage had deeper issues than that. So I could either try to convince him of the worth of our relationship, or I could put myself first for once and see whether he could find his way back to me on his own.

This was going against my very nature and denying how much I loved him and wanted to protect and cherish him. It dug a hole into my heart to deny him the reassurances he craved with such obvious fear. But in this moment, I needed a friend. I needed a partner. I needed strength and love and support. There had to be a balance in our relationship, or it would crumble for good.

While he stared at me, panting and upset, and waiting for my reply, I tugged a handkerchief out of my pocket and wiped my face. Fire singed my lungs every time I inhaled, but my cough had ceased. Then I folded my hands around my handkerchief and met Philippe's distressed gaze.

"I've told you before," I said in a calm tone that belied my inner turmoil. "I'm not going to die, and I love you. I'm not going anywhere. Whether you choose to believe it, and how you decide to act in response to these facts, is up to you. I don't expect our marriage to be perfect. You have your flaws and fears, and I certainly have mine. But I expect us to *try*. Can you?"

He let out a derisive snort, wiped his nose with the back of his hand, and sat down on my bed with his arms wrapped around his stomach.

"I just can't bear to lose you," he said, miserable. "But I can't see any way to prevent it. I can't . . ." His voice trailed off, and the tears welling in his eyes overflowed and ran down his cheeks. He wiped them in a quick, proud gesture, but he had bared all his insecurities in that moment.

I let out a sigh, unable to leave him in this state without trying to comfort him. I closed the distance between us to sit by his side and grab his hand. He let me touch him in silence, and we stayed motionless for a little while, as the noises of servants moving boxes and dragging trunks out of the room next door reached us through the thin wall. His clothes retained the smells of perfume, sunshine, and something that was just him, familiar and reassuring. The lace on his collar was askew, and I straightened it in an absentminded gesture. Silence stretched on.

It wasn't peace, but neither was it war.

* * *

"Henriette, wake up."

My mind still foggy with sleep, I blinked at my surroundings. Intermittent light illuminated the dark confined space of the carriage, and cold seeped into my limbs despite the heavy blanket in my lap.

"We're almost there," Philippe said.

My head rested against his shoulder, and his arm wrapped around my waist. I straightened on the velvet-covered seat and he let go of me, the sudden gap between us sparking a pang of regret in my chest. Touching him used to feel so natural, and now every contact held a tinge of awkwardness, like two butterflies bumping into each other and pulling back in fluttery embarrassment.

"Sorry I had to wake you," he added. "You were so peaceful in your sleep. But we're arriving at Versailles."

Outside the carriage window, the black shapes of trees stood against the dark backdrop of the starlit sky. The rumble of multiple carriages mixed with the clatter of numerous horses' hooves on the road as our convoy progressed through the forest by the guards' torchlight. But our pace was slow, and the sound of voices we shouldn't have been able to hear carried through the quiet night.

"What's happening?"

I opened the window to peek out, Philippe following suit by leaning against my back and poking his head out above mine. On the road ahead, a large traffic jam blocked the passage of oncoming vehicles. A confusion of elegant carriages, horsemen, and people on foot filled the space between the trees, their lanterns and torches bobbing like fireflies in the tumult. Within minutes our carriage stopped, unable to go farther.

"What's going on?" Philippe called out to the nearest guard.

The young musketeer urged his horse onward and disappeared in the crowd, his blue-and-red uniform swallowed out of view in an instant. I gave Philippe a gentle shove back and resumed my seat.

"Maybe the gates are closed?"

He remained at the window and shook his head. "The invitation said to arrive after nightfall. We should be expected. I don't know who these people are."

"They look like courtiers to me."

A rapid beating of hooves on the road signaled the return of our guard. He reared his horse back in front of Philippe.

"There appears to be a traffic jam ahead, Your Highness," he said. "Many courtiers hope to gain entry to the party."

Philippe huffed an irritated sigh. "What do you mean, 'hope to gain entry'? Either they're invited or they're not."

"That's what I meant, Your Highness," the young man replied. "People who haven't an invitation still came in the hope of a late admittance."

"Well, that's unfortunate," Philippe said. "What do you suggest we do?"

"I'm not sure, Your Highness. It seems many gentlemen and ladies have decided to finish the journey on foot. The king's estate is just ahead."

"Finish on foot?" Philippe repeated, scandalized. He sat back down at my side. "Can you believe this? Not only do I have to attend a weeklong celebration of my brother's greatness in the middle of nowhere, but now I also have to walk there? I've got half a mind to give my invitation to one of those courtiers and go home."

"I'm not surprised this happened," I said to distract him from his irritation. "There are three thousand courtiers, and I heard only six hundred were invited. And Louis has made sure to turn this party into the event of the year."

"So you're saying he won't notice if we're not there?"

I searched for a hint of playfulness in his features, but found none: as if he were seriously considering giving up on the whole endeavor and returning to Paris. I contemplated the idea for a moment. For weeks, the prospect of attending this entertainment at Versailles had loomed over me like a great dark cloud of daunting responsibility. I resented its imposition and dreaded its experience. Yet now that its beginning was mere hours away, an unexpected thrill of anticipation ran through me.

Yes, attending the festivities meant that I would have to face the French court after weeks of retirement, with very few allies at my side and when my health was still fragile. But it was also the opportunity that I had been craving to continue my investigation. I wanted answers about the vanishing spells and about

Lorraine, and what better time to do so but when every preeminent *magicien* and courtier in the kingdom were gathered in the same space? I could question guests, watch out for Lorraine, and reclaim my place at court all at once.

So I met Philippe's gaze and replied, "I'm saying I want to go. Are you coming with me or not?"

It was a hint, and not a very subtle one. But if Philippe wanted to mend things between us, he had to start somewhere, and taking my wishes into account was as good a place as any.

He paused, holding my gaze for a heartbeat, and it sliced at my heart again that his answer wasn't immediate and definite. "Yes," he said at last. "I'm coming."

I gave him a smile to acknowledge his effort, but it didn't hold its usual warmth. This had been a long day, and there were only so many olive branches for me to extend his way.

We both slipped on our gloves and fastened our cloaks, and he opened the carriage door to announce our intentions to the guards. Then he alighted and placed his hands on my waist to help me out after him. Yet as soon as my boots landed in the mud, he withdrew, hesitant again.

Our young guard nudged his mount forward, which diverted my attention to his anxious expression. "Your Highness, it's very crowded ahead. Are you sure—"

"I wager my wife is a better rider than you," Philippe interrupted him. "Now I'd rather not have her stand in the cold all night, so if you don't mind . . . ?" He shot him an expectant look, and the man gave a reluctant nod to his two nearest colleagues, who dismounted and handed the reins to us.

Contradicting my afternoon predictions, the weather had

turned after nightfall, with the temperature dropping and mist rising between the tree trunks nearby. A shiver ran down my spine, and my breath came out in cloudy shapes in the cold air. The musketeer who lent me his horse helped me onto the saddle of a beautiful chestnut mare that let me take her reins placidly.

Soon we were on the move at a trot, our guards surrounding us with torchlights. Either on foot or on horseback, they advanced with warning calls to cut us a path through the pandemonium of vehicles, horse riders, and pedestrians ahead. Everywhere courtiers in shimmering clothes and servants in uniforms competed for space on the road, either in the process of alighting from carriages, or while attempting to cover the rest of the ground leading to the royal estate. Torches, lanterns, and even a few magical lamps dotted the darkness, their bobbing lights like a hundred beacons on a river at night. The conversations of the walkers, the shouts of the guards, the clomping of the horses' hooves and the creaking of the carriage wheels all mixed amid the forest trees in a cacophony more reminiscent of a Parisian street than a country road.

We made good progress at first, but soon the crowd grew so thick, clearing a way through the throng became near impossible. With Philippe close behind me, I focused on guiding my horse forward, but the lack of space forced our guards to ride very near to us and it rendered my mount nervous.

When our pace reduced to near standstill, it hit me that no one in the multitude around us paid us any mind, and a strange hush had replaced the noise of the road at our back. Used to being in the public eye, either for better or for worse, being ignored was what caught my attention. Raising my gaze to see what captivated everyone, I gaped at what lay ahead.

The royal estate sat surrounded by gilded railings. Behind its open gates, Louis's father's old hunting lodge was gone. Last November, I had helped Louis create the first version of the *château* he wished to fashion out of magic. Now two symmetrical buildings encased the first castle, making it several times bigger than its original size. A vast paved courtyard preceded the royal courtyard, what had once been the lodge gate separating them.

And the entire place shone in the dark.

It gleamed in the night like a burning fire, countless windows sparkling in its bright facade and its two wings like arms held open to welcome the king's guests. I blinked and shielded my eyes against the glare.

"It's like looking at the bloody sun." Philippe groaned behind me.

"Let's just get inside," I said.

I urged my horse forward, and our guards resumed their efforts at clearing a path among the crowd. And even though the press of people was denser this close to the *château*, pedestrians and horse riders alike endeavored to let us through as soon as they recognized us.

"It's Monsieur and Madame!" several voices repeated. "It's the royal family," others said. "Let them through. It's Monsieur and his wife."

The words spread like a gentle wave inching its way toward the shore, and more people greeted us as we passed. I gave polite smiles to anyone who bowed or curtsied, and thanked the stars I had chosen to wear an elegant velvet gown for the journey. If news of this small incident ever reached my mother's ears at her convent, she would be pleased to hear I had followed her advice to dress the part of the princess in all circumstances.

We reached the open gateway, where a few musketeers ensured order by the *château*'s entrance. Yet as one of our guards announced our arrival, an odd shimmering between the gates caught my gaze. I halted my horse.

"Wait!"

Philippe let out an annoyed sigh. "What is it now?"

He maneuvered his horse to my side and I pointed at the opening. "A magic shield, here. The estate is protected against intruders."

Last spring, I had seen Fouquet put up such near-invisible wards around Fontainebleau, and I recognized now the same spell at work.

Philippe squinted in the distance. "If you say so. I can't see anything with this glaring monstrosity in the background."

"Her Highness is correct," said a guard by the gates. With graying hair and an impressive mustache, he strode forward with the air of a man in charge. He removed his hat with a flourish and sank into a deep bow.

"So we can't go in?" Philippe scowled.

The man straightened. "It is His Majesty's wish that anyone with an invitation may enter the palace grounds."

Philippe's jaw tightened and he cast the man an aggravated glare. I shot him a warning look. A crowd of onlookers stood at our backs, and if he lost patience, anyone within earshot would hear him. He acknowledged my stare with a nod and made an effort to relax his features into a sort of polite smile. He couldn't quite mask the sarcasm in his tone, though.

"Please be so kind as to stop speaking in riddles and tell us whether we may go in or not."

The older musketeer opened his mouth to reply, when an idea struck me.

"The invitation is the key," I said. "The shield spell lets through anyone with an invitation."

The older guard bowed again. "Her Highness is as insightful as ever and correct again. His Highness may use the king's invitation to pass through the gates and attend His Majesty's entertainment."

Philippe let out a muffled curse and patted his pockets. Trepidation ran through me. Louis's obvious effort at combining the protection of his *château* with the exclusiveness of an exceptional party sparked excitement in my chest. Like him, I liked games and riddles and magic, all things Philippe found at best tedious and, at worst, annoying.

"Aha!" Philippe brandished a cream-papered envelope.

"Make way for Their Highnesses!" the older musketeer shouted. The warning was unnecessary, since no one stood between us and the entrance.

Philippe handed me the envelope. "You're the one who knows about these things."

And for the first time that day, there was warmth in his voice, and something almost like pride. He may not understand magic or enjoy his brother's games, but it seemed he still loved the fact that I did. I gave him a conniving smile and nudged my horse forward to take the lead.

As I approached the ward spell, it glistened in the *château's* dazzling light. Following my instinct, I took off my glove and laid the spelled envelope in the palm of my hand. I presented it to the shield, as if I were producing a treat in front of a difficult horse's nose. The envelope warmed at the proximity and shivered against my skin. As a precaution, I held out my free hand to Philippe. He grabbed it without hesitation, as if he now feared I would enter the grounds alone and leave him behind. I had no hand left to guide my horse, but she seemed happy to carry on walking without my prompting.

One more step and the envelope hummed in my hand. The shield parted before us like curtains over a stage, and we walked through. A glance back allowed me to see the shield sealing behind us. Although only a few steps away, the faces in the crowd now appeared faraway and ghostly in the unnatural light of the *château*.

The clacking heels of an approaching footman turned my focus back to the building ahead.

"Welcome to Versailles!"

Philippe dropped my hand, and his face darkened, his sour mood returning. "Yes, we've been here before."

"Please follow me," the footman continued, undeterred. "I will guide you to your apartments in the palace."

"Oh, it's a palace, now, is it?" Philippe muttered to no one in particular.

I raised my head to embrace the entirety of the dazzling building with my gaze, and failed. Its main structure and symmetrical wings encircled us, and the shielded gates at our back prevented us from retracing our steps. The only way was forward, into the sunbright *palais*.

My excitement evaporated, an odd feeling of dread rising in its stead. Versailles had welcomed us, and would only let us go at the king's pleasure. As if a trap had been set, and it had now sprung.

CHAPTER VIII

A day later, the palace still shone in soft golden tones in the sunset, a striking background to the opening of the king's much anticipated festivities. The crowd of handpicked revelers gathered in the manicured gardens in their finest attires like a colorful flock of chattering birds.

"Welcome to 'the Pleasures of the Enchanted Island.'" Athénaïs read aloud a leaflet that servants in elaborate masks and glittering costumes distributed.

In preparation for tonight's entertainment, box trees had been magically grown at the end of the Royal Way where we stood, surrounding Apollo's Fountain with tall regular hedges that formed an outdoor theater. Courtiers gathered around it, as well as along the great lawn that led to the palace. A pang of sadness shot through me as I beheld the beautiful fountain. Creating it had been one of the first spells Louis and I had attempted together, and it had failed. Now he had found someone else to perform the enchantment, and the glorious result stood there for all to admire.

"What does that mean?" Olympe asked, yanking me back to the current discussion.

"It's the party's theme," Athénaïs explained. "We're on an enchanted island. It's all based on *Orlando furioso.*"

Louise leaned toward us with a perplexed frown. "Sorry, based on what?"

Athénaïs let out an impatient sigh. "*Orlando furioso.* It's a book. It's all the rage in the Paris *salons*. Everyone has read it."

"Obviously not everyone," Olympe muttered under her breath.

Louise shot me a helpless look, and I stepped in to rescue her. "It's an epic poem about brave knights and their ladies, and all the adventures they have. There's magic and love and battles against fantastical creatures and evil characters. I'll loan you my copy if you wish."

"Can she read?" Olympe stage-whispered to Athénaïs, who hid her smile behind a jeweled fan.

I shot her a warning look, but Louise replied, oblivious, "Oh, you don't have to. I'll never read it."

This time, Olympe snorted. I hurried to redirect the discussion before Louise could notice their rude behavior.

"So, what's tonight about?"

We all stood facing the sunset-lit palace in the distance, with Marie-Thérèse and the Queen Mother a couple of steps away. As this party was officially thrown for their benefit, they were the only two people seated in the crowd, on two gilded chairs decked with white feathers and white roses.

"Tonight is a procession," Athénaïs said, her eyes on her program. "The main character Roger is going to arrive with his brave knights, and the wicked *magicienne* Alcine is going to capture them and lock them on her enchanted island."

"Of course there's a wicked *magicienne*." Olympe rolled her eyes.

It was indeed interesting to note Louis had chosen to focus on the part of the story that involved a female magician hindering the hero's plans. Was it a subtle hint of his disapproval of the power of *magiciens* in general, and female ones in particular?

"So His Majesty will be Roger?" Louise asked, her eyes brightening with excitement. She wore a beautiful gown of silver silk that shimmered with magic in the dimming light, and she looked as lovely as I had ever seen her. Next to her, Athénaïs's dark blue dress and Olympe's burgundy one made them appear as two ominous birds of prey appraising a chickadee.

"Who else?" Olympe replied. "And all the kingdom's highest-ranking noblemen will be his knights."

Before leaving after breakfast to join the rehearsals, Philippe had complained about having to indulge his brother in this fashion, but I was looking forward to seeing him take part in what promised to be an outstanding spectacle. Wrapped in a white fur mantle that offset my yellow brocade gown, I felt warm and rested enough to face the evening with the proper enthusiasm and decorum.

"Well, I can't wait!" Louise announced.

Olympe and Athénaïs exchanged a snide glance, which reminded me of Olympe's idea that this whole entertainment was in fact a gift to Louise. No one else had mentioned this particular piece of gossip to me, which made me doubt its veracity. Surely Louis wouldn't be so blatantly disrespectful to his own mother and wife? As the light grew dimmer and the conversations of waiting courtiers louder, I moved toward the two ladies in question.

Marie-Thérèse had her hands folded in her lap and a bored expression on her face, while the Queen Mother's wan face stood out very white against her mourning clothes. They both sat in silence, and their features relaxed at my approach, as if they'd been waiting for someone to save them from the awkwardness between them.

"Isn't it a lovely night?" I smiled in the most encouraging manner I could devise. Given the queen's still-secret pregnancy and her mother-in-law's illness, I doubted either woman's first wish was to be here tonight, so I strived to direct their thoughts toward a positive outlook.

"It's cold." Marie-Thérèse pouted.

A chill indeed hung in the air, but the sky was clear, with the evening star already visible above our heads.

"At least it's not raining," I said in such a bright tone I sounded like Louise. "And I hear tonight's entertainment is an unprece-dented feat."

"My son has indeed worked very hard on it," Anne d'Autriche said.

Encouraged by their replies, I treaded toward bolder inquiries. I had come here with a purpose, after all.

"Yes," I said, "I heard his new Source is very good. A perfect match for His Majesty's great talent."

The Queen Mother remained composed, but Marie-Thérèse's features at once became more animated.

"He is very gifted. And so amusing! Have you met him? He tells the best stories."

So even the queen wasn't immune to Lorraine's charms, then. My posture sagged a little, but I stayed focus on my goal.

"And what's *his* story?" I asked. "Surely such a talented Source didn't just appear out of nowhere."

"He didn't," Marie-Thérèse said, warming to her subject. "His family is from Burgundy. He came to court to offer his services to the king. There are so few Sources in the kingdom; really, it's a blessing he came forward."

The Queen Mother shot me a sharp look. Her daughter-in-law ignored the truth about my own gift—there had never been a reason to share that secret with her—but I wondered how much she knew about her husband's magical plans. From Anne d'Autriche's expression, maybe not much.

"So he does magic with the king?" I asked to steer the conversation away from the topic of Sources.

"He does magic with everybody!" Marie-Thérèse replied. "Of course, most of his time is devoted to Louis, but he is so hard-working that he also aids the court *magiciens*."

"And His Majesty allows it?" I said with a pointed look at the Queen Mother. We both knew how much Louis hated to share anything in his life, and as the one who had taught him the importance of such behavior, she had to find Lorraine's conduct an unwelcome development.

"Louis is very generous," Marie-Thérèse said, and it took all my concentration to keep a straight face at the claim. She lowered her tone in a dramatic fashion. "And you know his gift isn't very strong. He doesn't really need a Source all to himself."

Letting everyone think his magical talents weren't very much developed had always been Louis's strategy: a way to let his enemies underestimate him, as Fouquet had found out last year. As it happened, letting everyone underestimate me was also my favorite tactic.

"So the man is a godsend, then?" I said in a teasing tone. "No annoying flaws? No dark secrets?"

This was more heavy-handed than I had planned, but helplessness made for desperate measures. Everyone—from the lowly footman to the queen of France—seemed to have the same things to say about Lorraine, and I needed more to go on.

"I don't think so," Marie-Thérèse said. "I think he's charming."

I turned to the Queen Mother, whose lack of interest in the discussion struck me as more concerning than her pale coloring. She had spent half her life working and scheming to protect and guide Louis. Yet now that a new adversary had appeared on the stage, she sat back and let everyone talk about the man like he was a blessing sent from above.

"I don't know him," she said. "I haven't met him. But as far as I've heard, he's the second son of an obscure provincial nobleman. What I know is that I trust my son's judgment. If the man proves unworthy or is hiding anything, I'm certain Louis won't be fooled."

I met her golden gaze and stared at her thin features, lined with more wrinkles than I remembered. She had really stepped back, then. After twenty years at the forefront of every decision taken on France's behalf, she was not only retiring from politics but also withdrawing from any sphere of influence around her son. As Louis had planned after Mazarin's death, he ruled alone, ignoring even his own mother's counsel. And for now, he was choosing to trust Lorraine at his side.

The situation was therefore clear: Lorraine wasn't going anywhere. As the Queen Mother pointed out, the man was one among many low-ranking courtiers. Yet he had climbed his way to the top, and unless he made a mistake—or I managed to prove his misdeeds—he would remain there. Whatever his means of action, which I suspected involved getting rid of the competition but still had to confirm, his goal appeared obvious: to become so indispensable to the king that he would be impossible to dismiss. He was ambitious, charismatic, and now powerful. How was I ever going to bring him down?

The blare of a trumpet snapped me out of my low spirit. All of a sudden, dazzling light replaced darkness as thousands of colorful magic lamps came to life on the gravel path and in the trees around us. A collective exclamation of delight escaped the assembled courtiers, and applause rippled along the crowd.

By Latona's Fountain in the distance, a herald and a small suite appeared, all dressed in magically enhanced outfits that sparkled in the night. They proceeded down the great lawn toward us at a slow pace, their features taking shape as they approached. I moved back next to my ladies, and Louise took my hand in her glee.

"Look! It's D'Artagnan!"

It was indeed the old musketeer on horseback behind the herald, surrounded by squires and a dozen drummers and trumpeters whose music filled the air with a bewitching rhythm. The blue and red of his uniform glittered in the magic light, and he waved at the greeting courtiers as he led his mount around Apollo's Fountain.

For an instant our eyes met, and he inclined his head in a

respectful nod. D'Artagnan had been there when Louis and I had defeated Fouquet for good. He was among the few people who knew who I really was, and he was one of the most respectful and loyal too. As far as I was concerned, he deserved this special place in the king's procession. I joined the general clapping, but already the first part of the pageant was dissolving to leave room for the main event.

"It's the king! It's the king!" Louise exclaimed. She squeezed my arm hard and jumped up and down with a squeal.

"Thank goodness she's here for the running commentary," Olympe said in an icy tone. "I would have no clue what's going on otherwise."

But loud music swallowed her words, and Louis appeared, riding what appeared to be a giant horse fashioned out of magic. If D'Artagnan and his retinue had sparkled, the king and his mount shone like a flame in the dark. Golden and silver fabric, colorful gems and precious garments covered him, and he wore a tall headpiece that was half-crown, half-feathered hat. It would have looked ridiculous if it hadn't been *magnificent*. Awe took over delight among the assembly, and if the clapping went on, the conversations died down. Even Olympe found nothing to say.

The magic horse, a huge beast made of shimmers or flames or sunshine, carried him forward at a regal pace, and the king rode it with his trademark impassive expression, neither waving nor nodding at anyone.

When he reached Apollo's Fountain, the rest of the procession came down the Royal Way at a trot. Princes, dukes, counts, and marquesses rode down the lawn in pairs, their bearing straight but with smiles on their faces. Philippe and Lorraine came first, resplendent in matching shining silver-and-blue outfits and feathered hats. Bitterness pinched my heart. As the king's brother and the king's Source, it made perfect sense for them to ride first and together. Yet I couldn't help but read mocking triumph in Lorraine's expression as he rode past me. Philippe waved at me, and I returned his gesture with a smile, because it was my duty and I would have hated for anyone to read my thoughts just then, but the look I gave Lorraine was the naive one he no doubt expected.

Thankfully the rest of the procession was there to distract me: I recognized Prince Aniaba in an impressive red-and-green outfit, and the Comte de Saint-Aignan rode with Olympe's husband, the Comte de Soissons. Armand came behind them, in a bold cream-colored ensemble and a magnificent white-feathered hat. He threw kisses at the crowd and grinned when our gazes met. Athénaïs's husband came next with the other marquesses, and I laid eyes on the man for the first time. Good-looking enough, with a straight nose and a happy smile, the young man was dressed all in red and sported golden gloves, boots, and hat that gleamed in the magical light. He waved at his wife, who was chatting with Louis's cousins Elisabeth and Françoise and pretended not to notice. I exchanged a glance with Olympe, who shrugged in helplessness.

After the noblemen came the comedians. Molière's troupe joined the procession in the most arresting way: like the king, they rode enchanted animals so big they sat far above our heads.

"Mademoiselle Du Parc is Spring on an enchanted horse,"

Athénaïs read from her leaflet, seemingly eager to avoid any mention of her husband at all cost.

The famous actress rode by with a seductive grin and a dress made of beautiful flowers and green ivy that moved about her body in a perpetual cycle of death and rebirth.

"Not covering much, that dress, is it?" Olympe said.

"Oh, do be quiet," Athénaïs snapped. "Du Parc is amazing, and I won't hear anything against her."

"You're in a mood," her friend replied. But she fell quiet after that.

"Next is René Du Parc as Summer on an elephant."

I had never beheld a real elephant in my life, but I doubted they were giant gleaming beasts that appeared made of water or a piece of the sky.

"Then it's La Thorillière," Athénaïs went on as we all gaped at Du Parc's mount. "He's dressed as Autumn, and he's riding a camel."

As with elephants, my experience with camels was limited to engravings in books, and I had never seen one pictured as a huge animal built out of copper leaves and tree bark.

"And finally, Louis Béjart is Winter, on a bear."

Wrapped in sparkling white fur, the comedian rode an enormous bearlike illusion, whose pelt seemed to be made of snow.

The courtiers' applause hadn't yet ceased when the trumpets signaled another event, and the herald called our attention to Apollo's Fountain. The king and Lorraine dismounted to meet in front of the gilded lead statue of the Greek god surrounded by water jets. They removed their gloves and joined hands, a hush falling over the press of guests now craning their necks and pushing to get a better view. Even the two queens left their seats to approach the scene.

In a theatrical gesture that I knew from experience to be unnecessary, Lorraine took a deep breath, threw his head back, and closed his eyes before whispering a spell. A dramatic shudder ran through him, and Louis extended his free hand toward the fountain in a commanding motion.

The assembly held a collective breath, and the statue moved.

Golden Apollo on his chariot slapped the reins of his four horses, which shook their heads and struggled to extricate themselves from the water. Their bodies shining with their own unnatural internal light, god and beasts splashed their way out of the shallow pool.

In the gathered assembly, courtiers gasped. A few cries rang out, and a commotion to the left indicated someone had fainted. Meanwhile, the statue of Apollo, god of the sun and Louis's favorite symbol, stopped his chariot in front of the king. In a symbolic gesture any guest would be able to read, he and his horses halted their race across the earth to bow to Louis. The Sun King acknowledged them with a curt nod, then snapped his fingers. Immediately Apollo guided his mounts back into the fountain, where they froze once more. Louis and Lorraine turned to receive the audience's applause.

The crowd clapped and whooped, eyes bright with wonder and cheeks red with elation. I felt the same as they did. If this was the opening of the celebrations, what did Louis have in store for the rest of the week?

Despite myself, some of my hard feelings toward Lorraine melted in the face of such grandiose magic. Maybe the Queen

Mother was right. The man had an incredible talent. His gift could be used for the good of the kingdom and the crown. He may have taken much from me, but was I really entitled to destroy him for my own gains when he could help France and its subjects with his magic, when my own gift faltered? Was my life meant to change anyway, and was his arrival the catalyst for such a difficult-to-accept but inevitable new era in my existence?

I had but an instant to ponder these thoughts when a sudden gust of wind found its way between the trees and blew through the courtiers, sweeping up skirts, knocking wigs askew, and ruffling feathers. Squeals and surprised exclamations punctuated the appearance of the draught, which I feared heralded a coming shower. I shivered, grateful for my fur mantle, when Louise let out a shout. Her jeweled silver hat, blown away by the wind, was skipping toward the fountain at great speed. Two guards rushed after it, but before they could get a hold of it, the elegant headpiece flew into the fountain and bobbed on the water like a toy boat made of cork bark.

"Oh!" Louise exclaimed, her face a picture of discomfiture.

Without a moment's hesitation, the king put one booted foot into the fountain to retrieve the hat. He plucked it out of the water in a deft gesture, and handed it back to Louise with a gallant bow.

Louise blushed and curtsied, accepting her rescued hat with thanks. Everyone stared. Marie-Thérèse stood a couple of steps away, her face pinched into a haughty pout. Oblivious, her husband exchanged a few words with Louise, who let out a happy giggle.

"Someone has to save them from themselves," Athénaïs whispered.

Olympe decided this someone was she, and she joined them as if Louise speaking with the king was the signal for every courtier to pay their own compliment to their sovereign.

"Your Majesty, what a wonderful spectacle!" she said, stepping between them in a deliberate gesture. "You spoil us!"

The rest of her words were lost to my ears as other guests stepped forward and called out to the king. A small gathering formed around Louis, while the rest of the spectators mingled with the noblemen who had taken part in the procession.

Just then the masked servants in glittering costumes emerged from the trees, this time carrying trays of colorful drinks and piles of food. They weaved in and out of the crowd to hand out the savory *bouchées* and sweet delicacies.

"I'm famished," Athénaïs announced. She grabbed Olympe's hand, and they both took off, chasing after a silver platter of meat and vegetables in the shape of a pyramid. I took one step in the direction they'd disappeared toward, when a voice called out behind me.

"Darling, you're here." Armand pushed a lady in a pink dress out of his way to reach my side and hand me a glass of wine. "What are you doing standing here all by yourself? Don't you have ladies to look after you?"

"I've been abandoned." It was becoming such a common state of affairs for me that I dismissed it with a wave of my hand and changed the topic. "Did you enjoy the procession?"

Armand grinned. "Did I enjoy it? Who doesn't love the clapping and cheering of an adoring crowd? No wonder our king is addicted to it. What was your favorite part? Please say when you saw me on my horse."

"When I saw you on your horse," I teased him obligingly.

His good mood was contagious, and I sipped some of my wine while he steered me toward the lawn, away from Louis and his gaggle of admirers by the fountain.

"Since you've been behind the scenes today, do you know what's in store for tomorrow?" I asked. "More illusions? Magical fireworks? Molière's comedians metamorphosing into fantastical creatures?"

Armand let out a chuckle and plucked a glazed cake off a passing slaver. "Wouldn't that be a sight?"

He placed it all in his mouth and chewed, but his reaction brought a puzzled frown to my brows.

"What do you mean?"

He swallowed the pastry and licked his fingers. "You said Molière's troupe could turn themselves into creatures. I just acknowledged your joke. Was I supposed to laugh out loud? I mean, it wasn't that funny—"

I scowled, my confusion increased tenfold. "Why do you think it's a joke? They did it for the ballet at Fontainebleau."

Armand blinked at me. "Wait. Is this one of those spells that you think exists but no one else has ever heard of?"

My fingers tightened around my fragile glass. It was happening again. Another spell had disappeared. I searched for a sign of Lorraine and, after a couple of seconds, spotted him talking with the lady in pink. He whispered at her with a playful smile, while the lady's cheeks turned the color of her dress in the torchlight.

"He's done it again, hasn't he?" Armand said. "Made another spell vanish."

With a nod, I drained my glass to steady my nerves. The ability to create portals. And now the metamorphosis enchantment. Whether it was Lorraine or not, *someone* was changing magic in the kingdom by taking away its most powerful spells.

And I needed to stop them.

CHAPTER IX

———————

The weather didn't improve the following day. Despite a clear sky, the temperature remained low and a brisk wind slithered between the hedges in the gardens and through any open window in the palace.

The second day of the king's entertainment involved a play by Molière and Lully. Much like the performance given the year before at Fontainebleau, the *comédie-ballet* mixed drama, music, and dance on a stage built on the great lawn, with the park in the background and chandeliers hanging from the trees on either side of the audience.

The story gathered onstage princesses and princes, fauns and shepherds, and if rumor was to be believed, a bear and a giant tree. Magic seeped into every aspect of the play, with dazzling illusions drawing gasps from the crowd every minute and constant costumes and sets changes keeping the spectators on the edge of their seats.

The program announced five acts and six musical interludes. By the time the third interlude started, with the melody of a harpsichord, violins, and flutes swelling into the air, cold had leaked into my bones and I shivered under my layers of clothes. I pulled my velvet cloak tighter around my shoulders, but a coughing fit wracked through me and I buried my mouth in my handkerchief.

Philippe pressed the back of his hand against my cheek with an anxious frown. "You're pale as a ghost. You can't stay here."

He sat between me and the rest of the royal family, who remained focused on the show in a concerted effort to avoid drawing attention to my condition. But my cough wouldn't abate, and within minutes courtiers behind us whispered and craned their necks to get a better glimpse.

Onstage, the musical interlude ended, and Molière's actors started the next scene with a few miniature fireworks. The noise and colors diverted the guests' focus for a minute.

"You need to go back to your rooms," Philippe said.

I opened my mouth to protest—I couldn't leave in the middle of the king's entertainment, with the whole court watching!—but instead of words, a gasp escaped my searing lungs. My breaths came out in a series of rasping noises, and I forgot what I was going to say.

Philippe turned to try to catch someone's gaze to help. For Louis's sake, he wouldn't leave the performance, but he seemed intent on making me go as soon as possible, and in that moment I couldn't find any reason to fight him. I would just have to apologize to Molière and Lully later.

Rushing feet on the gravel and a sudden presence at my side made me look up to see which of my ladies had answered Philippe's silent call for help.

Armand crouched in the space between the front row and the stage, his magically enhanced red velvet outfit shimmering in the lights from the stage.

"I'll take her back to her apartments," he said in a low tone.

"Where are her ladies?" Philippe whispered back, his jaw clenched in frustration.

"I don't know," Armand replied, before turning to me. "I'll help you back to the palace, all right?"

My cough prevented me from giving my opinion on the matter. The next step would be dizziness, possibly a fainting spell, or even worse, retching. I would *not* let this happen in public. Better to leave on Armand's arm and let people gossip about that.

Ignoring Philippe's scowl, I nodded at Armand and grabbed his proffered hand. He wrapped an arm around my waist to help me up, and we walked off as swiftly as one can when positioned between a brightly lit stage and an audience of six hundred nosy aristocrats.

"You sure know how to make an exit, don't you?" Armand whispered.

Gripping his hand like a life raft, I kept my head down and tried to control my breathing. Our heels crunched in the gravel, and we left the ephemeral theater behind us, the large shape of the palace looming on the horizon like a dark sleeping beast in the night.

"Nearly there," Armand lied. "You're doing very well."

My chest still hurt with every breath, but my cough had subsided for the moment. Hurried footsteps behind us made us pause. Prince Aniaba rushed toward us, waving a white handkerchief like a flag on a battlefield.

"Wait!" he said. "I have something for Her Highness!"

He caught up with us, out of breath and sweat beading on his forehead in the chandeliers' light. He handed me the handkerchief, which I pressed to my face without hesitation. The smells of grass, wildflowers, crisp air, and magic filled my nose. For the first time since the beginning of the play, my chest expanded and I took in a lungful of air. Tears of relief wet my eyes.

"Thank you," I told the prince.

He smiled. "You're very welcome. I saw you leave and thought the spell would help. I was sitting next to the Comte of Saint-Aignan, who was happy to assist me. He declined chasing after you, though."

I returned his grin at the idea of the poor count running up the slope toward the palace. I would have to thank him later nonetheless. That simple spell, which Fouquet had taught us before he betrayed us all for his greed, was proving time and again an immense relief.

"Let's get you inside now," Armand suggested.

We resumed our slow walk along the great lawn, and the prince fell into step with us.

"If you don't mind, I'll accompany you. I don't mind missing the play, and I'd rather see Her Highness to her apartments."

He was being as gallant as ever, and after what he had just done for me, I had no intention of arguing with him. I let him take my free arm, and the three of us made our way toward Latona's Fountain by candlelight.

"We have barely seen you lately," I said to the prince when my breath settled at last. "You've been so busy."

"I have indeed," he replied. "But working here has been a real pleasure, I must confess. I've been able to perform artistic spells I had never done before."

His comment about magic reminded me I had meant to ask for his opinion on the vanishing spells. Now seemed as good a time as any, with still a way to go before reaching the palace and no one to overhear us.

"You mention magic," I said. "I've been meaning to ask you a question about it."

Armand stiffened at my side, but I buried my misgivings under my resolve and went on.

"Have you noticed anything strange happening with certain spells lately?"

A silence followed, and my self-assurance faltered. Behind us, the outdoor theater shone in the distance, while the dark silhouette of the palace grew closer as we followed the curve around Latona's Fountain and headed for the steps leading to the water garden.

"You mean like tonight?" the prince replied at last, a note of caution in his tone. "With the play?"

His careful choice of words sparked hope in my heart, and my pulse quickened. "Yes."

"I attended a rehearsal of the play a couple of days ago," he said. "And I noticed the troupe wasn't using the metamorphosis spell they'd performed so well at Fontainebleau. When I asked Molière about it, my question confused him to no end. Our conversation was so awkward that I didn't dare mention it again to anyone."

A wave of relief washed through me, so intense I stopped in my tracks. The prince knew about the vanishing spells! I had been right. They weren't the product of my fevered imagination.

"Oh, I'm so glad to hear you say so," I said. "Everyone I mentioned it to acted as if I were talking nonsense."

We'd reached the water garden with its symmetrical pools and I started off again toward the palace terrace with a spring in my step.

"Why do you think you're the only two people who've noticed it?" Armand asked.

"Maybe because we're Sources?" I replied. "Magic comes from us, so we're not affected by it the same way you are."

"You might be correct," the prince said. "We should ask the Chevalier de Lorraine if he's noticed anything."

Armand and I exchanged a glance, both wondering how much to share with him. I opted to keep trusting him.

"I already asked Lorraine about this," I explained. "He denied the spells had ever existed. But Armand and I have reasons not to believe him and to suspect him of lying in this case."

"I see," Prince Aniaba said. "I won't mention it to him, then. And what about speaking to the king?"

I shook my head. "I already have. His reaction was the same as Molière's and everyone else's."

The prince let out a defeated sigh.

"Are you aware of any other spells disappearing?" I asked. "Beside the metamorphosis one?"

"I've wondered about the portal spell as well," he said. "When the Comte de Saint-Aignan and I were listing our ideas for this entertainment, I mentioned it in passing, and he didn't seem to understand what I was talking about. I put it down to overwork and tiredness, and moved onto another suggestion. But it struck me as odd, and now I see a pattern here."

"It definitely seems more than coincidence," I agreed.

We were now crossing the gravel terrace, and the silhouette of a guard detached itself from the shadowy palace to come to meet us.

"But who's behind this?" the prince asked. "And why?"

"That," Armand said, "we don't know."

Although now that the palace stood before us, empty of all its court, an idea grew at the back of my mind. There was no one there but servants and guards. Everyone else was at the play, and for quite a while yet. It was the opportunity I'd been waiting for.

"Your Highness!" The palace guard came to a halt before me, his weapons clinking as he bowed. "Is everything all right? Do you require any assistance?"

"Thank you," I replied. "But I just need to rest. The Comte de Guiche will accompany me to my apartments."

I turned to thank Prince Aniaba as well, who let go of my arm with a smile.

"Please, don't mention it," he said. "I was happy to help in my small capacity. If there's anything else you want me to do to help with the situation . . . ?"

I reached for his hand to squeeze it. "You've done far more than I ever expected, as always. Before we know more, I fear there's nothing we can do. And I do seem to be forever in your debt."

He kissed my fingers. "There's never any debt between friends. Let me know if anything else happens. Have a good night."

We parted ways, my heart lighter than it had felt in weeks. I didn't want to involve the prince more than he already was, but thanks to him I now knew exactly what to do.

Inside the palace, shadows filled every corner, chandeliers and lamps not yet lit for the return of the king and his guests. I declined the guard's suggestion to guide us back to my rooms but accepted his offer of a candelabra. Then, our arms still linked, Armand and I took off through the string of gilded rooms.

"Wait, aren't your chambers that way?" Armand asked after a minute, pointing to his left.

"They are," I said. "We're not going there."

"We're not?" Armand went up an octave in alarm.

"The palace is empty," I said. "We'll never get a better opportunity."

"Oh dear. You want to break into Lorraine's rooms, don't you?"

"You read my thoughts."

As proof of his unstoppable rise in status, Lorraine had been allocated rooms next to the Queen Mother's. We climbed the deserted staircase up to the facing doors of the neighboring apartments, our feet scraping against the marble steps. A guard stood on the landing, in the dim light provided by the window looking onto the gardens.

"Who goes there?" he asked.

Before I could think of an answer, Armand replied, "Who goes there yourself! Can't a man get some privacy in this place?"

His usual amiability abandoned, he charged up the remaining steps to spring upon the man in a dramatic move. Since his gesture seemed deliberate, I remained in the darkness on the stairs, my cowl up and my face buried in my magic-seeped handkerchief.

"My dear fellow." The candelabra in one hand, Armand wrapped his free arm around the guard's soldier, trapping him where he stood. "Please understand my predicament here. This lady and I have been looking for a quiet place, and everywhere we turn, there's a dutiful soldier like yourself. Will you take pity on me and go for a walk for a little while?"

"I . . . I can't leave my post," the guard replied, his voice wavering with uncertainty.

Armand released a theatrical sigh. "Listen—" Then he fished his purse out of his pocket, the coins jingling in the quiet staircase, and whispered in the man's ear.

Whatever he said worked, as the guard gave a muffled answer and hurried off, not even glancing at me as he walked past me down the steps.

"Come on." Armand waved me on as soon as the soldier disappeared around the corner. "We don't have much time."

"Isn't it a bit worrying how easy that was?" I joined him in front of Lorraine's door. "Does Louis know how quickly his guards can be bribed?"

"No matter." Armand gave me an expectant look in the dim light. "Well? I got rid of the guard. Now how are we getting in?"

"I don't know," I replied. My pulse quickened in consternation at the recklessness of this plan. "I thought we'd pick the lock or something."

Armand raised an eyebrow. "Can you pick a lock?"

"No," I admitted.

"Well, me neither."

I bit my lip. Time was of the essence. I needed an idea, and fast.

Meanwhile, Armand considered the door. "What if he has wards and magical shields in place?"

"One thing I learned with Fouquet is that men like him and Lorraine think they're untouchable. I doubt he has bothered to put up wards, especially if he always keeps his journal on him like his footman said."

"So what are you hoping to find here?"

"Anything else that might be useful."

And he kicked the door open. The gilded wood panel swung wide in a loud crack, part of the lock falling to pieces onto the floor.

I gasped. "What on earth?"

"What? You can't pick a lock, and you said there were no wards or shields!"

My heartbeat now frantic, I turned to the staircase. What if someone had heard this racket? Maybe we ought to abandon this rash endeavor now before anyone caught us in the act and a world of trouble found us. But no sound of rushing footsteps reached us, and the hallway remained empty and quiet. I glanced inside the dark anteroom, which yawned before us like the cave of a sleeping dragon, both frightening and tantalizing.

I drew a breath to calm my pulsing nerves. "We might as well go in now."

I plucked the candelabra from Armand's hand and took a couple of cautious steps forward. His hand on the small of my back, he followed suit, the parquet floor creaking under our heels.

"Do you want to check the bedroom while I have a look around here?" I said.

"Absolutely not," he replied in a low voice, as if the walls and mirrors could hear us. "This is the enemy's den. I'm staying with you."

His choice of words made it unclear whether he did so in order to protect me or to use me as protection.

A look around the room gave us a first clue about Lorraine's character: He was messy. Various articles of clothing and all manners of men's accessories—including a sword and a pistol—lay about the chairs and floor. By the window, a desk was piled high with books, letters, ink jars, and quills. We circumnavigated a large copper basin on the carpet and moved toward the back of the room, lined with bookshelves.

My heart jumped. "Tell me if you see any books about magic."

I brought the candlelight as close to the bookcase as was safe and read the titles off the volumes' spines.

"History books," Armand said. "Poetry books. Greek and Latin books . . . Maybe these aren't even his. This is a guest room after all."

My excitement waning, I bent down to look at the lower shelf. A title caught my eye, and my pulse raced again.

"Spell books!"

I grabbed the thickest one and handed the candelabra back to Armand. I laid the heavy book down on the desk and flipped through his well-worn pages. Just like in my missing *grimoire*, the incantations were organized in alphabetical order. I reached the letter *O* and found the page of the portal spell as blank as the one in my own handbook. But the enchantment on the page next to it was also gone.

"What's supposed to be there?" Armand asked.

I searched my memory to recall what I'd seen in my *grimoire*. "An incantation to force someone to obey an order, I think."

I turned over more pages, their yellowish paper crinkling under my touch. As expected, the metamorphosis spell was missing at the letter *M*. More concerning, other blank pages, whose enchantments I couldn't identify, dotted the book.

"There must be at least a dozen vanished spells here," I said with a sigh of dismay. "I don't know them all. I'll need to make a list of them."

Armand presented me with a quill and an unfinished letter from the pile. "Write them down, then."

Voices and footsteps resonated on the staircase outside, and we both froze. The light of a swinging lantern ricocheted against the window on the landing, fast approaching. My heartbeat thumping in my ears, I blew out the candles of our candelabra.

"The door is broken!" A male voice exclaimed outside. Booted feet pounded against the steps, and light was thrown onto the wreck of Lorraine's door.

Armand gripped my hand and crushed it in his, his breathing accelerating. I blinked and refused to panic. We still had a couple of seconds before discovery. The anteroom was dark as a pit. I had had worst odds against me.

In a deft gesture, I grabbed the spell book and pulled Armand toward the bedchamber. Its door had been left ajar, and I pushed it open with my shoulder, before barreling into the dark room. Behind us, shouts indicated our presence was known.

"Close the door!" I ordered Armand in a low voice.

To his credit, he slammed the gilded panel a heartbeat later, and turned the key in the lock. I prayed the king's guards would be more squeamish about breaking a palace door than he'd been. The bedroom curtains hung open, and thanks to the clear night, a dim light bathed our untidy surroundings. It was enough for me to judge the layout of the room to be similar to my own bedchamber. Without further hesitation, I tugged Armand toward the hidden passageway to the service rooms.

Behind us, the door rattled on its hinges as the guards shook its handle and pounded its panels. I wrenched open the concealed door, and we careered across the small unadorned rooms leading to the servants' corridor. Armand tripped on something and cursed, bumping into me.

"Nearly there," I said.

But my lungs were on fire, and finding my way in the dark was becoming increasingly difficult. Thanks to a small, round window above the servants' staircase, we were able to stumble our way down the wooden steps without breaking our necks, yet once we reached the low-ceilinged, brick-walled corridor at the bottom, my breaths came out in ragged rasps.

"Why are you slowing down?" Armand asked, his own breathing uneven.

I couldn't reply. Instead, I pointed at the rough door at the end of the hallway and signaled for Armand to mimic my unhurried steps. We were lucky to have encountered no one going through the palace's back ways. Now wasn't the time to ruin it by erupting out of the building like a pair of criminals on the run.

We paused behind the door to listen to the sounds of a potential search outside, but the coughing fit I had spent the last minutes trying to suppress tore through me. Prince Aniaba's handkerchief proved useless, its enchantment long dispelled.

"You need air," Armand said. "Let's chance it."

He hid the spell book under his coat and, still clutching hands, we walked out of the palace. We found ourselves under a stone archway leading to the gardens, with the clear night sky above us and the sound of the play reverberating in the distance. We moved to go around the building and find our way back to the main entrance, our heels clacking against the cobblestones. My cough wouldn't stop.

Two guards with lanterns emerged from the palace as we rounded the corner of the building. They rushed to us as soon as they spotted us.

"Her Highness isn't feeling well," Armand said. "I'm accompanying her back to her apartments."

The men fell into step with us, one offering to fetch a doctor while the other suggested asking the kitchens for hot drinks and food. A pang of guilt shot through me at their solicitude. We'd just played their colleagues for fools and likely got at least one of them into serious trouble. I promised myself to speak with D'Artagnan to ensure none of them would be dismissed for the events of the night. It would require some alteration of the truth, but it would be worth it.

By the time I made my way back to my chambers, however, the strain of the evening caught up with me. My body wracked with shivers and cough, I burned with fever and vomited as the doctor arrived. My brightly lit bedroom swayed around me, with servants buzzing about to bring linens and bowls of water. Reality became a series of flashes. A maid ushering Armand out. Another helping me out of my gown. The doctor feeding me a bitter potion. My lavender-scented sheets settling around me. Another maid telling me everything would be all right.

I closed my eyes, and the last thought that crossed my tired mind before sleep engulfed me was that, now that I had the spell book, the next step in my plan was to retrieve Lorraine's journal.

CHAPTER X

——————

The next day saw the conclusion of the Roger and Alcine story. The palace of the enchantress stood on an island in the middle of a vast artificial lake, conjured out of thin air in the heart of the park. The king's guests crowded along the shoreline at dusk, their luxurious outfits glittering in the fading light.

After sleeping until midday and resting all afternoon, I joined the festivities in my most lavish gown to date, ready to face the court and to find out Lorraine's secrets. Still, a shiver of anxiety ran over me as I made my way through the assembled courtiers, the layers of silk and tulle of my pale blue dress swishing around my ankles with every step.

The king was there, in conversation with his mother and Olympe. Farther away, Lorraine stood laughing with Athénaïs. Philippe chatted with Prince Aniaba, while Louise listened with rapt attention to some explanation given by the Comte de Saint-Aignan. Like an outsider arriving late to a party, I pondered which group to join, when Louis's cousins Elisabeth and Françoise found me and led me to mingle with the nearest cluster of young aristocrats dressed in their finest glittering apparels.

And although people were eager enough to talk to me, neither my untimely departure from last night's play nor the breaking into Lorraine's apartments was mentioned to me. What appeared to be the topic of every conversation was Louis's latest feat—the spell to create the lake. By all accounts, Louis had achieved his goal with this entertainment: all his courtiers praised his magical skills and lauded his powerful spells as if he were the first *magicien* in history to accomplish such wonders.

Fouquet was forgotten, Vaux-le-Vicomte gone from memory. After everything he had done, I didn't regret the Crown *Magicien*'s fall, yet it struck me how easily his existence had been erased from everyone's minds. Nine months ago these aristocrats had been applauding and admiring his magic. Now Louis had their attention, but how long would he be able to retain it?

"I'm so glad you're here." Armand hooked his arm with mine, and we moved toward a quiet spot on the bank of the lake. "How are you feeling?"

"Much better," I said, then lowered my tone. "Do you still have the spell book?"

He nodded. "I don't think anyone is looking for it though. This morning Lorraine's door had already been fixed, and that same guard was on duty—he didn't recognize me."

"You went back there?" I said, my eyes widening at the risk he'd taken.

"I wanted to know what Lorraine was up to. He was busy out here all day with the king. No one has said anything about an incident last night. It's as though they've swept it under a rug and chosen to forget about it."

"They might not even have noticed a book was missing." I pondered the news, far more reassuring than I expected. "Lorraine's rooms were a mess, after all, and it may not even be his own bookcase."

"So do we go to the king, then?"

I shook my head. "Not yet. All we have right now is a spell book with a few blank pages. Without Lorraine's journal, we don't even know the exact list of spells that are gone. We need both in order to compare them and prove Lorraine's guilt."

"What about going to the king with Prince Aniaba?" Armand said. "He will support your testimony."

It was tempting, but my first attempt at telling the king the truth had rendered me cautious. We couldn't underestimate how much influence Lorraine now had over Louis. He might not believe me again and make any further investigation near impossible. And I didn't want to involve Prince Aniaba in our schemes when that might put him in a difficult position.

"No," I replied. "I'd rather we focus on getting the journal and—"

Athénaïs materialized by our side and pushed her way between us. "You two," she said with a fixed smile and blazing eyes, "are drawing everyone's attention, standing there whispering by yourselves."

I startled and glanced behind me. Several courtiers had their eyes on us, hiding complacent smiles behind jeweled fans and exchanging knowing looks.

"There is such a thing as secret rendezvous, you know,"

Athénaïs said between clenched teeth. "Or are you two intent on becoming the court's latest scandal?"

"We're not having an affair," Armand protested.

"Tell that to someone who'll believe you," Athénaïs snapped. She gripped my arm and led me away, her voice rising in volume and fake brightness as we walked back toward the crowd. "This way, Your Highness. I have found the best spot to watch the ballet. I promise you won't be disappointed."

She drew me to an empty space by the shoreline, steeped in shadows now that the sun had set.

"I can't believe you, of all people, are being so reckless," she hissed in my ear. "You left with him last night with the whole court watching and now I find you together again!"

I bit my lip, guilt at deceiving her seeping through me. She was my friend, looking out for me. But she had been laughing with Lorraine mere moments ago. I feared I couldn't trust her with the truth of my association with Armand. And we had been reckless in our investigation, which made her scolding not entirely inappropriate.

Her features softened at my downcast expression. "I can understand falling for someone other than your husband," she said, her voice gentler. "But you two must be more careful if you don't want the king or his mother to find out."

Her effort at understanding, combined with Olympe's comment from the other day, woke a sudden doubt in me. Was *she* having an affair? So soon after her marriage? And with her husband at court?

A sudden blast of trumpets interrupted my thoughts. A hundred magical lights and torches burst to life on the lake, and the ballet began. From behind Alcine's palace, a giant beast appeared. Exclamations of surprise and delight erupted from the audience.

"What is it? What is it?"

I squinted at the approaching fantastical creature, followed by two more silhouettes. As if coming straight out of the pages of a book, or from the depths of a faraway ocean, a whale and her two calves came into view, made of seashells, water, and seafoam. A woman in an arresting gown of blue, pink, and silver fabric that sparkled with magic and jewels rode the whale around the lake, to the swelling music of violins, flutes, and drums.

"It's Mademoiselle Du Parc," Athénaïs said, sparks of admiration in her eyes. "She's amazing."

Soon the enchantress—for it was she—reached her island and alighted, the whales disappearing back into the churning waters. Several of Roger's knights and various nymphs, fauns, and naiads joined her in a complex dance in front of her castle, their costumes like gleaming gems on dark velvet fabric.

All of a sudden the king himself joined the ballet, dressed as Roger in a breathtaking golden outfit that shone like a flare in the night. He offered a ring to the *magicienne*, breaking the curse she'd kept him under. Just as she accepted the gift, Lorraine emerged from the crowd of dancers and took Louis's hand.

A small thunderstorm erupted above the enchantress's palace.

Even I gawked at the spell. Thunder boomed, and lightning illuminated the clear night sky, before striking the magical castle. All the dancers fled the island in magically powered small boats, feigning awe and distress. Alcine herself disappeared inside her palace. The storm doubled in strength, lightning lashing at the island and thunder echoing around the lake. Louis and Lorraine stood amid the chaos, unperturbed by this unleashing of natural forces they controlled seemingly without effort.

Alcine's castle crumbled under the repeated blows of lightning strikes, its towers collapsing and its walls dissolving under the assault. Then, as the enchantress's defeat was complete, fireworks exploded from the remains of her palace.

Their popping sounds replaced the rolls of thunder, and music rose once more above the lake to celebrate Roger's triumph. Magical shapes and vibrant colors filled the heavens, fantastical creatures and chimeras chasing each other across the firmament before dissolving into nothingness. Giant birds, fireflies, and butterflies spread their wings above our heads, trailing magic and wonder after them.

The audience cried out, cheered, and clapped with endless enthusiasm. "*Vive le roi!*"

Louis received the roaring approval of his court from his position on the enchanted island. After a few minutes, he and Lorraine linked hands once more, and a gilded royal barge surfaced from the waters. They boarded the boat, which moved of its own volition toward the shore, glitter of magic in its wake.

Once back on land, the king *magicien* and his Source greeted the two queens first, then received the compliments of the guests close enough to catch their attention.

"This was incredible," Athénaïs said, stretching on tiptoe to keep the two men in her line of sight. "I need to speak to them."

And without further ado, she took off to elbow her way through the crowd toward her quarry. Meanwhile, servants in faun and nymph costumes offered drinks in gilded goblets.

"There you are." Philippe grabbed two cups off a passing tray and handed one to me. "I was wondering where you were."

"I watched the show with Athénaïs," I said. The drink in my hand sparkled and changed color, and when I tasted it, a strange sweetness coated my tongue.

Philippe grimaced after his first sip. "What on earth is this? Why can't he just give us some wine?"

"I see you found the alcohol," a voice drawled, and we looked up from our experimental drinks. Lorraine surveyed us, dazzling in a green-and-silver costume and an amused twinkle in his eye.

I tensed, but Philippe didn't even pause. He thrust his goblet under Lorraine's nose. "What sort of poisonous potion is this?"

The other shrugged, unfazed. "How would I know? I'm not in charge of refreshments. The kitchens made it, and Saint-Aignan added the sparkle."

"Well, it's horrid," Philippe replied, waving over a servant to hand back his cup.

This was my chance. I faked a sneeze and bumped lightly into him just as he was about to set his goblet on the tray. Philippe in turn stumbled, and jolted the entire salver, which tipped over and crashed on Lorraine, smearing his costume with sticky colorful drinks. The now empty cups tumbled down onto the grass, and the tray skidded to the shore. Lorraine let out a loud curse, Philippe exclaimed an inarticulate sound, and the footman shouted a horrified apology.

Curious onlookers gathered, Philippe focused on Lorraine while I helped the shaken manservant gather his lost salver and cups and apologized to him. Drawn by the commotion, the Comte de Saint-Aignan and Prince Aniaba came to the rescue.

"A cleaning spell," the count offered, his voice muffled by the various conversations going on around us. "Very simple. No trouble at all if you will allow us . . . ?"

"Why not?" Lorraine said.

His usual smirk and self-assurance were back, and he proceeded to undress in front of everyone. Gentlemen chuckled and ladies giggled as he took off his stained coat and ruined shirt. His sculpted, broad chest bare in the torchlight for all to see, he handed his garments to the count and the prince, who went aside to perform the spell and returned it within moments.

Normal conversation resumed as he put his now-clean clothes back on, and I slipped off behind the gathering to meet with Armand.

"Well?" I asked.

He shook his head. "Sorry, nothing. The journal wasn't in his coat pockets."

"And it wasn't on him either," I said. "His breeches were tight-fitting enough for me to check."

"Scandalous," Armand said.

I let out a frustrated sigh. In the distance, Lorraine let out a loud laugh, all the light and gazes focused on him. Our scheme had unfolded exactly as planned, yet we still didn't have his journal. If he didn't keep it with him, where was it? And how were we going to find it?

* * *

The file of carriages halted in front of a blue and gilded gate, each vehicle unloading its passengers in the afternoon heat. I shielded my eyes against the glare of the sun and alighted after Philippe, my jewel-studded shoes landing in the dust of the road. I flipped my ivory-and-feathers fan open, and linked arms with my husband. Sweat already ran down my back under my pastel day dress. Philippe wiped his forehead with a handkerchief.

"At least that was a short ride," he said.

I glanced around at the green trees lining the road and the small building before us, seemingly sprung out of nowhere in the countryside. "Where are we?"

"We rode west of the palace," Philippe replied. "We've reached the edge of the Versailles estate."

Curiosity and puzzlement tugged at me. What was this slated-roofed building and why had Louis chosen to have it so far away from the palace?

"Let's go inside," Philippe said. "Before I faint and you have to carry me."

I acknowledged his joke with a smile, and along a gaggle of courtiers, I walked with him through the gate and a gravel courtyard, then up the main staircase of the central building, which was flanked by two symmetrical wings.

A day and a half had gone by since the ballet and pyrotechnic display on the lake, and we'd spent most of it together. While I searched for another way to get Lorraine's journal, I kept Athénaïs's advice in mind and remained away from Armand while in the presence of so many prying eyes. Meanwhile, Louis kept Lorraine endlessly busy, which meant Philippe sought my company again. I wasn't naive enough to think it meant everything was back to how it was before, but I enjoyed these moments with him nonetheless.

If the atmosphere inside the building was as stifling as outside, I appreciated the shade it provided. We climbed up another flight of stairs to access the gilded reception rooms, and followed a gallery toward the back of the building, which ended in an octagonal room. All the windows had been flung open, allowing access to a balcony that stretched around the building like a ribbon. Animal paintings covered the walls of the room, and strange noises reached us from outside. Realization prompted a gasp from my lips.

"It's a menagerie!"

I let go of Philippe and rushed onto the balcony. Sure enough, the land outside was divided into seven enclosures, where all manners of animals ambled around fountains and lavish green plants.

"I suppose that's not something you see every day." Philippe joined me, a glass of water in hand. "Now I see why Louis sent all of us here without a word of explanation."

I drained the proffered glass, the cool water a welcome respite from the unrelenting heat.

"Thank you," I said. "I needed that."

Philippe appraised me with a slight frown. "Don't take this the wrong way, my love, but I'm actually surprised you're not coughing right now."

The heat and dust didn't help my fragile lungs, but he was right: when any change in the weather or type of exertion used to spark a coughing fit, it had been three days since my last episode. There was no explanation for it, except the one provided by Armand that I still found too distressful to believe: that a spell cast by Lorraine was the cause of the worsening of my illness and that he had been too busy lately to renew his curse, which was therefore fading.

Casting aside those unsettling thoughts, I grinned at Philippe and turned to the enclosures below. "I'm just too excited to be unwell. Look at that! There's an elephant."

"Are Their Highnesses enjoying their visit?"

Charles Perrault, cheeks red from the heat and leaflet in hand, joined us on the balcony with a polite bow.

"Very much so," I said. "Do you know what all these animals are?"

"I don't." He held up his leaflet. "But I brought a script, and Your Highness will have to indulge me and pretend I'm not reading from this program." He proceeded to point out camels, crocodiles, a lion, and all sorts of extraordinary birds. "This is a pelican. And this one is an ibis."

"I believe I know this one." Philippe pointed at another bird. "Isn't it an ostrich?"

"It is," Monsieur Perrault nodded. "It comes from Africa and weighs twice the weight of a man."

"It can't fly," Philippe said to me. "I read it in a book."

"And," Monsieur Perrault added, "when pursued by a predator, it is rumored to bury its head in the sand and thus to believe itself to be unseen."

Philippe snorted. "A flightless bird that refuses to face its problems? Sounds like me."

Unsure how to react, Monsieur Perrault offered a tentative smile and made his excuses.

I gave Philippe a light slap on the arm. "You scared the poor man away. He's very knowledgeable, you know. He was giving us interesting information."

Philippe shrugged, his good mood evaporated. "It's too hot, and I'm bored now. You enjoy and let me know when you're ready to go back to the palace."

He moved away from me, but I gripped his arm before he could leave the balcony. We hadn't argued, and yet he scowled as if I had just upset him.

"What's wrong?"

"Nothing's wrong." He pasted a smile on his face, which I knew was false. "I don't want to ruin your day."

I clung tighter to his arm. "Just tell me."

"It's just—" He released a sigh and gestured at the enclosures. "It's ironic, isn't it? This place. Rare animals kept behind high walls and iron railings. Don't you find it the perfect metaphor?"

And his meaning struck me. "They're like us. That's what you mean."

He waved his hands in the air like a *magicien* who had just performed a great spell. "Ta-da! Whether it's a rich aristocrat or a wild bird, it doesn't matter. If my brother wants it, he'll have it. Then he puts it in a fancy cage and distracts it from escaping with magic tricks and good food. And nobody can stop him."

I glanced around to check whether anyone was within earshot, but all the guests were some distance away, their focus on the animals below. My spirits dampened by Philippe's reaction, I guided him back inside.

"You're right," I told him in a low voice. "I'm not sure I like this place after all. Let's go back to the palace."

"And now I've ruined your day," Philippe replied. "I'm sorry."

We walked back through the gallery and the reception rooms, navigating the courtiers mingling there. Then we went down the staircase. Philippe's observation replayed in my mind, its accuracy more striking with every step.

Since the beginning of the week, every activity provided by the king had been to lure, enchant and trap his court at Versailles. I wagered everyone would leave in two days wishing they could have stayed longer—or forever. Louis's plans to control everyone around him were at play here, and even I had overlooked it for a moment.

"You didn't ruin my day," I said to Philippe as we emerged into the sundrenched courtyard. "I just don't like to see you upset."

He kissed the top of my head. "You're too sweet for your own good, my love."

We left the menagerie through the gate, and walked along the dusty road toward our carriage in the line of vehicles.

"What would you like to do?" I asked. "If you could do anything right now, what would it be?"

I caught his gaze, determined to wipe the melancholy from his features. He pondered my question, as dust rose around our ankles and birdsong came down from the trees. The smell of dry grass and horse manure saturated the hot air.

"I don't know," he said at last. "What would you like to do?"

I grinned at him. The magic lake created by Louis still sat in the middle of the park, its presence taunting me for the past two days.

"I want to go swimming."

CHAPTER XI

I drifted on the cool water, my white shift billowing around my body.

A blanket of sparkles gleamed on the surface of the lake, enclosed by trees soaked in afternoon sunshine. Birds fleeted between the branches, their calls echoing in the quiet park. Bees buzzed among colorful flowers, whose soft scents wafted through the hot air. Like a slumbering giant brought down by an excess of heat and revelry, Versailles drowsed under a clear blue sky.

"What are you doing?"

The high-pitched voice came from the shore and cut through the peace of the moment.

"What does it look like we're doing?" Philippe muttered. He circled me at a slow breaststroke, his long dark hair pooled around his shoulders.

I blinked at the two small silhouettes on the bankside. "Who is that?"

"Elisabeth and Françoise, by the sound of it."

"You two are mad!" One of the girls shouted. "What about the whales?"

I let out a laugh and nearly swallowed water. The lake had a dark green tinge to it, and its depths were invisible. The enchanted island in its middle was gone, and if the remains of Alcine's palace or her fantastical creatures lay at the bottom of the waters, we had yet to encounter them.

Another question traveled through the distance. "What's the water like?"

I gave up on my floating endeavors and resumed an upright position. "It's nice and cool! Come!"

Giggles on the shoreline. Then two splashes and much squealing. Louis's teenage cousins swam to meet us at the center of the lake.

"You lied!" Françoise shrieked. "It's cold!"

"Stop shouting!" her sister replied. "You'll attract the whales!"

Their cream-colored shifts and long hair plastered against their skin, they swam in a complicated flailing of limbs that involved a lot of splashing water in each other's faces.

"Can you two even swim?" Philippe asked.

"Of course, we can!" Françoise said.

"We learned in the pond at Saint-Germain-en-Laye," Elisabeth added, slightly out of breath.

"That's reassuring," Philippe mumbled.

The noise now attracted other onlookers, courtiers who had found refuge in the park in search of fresh air or privacy. Elisabeth waved at them.

"Join us! It's very cool, and there are no monsters!"

"Is this allowed?" a gentleman in a tasteful brown and green outfit asked.

"No one said it wasn't!" Françoise replied.

A group was forming on the bankside, where some discussion took place before common ground was reached and people peeled off their layers of clothes. Elisabeth let out a gleeful laugh. Soon the courtiers made their way into the water, some more gingerly than others. The majority remained near the shore, but a few more daring ones joined us in the middle of the lake. They startled at Philippe's and my presence in the group.

"Your Highnesses." The courtier formerly dressed in brown and green attempted a bow in the water. "I didn't recognize you from the shore."

"I blame my wife," Philippe said with an ironic smile. "She's English."

I failed to see how this was any explanation, but Françoise added at once for the gentleman's benefit:

"Our governess was English. She taught us to swim in the pond at Saint-Germain-en-Laye."

"She also taught us embroidery," Elisabeth said.

Philippe grabbed my hand and gave me a pointed look. While the girls and the courtiers chatted and paddled in the water, we drew away from them.

After a few breaststrokes, Philippe stopped and took hold of my waist. I used my legs to keep me afloat and wrapped my arms around his neck. A half smile tugged at his lips.

"There," he said. "Much better."

Our noses were a handspan apart, flecks of sunshine reflecting in his brown eyes. The noise of conversation and splashing water became a droning sound in the distance. The sky and the water engulfed us like a protective bubble.

Once, in another life, we had been together like this in another lake, at another royal estate. It was dark, and Philippe had kissed me, and it had been perfect. But that was a year ago. Today the relentless sun beat on the waters, the lake was a temporary spell cast by a king, and Philippe gazed at me with melancholy in his eyes.

"Do you still love me?" I asked, the question escaping my lips before I could stop it.

"I do," he said without a hint of hesitation. "I'll always love you."

A pause. Flying insects alighted on the water for a second, then flew off or disappeared into the depths. I traced the faultless shape of Philippe's mouth with the tip of my finger. Other questions nudged me forward, and I was so close to the edge that I might as well take one more step.

"But you love Lorraine too," I said.

It wasn't an accusation or a reproach. Just a fact. Philippe lowered his gaze for an instant. I dropped my hand from his face.

"I love that he loves me," he replied.

It made sense. In a world that always reminded him there was nothing about him that made him worthy of care and attention, he was incapable of pushing away anyone who showed an interest in him. I wanted to question whether he could trust Lorraine's affections, but I wasn't the right person to do so.

"I thought we agreed no scandal," I said instead.

"Yes."

"But you're having an affair!"

He let go of my waist, his expression darkening. "Aren't you?"

My own temper rose, and I struggled to keep my voice low. "I've told you before. Armand and I aren't together."

He snorted, as if he didn't believe me, or it didn't matter whether I told the truth or not. An arm's length of water sat between us, but it felt like a chasm the size of an ocean.

"So is this it?" I asked. "You love me and I love you, but it's not enough?"

He met my gaze, defeat on his handsome features. "I suppose it's not."

"So what do we do?" I said, my voice wavering.

"I don't know, my love."

It might have been the words *my love*. Or his shrug. Or his lack of fight. My temper snapped, and I splashed water in his face as hard as I could.

Then I swam toward the shoreline, leaving him drenched in the middle of the lake. If he didn't know what to do, I, on the other hand, had a plan. I had played nice for long enough. It was time for Lorraine to return to Burgundy.

* * *

The weather cooled at sunset.

The last rays of sunshine painted the palace in fiery gold hues and turned the glass windows into hundreds of mirrors. In the gardens, the king's guests gathered under a canopy of magical branches and flowers. Ivy wound its way around colorful blooms above their heads, and the smells of roses and lilies permeated the air. Soft chatter and amicable laughter rose in the warm atmosphere, until the Comte de Saint-Aignan announced the start of the lottery.

Extravagant prizes filled the tables around the green enclosed space, from jewelry to art pieces, from rare books to baskets of fruit and delicacies. Excited courtiers mingled and reviewed the displays, and the press of people made it difficult to find anyone. The first familiar face I bumped into was Louise, in a lace-and-silk dress the color of a shimmering rainbow.

"There's ice cream," she announced, a porcelain bowl and spoon in hand. "Would you like some too?"

"Thank you, I'm not hungry," I said, still searching the crowd. I had come here with a purpose, and I wouldn't let myself be distracted.

But Louise remained at my side. "There's cake too, if you prefer. And all manner of drinks."

"No, thank you."

Athénaïs's husband walked past us, deep in conversation with D'Artagnan. A couple of steps away, Lully and Charles Perrault examined one of the books on display with serious nods. Farther down the table, Prince Aniaba said something to the Queen Mother that teased a smile out of her tired face. But the one person I looked for amid the crowd failed to appear.

"The king isn't here yet," Louise said as if he were the one I hoped to see. "The queen wasn't feeling well because of the heat. But he'll be here soon. They can't pick the winners without him."

"Yes," I said, distracted.

"I like your dress," she added. "It's very beautiful."

I wore a black satin dress, its bodice trimmed with an intricate gold pattern of leaves and its large skirts adorned with gold ribbons. I liked to think it offset my blond hair and agreed with my complexion, but the jump in the conversation still disconcerted me.

"Thank you," I repeated.

It occurred to me then that this was Louise's fourth attempt at starting a discussion with me in the last minute. We hadn't had a proper chat in months, yet she now stood before me with all her attention focused on me, and a puzzling eagerness to talk.

"Is there something you want to speak to me about?" I said, not unkindly.

She blushed and bit her lip. "Oh. No. I mean . . . it's nothing."

I widened my eyes at her, more perplexed by the minute. Was this about her relationship with Louis? Or about the queen, since Marie-Thérèse and she weren't on any type of speaking terms and seemed happy to use me as intermediary?

"It's just something Athénaïs told me." Louise said. She dismissed it with a wave of her hand. "It's silly."

I gave her an encouraging smile. "Now you have to tell me."

Her cheeks still crimson, Louise drew a deep breath then let out her confession. "I heard you and Armand are . . . *you know.*"

My heart sank. I should never have let Athénaïs think Armand and I were together. Now she'd told Louise, and who knew where this would end. This had been a mistake, and now I had to fix it.

"It's not true." I took her hand and met her gaze, my expression as open and honest as I could muster. "I'm not in love with Armand and there's nothing between us."

Louise squeezed my fingers. "It's all right. I won't tell anyone, I promise. Not even the king."

"But that's what I'm saying," I said, frustration at her lack of understanding growing in me. "There's nothing to tell."

"It's all right," Louise said. Her pretty mouth stretched into a reassuring smile. "I understand. I shouldn't have said anything."

I released her hand, unsure whether she believed me. Around us, the crowd was still too busy with the impending raffle to even glance our way or overhear anything.

"I'm sorry I mentioned it," Louise added. "I didn't mean to upset—"

Among the courtiers, Olympe's elegant silhouette appeared, snatching my attention. Clad in a gown of red and gold bright with magic, she greeted the Queen Mother and stopped to speak with the Comte de Saint-Aignan.

"Sorry," I said, "I have to go."

I left Louise standing amid the scintillating assembly and rushed toward my target. Without ceremony, I gave the count an apologetic smile and grabbed Olympe's elbow.

"May I speak with you, please?"

She turned, her face a mask of offended shock that softened into a surprised frown as she recognized me. "Your Highness. What can I do?"

I leaned into her ear to whisper. "How about a little spell?"

* * *

It was the perfect night for a stroll in the forest.

The canopy of leaves rustled under the clear sky and the fragrant undergrowth awoke with life after the day's heat. Twigs snapped underfoot as we made our way through the park, and

I let my fingers brush against the moss-covered bark of a tree trunk.

"Surely we could have done this at the palace," Olympe said, breathless.

I held up my lantern and paused to wait for her.

"We needed somewhere quiet where we wouldn't be disturbed," I replied. "It won't take long."

She caught up with me and cast dubious looks around her. "It's so dark. Are we lost?"

"We're not."

"What if we run into a deer? Or a wolf?"

I smiled, amused to witness the unflappable Comtesse de Soissons like a fish out of water. I linked arms with her in a reassuring manner and resumed our walk. "We won't. And if we do, we'll just cast a spell."

"But I thought you'd lost your magic," Olympe replied. "Because of your illness. That's the rumor anyway."

"I'm feeling better now."

This was true. I had been stronger in the past two days than in weeks. But I was also curious to attempt magic with someone other than Louis. After all, I had only his word that my magic had waned. The last time I had cast a spell, my body had weakened, not the power inside me. I hadn't tried doing any enchantment since then, so I still wasn't convinced anything was wrong with my magic. Tonight would be the best way to find out.

"I'm missing the lottery for this," Olympe muttered. "We better not be late for Molière's new play. I heard it's utterly scandalous. I don't want to miss it. I can't believe you convinced me this was a good idea."

She trudged alongside me, her skirts lifted up high so they wouldn't snag on any branches.

"Did I have to convince you?" I asked, keeping my tone light. "Admit it, you wanted to come. When was the last time you did magic?"

"Last year," she grumbled.

It didn't come as a surprise to me that the last occasion she'd performed a spell was when at the Crown *Magicien*'s side.

"And whose fault is that?" she added, bitterness in her tone. "There are barely any Sources left at court, and the only *magicien* who wanted to give power to female magicians is now rotting in prison."

"The reason there are barely any Sources left at court is because of that *magicien*," I reminded her, eager not to take the bait. I wouldn't apologize for helping bringing down Fouquet. "Let's stop here."

I led her into a small clearing, where an empty cart and piles of timber had been left behind by workers for the night. I set my lantern at the back of the cart and removed my silk gloves.

"This is all very pagan." Olympe surveyed the woods around us. "Two women performing magic in the heart of a forest at night."

I held out my hand. "Do you have it?"

"I do." She fished a folded piece of paper out of her dress pocket. "Although how stealing Lorraine's lottery ticket is going to do anything—aside from ruining his chances at winning a prize—I can't wait to hear."

"It bears his handwriting," I replied.

Olympe raised both eyebrows, a silent demand for an explanation.

"I want us to perform a finding spell," I said. "Lorraine has a journal. It's not in his rooms, and he doesn't keep it with him. I want to know where it is. I figured having something else bearing his handwriting would help."

A mischievous grin pulled at her lips. "Naughty. I like it."

I kept a straight face and let her assume my reasons for wanting the journal. "Can you do it or not?"

"Yes." Her expression turned thoughtful. "But what if we killed two birds with one stone? Find the journal *and* retrieve it?"

I frowned. "I don't know that spell."

"It's an old enchantment," she said. "Used by people to recover lost belongings. Not much use here when you have servants to look after your things but very convenient when you're a hermit wizard or an overworked housewife. I'll teach it to you."

The principles of the retrieving spell were the same as the finding one. Within moments, Olympe and I linked hands, Lorraine's lottery ticket held between them. The palm of mine was both clammy and cold in the warm evening. Olympe lightly clasped my fingers.

"Don't fret. It's just magic. You can do this."

I held her golden gaze, and here it was, the strange intimacy between a magician and their Source. That moment before a spell when both take a leap of faith and believe in what magic can do.

I took in a deep breath to calm my fluttering heartbeat. "Ready?"

"Whenever you are." This time, her smile was easy and sincere.

"*Rapporte*," I said.

Olympe drew my magic to her like a seamstress pulling a

yarn off a piece of fabric. The motion was gentle and precise, and the familiar golden flecks first touched the paper in our hands, then spiraled up into the night air. I grasped onto them with my mind to follow as they bobbed along the soft wind and dispersed around Versailles, searching for their quarry.

Soon the glittering particles reconvened in front of a palace window. In a dancing pattern, they went through the glass and carried on their luminous journey through all-too-familiar apartments. In Philippe's bedroom, they alighted onto a desk, where a leather-bound journal lay, closed by a golden clasp. The enchantment molded itself around the journal and lifted it up.

For a heartbeat it levitated there, wobbling slightly. Around it, the sparkling dots of my magic blinked in and out of existence, and somewhere in the forest, my body tensed.

"Stay calm." A whisper on the wind, like a kiss on my skin or a breath against my ear. "It's your magic. You control it."

The tension coursing through my limbs eased, and the golden flecks stabilized. Their purpose clear once more, they rose higher, and the journal with them. Immaterial as starlight, they floated through the window and into the night. Dancing above the shadowy gardens and the forest trees, they glided back to us and deposited their precious cargo down onto the back of the cart. Then they dispersed into the air, and I opened my eyes.

"Wow!" Olympe thrilled. "You *are* powerful. No wonder Louis wanted to keep you all to himself."

I gripped the side of the cart, bracing for dizziness or a fainting spell. But aside from some tightness in my lungs and shortness of breath, I felt . . . well.

"I'm all right," I said, almost to convince myself.

"Happy to hear it," Olympe said, her tone businesslike again. She put Lorraine's ticket back in her pocket and grabbed the journal from the cart. "For a second there I thought I'd lost you, but when I spoke to you, you calmed down and everything went as planned."

"It was you?" I asked, still baffled by the experience. "The voice?"

She paused to look at me. "Well, yes, who else would it be? Your magic is very strong, and it's a bit difficult to control, but I'm a very good *magicienne*." She shrugged off her boast with an unapologetic smile.

My gaze landed on our prize in her hands. "May I see the journal?"

"By all means." She dropped it in my outstretched hand.

"Thank you," I said. "One day soon I'll explain what it's all about."

"Anytime," she said. "I'm not very fond of Lorraine anyway."

Others might have pointed out that she wasn't fond of anyone save a very few people, but I kept quiet, my mind whirling from memories of the successful spell to hopes for what proof Lorraine's journal would provide.

Olympe took the lantern off the cart. "So this was entertaining after all. Let's do it again sometime."

Her tone was bright and playful, but a trace of seriousness lingered in her expression as she spoke. She meant what she said. She had missed performing magic, and she would do it again if I asked her. It had taken us a year, but we'd become allies after all.

I caught her arm before she could step away.

I now had proof my magic was as strong as ever, and a *magicienne* at my side willing to perform spells with me. This was the opportunity I had been waiting for.

"Actually," I said. "There is another spell I'd like to try."

CHAPTER XII

———————

"Accurate prophecies are extremely rare, you know."
Olympe surveyed me, her hands on her hips and her
mouth pressed into a doubtful pout.

"I have reasons to believe this one," I said.

After all, the *magicienne* who had told it to me was the most
celebrated seer in Paris, and the manner of the delivery had made
it all the more convincing.

"And you want to know who this prophecy is about?" Olympe
replied. "But you say you heard it over a year ago and you don't
remember the exact words?"

I bit my lip and shook my head, my hopes deflating in the face
of her incredulity. She rolled her eyes in a sarcastic motion.

"That's going to be easy."

My face must have been a picture of disappointment, for she
waved me over with a sigh. "Come and sit down, and tell me
exactly what you can recall."

We sat at the back of the cart, and I recounted as much as I
could of the old fortune-teller's words. Olympe listened to me

with an intent expression. When I was done with my description, she looked around her at the clearing.

"Shame we don't have playing cards," she muttered, as if to herself. I opened my mouth to suggest returning to the palace for a deck, but her mind had already skipped to another idea. "She talked about the elements, you said? One queen like air, one like fire?"

"Yes," I replied, my hopes swelling again at the light in her golden gaze. "Another like water and the last one like a precious gem."

She stood up, her index finger held up like a signal for attention. "I think I have it. We don't need the cards, or the exact words of the prophecy. We can use the four elements to symbolize the four maidens, and perform the spell the seer performed. This time, instead of her having the vision, *we* will."

I wasn't certain I followed, but she sounded so confident that I sprang to my feet to help her retrieve the four elements. The first three were easy to gather: we had our lantern for the fire, our jewelry for the gem, and air all around us. The water took a couple of minutes to find, but luckily the workmen had left behind a half-filled bucket before leaving the clearing earlier.

Olympe displayed one of her diamond earrings, the lantern, and the bucket at the back of the cart, and took my hand.

"Let's do this," she said.

My heart thudded against my ribs. After all these months, was I really going to walk out of this glade knowing who the four maidens were at last? Only one way to find out. I took in a deep breath.

"*Révèle*," I said.

Just like the previous time, Olympe tugged at my magic in the gentlest of ways, and the golden flecks danced up in the air like fireflies.

"A girl light as air," the wind whispered. "Of having her heart broken she should beware . . ."

The glittering particles of my magic gathered into a golden vision of a very familiar face: Louise, laughing and talking, yet no sound from her reached us. The apparition dissolved, and the sparks of magic twirled toward the lantern.

"A girl like fire," the light murmured. "The higher she rises, the harder she'll fall, and she should be wary of her desires . . ."

Again, the spell formed a shape in the air, and this time, Athénaïs's mocking grin appeared before dispersing once more.

They headed for the water, and a gurgling sound like a distant stream in the forest turned into a quiet voice.

"A girl as constant as still water, but secrets and betrayals will undo her . . ."

The silent face of Marie-Thérèse appeared, attentive as if she were listening to someone talking.

At last the bright dots settled on Olympe's earring, and a voice like tumbling stones echoed.

"A girl like a diamond. She will shine the brightest, but the world won't hold her light for long on earth."

At first the cluster of magic before us was so bright we couldn't discern a face in the brilliant mass. I blinked, and my eyes adjusted to the final vision.

Except it was like looking at a mirror, with my own face reflected, my expression both focused and slightly perplexed. As my puzzlement grew, so did the air of perplexity of my reflection.

Then it hit me. The visions had shown all the girls where and as they were now, and it was doing the same for me. Which meant . . .

I dropped Olympe's hand with a gasp. The link between us broke, and the magic vaporized in the air. My pulse thundered in my ears, turning my heartbeat frantic and tightening my lungs.

"Henriette!" Olympe gripped the sides of my face and forced me to meet her gaze. "You don't know if it's true, and if it is, you don't know when it'll happen. It might be years and years from now."

Her imperious tone helped prevent a full panic, but it wasn't enough to calm me down altogether, and I pushed her away.

"But I'm the one who dies!"

Of the four maidens, I had imagined I could be the one with her heart broken, or maybe the one undone by scandals. But I had refused to believe I could be the fourth one. The one who didn't survive.

"You're getting upset over nothing," Olympe said, still remarkably composed and serious despite the situation. "Prophecies are *warnings*. They're not set in stone. They're told so people can change their course of action and alter their fate. That's what the spell is for."

What she was saying made so much sense that it snapped me out of my frenzy. If *magiciens*' predictions of death and doom always came to pass, they'd have all been burned at the stake long ago.

"You mean it might never come true?" I asked, my voice small despite my slowing heart rate.

Olympe picked up the lantern and her earring. "I'm saying

you're going to die, like all of us, *at some point*. But the prophecy isn't a death sentence, and shouldn't be interpreted as one." She offered me her arm so I could guide her back. "Let's return to the gardens before anyone notices our absence. The lottery must be almost over and the play about the start."

Lorraine's journal and its secrets clutched against me, I led the way through the trees, my thoughts still in turmoil. If the prophecy was a warning, it meant I was in danger. A danger so great that it could cost me my life if I didn't find a way to prevent it.

My illness could be the source of my problems, but since I had been feeling better for the last couple of days, my mind went to the next most likely threat: Lorraine. I already suspected him of aggravating my symptoms. It wasn't too far a jump to conclude he might be wishing for a more permanent way of getting rid of me.

Thankfully, I now held the key to bringing him down before he could do me any further harm. Ahead, the light and noise of the finishing lottery grew amid the vegetation. My fears somewhat settled, I hid the journal under my skirts and waited for the night to be over—and for the opportunity to uncover Lorraine's secrets at last.

* * *

I met with Armand in one of the groves the next morning.

The king's entertainment was reaching its finale, and the weather greeted the news with another warm day of clear skies. The multiple water jets of the large Enceladus Fountain lent a fresh mist to the atmosphere, as the statue of the fallen giant struggled under a pile of heavy rocks sent by the gods to bury him for his arrogance.

Situated at the back of the gardens, the secluded grove was perfect for a chat away from prying eyes and curious ears at this time of day. I sat in the shade on a stone bench under the trellis colonnade, Lorraine's journal and spell book in my lap. I had spent half the night combing through them, and my excitement at what I had found was hard to contain. The seer's prophecy might foretell my demise, but at least I now had a weapon to take down the most direct threat to my life.

Footsteps crunched in the gravel, and Armand emerged through a passage in the trimmed hedges, his green and lace outfit a nice match for the vegetation and the foaming waters of the grove.

"Sorry I'm late, darling." He sank onto the bench next to me. "It's a labyrinth out there, and all those groves look the same."

I gave him a pointed look for his poor excuse but dismissed the matter as more pressing ones clamored for my attention.

"Did you hear the news?" Armand said, before I could speak. "The king and his mother had a major row last night after the play. She wants it banned."

It didn't surprise me: Molière's *Tartuffe* had proven as scandalous as advertised, an attack against bigots that many people chose to interpret as a charge against the Church. Louis had appeared pleased enough during the performance, but Anne d'Autriche had left before the end. Too occupied by my own problems, I had paid little attention to the show, and although this could be a setback for Molière, the playwright was still in charge of tonight's last entertainment.

"I'm sure it'll be forgotten soon," I said. "People at court move on very quickly. Tonight's play is a comedy about love and marriage that will get everybody to agree again."

"You're right," Armand said. "This morning's announcement certainly distracted everyone."

Hesitation made me pause. I had seen no one except my maids since waking up and had come straight here for our meeting. The courtiers I had passed in the hallways and garden alleys had all been in a flurry of excitement, but no more than usual at a court where something was always happening.

"What announcement?"

"That we're staying," Armand replied. "The king is moving the court to Versailles. Apparently the archives are on their way, and he'll hold his first official council with his government here tomorrow."

Again, the news didn't come as a surprise to me. Louis was following the plan he had set out a year ago, with each part falling into place with impressive accuracy like well-built marquetry.

"But where will everyone live?" I asked.

If hosting six hundred people for the party had been a challenge, how would thousands of courtiers find enough room to live in the same building?

"Apartments are going for a fortune, I can tell you that," Armand replied. "But it's rumored the king and Lorraine are planning a huge display of magic this afternoon. They are going to add two new wings to the palace."

His mention of Lorraine's name dragged me back to the point of our meeting. I handed him the journal and spell book.

"Lorraine might not, actually."

Armand's eyes widened as he leafed through the journal. "You did it! How?"

"Never mind how," I replied, anticipation swelling in my chest. "The right question is: What's in there?"

"Well?" Armand turned to me with an avid gaze. "What's in there?"

"A list of all the vanished spells," I said, a slight tremor in my voice that I blamed on my satisfaction at sharing the news at last, "with potential prices attached. Apparently, Lorraine has been planning on selling the stolen spells to the highest bidders at court."

Armand gaped. "So it was him! Which *magicien* helped him, do you think?"

"Someone in Paris, I suspect. I don't think a court *magicien* would take such a risk, when there are far easier ways to become rich and influential."

"So Lorraine has been making spells vanish in order to resell them later on for money?"

"Or for favors, or blackmail," I said.

"But that's . . . that's treason, isn't it?" Armand said, still torn between disbelief and astonishment. "The king is going to murder him himself when he finds out. He destroyed Fouquet for reaching for the throne. Imagine what he's going to do to someone who tried to take control of French magic!"

I wasn't certain I wanted to imagine Louis's reaction to these revelations, but it was out of my hands now. I had collected the proof he had asked for. Within an hour Armand and I would deliver it to him and explain everything. Lorraine would be out of my life, and I would start rebuilding what had been shattered in the last few weeks.

Armand stood up, tucking both volumes under his arm. "Let's go see the king, then. Let's show him all this."

A huge weight off my chest, I grabbed his offered hand, and we walked toward one of the openings in the surrounding trellis.

"Do you think—" I began—and didn't get a chance to finish.

Four dark figures barged into the grove and swooped on us like birds of prey. Clad in black from head to toe, masks covered their faces and blades glinted in their hands.

Armand let out a loud exclamation and dropped my hand. He stepped in front of me, but our attackers were already upon us. They brandished their weapons and one punched Armand in the jaw.

I screamed.

Under the force of the blow, he dropped the journal and book and stumbled against me. I grabbed him to prevent his fall, just as another of our assailants picked up the two bounded volumes off the gravel.

"No!" I shouted.

I reached for him, but a sword thrust in front of my chest stopped me short. My pulse wild and my breathing ragged, I watched as the proof of Lorraine's guilt was snatched from my grasp. The thief gave a low whistle, a signal for their flight. They took off one by one, the one threatening me with his sword the last to go. It had all happened in an instant.

I stood breathless, my mind racing for a quick solution.

Running after them in my gown was useless, but I could try the spell again with Olympe, if Lorraine didn't put up wards against it before we—

Hurried footsteps and shouts pulled me out of my thoughts. Alerted by my scream, a group of palace guards and gardeners rushed into the grove with their weapons and tools drawn.

"Your Highness! Are you all right?"

The mustached guard who had let me through the palace gate a week ago stepped forward, a look of dark suspicion lending on Armand.

"Thieves," I managed to say before he could draw any awful false conclusion. "Thieves in the gardens. They attacked us."

A bruise bloomed on Armand's cheek, and he wiped his forehead to dispel the dazedness brought on by the blow.

"There were four of them," he said. "Dressed in black. They went that way."

A few soldiers followed the trail he pointed at, while the old one with the mustache surveyed me.

"And you're not hurt, Madame?"

I shook my head. He assumed the thieves had been after my jewels, and I wasn't about to contradict him. I turned to Armand instead.

"How is your jaw?"

He grimaced. "I'll live. I've had worse."

From what I knew of his upbringing and of his father's violence, I believed it.

"We better take you back to the palace," the guard said.

Armand gave me a questioning look. He knew how important the journal and book were to me, and he was ready to follow my lead on how to handle the situation. Gratefulness expanded in my chest at his reaction, but there was nothing I could say or do in front of witnesses that wouldn't put us in a precarious position.

I forced a breath down my constricted lungs. There would be time later to think about a plan to retrieve the stolen items *again*. This was a setback, not a defeat. We were all staying at Versailles, and if it was Lorraine who'd organized this attack as I suspected—who else could it be?—he wouldn't get away with it for long.

So I nodded at the guard. "Yes, let's go back."

We all filed out of the grove, leaving Enceladus and his crushed hubris behind in the morning sunshine.

* * *

My plans to find Olympe immediately upon my return to the palace were thwarted by the guards who insisted on taking me back to my apartments, which Philippe stormed a couple of minutes later.

"Out! Everybody out!"

Pale with anger, he ushered out my maids and ladies, who didn't even dare a glance back. My mouth gaped in astonishment. In our thirteen months of marriage, I had never seen him behave like this.

"What are you doing?"

He opened his arms wide. "What did I ask you?"

I hesitated. Giving him the answer he sought would likely help settle him down, but I couldn't think of anything, and his furious expression wasn't helping. In the end, he answered his own question.

"I asked you to take care of yourself. That's *the only thing* I've ever asked of you." His voice grew louder and more distraught as he spoke. "All I want is for you to be safe and feel cared for. But you don't give a damn, do you?"

I took a step toward him to reply, but he cut me off, waving his arms.

"You'd rather do magic, and run about everywhere, and put yourself at risk every bloody day. The problem is, you're too nice. You can't say no to people. Not to Louis, not to anybody at court, and certainly not to Armand. So you know what? I'm saying no for you now."

"What do you mean?"

Apprehension gripped me. He was so upset that he didn't seem able to listen to me at all.

"You're going away," he replied. "Louis wants to trap all of us here, but he won't have you. I'm sending you away. Today."

"You want me to go back to Paris? For how long? And why?" My voice went higher in surprise. This was *not* part of my plan.

"I'm sending you away," Philippe said, his tone cutting, "so I don't ever have to walk into those apartments again thinking the worst has happened. I can't do it, Henriette! This court isn't good for you, so you're not staying here."

I opened my mouth to argue, but he interrupted me again.

"And you're not going to Paris. You're going to Saint-Cloud."

SUMMER

CHAPTER XIII

The afternoon breeze blew through the open window, filling the sheer curtains that billowed liked ship sails at sea. It teased my hair, rustled though the music sheets at my feet, and swept the open letters off my desk.

"Oh no!" the painter exclaimed.

His paintbrush in hand, he rushed to close the window. Mimi yapped at the disruption, and I took the momentary pause as an opportunity to stretch my neck. The portrait commissioned by Philippe showed me as Minerva surrounded by objects representing the arts. Dressed in a silk gown the color of a blood orange and an ermine fur cape, I sat with a blank canvas in my hands and a plumed helmet at my side.

"I'm so sorry about your correspondence, Madame."

The painter retrieved the letters from the floor and set them down on my desk in a reverent gesture. A short man in his sixties, his long wig always bounced about his thin face and gave him a youthful and dynamic look that his serious expression denied in a comical manner.

"Don't worry about those," I said. "They're nothing valuable."

They were just news from court, sent by people who believed the story that I had been taken too ill to remain at Versailles. Louise announced the king's next entertainment, set to take place mid-July for the benefit of every courtier this time; Athénaïs warned me Lorraine had all but moved in with my husband and they spent all their leisure time together; Olympe detailed the Queen Mother's failing health; and Marie-Thérèse complained about how crowded the salons had become at the palace. None of these missives provided me with a way back to court.

It had been two weeks since my exile.

I had spent the first few days at Saint-Cloud searching for ways to return to Versailles as quickly as possible, but in the end I had to admit my defeat: I had no means to prove Lorraine's wrongdoings or to regain any evidence of them; my health was as fragile as ever; I could perform no magic alone; and the chasm between Philippe and me was so large I couldn't see how to overcome it.

What was obvious, however, was that my situation wouldn't last. Philippe wouldn't be able to keep me away forever without raising questions and suspicions. I only had to bide my time.

"If Your Highness could look at me again . . . ?" the painter asked. Back at his easel, he gave me an expectant look that I returned with a smile as my dog settled again on the carpet. "Lovely," he added. "Simply lovely."

In his well-meaning yet misguided way of looking after me, Philippe had provided me with two distractions: a house and a painting.

An hour's ride from Versailles, the former was a sixteenth century building renovated ten years ago. A large country house with beautiful French-styled gardens, it operated as a retreat, not a place made for permanent living. It lacked the fanciful gilded decor I had grown accustomed to at the palaces, and the servants had never worked for a princess before. To their surprise, it suited me perfectly. I was mistress of a house that boasted gorgeous manicured gardens and was small enough to run as I wished, with staff eager to please yet uninterested in tracking my every move.

The latter also turned out to be a blessing in disguise. The painting meant to show both of us but didn't require my husband to be present: Philippe's portrait would be added later on the blank canvas I held in my hands. The irony of the whole endeavor wasn't lost on me, but it also gave me a lot of time to *think*.

"Madame, your guest has arrived." The maid gave a quick, perfunctory curtsy and waited for my reply.

I discarded my blank canvas and jumped to my feet. "Is he in the blue salon? Please tell him I'm coming."

I removed my ermine cape and agreed with the painter on our appointment the next day. Then, Mimi in my wake, I skipped through my apartments, which I had filled with flower arrangements. Like in the rest of the house, dozens of blossoms in vases greeted me with vibrant colors and delightful fragrances wherever I went. Saint-Cloud might belong to Philippe, but everywhere it was my presence that lingered.

My guest stood looking out the open window, his gloved hand resting on the handle of his sword and his large frame casting a long shadow onto the parquet floor. My entrance prompted him to turn around and to sink into a deep bow, his feathered hat in hand.

"Madame," he said, "you requested my presence?"

I clasped my hands together to hide my trepidation. After two weeks of idleness, I was moving forward again of my own volition, instead of being cast about by fate and duty like a leaf in a stream.

"D'Artagnan," I replied. "Thank you so much for coming."

I gestured toward a chair, and he took a seat with his back straight and that slight awkwardness of soldiers more used to riding a horse than sitting on silk-covered furniture. A middle-aged man with a thin mustache and the golden eyes of a *magicien*, he still displayed the handsome features that had made him famous in his youth, but his hair now showed more silver than brown and lines traced his brow and mouth.

"I heard you were poorly," he said, kindness in his tone. "I'm pleased to see you're better."

"Indeed. The country air does wonders for my lungs."

It wasn't a lie: although still present, my symptoms weren't now as much a cause for concern as they had been since April. I took a seat opposite him and lifted Mimi into my lap.

"I grew up in the countryside," D'Artagnan said, the hint of a smile crinkling his face. "You don't have to convince me of its advantages."

Under other circumstances, I would have loved to hear about his youth in Gascony and his time serving the Crown as a musketeer, but pleasant conversation or tales about his past weren't why I requested he come to me. My reasons were far more self-serving.

"There's something I must ask of you," I said.

The change in my tone brought a crease between his brows. "What is it, Your Highness? You know I'm always here to help."

His devotion to the royal family was indeed legendary. Louis wasn't even born when D'Artagnan already served his parents, and he'd spent all his life showing indefectible loyalty to the young king. This was why Louis had trusted him, and no one else, with Fouquet's arrest last year. The musketeer had witnessed our spell to defeat the Crown *Magicien*, and been put in charge of his custody since then.

"I need to speak with Fouquet," I said, choosing bluntness over flattery.

His eyes widened in shock. Since his arrest in Nantes, the former Crown *Magicien* was under the heaviest of watches. Kept in solitary confinement, he was moved between prisons while awaiting his trial, and I knew from Louis his latest jail was the Bastille in Paris, an hour away from Saint-Cloud. And his jailer was D'Artagnan.

"I'm afraid no one can see him," the musketeer replied, ever polite. "Unless I receive direct instructions from His Majesty, I can't—"

"I know."

Interrupting him was rude and not something I wished to make a habit of, but I could already guess all his reasons for refusing me, and I had no time for them. I had spent two weeks hatching this plan, and I wouldn't be deterred.

"I know you have to answer to the king, and I wouldn't want to put you in a difficult position with him. But it is *imperative* that I speak with Fouquet. Today. It has to do with my health.

It has to do with my magic. And it's urgent. So you're going to take me to him, and afterward you'll tell the king everything and blame it all on me."

The assertiveness in my tone surprised even me. D'Artagnan blinked, hesitation and counterarguments battling on his features.

"It would be my responsibility—" he started.

As I thought, the gentleman in him refused the idea of not endorsing the blame, so I cut him off once more.

"The king won't be happy. But we are not going to do anything wrong. We are not going to set Fouquet free, or tell him anything he shouldn't know, or help him in any way. I'm going to ask him questions and hopefully get answers only he, in the whole of France, can provide."

D'Artagnan opened and closed his mouth, wavering. I held his gaze, as sincere and firm as I could, my heart thumping against my ribs despite my outward composure. He had to agree. I had to see Fouquet.

"We don't know each other very well," I added. "But I don't make a habit of lying, or of getting people into trouble. I would never ask this of you if it weren't my last resort. Believe me when I say I don't want to see Fouquet—the man nearly destroyed everything I hold dear—but I *need* to see him."

He dropped his gaze, and released a sigh. "I know you're not a deceitful person, Your Highness. Are you certain this is what you want?"

My heart jolted in my chest. He was giving in.

"Yes," I said. "I'm sure."

He nodded, his expression grave. "Then I'll take you to him."

Somehow, this didn't have the feel of victory I anticipated. Instead, dread descended over me like a cold draught. I was going to a prison, to meet with a man who haunted my nightmares and whom I'd thought never to see again.

But if I wanted answers to the questions that plagued me, I had to set aside my fears, and enter the lair of the beast one more time.

* * *

A complex web of torchlit corridors and winding staircases made the Bastille fortress an endless labyrinth I would have been lost in within moments without D'Artagnan at my side. I held on to his arm as he guided me past countless reinforced doors, decay and hopelessness permeating the stale air.

"The prisoner is held in a wing that we've emptied for him," the musketeer said in a low tone. "Only my men guard him, and half the garrison is here day and night: His Majesty is worried about an escape."

I failed to see how anyone could leave this maze without outside help or magic, but underestimating the former Crown *Magicien* was a mistake no one was willing to make, it seemed. My cowl low over my brow and my black cloak tight around my body, I followed my guide without a word, the rustle of my dress the only sound accompanying the echo of our footsteps in the low-ceilinged hallways.

At last, we stopped at the end of a corridor where four musketeers stood sentry, their shadows quivering in the torchlight. They all stood at attention at D'Artagnan's approach.

"We're going to speak with the prisoner," he announced. "It won't take long. Stay outside, and be ready to come in upon my order."

"Yes, sir," his men replied, and one moved aside to allow him access to the heavy locks.

The thick metal door grated on its large hinges and opened onto a small cell whose only furniture were a single bed and a low wooden stool. Cold seeped into every corner of the confined space, as if summer and sunshine were concepts the citadel had never heard of. A small aperture, high up in the wall, provided the only source of gray light, lending a gloomy shade to the stones of its walls and floor.

Fouquet sat on the bed, his face turned toward the window. In truth I assumed it was the former Crown *Magicien*, for nothing in the diminished white-haired figure reminded me of the man who'd attempted to seize the French throne a year ago.

"Two pairs of footsteps," he said, his voice gravely. "Who have you brought me, musketeer?"

He tilted his head toward us, his black outfit and his stance lending him the silhouette of a raven. The door slammed shut behind us, and my heartbeat thundered in my chest. Despite D'Artagnan's reassuring presence at my side, the situation was too reminiscent of my time facing Fouquet in the dark grotto at Vaux-le-Vicomte. I swallowed my fear and pulled down my cowl.

Fouquet sprang to his feet. I startled, and D'Artagnan jumped in front of me, his hand already at his sword. But the former Crown *Magicien* didn't move toward me. Instead, he stumbled away and crashed against the far wall as if he could magic his way through to get away from me. Shock and fear clashed on his gaunt face, and he let out a strangled cry.

"You!"

Never in my life had I been greeted by such a reaction. My pulse ceased its trepidation all at once, and calm washed over me. There was nothing to fear. Without magic, without wealth, without support, the *magicien* who had nearly killed me and my family was just an old man imprisoned for his crimes.

"Why . . . why have you come?" he asked, bewilderment winning over panic on his features.

I relaxed my shoulders and moved around D'Artagnan to sit on the low stool. I gestured toward the bed.

"Sit down," I said, my voice clear and calm. "I want to talk."

Fouquet's gaze flicked between D'Artagnan and me, and some of its old shrewdness returned. He resumed his seat on the bed, and leaned toward me with a half grin.

"You shouldn't be here," he said. "I'm not even allowed a priest or a doctor. So . . . what are you doing here, Madame?"

He made my title sound like an insult, and D'Artagnan stiffened at my back, but I ignored it. I had come here with a purpose, and I wouldn't let myself be distracted. In my experience, Fouquet had two weaknesses: He loved to hear himself talk, and he always thought he had the upper hand. I was ready to take advantage of both.

"I'm not here on behalf of the king, if that's what you're hoping," I replied.

His nostrils flared at the mention of Louis, but he gritted his teeth and didn't pick up on it. "So you're here on your own behalf," he said. "You want something."

His calculating gaze swept my face and cloak, as if looking for clues. His scrutiny unnerved me, but I kept a straight face. I would *not* be intimated by him ever again.

"I have questions about magic," I said. "Questions no one seems able to answer. You once boasted to be the most knowledgeable scholar of magic in the kingdom. I hoped you might have the answers I seek."

His face darkened. "You have some nerve," he spat. "After what you did to me, coming here to ask about magic?"

D'Artagnan unsheathed his sword and stepped forward. "You move from that bed and you'll regret it."

Fouquet shot him a loathing glare, but he stayed where he was as commanded, and made a show of relaxing his stance by holding up the palms of his hands.

"No need for threats," he said, a mirthless grin on his lips. "We're only talking."

"I am aware of the irony of the situation," I replied. "Believe me when I say I had no other choice. But I have questions, and I'd like to know if you have answers to them."

Fouquet shrugged. "Very well. What do I get in return?"

"Nothing."

He scoffed, and I folded my hands in my lap to gather my resolve. My mother always praised my diplomatic skills. Now was the time to put them to the test.

"There is nothing I can promise you without lying," I said, "and nothing I can give you without committing treason."

"Then why should I listen to you, let alone answer your questions?" Fouquet growled.

"You don't have to, but I trust you'll want to."

He snorted. "Then your trust is wrongly placed. Now leave me alone." He looked up at the window again and made a point of ignoring me.

"Alone," I said, my tone gentler. "That's what you are, isn't it? Nine months in near isolation, when you used to spend your days talking, debating, arguing, seducing, coaxing, convincing. I'm offering you conversation, on your favorite topic."

His golden gaze returned to me, longing lingering behind them. I had touched a nerve.

"Sweet, unassuming Madame," he said, a mix of sarcasm and defeatism in his tone. "Are you still the most overlooked person at court? Or have you taken your rightful place at the heart of it all?"

"I'll be the one asking questions today," I replied.

He inclined his head in pretend deference. "Of course."

I paused, half for dramatic effect and half to gather my wits. I had had two weeks to prepare this discussion, and to decide on the phrasing of my questions. Despite his weakened position, Fouquet still struck me as cunning and alert. I didn't want to divulge any information he could use later.

"To your knowledge," I asked, "is there a spell to ward off death?"

He startled, and what appeared to be a genuine smile spread across his thin lips. "Now, that's a very interesting question."

"Will you answer it?"

He tapped his knee in an absentminded gesture, his focus on the gray stone floor for a moment. I kept my attention on him, ready to call him out on his theatrics, but he inhaled a deep breath and met my gaze with the first frank expression to settle on his face since I had entered his cell.

"Others have wondered about this long before you have," he said. "Throughout history, *magiciens* have focused their efforts on a few recurring obsessions: power, wealth, youth and beauty, and of course, defeating death. I'm afraid that, regarding the latter, their efforts have been in vain. Much like we can't cure illnesses, we can't stop death."

Despite my resolve to hide my emotions, my chest deflated. There was no fighting the prophecy this way, then. Still, I pressed on.

"My understanding is that for every spell," I said, "there is a counterspell. A spell to kill someone exists. Surely this means a spell to protect oneself against it is available too?"

Fouquet nodded. "Some *magiciens* tried to make themselves impervious to harm," he said, warming to his subject as I had hoped he would. "But somehow fate always found a way to cut them down in the end. There's always a loophole, or some unforeseen circumstance that renders the ward spell useless."

"There's no fighting fate, I understand, so what about a spell to make someone less vulnerable? Less . . . weak?"

He tilted his head to the side. "You would have to be more specific."

I bit my lip, unwilling to give him any details about my life that he could use to his advantage. As if reading my mind, he went on without waiting for my answer.

"The crux of the matter is that no, no one can protect themselves in any long-lasting manner. I tried, and failed, as you're aware."

Bitterness crossed his features, and I asked another question before he could dwell on his past mistakes and the reasons behind his fall.

"Can a Source's magic wane?" I asked. "Disappear, even?"

Interest sparked again in his eyes. "Why?"

"I'm the one asking the questions, remember?" I gave him a stern look, and he relented with a sigh.

"I'm only asking," he said, "because I've never heard of such a thing. A Source's magic is there at birth, and it grows as the child grows. For some, as you well know, the power becomes very strong. Some *magiciens* access that power more easily than others. But the magic itself doesn't change."

I surveyed him, trying to gauge if he was telling the truth. He read the misgivings in my gaze.

"Think of your magic as a block of marble by the side of the road," he added. "For most people, it's just a block of marble, something they have no use for and barely notice as they walk by. Only a sculptor can come along and shape something out of it. A very gifted sculptor will create a wonderful statue of a Greek goddess. A less gifted one will just turn the marble into a smooth slab of stone used in a staircase. But in the end, whether the marble is sculpted or not, whether the result is beautiful or not, the marble is still there. Its inner qualities haven't changed."

"So a Source's magic shouldn't be affected by any outside factors?" I said. "Or any spell?"

"*Nothing*"—he emphasized the word—"can have an impact on your magic. However . . . There are outside elements that can affect your ability to *use* that magic to cast spells. One of them is poor health. Another is tiredness."

"You mean the Source's body has an effect on the magic it contains?"

"Yes," he said, animation turning the gold in his eyes more

vivid. "Your body is the vessel for the magic. Anything, anything at all, any change, that affects your body, will influence your capacity to use your magic. For example—"

He stopped, his eyes widening as a sudden realization settled over his features. My heart rate picked up.

"What?"

Hesitation crossed his face, devoid of any malice this time. He glanced at D'Artagnan, still as a statue at my side. He wanted to speak, but the musketeer's presence stopped him. What could he possibly have to say that required privacy, when he'd had no qualms having the rest of the conversation before witnesses? I replayed his last words in my head. He'd been talking about the link between the Source's body and their magic. About how changes in one affected the other.

Changes . . .

I blinked.

"Your Highness," Fouquet said, his tone so soft as to be almost unrecognizable. "Is there any chance that you might be with child?"

The wooden stool clattered to the floor, the sound jolting me to the fact that I now stood in the middle of the cell. Fouquet startled back on the bed, and D'Artagnan reached for me.

Is there any chance that you might be with child?

Jumbled thoughts whirled through my mind, yet everything was clear for the first time in weeks. Everyone, including myself, had attributed the worsening of my symptoms to my illness, ignoring the fact they pointed at another truth. It was obvious now that the words had been said—it would have been obvious to everyone, including the doctors and *magiciens* brought to my bedside, if I had been any other woman. But I was Madame, always faint and tired and grimacing at the smell of food, with a husband known for his indifference toward me. The thought hadn't even crossed anyone's mind. Yet it made perfect sense.

I was pregnant.

CHAPTER XIV

After the confinement of the Bastille, the ride back to Saint-Cloud was a confusion of loud noises, bright lights, vibrant colors, and conflicting thoughts.

The matter of the prophecy, still unresolved, weighed heavy on my mind, but my first order of business was now to send a message to Philippe, and to see a *magicien* to confirm the pregnancy.

"Do I have Your Highness's leave to speak with the king, then?"

D'Artagnan's question pulled me out of my anxious considerations. My carriage was rumbling through a village, the Parisian buildings left behind a while ago already, and the musketeer had remained silent until now. A wave of appreciation for his thoughtful behavior in the face of my tumultuous state of mind washed through me.

"Yes," I replied to ease the concerned frown between his brows. "Feel free to tell him of my visit to Fouquet. However I would be grateful if the . . . other matter could stay between us until I have had time to speak with my husband."

He inclined his head. "Of course. You have my word."

"Thank you, for everything."

I gripped his gloved hand in a rush of gratitude. The man had gone out of his way to help me, and even if my conversation with the former Crown *Magicien* hadn't yielded the expected results, I still owed the musketeer a great deal. The shadow of a timid smile tugged at his lips.

"Your request wasn't made lightly, I know," he said. "It was my pleasure to accede to it."

Once at Saint-Cloud he didn't come into the house, choosing to ride out immediately to Versailles on his horse instead. I took off my black cloak and gloves, too hot for the weather, as I made my way inside the cool and fragrant building. The late-afternoon sunshine lent every room a golden glow and welcoming warmth, and Mimi greeted my return with a wagging tail. I picked her up under my free arm and walked toward my apartments.

"Madame!"

A maid caught up with me on the grand staircase, breathless and strands of hair escaping from her white cap. I longed to hide in my chambers to think and write letters, but I gave her a smile nonetheless.

"I'm glad you've returned," the girl said. "You have another visitor. She's waiting for you in the blue salon."

Confusion pushed my brows together. An unannounced guest? Questions pressed against my lips, but the maid spoke again before I could ask any of them.

"We did say Your Highness wasn't home, but the lady insisted. She's in such a state we didn't have the heart to turn her away, and she's been waiting for an hour."

Dread added to my perplexity. A lady? In such a state as to not be turned away?

"What on earth are you talking about?" I dropped my cloak and gloves in the maid's arms, and retraced my steps toward the salon. "Who is this lady?"

The maid trotted behind me, her explanations more unclear by the minute. My skirts swishing after me, I hurried into the blue room. Louise sat on the silk-covered sofa, in tears. I put Mimi down to rush to her.

"What's happened?"

She fell into my arms with heart-wrenching sobs. For a moment her crying filled the salon, and I dismissed the maid with a discreet nod. The girl called Mimi and closed the double door, leaving us alone. I handed Louise my handkerchief, as hers was already soaked, and forced her to sit down again and to drink a sip of the tea brought in by my servants. Her weeping eased down, punctuated by small hiccups.

"Will you tell me what's happening?" I asked, my hand tracing gentle circles between her shoulders.

"I left him," she said at last, her eyes swollen and her nose red. "We argued, and I left him."

It took me a heartbeat to understand her meaning, and I gaped. "You left Louis? But . . . you can't!"

No one *left* the king of France. No one could; no one did.

"I don't care." Louise sniffled, a hint of defiance in her eyes. "I couldn't stay there a minute longer."

My earlier dread returned. Louis would be furious when he found out. Louise was my lady. I couldn't let her make such a rash decision that would impact her whole future life. I had to fix this before the situation got out of hand.

"Just tell me what happened," I said.

She blew her nose, and took in a deep breath to gather her courage. "You remember how Athénaïs told me about you and Armand?"

Annoyance rose in my throat. How long was this small lie going to pursue me? I needed to have a serious chat with Athénaïs.

"I promised to keep it a secret," Louise went on, oblivious to my rising temper. "And I meant to, you know I did. But Louis . . . I can't lie to him. He knew I was hiding something, and he wouldn't let it go. So I told him."

I froze. She'd told my brother-in-law I was having an affair? This was a disaster. My breath caught in my throat, and I coughed.

"He was so angry," Louise carried on, lost in her tale. "He said I had betrayed his trust by hiding this from him, and he said the most horrid things. We argued, and I was so upset that I left!"

I stood up, too restless now to sit down. I poured a cup of tea to ease my cough, while Louise blew her nose once more. Now, on top of everything else, I needed to stamp out this fire before it spread. I couldn't let Louis believe this rumor was true, not when I was pregnant, not when it could jeopardize everything I had built since my arrival at court.

"I love him so much," Louise added, still intent on her monologue and unaware of my reaction to it. "But I have committed so many sins in the name of that love. I know it's wrong. That's why I left. I'm going to a convent in Paris to pray for my soul's salvation."

So that was her solution. After creating a mess at court, she would leave it all behind for others to deal with the consequences and retire to a life of solitude and prayer. The thought brought up an ungenerous mood in me, which I pushed down. Louise was in love. From the beginning, it had shut out anyone else's feelings, including mine. She didn't care that her passion for Louis hurt Marie-Thérèse, or that her promise to keep nothing from him could harm me. Even now, she came to me to share her distress, not to help repair what she'd broken.

"You do realize there's nothing between Armand and me?" I replied, my tone more controlled than my building emotions. "And this whole argument with Louis has no basis?"

She blinked at me, her red-rimmed eyes owlish in her pale face. There was a brief pause, as my words registered with her, before she dissolved into tears once more. "But it doesn't matter! I can't forget the horrible things he said to me. I have to get away. You have to understand, I need your help!"

Her single-mindedness astounded me. For a second, I was close to shouting at her and throwing her out of the house to leave her to her own fate. But I couldn't afford a fit of temper; I had to fix this before the damage was beyond repair. So I drew a calming breath, and used the royal tone I seldom resorted to.

"Stop crying," I said. "I'll write you a letter of introduction to the Chaillot convent if that's what you wish. But in return, you'll write a letter to Louis explaining why you left and how this whole story about Armand and me is pure nonsense."

I stared at her, and for a moment she gaped at me, before nodding and wiping her cheeks with my soggy handkerchief. I refilled her cup of tea and called for ink and paper.

* * *

I lay in bed, the night air coming through my open window and settling over my dark bedchamber like a comforting blanket. In the gardens below, a fountain gurgled in the quiet and an owl called out through the moonlit trees. Mimi dreamed at my feet, her ears shivering. Sleep eluded me.

Louise had left before supper, in a state of less agitation than she had arrived in. A messenger had departed at the same time for Versailles, carrying with him my note to Philippe and Louise's letter to the king. Afterward, my anxiety had prevented me from eating anything of the evening meal, and I had retired to my bedroom to rest.

But one thought chased after another in my overactive mind, and I turned between my bedsheets like a trapped butterfly.

A knock resounded at my door, and I sat up, my heart racing. Jolted awake, my dog barked. I shushed her with a word, and the white wooden panel creaked open, allowing a slim shaft of light to grow on the parquet floor, and a head atop a candle to appear.

"I'm very sorry to disturb you, Madame," a blond-haired maid said in a low tone. "But you have visitors again."

I sprang to my feet. Philippe had come. I grabbed my nightgown and fumbled for my sleepers, Mimi barking again on the bed. The maid rushed to help me.

"Has he come with a *magicien*?" I asked her.

Her eyes widened in the candlelight. "A *magicien*? No, Your Highness. Why?"

I paused in my haste. "You said 'visitors.'"

"Yes," she replied. "His Majesty and the lady who was here earlier. Shall I help you dress, Your Highness?"

My pulse became frantic again, but for a different reason. The king was here? With Louise? In the middle of the night? After two weeks of near isolation, I was receiving more guests in one day than in my whole stay at Saint-Cloud. Sensing the general confusion, Mimi's barking grew erratic. I calmed her and put her down on the floor.

The poor maid still stood bemused, her candle in hand and her mouth pursed into a worried line. I took her candleholder and met her gaze.

"I'll just wear the same dress I wore this afternoon for my ride."

It was a plain blue afternoon dress that had seemed appropriate to visit Fouquet, a million years ago, it seemed. The maid helped me squeeze back into it, and we left my long hair in a simple plait. I threw a light shawl over my shoulders, left my dog and my maid behind, and hurried downstairs.

My expectation when I walked into the grand salon was to find Louis angry. Whether because of my interview with Fouquet or my supposed affair with Armand, the king had many reasons to be unhappy with me. So I made an effort to hide my distress behind a placating smile, and stepped into the receiving room.

In a gold-trimmed cream outfit, Louis sat in an armchair, his gilded cane propped up at his side and his feathered hat lying on a pedestal table nearby. Louise was on the sofa next to him, her demeanor from the afternoon altered beyond recognition. Both beamed at me.

I curtsied to the king, and surprise must have shone through my careful mask as I surveyed them, for Louis said, "I apologize for startling you in the middle of the night, but it couldn't be helped."

"Oh," I said, my wits temporarily deserting me. "It's all right."

"We're here to thank you," the king said.

These weren't the words I thought to hear from him. My legs unsteady, I sank more than sat next to Louise, and waited for an explanation to be provided to make sense of what was turning into an extraordinary day.

"As you're aware," Louis went on, unperturbed, "Louise and I had a misunderstanding earlier today. She came here for counsel, and the letter you recommended she write to me allowed me to meet her at Chaillot and to convince her to return to court."

There was so much left unsaid here that my gaze flicked between them, and I waited for someone to fill in the gaps.

"His Majesty rode to Chaillot," Louise said, her eyes bright and her cheeks pink at the retelling of the events. She giggled. "He came after me, like a knight in a story. And of course I agreed to come back to Versailles."

"Of course," I repeated, mystified.

The king of France had left court and ridden off on his horse after supper to fetch back his mistress in Paris? Surely these things only happened in novels. But Louis nodded, his golden gaze warm with affection as it beheld Louise.

"I'm happy you resolved your misunderstanding," I replied, gathering my faculties at last.

"Yes, this rumor about the Comte de Guiche was quite unfortunate," Louis said, his attention turning to me and his tone becoming colder.

I held his gaze and refused to be cowed. "I can assure you it is completely unfounded. The count is a dear friend, and anyone who says otherwise is lying."

He stared at me for a heartbeat in that unnerving way he had to look as if into someone's soul. Then his mouth relaxed into his trademark smile that didn't reach his eyes.

"You know I trust your word, Henriette. If you say the count is no more than a friend to you, then I believe it." A weight lifted off my chest, but he wasn't done talking. "I'm delighted to find you looking so well. I'd heard you were most ill."

"Exaggerated rumors as well," I said. "I have rested, and I'm much better now."

"It's a relief to hear it," he said, his expression inscrutable again. "I hope this means you'll return to us very soon. Your absence from court has been keenly felt."

This was a command, not an invitation, and Louise heard it as well.

She gave an emphatic nod. "Yes, we've missed you terribly."

"And upon your return," the king added, "it would make me very happy if Louise could be your lady-in-waiting again."

So that was why he'd come. Louise had refused to go back to court without an official place waiting for her there. He couldn't make her an official mistress, not when Marie-Thérèse was pregnant and his mother judging his every move, but I could give her a legitimate status without anyone questioning my motives.

I recognized a trade where there was one: He would support

my return to Versailles against Philippe's wishes and forget about the rumors about Armand, and in exchange, I would help him carry on his relationship with Louise.

I made my decision in an instant. There was too much at stake for me to stay hidden at Saint-Cloud forever.

I was going back to Versailles.

CHAPTER XV

———————

The *magicien* pressed his lips together in an indecisive pout. Dressed in a sober gray outfit with a lace collar that must have been the fashion during the reign of Louis's father, he had long, straight dark hair, a thin mustache, and polished buckled shoes that made him look like he'd just stepped out of a thirty-year-old painting.

"Well?" Philippe asked. "What's taking so long?"

He paced the length of my bedroom at Saint-Cloud, the morning sunshine making his shadow dance along the parquet floor. Following my message last night, he had arrived at dawn in a gilded carriage with a handful of guards and dark shadows under his eyes. I had barely slept myself, too agitated after the king and Louise's departure to find rest. Hours later, there was still no word from Louis about my visit to Fouquet, and my hope was that he'd been kept too busy by the private events in his life to care about my misdemeanor.

So I sat against my pillows in the large canopy bed, fully dressed and awaiting the *magicien*'s instructions. Famed for his healing spells and knowledge of the human body, he came highly recommended by all the mothers at court, including Marie-Thérèse, who had given me his name shortly after my wedding.

"I thought this was a simple spell?" Philippe added, opening his hands in impatience.

The *magicien* exchanged whispers with his Source, a woman maybe ten years older than me who wore a brown dress of homespun fabric and a white bonnet.

"The way we usually perform this spell," the *magicien* said at last, his voice deep and with a faint accent I couldn't place, "uses the subject as the conduit."

"What?" Philippe said, his gaze darting between the man and me for explanation.

With the calm and patience of a professional who has had to give the same talk a thousand times before, the *magicien* folded his hands in a pious gesture.

"A spell requires a conduit, to guide the magic and allow for the spell to work. To ascertain a pregnancy, the obvious conduit is the mother-to-be."

Philippe gestured toward me. "Well, there you go."

"Because your wife is a Source," the *magicien* replied, undeterred by the interruption, "her magic will interfere with the spell when I use her as a conduit."

A memory of the fortune-teller in her Parisian flat fleeted through my mind. Unaware of my condition, she had used my blood as a conduit and derailed her own prophecy spell more than a year ago.

"So what do we do?" Philippe asked.

"We proceed cautiously," the man said.

He and his Source moved to stand at my bedside with grave faces, and my heart rate quickened despite myself. This was such an ordinary spell, performed every day across the kingdom. There was no reason for me to feel nervous, yet this pair rendered me anxious with their whispered deliberations and side glances.

Philippe was of the same opinion as he approached the bed, his fists on his hips and a tense expression on his face.

"Maybe it would be better if His Highness waited outside?" the *magicien* said.

"No," we replied both at the same time, in an unusual display of mutual understanding.

The man relented and turned his attention toward me. "Your Highness, I will need you to control your magic when I perform the spell."

His use of the singular pronoun bothered me—he wouldn't be doing the spell alone, after all—but I let it slide in order to focus on the greater matter at hand.

"What will you need me to do?" I asked.

"I'm told closing your eyes will help," he replied. "And then you may focus on the magic inside you and try to keep it contained with your thoughts so it doesn't affect the magic in my spell."

I shot him an uncertain look, and his Source stepped in. "Maybe think of a box, Your Highness. Or a bubble. And picture your magic inside it. Stay focused on that thought until you're told to stop."

Her gentle tone and reassuring smile eased my throbbing heart. This didn't sound as complicated as the *magicien* made it sound.

"Do you think you can do that?" the man asked, and there was enough condescension in his tone to irritate me.

The real question was: Would he be able to handle my power if I *didn't* keep a hold on it? For all his great reputation, would he manage such a surge of magic, or be swamped by it? An unkind part of me wanted to put his arrogance to the test.

I inhaled through my nose and ignored the temptation. Instead, I pasted a polite smile on my face, and held out my hand to him. "I'm going to do my best."

We all linked hands and closed our eyes. In my mind's eye, I pictured the golden flecks of my magic, like a cloud of stars at my core. I took in measured breaths and imagined the particles of magic drifting into a transparent container, a thousand miniscule fireflies caught in a glass jar.

"Now," I whispered.

The sparkling specks bumped against the sides of my imaginary vessel, more intent at escaping every second. My pulse picked up. I didn't know how long I would keep them contained.

I squeezed the hand of the Source. "*Now.*"

She said the spell. From my point of view, nothing happened except the relentless knocking of my magic against the walls of my mind. The dots became brighter, their incandescent light filling the fictional prison that held them, and blinded me. I kept my eyes closed, my entire body stiff against the pressure, and stifled a moan. A couple more seconds and I would have to let go. Why was this spell taking so long? The *magicien* and his Source both crushed my hands, as if they too struggled to keep control of their own enchantment.

The glow of my magic turned bright as a shooting star.

My hands shook.

I held my breath.

The imaginary vessel inside me shattered.

The *magicien* let out a yelp and snatched his hand back, as if he'd put his fingers into the fire and been burned. I opened my eyes. The Source swayed on her feet, pale as a ghost, and Philippe caught her before she could swoon.

"What happened?" he cried.

His panicked gaze was on me, but now that the pressure on my magic was gone, my pulse was calm again. I wiped my sweaty palms on my bed sheets, and took in a breath in an attempt to ease the familiar tightness in my lungs.

Breathless, the *magicien* rested his weight against my bedside table, while his Source dropped onto a chair. Philippe abandoned her to rush to me.

"What happened?" He cupped my face between his palms. "Did it work?"

"I don't know," I said. "I didn't feel the spell."

Reassured that I wasn't in any immediate danger of collapsing, he turned to the *magicien*, whose skin was now as gray as his clothes.

"Well?"

With shaking hands, the *magicien* pulled a tattered handkerchief out of his pocket to wipe his brow.

"I apologize, Your Highness," he told Philippe. "Sometimes a familiar spell proves it can still surprise you."

It was a poor lie. What had surprised him was the strength of my magic, but he was too proud to admit it. He coughed and regained some of his composure.

"Her Highness is indeed with child," he added, his voice more assertive.

Philippe clasped his hands with a gasp. My heart soared. Out of a similar instinct, we threw ourselves at each other. He wrapped me in a fierce embrace that lifted me off the bed, and we both laughed.

"We're having a child!" he said, delight and disbelief mixed in his tone. "We're having a child."

We kissed. The past vanished, and for an instant only us and our child remained, along with all the potential threads of our future ahead of us. There was only Philippe, and there was only joy, and there was only hope.

The *magicien* cleared his throat. The moment ended. Reality rushed back at us, and all of a sudden it became necessary to pay the man for his services, to offer his Source some refreshments, and to call for servants and messengers. Philippe let go of me, and my heart ached for more of his touch, more of his presence, more of his words.

Soon, a voice at the back of my mind promised.

I hoped it was right, and this kiss was the first step on walking the path back toward each other.

* * *

A parasol in one hand and a pair of scissors in the other, I picked flowers to take back to Versailles. The tidy gardens of Saint-Cloud slumbered in the afternoon sunshine, bees buzzing among blooms and Mimi sniffing every crack in the ground.

After the *magicien*'s visit this morning, Philippe had stayed to check on the running of the household, while I supervised the packing of my luggage. But the hive of activity inside was such that it rendered my presence unnecessary, and I had found refuge in the haven outside the house.

All of a sudden, loud voices ripped through the peace of the gardens. I turned toward the house, while Mimi's ears perked up. Most of the windows stood open with the indoor shutters shut, to keep the sun out but let in the warm air. The breeze carried more noise through the evergreen hedges, as the shouts crescendoed to a full argument inside. The sound came from the ground floor, and I abandoned my scissors and cut flowers to lift my skirts and hurry back to the building.

Several servants hovered in the hallway amid cases and boxes, craning their necks and exchanging whispers as echoes of the commotion spilled out of the grand salon. They scattered like frightened birds at my approach, and I dropped my parasol onto a half-packed trunk before walking into the large receiving room.

Philippe and Armand stood nose-to-nose, red with anger and out of breath.

"What is going on?" I marched to their side and stared them both down. "Do you realize people can hear you shouting in the next village?"

Paper crinkled under my feet. I picked up the printed sheet, but Philippe snatched it from my hand with a growl.

"Don't look at it."

My temper rose. "Why? What is it?"

"Armand will explain," he spat with such ferocity it was hard to believe they had once been best friends and lovers.

Armand ran his fingers through his hair, and struggled to meet my gaze. Alarm replaced irritation in my chest.

"It's probably better if you don't read it," he said.

"But what is it?"

"An anonymous pamphlet." Armand sighed. "It's been circulating at court and in some of the Parisian *salons* for the past couple of days. And it's about . . . us."

My gaze went from his embarrassed expression to Philippe's fuming one, uncomprehending. "Us?"

"It's a tale of our supposed love affair," Armand said, defeat in his tone.

A silence greeted his reply, and he let his words sink in. My shoulders relaxed.

"That's it?" I asked. "That's all?"

"*That's all?*" Philippe repeated, incensed again. "You think this is nothing?"

His furious tone brought out the coolness in my nature. I would not stoop to his level and argue with my husband like a screeching wife.

"It *is* nothing," I replied. "Slander like this gets printed and circulated all the time. It doesn't make it true or memorable."

"Half the court has read it!" Philippe shouted. "They'll think you cheated on me. Reputations have been ruined for less than that. Marriages have ended for far less than that."

"Don't shout at her," Armand said.

Philippe pushed him. "You, shut up."

Armand righted himself, his fist raised. I leaped between them.

"Don't you dare fight in my presence." I used my royal tone, which always seemed to work. "You're noblemen; behave as such!"

They stood down, glaring at each other. I raised my index finger at Philippe to regain his attention.

"The only pamphlets," I said, "that ruin reputations and break marriages are the ones that are true. This one isn't. We'll ask the king to have it destroyed and to spread the word that it was mere slander meant to harm the royal family, or France's relationship with England, which both might be the case."

Philippe snorted. "So you're denying it's true?"

Red-hot anger spiked through me, with force I had seldom felt. My tone turned ice cold and I stared him down.

"Now you listen to me, because I will not say this again. I am not having, and I have never had, an affair with Armand. All I've done since marrying you is love you, be patient with you, accept *your* affairs, and be a dutiful wife. So if you accuse me of infidelity one more time, I swear I will leave French court and go to my brother in England, and *you* will have to explain why to your brother."

To punctuate the end of my speech, I grabbed the pamphlet from his hand, crumpled it, and threw it in the empty fireplace. It was the most theatrical I had ever been in my life, and my threat was mostly an empty one, but they didn't have to know that. Armand gaped at me. Philippe stared at the ball of paper in the bare hearth.

"And while we're on the topic of who's to blame for this," I said before my anger vanished and my boldness deserted me, "you might want to ask yourself who would benefit from publishing such a pamphlet and wrecking our marriage."

Philippe raised his gaze to me at last. "You think Lorraine is behind this?"

"There aren't many other candidates," Armand replied.

"I thought I told you to be quiet," Philippe snapped. "You've said and done enough, don't you think?"

Hurt fleeted across Armand's features, and pain pinched my heart at the hostility between them. They used to be so close; surely they missed that familiar bond. But Philippe's focus had already drifted back to me.

"I don't believe Lorraine is behind this," he said.

Armand threw his hands up and let out a frustrated groan, as if he'd argued this point many times before. I chose a more diplomatic approach.

"What makes you say that?" I asked.

"First, it's not like him," Philippe replied.

Armand and I exchanged a glance. He would never want to hear anything against Lorraine, not without solid proof to back our claims.

"You don't know him as I do," he went on. "And second, what would be the point? He doesn't need to break up our marriage. He already—" He stopped, as if realizing what he was about to admit.

He already has me, was what he'd meant to say. This half confession hit me far harder than I anticipated. A painful pang reverberated from my heart through my body, and I coughed. Both men moved toward me out of instinct, but I held up my hand to prevent them from drawing closer. I needed space. I needed air. I certainly didn't need either of them to touch me.

My cough stopped after a few seconds, and I cleared my throat to speak. I turned to Armand first.

"Would you leave us for just a moment?"

His focus traveled from me to Philippe, his expression uncertain. Then he nodded, and walked out of the room. Once the door had latched into place behind him, I held Philippe's gaze.

"This is what's going to happen," I said. "We are going back to court. Together. I'm not going to see Armand. You're not going to see Lorraine. There won't be any scandal, and we're going to put all this behind us. Do you agree?"

Philippe bit his lip and shifted his weight from one foot to the other. His hesitation was a knife through my heart, but this time I wouldn't retreat.

"We can try," he said at last.

This wasn't the resounding agreement I sought, but it was a start. Whether the pamphlet was Lorraine's doing or not, it was another dent in the fragile equilibrium of my life. It was time for me to regain control of it.

CHAPTER XVI

───────────

The palace terrace was a ballroom.

Checkered columns sprang between the symmetrical pools of the water garden and the candle-lit facade to support a gauze canopy sprinkled with sparkling gems. A smooth parquet floor covered the gravel, and heavy chandeliers cast a dazzling light that chased all the shadows away. On a platform in a corner, Lully's large orchestra performed lively music that swelled in the open-air gallery and led the French court into an endless string of dances. And everywhere, the sweet scent of magic mixed with the guests' perfumes, as spells increased the brightness of the lights and helped white feathers and golden leaves float above the guests' heads.

"Here." Philippe handed me a glass of water. "I don't trust any of those magically tempered beverages."

Arrived only minutes ago, we stood by the fully laden buffet that teemed with cakes and delicacies piled high on silver plates. I took a sip from my drink and waved my gem-studded fan, scanning the thick crowd. As per the king's instructions, everyone wore black and white, which rendered the French courtiers akin to giant chess pieces.

"Is my brother here?" Philippe asked.

In an absentminded gesture, he slipped his arm around my waist and drained his own glass. Since our return to Versailles a week ago, he'd kept his promise to present a united front at court. Louis had helped us quash the rumors of our mutual infidelity by having the pamphlet destroyed and—albeit inadvertently—by keeping Lorraine busy. We still waited to make the news of our upcoming child public, but in the meantime our behavior was beyond reproach enough to make everyone yawn and seek new gossip elsewhere.

"Not yet," I replied.

If her husband was absent, Marie-Thérèse was already sat in a black armchair by one of the columns. Wrapped in white lace and tulle that didn't agree with her pale complexion, she ate pastries off a porcelain plate with industrious gravity. Crumbs fell on her prominent belly, and she brushed them away without a pause. The mere idea of food made me nauseous, and a pang of envy ran through me at her appetite and carefree pregnancy.

"Shall we dance?" Philippe said.

That wrenched me out of my melancholy thoughts faster than any other question could. I raised my eyebrows at him.

"You want to dance with me?"

Philippe and I never danced together. In public, it was his way of showing his aloofness toward me, and in private he claimed I was too good a dancer for him to match my skills. In truth, and with the growing distance between us, it had become an activity we never engaged in together.

Hurt flickered in his eyes at my surprised tone, swiftly replaced by indifference. He put down his empty glass to avoid my gaze.

"We don't have to. It was just an idea because I'm bored."

Remorse swept through me. He'd taken a step toward me, and I had pushed him back.

"We can," I said more gently. "You know I love to dance. But are you sure?"

He shrugged. "Never mind. I just thought we looked very stunning tonight and we might gift the crowd with a display of our combined attractiveness."

The offhand irony in his tone, which he used whenever he wanted to hide his true emotions, increased my guilt. It had been a long time since he'd resorted to it in my presence. And we did look good together, he in white and gold silk, I in black and silver, our outfits matching with intricate embroidery and pearls.

"I see your point," I replied, fumbling for a way to justify my reaction. "It's just people will notice and may find it odd. We agreed not to draw attention to ourselves. But if you—"

He gave me a smile that didn't reach his eyes. "You're right, my love. Let's keep a low profile. I see Jean Aniaba is here. I should go and say hello."

Before I could argue, he released his hold on me and turned away, dragging a piece of my heart with him. He strode away through the glittering revelers to reach the prince clad in a shimmering cream-colored outfit.

"His Majesty, the king!" the herald announced, his voice carrying over the music and the general chatter, and distracting me from Philippe's desertion. The dancing stopped and everyone sank into bows and curtsies, as the herald went on: "And Mademoiselle de La Vallière."

A stunned silence greeted the announcement. I glanced up as Louis entered the ephemeral ballroom with Louise at his side. Their arms linked, they walked in like a royal couple, her gold-trimmed white dress a perfect echo of his flamboyant outfit. His face a serene mask, Louis held up his gold-plated cane to signal Lully to resume the ball. Music ascended under the gem-filled canopy once more, and people rose from their greeting stances with wide eyes and whispered comments. My gaze went to Marie-Thérèse, who stood with her colorless features halfway between mortification and rage. Her ladies gathered around her to distract her, and she sank back into her seat, but the damage was done.

My irritation with Louis and his unforgiving conduct mounting in my chest, I took a step toward her to grant her my public support in the face of such humiliation. A hand on my arm stopped me.

"Did you see that?" Athénaïs hissed in my ear.

"I did," I replied in the same low tone. "What on earth has possessed them to behave like this?"

Until now, Louis had always strived to spare Marie-Thérèse's feelings and to hide his liaison with Louise. This unexpected show went against every effort he'd made to avoid a scandal and to keep everyone oblivious.

"Is it because his mother isn't here to lecture him?" I asked. "He thinks he can do whatever he wants because she's unwell?"

Her hand still on my arm, Athénaïs grabbed a green-colored drink from the buffet and swallowed a sip.

"It's a factor," she said, still in hushed tones. "But this is all Olympe's fault."

A devilish look sparkled in her eyes at her imminent revelations, and she bit her lip in anticipation. I wasn't one to encourage gossip, but since the situation involved my closest friends and family members, I relented and let out a sigh.

"Oh, go on, you're obviously dying to tell me."

"It's all out of a novel, really," she said at once. "Olympe never forgave Louise for seducing the king when she always failed to bring him back to her after his marriage to the queen."

I cast a quick glance around to ensure we weren't overheard, but everyone was engrossed in their own conversations or the dancing, and the music covered our words.

"So she hatched a plot to reveal the affair to Marie-Thérèse," Athénaïs continued, "hoping this would lead to the king breaking up with Louise. Except she didn't want the queen to know she was behind it. So she had a servant steal an envelope from the queen's chambers, one addressed to Marie-Thérèse from Spain. She wrote a letter explaining the affair and used the envelope to have it delivered to the queen."

I pursed my lips in attempt to follow the intricacies of the scheme. "She wrote a letter pretending to be Spanish? I thought Olympe didn't speak Spanish."

"She doesn't," Athénaïs replied, still gleeful. "But guess who does?"

Ice spread through my stomach. "Armand."

"Yes." She chuckled in delight at the enormity of the anecdote. "Olympe asked Armand to translate the letter, except he isn't as fluent as he pretends, the rake. And the envelope they used was all creased from the various handling."

"So? How does this lead us to the king making Louise his official mistress in front of the whole court?"

My patience was running thin with her long-winded story, and alarm rose in me as the scheme seemed to involve everyone in my life.

"The letter was delivered to the queen this morning," Athénaïs explained. "Except the head of her household thought it might be bad news from Spain, so she read it instead of handing it to Marie-Thérèse straightaway. And when she realized what the letter contained, she brought it to the king."

"How do you know all this?"

Athénaïs shrugged, feigned innocence all over her pretty features. "I talk to people. And the queen's servants like me. Anyway, the king was furious. He shouted at Olympe, and—" She gestured at Louis chatting to the Comte de Saint-Aignan, Louise all smiles at his side. "The whole business prompted him to make his affair public, apparently."

I shook my head, too flabbergasted to speak. I had assumed Olympe's absence from the ball was due to her tending to the Queen Mother tonight. It hadn't crossed my mind that she could be back to her old plotting and deceiving ways. Would Louis forgive her this time? I wondered. And Armand? Why in heaven would he take part in this ridiculous conspiracy, when his situation at court was precarious enough as it was?

"This is all a secret, of course," Athénaïs added. "The queen knows nothing of it, and I doubt the king will want the whole story to be known at court."

"Of course," I replied.

I wanted to ask about Armand—who was also conspicuously absent tonight—but I had promised myself not to utter his name in public anymore, *especially* in front of Athénaïs. Instead, my mind jumped to the prophecy. Louise's fate was supposed to be a broken heart, yet the events of this evening gave me hope. When everything had conspired to ruin her love story with Louis, fortune had intervened in the most dramatic way to save her from a heartbreaking separation. If her fate could be altered, then why not mine?

A glimpse of Marie-Thérèse's sullen face in the crowd deflated my hopes. The prophecy foretold betrayals and secrets would be her undoing, and tonight's events were a grim fulfillment of that prediction. Maybe there wasn't escaping every part of the prophecy after all.

"You're feeling sorry for her, aren't you?"

Athénaïs's question pulled me out my musing. She followed my gaze toward Marie-Thérèse, and gave me a pointed look.

"Who wouldn't?" I replied, harsher than I intended.

This might all be entertaining to Athénaïs, but the queen's situation brought out compassion and kinship in me. She was a foreigner at a French court that relentlessly mocked her, where she was the constant object of gossip and now humiliation. As a fellow princess and sister-in-law, it was my duty to side with her.

"I have to go and talk to her."

I disentangled my arm from Athénaïs's grasp, put down my glass, and moved through the throng of dancers toward Marie-Thérèse. A firm grip caught my wrist, and I stopped in my tracks, my pulse spiking at the audacious touch.

I raised my gaze to the tall silhouette now standing between me and my objective. Lorraine's smooth smile greeted me.

"Your Highness." He bowed. "May I impose on you and have this dance?"

He still clutched my wrist, and I would have been within my rights to slap him for insolence and to walk away. Instead, I paused. Since his arrival at court two and half months ago, it was the first time he had sought me out. My body recoiled at his touch, and my instinct screamed at me to stay away from him, yet curiosity nagged at me. Here was the man who'd thrown my life into upheaval yet stood before me grinning as if he thought he would get away with it. Fouquet had made the same mistake, once.

I slipped from his grasp and held out my hand with a harmless expression. "Are you a good dancer, sir?"

His smile grew in impertinence. "I've been told I'm passable."

A new dance number had just started, and I allowed him to lead me around the room. Heads turned along the way, bending to catch a better view or to hide whispers behind feathered fans. As Athénaïs had predicted all those weeks ago, Lorraine and I did make a perfect duet. He was as good a dancer as the king, and his exquisite black outfit matched my own dark dress. We moved in coordinated harmony to the rhythm of the violin music, our footsteps decidedly synchronized. Within moments my lungs tightened and my breaths struggled, but I had enough experience with my condition to ignore its symptoms for a little while.

"I'll admit," Lorraine said after a minute of silence, "I underestimated you."

I shot him a bold look to hide my disappointment. His use of the past tense meant he likely wouldn't make that same mistake again.

"Your attempt at taking hold of my journal took me by surprise," he went on. "And I didn't think you'd draw Philippe back to you so quickly."

I gave him my sweetest smile. "I suppose you don't know me very well."

We spun among the other dancers, his hand letting me go and catching me again with ease.

"I didn't," he replied.

Again, his use of the past tense flooded me with apprehension. Fouquet hadn't realized my power until very late in the game. Lorraine wasn't as arrogant, it seemed.

"I did believe the whole wide-eyed princess charade for a while," he went on. "A wisp of a woman with a kind smile and a generous heart."

"That's me." I punctuated my reply by my trademark grin.

"It is," he said. "Which is why it took me a little while to understand the truth. Take women like Olympe de Soissons, or Athénaïs de Montespan. What they show to the world is all a facade. But you . . . it's actually who you are." He bent down to whisper in my ear. "It's just not *all* you are."

I cringed at his breath against my skin, but he withdrew at once, and carried on the dance.

"You know what your problem is?" he asked, the question obviously rhetorical. "Everyone loves you. That means everyone loves talking about you. Everywhere I turn, I find someone more than happy to tell me all there is to know about the wonderful Henriette d'Angleterre."

We reached the end of the ballroom, and he let go of me so we could turn in time with the music. The short respite allowed me to relax my stance. I wouldn't let him see how much his words rattled me. He grasped my fingers again.

"Another thing I didn't realize was how much Philippe loves you," he added.

Hearing my husband's name on his lips was like a slap in the face, but I kept a placid expression. I would hear what he had to say and find out as much as I could from this flow of words.

"He hides it very well," he said. "And it was my fault for assuming he didn't care about you. But you know what gave him away?"

Again, the question didn't require an answer, and I simply shook my head with polite inquisitiveness, despite my actual curiosity. Much like with his brother, Philippe had strived to protect me, it appeared. What had exposed his intentions?

"His insistence at keeping us apart." Lorraine released me for a twirl, then grabbed me once more. "Did you notice? I arrived at court some months ago, and it's the first time you and I have the opportunity for a chat. It puzzled me, how out of reach you seemed."

The dance ended, but the orchestra launched into another number without pause, and Lorraine guided me through the ballroom again. I didn't mind. I wanted to hear everything he had to say, now.

"You were unwell," he carried on. "You were busy. You were away. At first I didn't mind. It meant I'd won, didn't it? I was the king's Source. I had Philippe. I forgot about you. But then, you stole my journal, and I understood I hadn't won. Contrary to what the king said, you still have magic. And Philippe still *adores* you." He sneered at the word as if it were an insult to his person. "That's when it all became clear: Philippe kept us apart because he feared the reckoning that would come about if we ever met."

His expression darkened, and his hold on me stiffened. For the first time, I was glad we stood in a brightly lit ballroom with the entire French court around us. The dance sent me twirling away from Lorraine, then back to his arms that enclosed me in a rigid embrace. My heartbeat ricocheted against my ribs, and although he was taller than me, I channeled all my mother's haughtiness to stare him down.

"Are you threatening me, Chevalier?"

His suave grin was back, but his eyes were cold. "Would I dare?"

He spun me away from him again, and to any outside observer, our moves were as smooth as if we were having a lovely time dancing together, which rendered our conversation even more surreal.

"Let me tell you a story instead," he said as we glided along the ballroom. "Have you ever had the pleasure of meeting the Duc de Gramont? Charming man."

I knew Armand's father only in passing, but nothing about the man could be described as charming. Lorraine's words awoke an awful sense of foreboding in my chest.

"The duke and I share similar views on many topics," he went on. "And the last time we were chatting, the matter of his son came up. You see, the duke is in despair when it comes to his wayward offspring."

Despite myself, I felt all color drain from my face. What had he done to Armand? *What had he done?*

"The problem, I told him," Lorraine explained, "is that Armand is an idle man. He needs a purpose in life. So I wondered if the king could be persuaded to give the young man some military command in his army. There always is a war going on, after all. Next thing you know, the duke is speaking with the king, and it so happens that for some unfathomable reason, His Majesty has had it up to here with Armand as well! So it's done: Armand will be off to the front by the end of the week, and isn't this a happy ending for everyone?"

A buzzing in my ear overtook the ballroom's music and chatter. I halted my steps in the middle of the dance floor and ripped my hands out of Lorraine's grasp. He'd gone after *Armand*.

Triumph twinkled in his gaze, and it was all I could do to stop myself from scratching his eyes out right there and then. My breathing came out ragged and my hands shook with fury.

"Philippe won't allow it," I said.

Lorraine gave a theatrical helpless shrug. "I don't believe Philippe cares anymore."

"You've made a mistake," I growled.

I didn't sound like myself, but this man seemed to bring out the worst in me. A cough tore through me then, giving me an excuse to get away from him without causing a scene. I buried my mouth in my handkerchief and slid between the courtiers to slip through the gauzy drapes of the ballroom's walls. I stopped by the pools, which reflected the starry night sky and the moon crescent in a peaceful manner that was at complete odds with my inner turmoil.

I had been such a fool. Lorraine could not only threaten me but he could also act on his threats. Now Louis would never listen to me if I asked him to rescind the honor he had bestowed Armand. And Philippe was so angry with his former lover that he would be glad to know him gone for a while, never mind that Armand could die in the meantime.

The thought sparked another fit of anxiety and my coughing redoubled. Lorraine had played his hand to perfection, and with an ease that would have awed me if it hadn't been terrifying. From then on, I would be scared of what he might do to my other friends, and I had lost my main ally in my fight against him.

The next royal entertainment was a month away, where he no doubt planned to establish even further his influence over the French court. He would be even harder to challenge after that, which meant I had only a few weeks to show his real face to the king and my husband.

"Henriette!" Philippe jogged to my side, his feet crunching in the gravel. He extended his hands toward me, but my cough subsided and he pulled back, hesitant. "I saw you dancing with Lorraine. Did he upset you?"

A dozen replies came to me, from reassuring to irritated. In the end, I settled for the truth.

"Yes," I said. "But it was for the last time."

And I marched back into the ballroom, ready to formulate a plan.

CHAPTER XVII

Light rain pattered against my windows, lending a melancholy gray light to my bedchamber that matched the state of my thoughts.

Following the ball three days ago, I sat at my desk with my quill poised above paper and the intention to write a letter to my mother describing my return to Versailles. Instead, I stared at the raindrops trickling down the glass panes and pondered how to reveal Lorraine's dark secrets to Louis and Philippe.

If I now knew he likely had nothing to do with my ill health, it was still my duty to expose his plot to steal spells and sell them for profit. How to do this, however, without written proof, or getting Prince Aniaba involved? Ink dripped onto my blank page, and no epiphany came.

A soft knock yanked me from my reflection. The maid at the door curtsied.

"Your Highness, the Comtesse de Soissons is here to see you."

My heart lifted at the interruption. Olympe might momentarily be on bad terms with Louis, but she could be relied upon to come up with inventive ways to tackle problems. I moved to meet her in my salon, where she stood taking off her wet cloak with a manservant next to her. I paused on my way to greet her. The man in a valet's uniform was Armand.

My maid slipped out of the room with Olympe's coat, and I let my mouth gape.

"What are you doing?"

"Don't blame me." Olympe pointed at Armand. "He's the one who convinced me to go along with this scheme. Now I'm going to wait in your antechamber until you two are done."

And before I could protest, she sashayed out of the salon and let the door click shut behind her. I turned to Armand, who gifted me his rakish grin.

"You shouldn't be here," I said, still debating between bewilderment at his eccentric apparition and worry that he would be recognized.

His face fell at my greeting. "But I had to see you! And I thought you'd be pleased. You didn't really expect me to leave the country without saying goodbye?" Taking my hands, he led me to the chairs before the fire and sat down opposite me.

His hopeful gaze melted the anxiety in my chest. "*Of course* I'm pleased to see you, but we made a promise to Philippe, and I don't want rumors to start again."

"Hence my clever disguise!" Armand replied, his self-confidence returning. "And Olympe was happy to help, or rather, she didn't have a choice given how much she owes me for the whole Spanish-letter fiasco."

"Speaking of which," I said, "you two couldn't help your-selves, could you? Left to your own devices for two weeks and you had to go and do something ridiculous."

"I was bored." Armand pressed his lips in a pout. "You don't understand, darling, it's been dreadful without you and Philippe."

There was a hint of sincere dejection in his expression that sparked compassion in my heart.

"And look where it's led you," I said in a kind tone. "Promise me you'll stay safe."

Sparks of excitement shone again in his eyes. "Oh, don't worry! I plan on being a war hero and coming back with a small wound that'll increase my charisma. A scar on my face would do nicely, I think."

"Oh, stop it." I bit the inside of my cheeks to prevent a smile.

"I promise I'll write often," he went on. "And while I'm single-handedly saving the French kingdom from foreign enemies, you'll have to carry on the fight against our foe here and keep me apprised of the situation. I'm leaving you in charge, Henriette. Don't let me down."

I sighed. "I'm not certain how to do that. Whatever I try, he seems to be able to counteract."

"You'll find an idea." He patted my hand. "And Athénaïs will help if you need her. She'll have plenty of time to do so, won't she?"

I frowned. "What do you mean?"

"Didn't you hear? Her husband is coming with me." He leaned in to stage-whisper. "Apparently he has a hoard of gam-bling debts and he needs money." He resumed his seat and his normal voice. "Not that I'm one to judge, but the man seemed quite keen on a speedy solution to his problems, and the army offers just that, doesn't it?"

That was an unexpected development. *What did Athénaïs think of it?* I wondered.

"Do you know where you're going?" I asked, more concerned with Armand's fate than the Marquis de Montespan's.

"Poland," he replied. "Apparently it takes ages to travel there. Who knows, the war might even be over before I arrive."

His offhand tone did nothing to assuage my fears. Behind all his bravado, he was going to *war*. There was a chance he might not come back. Tears filled my eyes despite my resolution to remain cheerful for his sake.

"Oh, darling, don't get upset." He knelt in front of me and offered me his lace handkerchief. "You know how the army works. The people in charge don't even see the frontline. I'll be in my tent all day, studying maps and complaining about the weather. I'll only be heroic if it's safe."

His mischievous smile was back, reassuring in its familiarity.

"I'll miss you," I confessed, my eyes dry again.

He pocketed his handkerchief with a flourish. "Of course you will! But I was exiled from court once before, and you managed perfectly well without me."

"On the topic of managing well without you," I replied, "did you remember to tell your future wife you're leaving?"

Armand grimaced. "Oh, I'm afraid the countess gave up on me a while ago. I heard she married a marquess and is quite happy. But no doubt my father will use my military exploits to convince some other poor soul I'm the perfect match. Too bad I—"

The door slammed open.

"Philippe is here!" Olympe hissed. "He's coming up the stairs right now."

My heart took a dive in my chest, and I stood up.

"But he's supposed to be in Paris all day," Armand said, as if refusing to face reality would change its course.

Like panicked chickens aware of the fox's arrival in the henhouse, the three of us shuffled our feet and glanced around, desperate for a solution. Panicked thoughts chased one after the other in my mind, with one thing for certain: finding Armand in my apartments would cause Philippe anger and pain, which I wanted to avoid at all cost.

"We have to leave," Olympe whispered, her tone urgent. "Can we get out through the service rooms?"

Footsteps echoed in the antechamber. It was too late. They'd never slip out without being heard or seen. Blood pulsed against my temples, and I forced a breath down my throat. If I let myself get flustered we were lost.

The door handle moved. I pointed a chair to Olympe.

"Sit down."

I grabbed the nearest flower vase, and threw its water on the fire, which sizzled and smoked, half-extinguished.

"Tend the fire," I said to Armand.

Bafflement all over his features, he dropped to his knees in front of the fireplace, and I resumed my seat. The door opened.

"It's a downpour out there," Philippe said, taking off his hat. "I made it halfway to Paris before I told the driver to turn the carriage around." He caught sight of Olympe and paused. "Oh, I thought Henriette was alone."

My heart slammed against my ribs, deafening to my ears. At my feet, Armand kept his head down and poked the dying embers. Olympe stood up with a tight smile, the large folds of her dress hiding him from Philippe's view.

"I was just leaving."

She gave a quick curtsy and bid us goodbye. As she walked out of the room, I maneuvered so I kept Armand out of sight. Whatever he was doing to the hearth, the fire had completely gone out, now. His uniform was a good disguise, but his clumsiness was going to bring an end to this charade if I didn't divert Philippe's attention.

"I thought you didn't like her," my husband said, his mind still on Olympe.

I gave an awkward shrug, and tried to sound relaxed. "I have to be polite to her. She's head of your mother's household."

Lying wasn't my strong suit, and guilt at deceiving Philippe of all people didn't help. But other preoccupations distracted him, for he gave me only a passing glance on his way to my bedroom.

"It's cold in here," he said. "You should stay in your bedchamber in this weather. It's warmer."

He disappeared next door, clearly expecting me to follow him. Armand sprang to his feet.

Go, I mouthed.

He blew me a kiss and tiptoed out. The door clicked shut behind him, and for an instant my heart split between relief at a crisis averted and grief at his departure.

"I found your shawl," Philippe called out from my bedroom.

I joined him as he pulled out one of my stoles from a trunk at the foot of the canopy bed. With the fire crackling and lit sconces on the walls, warmth did chase away some of the gloom of the day in this part of my apartments. I wrapped the shawl around my shoulders and sank in an armchair in front of the fireplace, the strain of the last few minutes catching up with me.

"I stopped by Mother's chambers on my way up," Philippe said.

He took off his high-heeled shoes and coat before sitting in the chair opposite mine with his legs stretched out before the hearth.

"How is she?" I asked.

Renewed guilt shot through me. I had been back at Versailles long enough to pay a visit to the Queen Mother yet had failed to do so. I ought to remedy this as soon as possible. She and Louis were the first people who should be informed of my pregnancy.

"Not well at all." Philippe shrugged with a dismissive smile.

I wanted to shake him for trying to hide his feelings from me and to embrace him for comfort at the same time. Taming my temper, I took hold of his hand and kissed his long fingers.

"Did you two speak?"

He snorted. "Yes. And guess what she wanted to talk about?"

Disappointment gripped my heart on his behalf. "Your brother."

"They had an argument," he said, his eyes on the fire and his voice low. "She's heard about Louise, and she wanted him to end the whole affair. He refused, of course. I think it was a proper row. He shouted at her, and she threatened to leave for a convent, but he forbade it. She was still upset." He let out a sigh. "He's really stopped listening to everyone, now."

He was right. The Queen Mother was the last person to still have some influence over Louis. If he refused to heed even her advice, there was no one else left to oppose him.

"I told her about the baby." He glanced at me. "I know it wasn't right to do it in your absence, but I just wanted to distract her and—"

I extended my hand toward him. "It's all right. I don't mind." Anne d'Autriche knew about the pregnancy, which was what mattered.

Yet Philippe met my reply with a grim face that made me pause. "What did she say?"

"She's happy for you," he said, which left so many things *unsaid* that suspicion gripped me and I frowned.

"*She's happy for me?* Philippe, what did she say?"

He stared at the fire. "She said she was disappointed I was once again trying to draw attention to myself when the focus should be on my brother's situation. I suppose it was my fault for expecting a different reply from her."

The dejection in his tone tightened my throat. Never mind who she was—I wanted to shout at the Queen Mother's that no matter how much she wanted to protect Louis, doing so by belittling Philippe was wrong and someone should have told her so long ago.

I moved to sit in his lap, and he let me, wrapping his arms around my waist and leaning his chin against my shoulder. It was the most intimate we'd been in weeks, and I wished it wasn't because he was miserable.

"Nothing about this is your fault," I said. "You know that. You've given your mother every reason to be proud of you, and the fact that she isn't is her loss."

But his expression remained disconsolate. "I'm going to be a terrible parent, aren't I?"

"You're not." My voice rose with my temper. His mother had let her fears overrule her heart, and I refused to let him do the same. "Our child will love you, just like I do."

He tensed against me. "That's the problem, isn't it? I've done nothing to deserve that trust, that love."

Exasperation pushed me to my feet. "Will you stop saying that?"

Fighting against his insecurities was like bailing out a skiff in the middle of a storm. No matter how many times I repeated reassurances, he always circled back to the belief that he didn't deserve the good in his life, and that it should be taken away soon. It didn't help that both the Queen Mother and the king worked against me, pushing the boat further at sea at every turn.

I paced the length of the bedroom, my feet bringing me to my desk, where the letter to my mother waited, unfinished. It sparked an idea in my mind.

"Since you've told your mother about the baby," I said, "I want to tell mine. I want us to go see her when the rains stop."

Surprise at my sudden shift in mood flickered across his features, but he nodded. "As you wish."

If his mother couldn't tell him what he needed to hear, maybe mine would.

* * *

After spending the winter at the convent that had sheltered us in my youth, my mother was back in Paris for the warmer months and staying at the Palais-Royal. Sunshine bathed the small palace where Philippe and I had been wed fifteen months ago, but the windows were shut in the salon that my mother had chosen to receive us.

"It's because of the noise," she said with a wrinkled nose as a servant handed out teacups. "If I'd known, I would have stayed somewhere else."

Banging and shouting resounded outside to illustrate her words, and she winced. The servant left, and Philippe grabbed a piece of cake off a porcelain plate before moving to the window to peer at the gardens below.

"What's going on here?" he asked.

"The king is having a little house built at the back of the gardens," my mother explained, disdain all over her features. "Now, one could wonder why he has need of such a dwelling hidden in the heart of Paris, but I won't be repeating gossip in your presence."

Straight-backed and pale in her black mourning clothes, she sipped her tea with a prim air. Mimi, who I had brought along, sat in her lap, and she petted her distractedly.

"It's for Louise, isn't it?" Philippe asked, craning his neck to see the construction site in the distance. "He's building the house in case he needs to send her away from court."

I suspected he was correct. It made sense for Louis to have a contingency plan should the revelation of his liaison turn into a full-blown scandal. Philippe bit into his cake and resumed his seat, unflappable in the face of his brother's plans. I swallowed some of my tea, but my throat and lungs were tight in the room's stuffy atmosphere. My mother surveyed me with a critical eye.

"You don't look too well. Have you been eating? And taking

the cordial I sent you?" She looked at Philippe, her sharp gaze turning accusatory. "Do you look after her at all?"

"Mother." I interrupted her embarrassing line of questioning before my husband choked on his cake. "I'm expecting a child."

Her expression froze, then lit up. A smile broke across her thin lips, and she put down Mimi to embrace me. "Oh, my sweet girl. What wonderful news."

I sank into her arms, welcoming the reassuring touch. She pulled back a fraction to kiss my hair and extended her hand to Philippe to draw him into our fold. He stiffened for a heartbeat, before allowing her to grab him. He wrapped his arm around my shoulders and kissed my temple. Time slowed, the three of us suspended outside of constraints and fears. *This is it*, I wanted to say to Philippe. *This is what family is supposed to be.*

He was the first to break away from the embrace, pulling us back into the reality of construction noises and cooling tea.

"How did it go with the *magicien*?" my mother asked as she resumed her seat and lifted Mimi into her lap again. "I always heard it makes it difficult when the expecting mother is a Source."

My being a Source had always been one of my mother's constant causes for worry. She feared I would be used for my magic and ultimately destroyed by it. A positive aspect of my life at French court had been to show me that a Source could do more than live in perpetual fear.

"The spell was a bit of a struggle," I replied, "but all in all, it went well."

"And how are you feeling?" my mother went on. "I heard you cough when you came in, and you look awfully pale."

"I'm all right," I lied. There was no use worrying her, and

admitting the truth would only lead her to spend the next months sending me every potion and doctor she came across.

"And you." She turned her dark gaze to Philippe, who was drinking his tea and stopped moving at the sudden attention. "I must say one hears all sorts of rumors about you. It would be reassuring to know they're not true."

And here she was, the former queen of England and now Queen Mother to the English king. Politely blunt and protective of her family to a fault. Philippe put down his cup, either to keep his countenance or to gather his thoughts, I wasn't sure. In the end he held her stare.

"There haven't been rumors only about me."

I stiffened. Snapping back was his usual way to defend himself, but it was my mother he was talking to. I loved them both too much to see them argue. Yet my mother remained as composed as ever.

"I know two things about my daughter," she said, the meaning behind my husband's words clear to her. "She loves you, and she would never do anything that could jeopardize her marriage." Her resounding support nearly brought a smile to my lips, until she added: "Unfortunately, I can't say I know the same about you."

Philippe's jaw tightened, and his gaze turned hard. "I suppose you don't know me well."

"Arguably," my mother replied, unperturbed. "Hence my request for reassurances."

Philippe's mouth pressed into a thin line. Sensing the tension in the room, Mimi whined and I stretched out my hand to soothe her with a caress. It gave me an instant to collect my wits despite the thumping of my heart.

"Let's not dwell on what happened in the past," I said. "We came here to talk about the future, Mother."

She gave me her gracious queenly smile, which didn't quite reach her eyes. "Of course, sweetheart. What else did you want to talk about?"

I launched into a description of the new palace at Versailles to steer us away from the dangerous waters of rumors and accusations. My mother prompted me with questions, and after a while, Philippe rejoined the conversation with a few remarks on the king's upcoming entertainment. My pulse settled, and the tension in my neck relaxed.

We'd avoided an argument, but the heart of the matter remained. Lorraine was still at court, a constant shadow cast over any plans we made for the future. And I still didn't know how to dispel it.

CHAPTER XVIII

We can't stop death, Fouquet had said.

Not *magiciens*. Not kings.

And so death came for Anne d'Autriche at last.

White clouds chased each other in the pale sky as her coffin arrived at the Saint-Denis basilica. A large crowd greeted the procession in silence, throwing flowers onto the cobblestones and the casket's fleur-de-lis velvet cover.

Inside the tall white building, the black-clad French court filled every pew, as murmurs and quiet sobs rose under the gothic arches of the high-ceilinged church. The heady smell of incense saturated the air, and I had to press my handkerchief against my nose to keep from coughing.

Pale and tense, Philippe stood by the bier and nodded at a whispered word from Bishop Bossuet. In his brother's absence, the overseeing of the ceremony rested on his shoulders, and the weight of it all carved lines around his mouth and smeared dark shadows under his eyes. The priest left him to take his place behind the pulpit. For an instant Philippe's attention snagged on the coffin, and a lost expression fleeted across his face. Then he lifted his gaze and caught my stare, which drew him to me like a magnet. His gloved hand gripped mine, and the service began. The choir sang a hymn, seconded by the congregation. Bossuet spoke next, and the funeral unfolded, comforting in its predictability.

Marie-Thérèse, Olympe, and my mother occupied the front row next to us with the Spanish ambassador. A little farther behind, D'Artagnan acknowledged me with a respectful nod, quiet tears running down his cheeks. How odd it was to think that he and the Queen Mother had known each other for decades. How even stranger the notion that they'd once been as young as I was. What had Anne dreamed of then? I wondered. Before the birth of her sons, before the loss of her husband, before the regency, before the Fronde, before the death of Mazarin, before Louis the Sun King? A Spanish princess brought to France at fourteen to marry a man who never showed any interest in her, what had her first years at French court been like? Would anyone care to remember it?

Philippe shifted on his feet as the assembly sang another hymn, nearly drowned out by the organ. He had let go of my hand, but held his leather-bound prayer book in a stiff grip. I rested my fingers on his forearm, which he acknowledged with a mirthless smile.

His mother's passing was a tremendous blow, of course, but I knew what added to his inner turmoil: for the first time in his life, people looked to him for decisions and instructions. Indeed, a few days ago, Louis had fallen apart at the news of Anne d'Autriche's imminent death. He had fainted as she received the last rites, and from then on it was Philippe who stayed at their mother's bedside until the end, Philippe who dealt with the wake and the funeral arrangements, Philippe who rose from his bed to face the court each day, while Louis remained in his apartments and hid behind protocol to avoid his own mother's burial.

By his own admission, my husband didn't mind doing all this for his family, but I knew him well enough to guess what grated him in this situation: everyone's heartfelt compassion for the king's bereavement. Even as we filed into the basilica earlier today, courtiers talked about Louis's behavior with sympathetic nods and earnest understanding. Who could blame the king for grieving his beloved mother? What son wouldn't react the same way? Meanwhile, Philippe's brave front was taken for granted and his own loss ignored by most. Even in death, Anne d'Autriche appeared to have one son, and a spare child who could be relied upon to fulfill whatever duty was required of him at the time.

Bossuet's sermon dragged on, so my mind wandered as my attention drifted along the crowd. Louise, her rosary tight in her grasp, had her head bowed and her eyes closed. Nearby, the Comte de Saint-Aignan stared at the stained glass windows, lost in thought. Lorraine sat next to him, magnificent in black clothes, his face a mask of neutrality.

To my surprise in this time of crisis, Philippe hadn't run to him, but sought my company instead. Perhaps with a child coming he did mean to salvage our relationship, or he simply looked for the reassuring stability that our marriage provided in his upended life. In any case, this brief separation gave me hope that the reveal of Lorraine's treachery wouldn't hit him too hard.

Another hymn swelled under the vaulted ceiling of the church, drawing me back to the present and bringing an end to the service. The bishop stepped aside, and a ripple of anticipation ran through the crowd. My heartbeat sped up too, despite the solemnity of the moment.

In spite of her condition as a woman, Anne d'Autriche had been a *magicienne* too. And in the kingdom, no one with magic was laid to rest without a final spell.

A hush fell over the assembly as the court *magiciens* and Sources stepped out of their pews to gather in the transept. The Comte de Saint-Aignan, Prince Aniaba, Lorraine, and the artist *magiciens* from Versailles joined hands around the casket with an unfamiliar man that I assumed came from Paris.

Olympe and I stayed in our seats, but we exchanged a glance. Her eyes were red from weeping, but her gaze was sharp. I had planned on this moment, and last night I had met with her to explain how I intended to use it as an opportunity. The loss of her mentor and her exclusion from the present magical ceremony rendered her combative, and her desire to protect Louis and to find herself in his good books again had done the rest. She'd agreed to my plan.

By the Queen Mother's coffin, the *magiciens* mixed with the Sources. Lorraine stood between the count and the short, portly man in old-fashioned mourning clothes I had never seen. Olympe shot me a pointed look. She'd noticed the stranger as well.

All the men around the casket assumed stern frowns and earnest focus. Then the Sources said the spell, Lorraine's voice clearer than the others'.

A flicker of light appeared above the coffin, like a star winking into existence in the vast expense of the universe. The audience held a collective breath, mesmerized by the spectacle. Within moments the light turned brighter and grew into a glittering shape suspended midair above the transept. The tiny brilliant dots coalesced into the form of a small golden tree, with roots hanging in thin air and leafy twigs wavering in an invisible breeze. The tree flourished and matured before our eyes, casting a shining light all around its strong branches and sturdy trunk. The sweet fragrance of magic took over the smell of incense under the vaulted ceiling, and the unnatural warmth of a hot summer day spread along the pews. But soon a gust of magic wind dispersed the leaves and dissolved the branches into nothingness. The trunk twirled and turned back into innumerable specks of light that merged into a glowing orb. The sphere of magic hung above the casket like a bubble, its size shrinking until it was a tiny fleck of light again, which slowly lost its brightness before disappearing.

The crowd released a collective breath in the silent stone building. Next to me, Olympe was weeping again. Philippe's expression was stone-cold, his gaze lost on something ahead of him.

The *magiciens* and Sources gave each other congratulating nods. The symbolic spell was an easy one, but for a royal funeral they still must have felt the slight pressure of their distinguished audience. Feet shuffled and noses were blown as the courtiers relaxed and the bishop walked up the aisle to signal the end of the service. Later today the Bourbon family vault in the basilica's nave would be opened and the Queen Mother's coffin lowered next to Louis's ancestors.

As people filed out of the church, Philippe sat back down. I gave Olympe a conniving look.

"I'll be back in a moment," I whispered into my husband's ear.

His reaction to my announcement was minimal, and I let him assume I was going to speak with the bishop or the English ambassador, as could be expected of me under the circumstances. Instead, I linked arms with Olympe, who wiped her eyes with an embroidered handkerchief and followed me down the side aisle.

The *magicien* Lorraine had lent his magic to for the tribute spell made his way out ahead of us, cutting a brisk path through the crowd. I kept a close eye on his black wig and stout figure, and ignored the sympathetic members of the assembly who tried to stop me along the way. Both Olympe and I had our handkerchiefs over our noses, and anyone would assume we were too grief-stricken to speak with them.

We trailed the stranger to the square outside, where a chaos of carriages now awaited courtiers eager to return to Versailles. Our quarry made for a simple one-horse vehicle at the mouth of a side street, and we hurried after him among the throng of mourning-clad people too busy chatting to notice us.

"Ready?" Olympe asked, her expression purposeful.

I squeezed her hand to signal my agreement, and she grabbed the *magicien*'s arm.

"*Divulgue*," I said under my breath.

A sliver of my magic ran from my core to Olympe's, and a veil of gleaming magic layered over our vision.

"What . . . ?" The *magicien* halted with his foot on the carriage footboard, his plump face reddening at the unexpected impediment on his progress. "What's the meaning of this?"

The spell took hold, and to Olympe's eyes and mine, his words took literal shape. They danced out of his mouth in a ribbon of golden letters that spelled out his question.

"Do forgive us," Olympe gave him a saccharine smile. "We only want to speak with you for an instant."

With the authority of a woman who seldom didn't get her way, she pushed him inside his carriage and we crowded in after him. My pulse thumped against my temples. We didn't have long: the spell wouldn't last more than a couple of minutes, and we would be missed within the same amount of time.

"Who are you?" the *magicien* asked, more flustered by the second. "What do you want? I don't have any money. I'll scream!"

All his words tumbled out of his mouth like a torrent of gilded letters and floated up under the dark ceiling where they dissolved.

"You'll do no such thing," Olympe replied, her eyes blazing. "If you don't know who we are, then it doesn't matter. We only want you to answer our questions and let you on your way."

A survey of our clothes made him relax a fraction. In our fine mourning outfits, we didn't look like robbers, and as women, he likely surmised we couldn't be such a threat to his personal safety.

"What questions?" he asked, unaware of our invisible spell that turned his speech into magic. It was a peculiar enchantment that I had found in my now-lost *grimoire*. An old yet simple truth spell that allowed the spell casters to see whether someone spoke true or not. As long as the *magicien*'s words came out of his mouth in golden tones, he was telling the truth. Should the letters turn black, he would be lying to us.

"You performed today's spell with the Chevalier de Lorraine," Olympe said.

Puzzlement crossed his features and sweat ran down his temples. "Well, yes."

"You reside in Paris, don't you?" Olympe went on. "What's your magical line of work?"

"Yes, yes, I do." The man's voice shook at the fierce intensity of her questions, but his answer was truthful. "I perform mainly illusion spells, at parties and in the *salons*. Is that why you want to speak to me? Do you need an enchant—"

"I ask the questions," Olympe snapped.

Whatever the man saw in Olympe's eyes, it prompted more sweat to pour out of his forehead and his golden eyes to turn fearful. He cast me a desperate glance for help, but I was focused on the truth spell and on providing a steady stream of magic to Olympe. My lungs were already tightening, and I breathed through my nose to delay a coughing fit.

"I'm not a very gifted *magicien*," the Parisian *magicien* admitted. "I can't do healing spells or anything too complex. Whatever you need, I—"

"How do you know Lorraine?" Olympe cut him off again. "Why did he invite you here today? You're not a court *magicien*."

"For the tribute spell! I told you, illusions are my specialty. The *chevalier* knows it, that's why he invited me."

"How do you two know each other?"

I stifled a cough. My muscles strained as my magic flowed toward Olympe, and each heartbeat sounded louder in my ears. We were running out of time.

"We met at one of the *salons*," the *magicien* said, his words more rushed in his inflating panic but not less golden. "I can't remember which one. Madame . . . Madame de Montespan introduced us."

"And have you performed other spells together before?"

"A couple of illusions at those *salons*! Nothing more. I barely know the man."

His words shone gold in the dim carriage. He was telling the truth. He wasn't the *magicien* who'd helped Lorraine make spells vanish. My shoulders slumped, and Olympe cast me a worried look before attempting a last question.

"Do you know if Lorraine has worked with any other *magiciens* in Paris?"

He shook his head. "Not that I know of. He wasn't even happy to perform spells with me. I think he thought it was beneath him to entertain those people. He said he only worked with court *magiciens*, and I hear nowadays he only casts spells with the king."

Again, his words drifted up inside the carriage, shimmering gold in the shadowy interior. No lies. Based on his footman's testimony, Armand had convinced me Lorraine's scheme rested on the complicity of a Parisian *magicien*. Yet the spells had started to vanish after the man's arrival at court. However hard to believe, it made sense for Lorraine to have collaborated with a court *magicien* to make spells disappear, rather than dealing with the inconvenience of meeting a *magicien* in Paris. Which meant my investigation had to focus on the *magiciens* of Versailles. Like last year, the traitor stood on my doorstep, not leagues away from my home. A chilling thought indeed.

A coughing fit rose in my chest and cut short my musing. I buried my mouth in my hands, breaking the connection with Olympe. I didn't hear her parting words to the *magicien* over the noise of my rasping breaths, before she ushered me out of the vehicle.

As we walked back toward the basilica, we ran into the Comte de Saint-Aignan and Prince Aniaba amid the mingling crowd of mourners. The prince insisted on performing the spell with my handkerchief, which soothed my lungs enough for me to recover for a moment. I left Olympe with them before going in search of Philippe inside the church.

My footsteps rang out in the now near-empty building. In the middle of the nave, men in workmen clothes were already busy piling wooden planks and collecting tools for the opening of the vault.

Philippe still sat in the front pew, but Lorraine had joined him, his blond hair a stark contrast to his expensive black clothes. He whispered in my husband's ear, his arm around his shoulders. Philippe didn't relax into the embrace, but my heart sank nonetheless at the sight of the two of them together. My steps slowed, and I hovered by a pillar, uncertain.

Philippe craved support and love. Very few people in his life provided him with it, and here I was, plotting to remove one of them. Lorraine might be a treasonous snake that threatened French magic, but he was also there for my husband when very few were. A wave of guilt and doubt washed through me. For the first time since I had resolved to reveal Lorraine's secrets, it occurred to me that Philippe might not thank me for it. I had expected him to be hurt at Lorraine's betrayal at first, then to understand my motives and be grateful for my intervention. Only now did it strike me that Lorraine stood among the handful of people Philippe cared about and trusted.

And my husband might not forgive me for taking that away.

CHAPTER XIX

"No, ladies and gentlemen, no!"

The Comte de Saint-Aignan threw his hands up, suppressed giggles greeting his despair. The king's next entertainment was a week away, and the July heat had seemingly melted all memories of the Queen Mother's funeral in the courtiers' minds. Even the king had been seen smiling and humming to himself during a recent horse ride.

The dance rehearsals took place in the palace *orangerie* to escape the oppressing temperature. All the citrus trees that the long gallery housed in the winter months now moved outside, the large and cool space had been deemed the perfect place to practice the latest fashionable dance.

"Let's try again!" the count said.

He wiped the sweat off his forehead with a lace handkerchief and trotted down the length of the gallery to organize the dancers in three straight lines. Nearby, a quartet of musicians awaited his signal to resume the right movement. Marie-Thérèse, her round belly now prominent under her yellow silk dress, sat in an armchair next to them, her dogs at her feet and Mimi in her lap. Waving a jewel-studded fan, she caught my gaze and gave me one of her rare smiles as I stood side by side with my friends.

"You start with your left foot." Athénaïs demonstrated the first four steps.

Elisabeth watched her with a skeptic pout. "It's ridiculously complicated. I'll just hide behind Madame and copy her."

"Don't be silly," Olympe replied. "If Louise can do it, anyone can."

Louise cast her a hesitant glance, and I would have dismissed the encouragement as innocent if Olympe and Athénaïs hadn't shared a mocking smile just then. Louise's discomfited expression prompted me to intervene.

"We need to listen to the count," I said, pretending obliviousness. "He is working hard and he deserves our support."

"You're right," Olympe said. "He's red as a lobster, poor man."

Athénaïs and Elisabeth giggled again.

"From the beginning, everyone!" the count called out, cutting short their mirth.

The violin music built up under the *orangerie*'s high ceiling and along its white walls. The lines of courtiers moved in a synchronized motion for six steps, but the first turn broke the pattern as some headed the wrong way and others tripped over their feet. Elisabeth collided with Louise, who let out a surprised cry.

"Stop!" The count waved his arms like a flapping bird, and the quartet paused again.

Elisabeth apologized to Louise. Athénaïs and Olympe snickered, and Louise flushed.

"Oh, why do you have to be so horrid?" Her voice broke on the last word, her eyes filling with tears.

To my astonishment, her reaction drew loud laughter from the other two. Louise picked up her skirts and fled, her heels clacking a staccato against the flagstones.

"What is with you two?" I chided.

I couldn't let Louise go off alone in such a state. Signaling the count to carry on without me, I pursued her outside. The afternoon sunshine turned the *orangerie* garden into an oven. Gravel crunched under my feet as I wandered along the short alleys lined with fragrant orange and lemon trees in wooden pots. The sound of Louise's loud sobs guided me to the center of the *parterre*, where a water jet in the middle of a round pool pulled all the lines of the symmetrical garden together.

The dust and heat clawed at my throat and I coughed. Louise turned around, her eyes swollen with tears and her face splotched with red.

"What's wrong?" I asked as soon as my cough eased.

"Everything . . . is . . . horrible," she hiccupped.

The low stone edge of the pool was just large enough to accommodate us, and I coaxed her to sit next to me with gentle guiding gestures. She blew her nose in the handkerchief I offered.

"They're all vipers," she said at last.

My heart swelled with compassion at her unhappiness, but the bitterness that suffused her words caught me unaware.

"They were just teasing," I replied, soothing. "It's hot and we're all a bit bored. They didn't mean any harm."

"Of course they mean harm!" Louise's voice rose with a fierceness I had seldom witnessed in her. "Can't you see?"

"I suppose I don't," I said, my tone clipped. My mother always warned me against my tendency to see the best in everyone. It appeared Louise also regarded it as weakness.

More tears brimmed in her eyes, and her voice came out strangled. "He's sending me away."

"The king?"

She nodded. "He's sending me to Paris."

I wrapped my arm around her shoulder to comfort her despite my confusion. Louis had just made her his official mistress. Why would he send her away now? The memory of the renovated house at the Palais-Royal came to me then. I had thought it would be a place for the king to visit his mistress away from prying eyes. It seemed it was somewhere to banish her instead. "Did you two have an argument?" I asked.

Tears rolled down her cheeks, but she answered me without wiping them. "In a way. He says it's the best thing to do until the baby comes. But I know it's a lie."

My heart stuttered. "The queen's baby?"

"No." She stared at a nearby olive tree, avoiding my gaze. "Mine."

"Oh, Louise." I sighed.

Of course Louis was sending her away. She might be his official mistress, but having her with child at court at the same time as Marie-Thérèse would be too much of a scandal, even for him.

"But it's only temporary," I said to reassure her. "And in the meantime, are you well? Are you . . . happy?"

More tears spilled from her eyes and they were answers enough. "I'm happy about the baby." She sniffled. "Everything else is a disaster."

"It's not all bad," I tried again. "You have a beautiful little house waiting for you in Paris. And when you return to court—"

"But don't you see?" she cut me off. "I may never come back. She won't let me, once I'm gone!"

I blinked at her, too confused to be angry about her rudeness. "The queen?"

"Athénaïs!" she exploded. "Who else do you think has spent the last months undermining me, whispering poison into everyone's ears and seducing the king?"

I gaped. Images and words flashed through my mind. Athénaïs and Louis meeting at the Tuileries all those months ago. Her comment on understanding how one could fall for someone other than her husband. Her indifference in the face of Marie-Thérèse's humiliation at the ball. And her husband's timely departure for the front. Athénaïs was indeed having an affair, as I had suspected all those weeks ago. Except it had never occurred to me it was with the king.

"They're all in on it," Louise added, unfazed by my shocked silence. "The queen and Olympe want nothing more than to see me gone, so they've done everything they could to have me pushed aside. And Athénaïs waited in the wings to slither her way into the king's life. She's convinced him she's in love with him, but I don't believe it. She would lie to the pope himself if it got her where she wanted."

"But," I said, finding my voice again despite this avalanche of revelations, "have you tried speaking with Louis? What does he say?"

She wiped her nose with my handkerchief. "He says he loves me, and he can't wait to meet our son. Except it's very convenient for him that I'm pregnant now, isn't it? He has an excuse to send me away."

Was she being paranoid? I couldn't decide. It seemed awfully selfish, cold, and calculating of Louis to use one mistress's pregnancy to send her away while making room for a second mistress at his side, and with his wife also expecting a child at the same time. But Louis had proven in the past he *was* selfish, cold, and calculating. He took what he wanted, regardless of the hurt it caused, even to those closest to him.

"What can I do to help?" I asked, powerlessness washing over me like a wave.

She shrugged. "Nothing. Everyone warned me to be careful, and I didn't listen. Now the king has lost interest in me, and it's my punishment."

Her reply made me sigh. Louise and her ideas about good and evil, about guilt and innocence. It struck me then that she had indeed never listened to me. She wasn't about to start now. The flow of her tears had run dry, at least. I linked arms with her, and we walked back toward the *orangerie* in silence.

As a sunken garden, it lay below the level of the palace terrace, with the sprawling buildings of Versailles looming over the grounds in the distance. In the bright afternoon sunlight, they sparkled like precious gems—a sight that should have filled me with awe but awoke in me sadness instead. Louis had designed this place as a dream, yet no one dwelling here seemed able to find any happiness within its walls. Heartbreaks and betrayals lurked at every corner. Friendships frayed in every garden grove. Relationships fell apart in every room. Unfulfilled aspirations mixed with greed and frustration in the salons. And magic, everywhere, served as smoke and mirrors to hide all the little tragedies unfolding backstage.

A queen humiliated and isolated, undone by betrayals and secrets.

A young provincial girl with a broken heart.

A shrewd noble girl whose rise was as swift as it was unforeseen.

The reality of the situation drenched me with ice-cold realization: the seer's prophecy was all unfolding as predicted, and nothing had stopped it. The only part left to come true was my death.

* * *

By the time we reached the *orangerie*, all desire for dancing had left me. Louise put on a brave face and rejoined the rehearsal, but I picked up my dog from Marie-Thérèse's lap. Her mouth puckered in a worried pout.

"Is it the heat?" she asked over the swelling music.

"Yes." It wasn't really a lie. My lungs felt tight and sweat ran down my spine. "I think I'll retire for now."

I waved Athénaïs over. She broke away from the dancing line with her eyebrows raised in inquiry.

"I think it's better if I go and lie down," I said. "Will you accompany me?"

She gave the practicing dancers a mournful look, but she couldn't very well refuse me. My desire to have a private word with her overpowered my remorse at drawing her away from the fun. Mimi in my arms, I left the cool gallery to walk back through the water gardens to the palace. The sun beat on the gravel paths, and Athénaïs shielded us with a lace and ivory-handled parasol.

"Is it true?" I asked as soon as we were out of anyone's earshot. "Are you having an affair with the king?"

An amused smile teased her red lips. "What if it is?"

I struggled not to roll my eyes. This was as good as a confession, yet in true Athénaïs's fashion, she displayed no embarrassment or regret. It fell to me to point out the obvious.

"What about Louise?"

She shrugged. "He tired of her long ago. I wouldn't have been able to distract him otherwise."

Whether this was true or not, the result was the same. Louise was distraught and exiled from court. Since her fate didn't appear to affect Athénaïs, I chose another angle of attack.

"But you're both married! It's going to be a scandal when this comes out."

"I can handle my husband." She waved the matter away with a flick of her hand. "And the queen is so happy with her supposed victory over Louise that it's going to take her months to work out she defeated the wrong adversary."

Her unconcerned tone left me speechless. Had she always been this selfish and self-serving? We reached the palace, and the stuffiness inside was only a minor improvement compared to the furnace outside. Our wooden heels struck the parquet floor as we made our way to my apartments.

"Are you in love with him?" I asked, still trying to wrap my mind around the fact that Athénaïs, of all people, had seduced Louis.

"Of course."

Her smile would have made a sphinx proud. Whatever she read on my face, it brought a hint of seriousness to her features.

"I understand you're shocked," she added. "But I've always done what I was told. Can you blame me for now putting myself first?"

Her question struck a chord in me, because I had been struggling with it for the past few months too. We lived in a world where duty controlled every part of our existence. We were expected to obey our family, serve the king, marry whom we were told, have children, and display a behavior beyond reproach. And the moment one of us stepped out of line, we turned on her with the rest of the crowd. I had blamed Olympe for seeking power. I had blamed Louise for wanting love. Maybe Athénaïs was right and I shouldn't blame her for desiring more than what our society had given her. But my mind spun with the words of the prophecy. *The higher she rises, the harder she'll fall . . .* Too much of the seer's prediction had already come to pass. I had no wish to witness her destruction. Where would this new path lead her?

"Just . . . be careful," I said.

Her confident grin was back in a flash. "I always am."

We arrived at my apartments, and she left me without a backward glance, flying down the staircase with her skirts flowing at her back in her hurry to return to the dance rehearsals. I stepped into my antechamber, and Mimi barked at a visitor waiting on the silk sofa by the window.

"My apologies."

I glanced around in search of a maid to introduce the stranger, but we were alone. The indoor shutters drawn against the sunshine, the room sat shrouded in dimness, and the woman's features were shadowed. Still, her face didn't spark any recognition in me.

"It's me who should apologize, Your Highness." She curtsied. "I know this is most irregular, but I had to see you."

A glimmer of trepidation quickened my pulse. The woman stood unthreatening a few steps away, yet her dark silhouette and solemn tone sent a shiver down my back.

"Have we met?" I asked, glad to have Mimi in my arms to help me keep my composure.

"No, Your Highness."

A sort of sadness tinged her every word, as if the weight of the world rested on her shoulders. My eyes became accustomed to the room's shadows, and she stood out with more clarity. Maybe ten years older than me, sorrow or exhaustion etched lines on her pale face framed by dark hair, and her dress was a deep blue that appeared almost black in the dark antechamber. This wasn't a gown for court, I realized with a renewed pang of worry, not even a summer dress.

"Who are you?"

She sank into another curtsy, each gesture slow and careful, as if she were used to not draw attention to herself. "I'm Marie-Madeleine Fouquet."

I froze. A confusion of thoughts and emotions tumbled through me.

If anyone had asked, I would have been able to tell them Fouquet was married. Yes, I would have said, to a woman twenty years younger than him, I believe. They have several children—the repeated pregnancies keep her away from court.

I knew Marie-Madeleine Fouquet existed. Yet to my shame, the fate of the former Crown *Magicien*'s wife had not crossed my mind once in the past year. Fouquet had nearly shattered my family. But his actions had most definitely ruined his. And his wife, disgraced and alone, was paying the price.

Regret and sympathy propelled me forward, and I put Mimi down to seize the woman's frail hands in mine.

"Please sit down, and tell me what I can do."

I guided her back to the sofa and took a seat next to her. Mimi, reassured by my reaction, sniffed her shoes and wagged her tail tentatively.

"You don't want me to leave?"

The genuine disbelief on the young woman's face nearly broke my heart.

"Obviously you can't stay long," I said, "but I won't turn you away before you've said what you came here to tell me."

Her hands shook in my grasp, my words not what she expected, it seemed. She folded her fingers in her lap and nodded to herself, as if for focus or courage.

"Nicolas said you were kind and you would listen," she said. "But I suppose I didn't believe him."

"You've seen him?"

I couldn't hide the surprise in my tone. Given what I'd witnessed during my own visit to the fallen *magicien*, I didn't think the king allowed him conjugal visits.

"I was allowed to see him briefly," she replied, "before his transfer out of Paris."

"He's not at the Bastille anymore?"

She shook her head, her eyes wet. "I was told he was taken to a fortress in the Alps and I won't be able to see him again."

Louis really wanted the man out of his life, then. Before I could comment on the news, Madame Fouquet went on.

"He said the king listens to you. You could intercede on our behalf, to allow me and our children to visit."

"I can ask," I said. "But your husband gives me more credit than is due if he thinks His Majesty agrees with everything I suggest."

I would ask Louis, of course, but I didn't want the poor woman to hang all her hopes on my intercession. Still, her eyes shone and she leaned forward.

"You will? Oh, thank you, thank you. Nicolas did say you would help."

The former Crown *Magicien* still knew me well, then. He had counted on my guilty feelings and good heart, and it annoyed me to prove him right, but I would do what I could for his wife, if not for him.

She fumbled with her dress pocket, and I puzzled over what she was doing for a moment, until she pulled out a piece of paper. She unfolded it with an apologetic smile.

"This is for you. I wrote down what Nicolas said as I feared I wouldn't remember his exact words."

I glanced at the scribbling in her hand. "What is it?"

"Nicolas said it's a thank-you," she replied, and held up the paper to read it out to me. "He said it's a spell, and it would help you."

A spell? My heartbeat quickened. Was this Fouquet's last

attempt at destroying me and Louis from his faraway prison? One last trick to get his revenge on us?

"The spell," his wife read aloud, "is *Déverrouille*. It's used to temporarily unlock the power of a Source so they can perform another spell by themselves."

"*What?*" I snatched the paper.

My eyes skimmed over the two lines of text, which read exactly as Madame Fouquet had spoken them. I gazed back at her, and she tensed at the fierceness in my expression.

"What else did he say?" I pressed on. "Is this a real spell? Why does he think I might need it? When?"

Was he planning something from his jail cell? Another attack against the king, against the royal family? My suspicions must have been clear on my face, for his wife's eyes widened and she shook her head.

"I don't know much about magic," she said. "And I know Nicolas hurt you in the past. But we need your help, and he's trying to make amends. I wrote down everything he said, and I wouldn't have delivered his message if I thought it might bring you harm. All I want is for my children to see their father."

Her voice broke, and tears brimmed in her eyes again. Her sincere demeanor calmed my beating heart. I folded the paper and slipped it in my pocket. Madame Fouquet inhaled a breath to regain her composure.

"My husband knows nearly everything there is to know about magic," she added. "And from what I understand, you share his interest in forgotten spells and ancient enchantments. I think he means this message as a peace offering, a parting gift, even."

All those months ago in the cave at Vaux-le-Vicomte, Fouquet had wanted me to join his side. *In all my life*, he'd said, *I have never encountered a more powerful Source in this country than you.* He had dreamed of a future where he and I performed magic together. I didn't doubt he wished to alter many of the events that had unfolded last year. But it occurred to me now that, out of all these regrets, the man who had once been a young *magicien* poring over countless books of magic to unlock its secrets might mourn the loss of my friendship most of all. The idea of what could have been—thrust against the reality of what he had done, alienating me forever.

Maybe he hadn't changed, and he was using his innocent wife as a messenger to wreak havoc in my life one last time.

Or maybe the spell was genuine, and it was the last attempt of an old *magicien*, alone with his regrets and gloomy prospects, at sharing his encyclopedic knowledge of secret magic with a kindred soul.

As much as I hated to think of it, Fouquet and I did have a common curiosity for the possibilities magic offered. And in my upcoming fight to regain control of my unraveling life, a spell history had forgotten might be the key to unlocking my future.

CHAPTER XX

———————

I only managed to speak with Louis on the morning of the
Grand Royal Entertainment.

In the days leading up to the party, the king oversaw the
preparations from dawn till late at night, moving about the
Versailles estate, issuing orders, and casting a critical eye on
everything. Always busy and surrounded by people, he proved
impossible to isolate for a private conversation about magic and
threats. However the looming menace of my prophesized death
rendered me bold and inventive.

The king's entertainment wasn't due to start before late
afternoon, but from one of Philippe's passing comments, I
knew Louis planned to check on the hydraulic pumps by the
Clagny pond early. Never one afraid of rising at the break of
day, I donned a summer riding dress and a large hat, before
heading for the stables. Louis and a handful of musketeers
stood in the paved courtyard, while grooms led out the horses
in the rising sun.

The king scowled at me, the gilded ornaments of his brown

leather outfit glinting in the slanted sunshine. "What are you doing here?"

"You know I like exercising in the morning, Sire," I said, innocent cheerfulness in my tone. "Are you going for a ride as well?"

"I'm going to the Clagny pond," he replied, his demeanor still gruff. "You might as well come along if you're intent on riding somewhere."

I greeted his offer with a smile and hid my delight at how easy this had been behind a grateful reply. I knew the king liked the fact I was as much of an early riser as he was. And I had planned on him being too focused on his own plans to care much about me. It seemed I had bet correctly.

Soon we were off along the northward road, squirting the palace buildings toward the large pond that fed water to the estate fountains. Dew evaporated in the early warmth, thin mist rising above the fields in a shimmering haze. The horses' hooves clopped on the dry dirt, and birds chirped in the branches of the trees lining the road.

"May I ask you a question?" I said after a moment of silence.

The musketeers rode ahead and behind us, far enough to be out of earshot. His face his usual neutral mask, Louis turned his golden gaze to me with a brief nod.

"Did you move Fouquet because of me?"

He had never mentioned my interview with the former Crown *Magicien*, but I wasn't naive enough to think D'Artagnan had kept it a secret. Louis's silence on the topic had been reassuring at first, but after Madame Fouquet's visit, it had woken an anxious feeling in the pit of my stomach.

"I understand why you went to see him," he replied. "But it couldn't happen again."

I bit my lip, misgivings rising in me at his choice of words. Was his decision to move Fouquet to a faraway prison a way to protect me, or to ensure the man's knowledge would be lost forever?

"Surely you could let him see his family?"

I had promised Madame Fouquet to ask, yet all hopes of clemency died at the uncompromising look he gave me then.

"You have a generous heart, Henriette," he said. "And Fouquet has used this to his advantage too many times already. Every time I have shown the same weakness and let the man see his wife and children, he has used them to send messages or try to gather support. You understand this had to stop."

I gave a grim nod, my thoughts cast back to the spell Madame Fouquet had told me about on behalf of her husband.

"I wish there was something I could do for them," I said.

"The woman isn't destitute," Louis replied, his tone stern but not unkind. "And even if I have banned her and her children from court, they are not without friends. I encourage you not to worry about them unnecessarily. There are more important matters for you to focus on."

He glanced at my stomach, a clear indication that he knew about my pregnancy and that this was the "important matter" at hand.

In the distance, the surface of the three large reservoirs gleamed in the sunlight. The rectangular tanks sat at the foot of a tall tower.

"The cistern is inside this building." Louis pointed. "We use magic to draw water from the pond and keep it in the reservoirs.

They are above the level of the gardens, so we have enough pressure once the water reaches the fountains."

We guided our horses toward the tower, where a few men stood with their hats in their hands, waiting for the king. I let Louis approach them and led my horse around the reservoirs while they went inside. A faint shimmer of magic remained on the surface of the water, remnant of the spell that had drawn it from the pond. Along the edges of the tanks, wooden crates sat in the grass, all labeled "fireworks." So this was the reason behind Louis's visit here, then. The men were preparing tonight's fireworks display. I expected his conversation to last a while, but within minutes he emerged from the building, and we rode back to the palace.

"How often does the *Pompe* spell have to be done?" I asked to steer his mind toward magic.

"Every few days," he said. "Obviously it lasts longer if Lorraine and I perform it together, but I often lack the time for it, so the fountain engineer does it."

I had come across the intendant of water and fountains to the king, François Francine. An artist *magicien* discovered by Fouquet, he could turn any fountain into a marvel of water jets and music.

In the half hour since we'd left the palace, the sun had risen enough to blanket the estate with heat. Perspiration dampened my back and breathing in the hot air became difficult.

Yet I still had a few minutes before we reached the stables, which I intended to use well. And since he had brought up Lorraine's name first, I jumped in with both feet.

"So you're pleased with your association with Lorraine?" I asked. "He understands your vision for Versailles?"

Louis's eyes took on an excited glint. "He really does. And his magic is so smooth, so malleable. Yours was very powerful, but his is perfect for my work."

My work. The use of the possessive would have made me wince if I hadn't known about Lorraine's true intents. As it were, I needed to obtain information about him, and find out who was the *magicien* helping him to make spells vanish. I pasted an innocent expression on my face.

"Does he perform spells with anyone else?"

"Not anymore," Louis replied in the self-assured tone of a king who doesn't doubt he's being obeyed. "I asked him to focus entirely on my spells and he has done so. His association with me is obviously very beneficial to him."

His utter confidence made me pause. Of course Louis couldn't accept to share his Source with anyone else, and he had kept Lorraine very busy since his arrival at court. He would have found out if the man worked with other *magiciens*. But how did Lorraine make spells disappear without a *magicien*?

A thought struck me so suddenly my hands jerked and my horse sidestepped in disapproval. I regained control in a heartbeat, but the idea wouldn't leave me now.

The spell, Madame Fouquet had said, *is* Déverrouille. *It's used to temporarily unlock the power of a Source so they can perform another spell by themselves.*

Somehow, Fouquet had known. Through his few contacts with the outside world, he'd heard about the king's ambition and his new Source. It was in his interest to prevent Louis from achieving his goals, and what better way than to take away his Source by exposing his darkest secret?

Lorraine had used the unlocking spell to make powerful spells vanish alone. Since no one knew about the *Déverrouille* spell and couldn't suspect him of doing magic by himself, it would have been the perfect plan, except it didn't work on other Sources, and likely not on Fouquet either. And so the Crown *Magicien* had elected to use me yet again for his own gain, by letting me know about the ancient spell.

However, this time, I didn't mind, because his plans aligned with mine. He thought exposing Lorraine would weaken the king. I thought it would allow me to regain my place as the king's Source.

"I know you're not fond of Lorraine," Louis said, dragging me out of my thoughts. "And I understand why. But he has been a faithful servant to the crown and performed his duty without any difficulty or question. He's incredibly valuable to me, and as a loyal subject yourself, I hope you see it."

His meaning was clear: Doubting Lorraine was almost akin to doubting the king, and it wouldn't be permitted, even from a princess. If I wanted to defeat Lorraine, I had to have tangible proof of his treachery. In the absence of a *magicien* accomplice, I circled back to the other solution available. I needed the list of vanished spells.

Thankfully, a royal entertainment was the perfect setting for larceny.

* * *

Heat still permeated the atmosphere when the French court gathered on the palace terrace for the Grand Royal Entertainment late in the afternoon. Unlike the Pleasures of the Enchanted Island two months ago, every courtier was invited this time, and the crowd was so thick one found it hard to see their own feet. Mingling conversations rose under the clear sky and jewel-studded fans snapped in the still air. Philippe held a parasol above both our heads and let out an impatient sigh.

"Where is he?"

He meant his brother, of course.

"He's not late," I replied in a soothing tone.

Everyone had come early to the meeting point, either fearing to be late or eager to join the festivities. There was no theme to the party, and courtiers had taken this as leave to rival in extravagance and magnificence. Everywhere, magically enhanced fabric shimmered, gem-adorned coats and gowns sparkled, feathered hats and ornate canes attracted glances with features moving with spells, and lavish shoes peeked out from under long dresses.

Never one to be outdone, Philippe wore an outfit the color of the rainbow that reminded me of the clothes he'd had at our wedding. This time, silver ribbon and white lace trimmed the coat and breeches, enhancing the colorfulness of the interwoven fabrics. Upon his suggestion, my own gown was the opposite: a silver and lace dress with colorful ribbons and jewels. We matched without being obvious, which summed up our relationship quite well.

A happy exclamation rippled through the courtiers. "The king! The king!"

The crowd parted as Louis advanced in a glittering gold outfit and hat, his diamond-studded cane punctuating his steps. The sun glinting off the palace windows at his back framed him with light, like a confirmation of his nickname.

"Welcome!" His poised voice carried over to the assembled guests, who hushed to hear him. "Welcome to the Grand Royal Entertainment. I invite you all to follow me for a walk in the palace gardens, where we may encounter a few surprises . . ."

A walk. After the elaborate splendors of the Enchanted Island, the simplicity of a promenade among the Versailles groves appealed to me. Whatever I thought of Louis, I couldn't deny him a gift for wonder and entertainment.

Accompanied by a small group of courtiers, among which Athénaïs, the Comte de Saint-Aignan, and Prince Aniaba, the king led the way down the staircase and turned right into the gardens. The large crowd shuffled after him, eyes shielded against the glaring light and excited whispers on their lips.

"Where is the queen?" I asked Philippe as we followed his brother, our arms linked.

"Pregnant," he said, as if this was explanation enough.

She was only two months further along than I was. And in her absence, Louis was making polite conversation to Athénaïs in full public view. My heart went out to Marie-Thérèse, confined in the palace, and Louise, hidden away in Paris. The seer's prophecy tugged at me, then, and I focused back on tonight's goal: to expose Lorraine and in doing so reduce my chances of an untimely demise. I had no proof that the man wished me harm, yet his veiled threats at the ball made him the likeliest candidate when considering how I could come across death.

Hundreds of feet crunched on the gravel path as we reached a new fountain, and my foe appeared at the king's side. The crowd spread along the edge of the circular pool, and its enthusiastic chatter died down as Louis raised his cane.

"Once," he said, "the young god Apollo killed with a single arrow the serpent Python that threatened the Greek city of Delphi. Today, I give you the Dragon Fountain."

Ladies craned their necks and gentlemen squinted in the sunlight, but for now the name of the fountain remained a mystery, as the water of the pond before us appeared empty. Anticipation ran along the guests, however, as Louis and Lorraine linked hands.

The pool began to bubble, and out of the churning waters a large bronze dragon reared its head. Louis then threw his cane like a lance, and the diamond-studded staff turned into an arrow that pierced the dragon's neck. The giant serpent splashed in the water and let out a mighty roar, which released an incredible jet of water into the skies. Around the beast, cherubs on swans' backs emerged from the roiling waters and launched their own tiny arrows at the thrashing dragon.

I squeezed Philippe's arm before I realized what I was doing. Once, Louis and I had performed a similar spell not far from here, to create the Apollo Fountain out of magic. We had failed, but it had been our first attempt at turning Versailles into the place it was today. A hint of regret tugged at me at the thought that he now succeeded in doing the spectacular enchantment with another Source. A tiny piece of me wished I was part of it.

Soon the creature stilled, defeated, and froze in the middle of the pool with its head reared back and the water exploding from its open mouth falling back onto the fountain in a thin mist. Dolphins joined the cherubs and became motionless, forever standing guard around the trapped beast.

Thundering applause rose from the crowd. Once again, Louis had amazed them with magic, and everywhere I turned I saw eyes wide with wonder and clapping hands.

Philippe didn't let go of our parasol to clap politely. "That was impressive," he said. "If one likes that sort of things."

I nudged him playfully and earned a smile that warmed me to the core. I had been back at Versailles for five weeks, and in all that time he had kept his promise to try to give us a chance. He slept in my bed every night and never sought out Lorraine in public. I didn't know if that meant things were over between them, but it felt like a small victory already.

But the king was on the move again, distracting me from my train of thought. His court trailed after him like loyal puppies, eager for the next treat. Our stroll didn't take us far, as we walked through a tall hedge into a hidden grove. A circular lawn greeted us, where tables had sprouted from the ground like trees. A giant open-air buffet displayed piles of meat pastries, cakes, and fruit, along with carafes of colorful wines and liquor. Guests helped themselves to the food before settling in the grass.

Philippe grabbed Elisabeth and Françoise as they walked past. "Find a place in the shade with Henriette. I'll bring us food and drinks."

We sat beneath an oak tree, and I took off my jewel-speckled shoes with a sigh of relief. Louis's cousins babbled about the fountain spell, and within moments Philippe joined us, a servant with a large tray on his heels. The glittering pastries and cakes made me wince—whether because of my illness or my pregnancy, I was nauseous more often than not, lately. I managed to eat strawberries dipped in whipped cream, and drank water to soothe my parched throat.

"What do you think is next?" Elisabeth asked, her eyes bright with anticipation.

"There has to be a ball," her sister replied. "We didn't learn that new dance for nothing."

"I heard there'll be fireworks," I said to contribute to the discussion, although my attention strayed as a strange ballet caught my gaze.

Every so often, one of the guests rose from their spot in the grass in a seemingly innocent fashion and ambled toward a white birch tree at the edge of the grove. They stayed there for an instant, too far away for me to see what they were doing besides casting furtive glances about them, before returning to their party. The first person I noticed was Madame de Châtillon, who I assumed had seen something in the bushes and wanted to investigate. But moments later the playwright Molière performed the same strange move, promptly followed by the Comte de Soissons. In the next half hour, a dozen courtiers behaved in the same odd manner. With such a large crowd assembled in the grove, however, the palace guards and musketeers on duty stood oblivious, more focused on the various exits, and on the king in the heart of the clearing.

"You're quiet," Philippe said. "Are you feeling all right?"

"Yes," I replied, distracted. "I just need to stretch my legs. You stay here."

I put on my shoes, grabbed our parasol, and pushed myself off the grass before he could protest. My gaze on the birch tree, I circled the grove, just as a short marquess I knew by sight made his way to the suspicious spot in a crab-like walk that attracted my attention even more. This time when he reached the tree, I was close enough to see him throw an envelope against the white trunk, where it disappeared.

I stopped in my tracks. The only way the envelope could be gone in an instant was because of magic, and I would have bet my wedding ring said magic was a portal spell. One of the *vanished* spells.

His deed done, the marquess hurried away, and I carried on my stroll around the grove until I reached the birch tree. There, at the bottom of the trunk, the air shimmered with magic. This was the portal. All these courtiers were depositing envelopes there as if it were a messenger bag, taking their post to its destination in the blink of an eye. What was in those envelopes though? And where were they being delivered?

One thing was certain: I had to tell Louis about this before the spell disappeared. I turned on my heels, and ran into a broad chest.

"Why do you have to spoil *everything*?" a familiar voice grumbled in my ear.

I stiffened and stepped back—too late. Lorraine had my wrist in his grip.

"Is this your spell?" I hissed back, although I was quite certain I knew the answer. "What are these people giving you?"

His eyes widened in fake innocence. "What spell? What people?"

I glanced back at the tree trunk, where the telltale glimmer faded before my eyes. Air drained from my lungs. Now it would be his word against mine, unless one of the courtiers supported my testimony.

"Don't even think about it," Lorraine said, reading my mind. "No one will support or believe you, and the king won't be happy you tried to spoil his evening. All you'll get is being sent to bed to rest your feverish mind. Sunstroke is so common among women."

His sarcasm and self-confidence made my blood boil, but he was right. The proof of the spell was gone, and Louis wouldn't look kindly on anyone causing a scandal at his party, even if it was his sister-in-law.

"Let go of me," I said through gritted teeth.

I wrenched my wrist out of his grasp and marched back to Philippe and his cousins. At that moment Louis clapped his hands twice, to announce the next part of the entertainment. Everyone rose to their feet at once with exclamations of delight, and it took me longer than expected to join my husband. When I did, Lorraine had melted into the crowd, any opportunity for me to call him out on his deed gone in the commotion.

So I schooled my features into a calm mask and linked arms with Philippe again.

All these courtiers had given Lorraine something in those envelopes. My guess was that it was in exchange for something else—a favor, a spell, or information? Whatever it was, they likely expected it to be handed over to them tonight. A party like this, with such a large crowd mingling in a labyrinthine garden at dusk, was the perfect setting for nefarious activities. My own plan had been to use the general confusion to steal Lorraine's journal again. It made sense he had had his own goals for the evening. I was nothing if not ready to adapt my strategy to catch him in the act.

I may have lost the first hand, but the game wasn't over yet.

CHAPTER XXI

Outside the grove, a long line of horseless carriages and sedan chairs sat ready to shuttle the king's guests to the next part of the entertainment. The rush to gain access to a magically propelled vehicle caused some confusion, and Philippe stretched his neck to spot an empty one that would fit his two cousins and us.

"Stay here a minute." He shoved our parasol in my hands. "I'll fetch one of those enchanted contraptions."

Just as he strode away, slicing through the crowd, the line moved forward, most of the vehicles already full. A few courtiers, loath to be left behind, jumped into already moving carriages amid the shrieks of their occupants. Fortunate passengers waved their hats and handkerchiefs at the people stranded by the side of the road.

"Better luck next time!" Their laughter rose under the clear evening sky. "You can still walk, you know! Or go home!"

Elisabeth met their hilarity with an outraged open mouth,

while Françoise threw her fan at a mocking young man in feathered hat.

"Don't they know who we are?!"

Part of me knew I should be fuming at the courtiers' behavior along with the king's cousins, yet at the forefront of my worries was the fact that I was being left out of the action and would arrive late at the following stage of the party, possibly missing Lorraine's next move.

I scanned the passing vehicles, and my gaze landed on a sedan chair that held the short marquess who had left the last envelope in Lorraine's trap. The seat opposite him in the *chaise à porteurs* was free. Without giving my reckless instinct a second thought, I took off after it, wrenched open the sedan chair's door, and threw myself onto the empty seat. The small man let out a yelp.

"Good evening." I gave him my warmest smile.

Outside, Françoise's and Elisabeth's surprised shouts already faded in the distance, our magically driven vehicle effortlessly gaining speed along the graveled path.

"I . . . I—" The poor marquess spluttered, sweat running down his paling features and panic widening his beady golden eyes.

"Can you believe I missed my carriage?" I went on in a bright tone, as if oblivious to his reaction. "I'm certain the king will be very grateful to you for rescuing his stranded sister-in-law!"

The marquess's chest deflated at the mention of the king. "Oh. Yes, I suppose, I—"

"I don't want to miss anything, you see?" I added in the same cheerful manner. "This is all so very exciting! Wasn't that water dragon a marvel? And the food! I wonder what's next, don't you?"

"Yes," the marquess stammered. "Yes, indeed—"

Overwhelmed, he stared at me with blinking eyes. However, the shaking in his hands faded and his stance relaxed as I babbled on. Although we'd never met, I played the part the man no doubt assumed to be mine: that of a harmless coquettish princess with an eccentric streak. Which was exactly what I wanted him to believe, before I went in for the fatal blow.

"And of course," I said, "I can't wait for the Chevalier de Lorraine to deliver on his promise."

He startled like a fish out of water. "I . . . I beg your pardon?"

I gave him a conniving wink that would have appalled my mother. "Dear *marquis*, don't play coy. You and I have a friend in common, don't we? Someone who asked for a certain something delivered in an envelope in exchange for another certain something tonight?"

It was very heavy-handed work, but both my presence in his sedan chair and my words so flustered the marquess that he didn't pause to question it.

"So you are—" he said. "I mean you're also—"

"Yes," I replied. "I saw you drop your envelope just before mine, and I thought: here is a man who's also in on our secret."

As expected, pride puffed up his chest and crimson crept over his cheeks at the mention of his inside knowledge. Courtiers could be so easy to play, sometimes. No wonder Lorraine had forgotten it was wrong to take advantage of it.

"Well," he said, "I'm not one to pass a good opportunity. I only hope my bid was high enough for the metamorphosis spell.

That's the one I'm interested in, you see. But I know some of the artist *magiciens* are also eager to get their hands on it."

Of course. The envelopes contained money. Silent bids for a spell, with the highest bid the winner. Just as his journal had suggested, Lorraine was selling off the spells he'd made disappear.

I glanced out of the sedan chair window. The sun sat low in the sky, casting orange and golden hues over the gardens. After heading westward, the line of vehicles had turned left and now rode southward past Apollo's Fountain, which glowed in the sunset as if on fire.

"Do you think we'll be on time?" I asked the marquess, keeping my question vague on purpose.

He pulled out a silver pocket watch. "I think so. We should be able to enjoy the next part of the entertainment. The *chevalier* promised we'd know if we'd won after sunset, so we have a little while yet."

I kept a straight face despite the importance of the revelation. Lorraine meant to hand over the spells to the highest bidders after dark, then.

Our chair turned left again, continuing its smooth magical ride eastward. But within moments it came to a halt, and a servant rushed to welcome us into the southernmost part of the gardens.

We stood at a crossroads, where a large area opened before us—a part of the gardens that had clearly yet to be designed. Tonight it housed a temporary open-air theater that drew gasps from the crowd. Dozens of glass lamps lit the place, infused with magical light. Large tapestries hung around the clearing, creating the illusion of walls, and canvas covered the ground, hushing our footsteps. Blue fabric dotted with fleur-de-lis adorned the stage lit with magically enhanced candlelight.

"How baroque!" the marquess at my side said.

"Can you see the *chevalier*?" I asked, eager to keep on task.

Between the courtiers still alighting from their means of transportation and the guests already mingling about the improvised theater, it was a challenge to spot anyone in the throng of people.

"There you are!" Philippe grabbed my hand and gave it a distracted kiss. "Why didn't you wait?"

"I didn't want to miss anything." It wasn't exactly a lie. "And the marquess had a free seat in his chair."

"Come on," Philippe replied. "We have seats in the front row, and my brother is already waiting."

He guided me toward the stage as the last rays of sunshine crested the treetops. Around us, the guests shuffled along the rows of velvet-covered chairs to find seats, and the noise of their conversation rose under the darkening skies. I cast anxious glances around me, but the marquess had been swallowed by the crowd, and Lorraine was nowhere to be seen. A pang of anxiety shot through me. Avoiding watching the play was impossible, yet with every passing minute, the sun set lower beyond the trees of Versailles, burning my chances of catching Lorraine in the act. With reluctance, I took a seat between my husband and Olympe as a hush fell over the audience and Molière appeared onstage in a peasant's costume.

"You're frowning," Olympe whispered in my ear over the playwright's introductory speech.

Sudden inspiration struck me. "I'm going to need you soon," I replied in the same tone. "For a spell."

Her eyebrows rose in surprise. "What spell?"

"I don't know yet. Will you be able to improvise?"

A mix of curiosity and challenge shone in her golden eyes. She didn't owe me any help, but the prospect of playing with magic was enough to make her side with me again, it seemed.

"Whatever are you up to now?" she said with an amused smile, her gaze returning to the stage and the actors moving in time with Lully's music.

If only I knew the answer to that question.

* * *

My mind too busy with twirling thoughts, I paid very little attention to the play. I caught only fragments of the plot, which involved an arranged marriage, a husband cheated on by his wife, and an unexpectedly depressing ending that left most of the audience puzzled.

Louis applauded the playwright and his troupe with his usual well-mannered approval, but the crowd buzzed with comments as people rose from their seats.

"What's happening to Molière?" Olympe muttered, her fan swishing in the warm evening atmosphere. "Can't the man put on a good comedy and make us laugh anymore? His plays used to be hilarious."

"He wants to show the world the way it is," I replied.

She linked her arm with mine and led me away from the stage, Philippe on our trail with Elisabeth and Françoise.

"I'm well aware the world is a miserable place," she said. "I expect the theater to make me forget it."

I was about to reply, but a commotion ahead caught my attention. People pressed forward with excited cries, eager to reach the edge of the clearing. Olympe put away her fan and hurried up, dragging me in her wake.

"What's happening?" she asked the first lady she pushed aside.

"They're giving out candles for the procession," the woman in an impressive purple gown explained. "We are going to light our own way to the feast, apparently."

Based on this information, Olympe elbowed her way through the crowd, my arm still in her grip, until we reached a long table strewn with taper candles in glass holders. Servants lit each candle before handing them out to courtiers, and Olympe meandered through the gathered guests to find a less crowded spot by the end of the table.

"We'll take two," she told the man in livery behind the rows of candles.

He shook his head. "I'm sorry, my lady, but these are reserved for special guests. You'll have to queue over there."

He pointed at the place we'd just come from with an apologetic bow.

"That's ridiculous," Olympe said. "I'm the Comtesse de Soissons and this is Madame. Who's more special than us, here?"

I would have cringed at her boast, if she hadn't had a point. Who were these special candles for, if even members of the royal family weren't to have them?

The manservant stiffened at Olympe's tone, his expression wrapped in offended dignity. "I'm sorry," he repeated, "but I've been given clear instructions and these are for special—"

I cut him off before the incident escalated into a whole scene.

"Maybe they're for the ambassadors and foreign dignitaries," I told Olympe, tugging her back to the busiest part of the table. "Never mind."

She mumbled under her breath about rude people and boring parties but let me lead her away. Within moments she was focused on fetching us another set of candles, and while we queued with the rest of the courtiers, I kept my focus on the manservant and his special candles at the end of the table. Something suspicious was afoot there, and experience told me there was a high chance this had to do with Lorraine.

We had barely moved forward in the line, much to Olympe's dismay, when Madame de Châtillon crept to the special-candles display and whispered a word to the servant. With a polite bow, he acknowledged her request by lighting a candle and handed it to her. As soon as her fingers clutched the holder, sparks erupted from the flame and twirled in the warm air to take on a strange shape that looked like letters, too far for me to see. Madame de Châtillon beamed at the spell and hurried away with her candle.

A smile tugged at my lips despite myself. Madame de Châtillon had been among the courtiers throwing an envelope into Lorraine's portal. Having won her bid, she claimed an enchanted candle that revealed the purchased spell at her touch. This was such an elegant, clever trick.

Madame de Châtillon was barely gone before my marquess made his way to the special candles. Throwing nervous glances around him, he leaned forward to give his password to the servant, who repeated the same process for him. However, this time, the candle didn't spark, and the marquess's face fell in disappointment. He asked a question to the man behind the table, who shrugged in ignorance and dismissal. The poor marquess made his way out of the clearing, his shoulders sagging and his steps slow.

So all the bidders had been instructed to retrieve a special candle, but only some had been enchanted with a vanished spell for the winners, while the others were left magicless for the losers. A cruel, but efficient way for the organizer of the silent auction to let people know the outcome of the bidding war while remaining anonymous.

Except I knew exactly who the mysterious organizer was.

I grabbed Olympe's arm. "I need you to come with me."

Her mouth opened in protest. "But we're almost there!"

Indeed the only obstacle between the procession candles and us was the purple-clad lady, but I pulled Olympe away nonetheless.

"Forget the candles," I said in a hushed tone. "We have to perform the spell now."

That cut short her objections, and she let me lead her to Prince Aniaba waiting at the back of the crowd.

"Have they run out of candles?" he asked with a frown at our empty hands.

Having no time to spare, I dismissed his question and went straight to the point. "Do you remember the vanished spells?"

Faint surprise fleeted across his features, but he recovered and nodded.

"I'm going to reveal them now," I said, trepidation quickening my pulse at the boldness of my claim. "But I need everyone to pay attention, especially the king. Can you help me?"

To my relief, he didn't hesitate. "Of course."

I squeezed Olympe's arm to guide her behind the table and into the trees. Twigs crunched underfoot and shadows engulfed us, giving us the privacy I wanted for us to perform the spell.

"Can you perform a repetition spell?" I asked her, out of breath after all this exertion and tension.

"I suppose," she said, her tone halting. "It's a little difficult to control, but if I can focus it on something . . ."

"Focus it on the candles," I replied. "All the candles in the clearing. Can you do that?"

Her golden eyes shone bright in the dim undergrowth, and a smile stretched her lips. "Oh, yes."

"Ladies and gentlemen!" Prince Aniaba's clear voice carried above the open-air theater, and silence spread over the crowd as courtiers exchanged curious glances, unsure whether this was part of the entertainment or not. The prince stood on a chair, his tall silhouette rising above the heads of his audience.

"It is my regrettable duty to inform you that His Majesty has uncovered a most heinous crime," he went on, his tone strong and poised. "A crime against magic!"

Olympe's eyes widened in the dim light. "He certainly knows how to get everyone to pay attention, doesn't he?"

Utter silence filled the clearing now, all the guests frozen in their spots with their gaze on the prince.

"Someone," he added, "has been stealing spells. Making them disappear! Making people forget they ever existed! But tonight, this lost magic is going to be returned to the kingdom! Tonight—"

I didn't wait for him to run out of ideas for his speech. I turned to Olympe, and took her hands in mine.

"Now."

She inhaled a deep breath, held my gaze in the dark, and gave a brief nod.

"*Répète*," I said.

My magic twirled out of me on a gentle breeze of golden flecks, making its way to the enchanted candles on the table and in the courtiers' hands. In my mind's eye, I followed it as it rekindled the enchantment cast by Lorraine and ignited the sparks that revealed the lost spells.

Golden letters shot up in the night sky, forming words under the stars.

Métamorphose.

Transporte.

Obéis.

Disparais.

Écoute.

Dozens of spells like glittering shapes illuminating the darkness with knowledge and filling the air with the sweet smell of magic. The letters curled and danced above the courtiers' heads, casting their upward faces in a golden glow as they gasped and cried out.

"I remember that one!" someone shouted.

"And that one!" another echoed.

Awe and excitement rippled along the crowd, and people began to clap and call for the king.

"Thank you, Your Majesty! Bravo!"

The noise filled my mind. A strange buzzing took over my ears and my lungs tightened in protest at the lack of air. A coughing fit tore through me, so violent I let go of Olympe's hands and let the spell dissolve into the air.

"Henriette," Olympe's voice urged me from far away. "Don't panic, I'm here. Take your time and breathe. Just take your time and breathe."

Shapes took form again out of the darkness, and it struck me how close I'd been to losing consciousness. Olympe's hands held me up in a firm grip as she drew deep breaths in time with me.

"There," she said, her tone soothing. "There, you're all right. Just breathe."

My panicked heartbeat settled and I blinked at my surroundings. The tree trunks and the underbrush still hid us from view, a few steps away from the brightly lit clearing. By the open-air theater, the crowd had shifted to form a circle around the king, a few musketeers, and a handful of courtiers with extinguished candles in their trembling hands. Madame de Châtillon stood among them, tears streaming down her cheeks.

"Arrest these traitors," Louis ordered.

The musketeers moved forward to seize the winners of the silent auction.

"We were tricked!" shouted a deep-voiced gentleman I knew in passing when a guard landed a heavy hand on his arm. "We were duped!"

"By whom?" the king asked, his tone commanding and cold.

The man stammered, at a loss, and shot appealing looks to his companions in misery. "We never met anyone," he said. "We received letters. Written instructions—"

"Where are those letters?" Louis said, his expression a rigid mask. "Those instructions?"

The barrel-chested man deflated in defeat. "Destroyed."

Louis signaled for the prisoners to be led away, and turned to his guests. "An investigation will be led to find out who was behind all this. In the meantime, let us enjoy the rest of the evening. A feast awaits us not far from here, if you would do me the honor of lighting the way with all your candles."

No, no, no, no. I stepped forward with no clear plan in mind, only a deep-seated conviction that things couldn't end here and now like this. I had done all this to unmask Lorraine. I would shout his name in the middle of the clearing if I had to.

The crowd was already moving out of the open-air theater, their loud conversations filled with bewildered comments on the recent events. Olympe on my heels, I emerged from the tree line, my focus on Louis and my steps confident despite my shortness of breath.

"Where have you been?" Philippe stepped in front of me, blocking my path and my line of vision with a concerned frown.

"She felt unwell," Olympe lied. "I took her aside until she recovered."

"Are you sure you're all right?" Philippe cupped my face in his hands, his anxious gaze roaming my features and his fingers testing the temperature of my skin.

His solicitude, so genuine and kind, nearly undid me. Here he was, thinking only of me, worrying only about me, when I plotted to take down a man he had cared for and likely still did. Could I be responsible for Lorraine's arrest, when it would hurt Philippe, the one person I had sworn never to harm?

A shout took the choice away from me.

"It was the Chevalier de Lorraine!"

Olympe walked out of the crowd to curtsy before the king. "Sire, I will swear to it before a court of law. It was the Chevalier de Lorraine who made the spells vanish and attempted to sell them for profit tonight."

Louis appraised her with a cold, calculating expression. "Can you prove this claim?"

She straightened to hold his gaze, as bold and proud as ever. "I can. I held in my hands the journal he used to keep a record of the stolen spells. I heard him threaten a member of the royal family should they divulge what they knew."

Louis stared at her, impassive. Astonished murmurs spread along the gathered courtiers at these new revelations. My pulse thumped against my temples, out of control. Now that the truth was out in the open, my heart should have been swelling with relief and delight. Yet Philippe's ashen face stole any triumph from the situation. Much like everyone else present, he scanned the crowd for Lorraine. The man was nowhere to be found.

"The *chevalier* is helping to prepare the feast," the king announced, his voice controlled despite the threatening glimmer in his eyes. "He shall be arrested immediately, and an investigation will be launched. Let us not have this spoil the rest of the evening."

His word was law, and everyone resumed their walk to the grove where the rest of the action was to happen. However, Philippe marched against the tide until he reached his brother and Olympe.

"Those are vile lies," he spat. "How can you trust anything she says? She used to be Fouquet's pet."

Louis grabbed his brother's wrist in a viselike grip that turned his knuckles white. "Be quiet," he commanded through gritted teeth. "Don't you dare make a scene. Do you think me a fool? Do you think I would base my decision on the word of one woman? I have my own reasons for having Lorraine arrested, and I will *not* have you question them in public."

Philippe shook in his grasp, his own hands curled into fists and his lips thin with barely contained rage and pain.

"You couldn't let me have him, could you?" he said.

Louis let go of him so brutally Philippe staggered back. "I couldn't." Louis's tone cut like steel. "You have enough as it is. Don't make me take it away too."

And without a backward glance, he strode out of the clearing, his musketeers in his wake. Philippe's breath was as labored as mine in the quieting atmosphere.

"I'm sorry," Olympe told him, her tone too confident to sound truly apologetic. "I had to speak up. Lorraine can't be trusted, and it was time everyone knew about his lies."

Philippe stared at his brother's disappearing silhouette in the distance, seemingly oblivious to her words. She gave me a help-less shrug and clasped my hand in a quick parting gesture, before heading toward the feast with the tail of the crowd.

Around us the air settled and the open-air theater sat empty, its chairs overturned, its canvas floor trampled to shreds, its magic lights half-extinguished, and his dark tapestries like mourning drapes on the walls. Silence replaced the earlier hustle and bustle of the crowd, and the warm evening breeze swallowed forever the words the comedians and the exclamations of the audience. Nothing remained of the play performed on the stage, nor of the dramatic incident that had followed—only the feelings they had awoken in us.

Curiosity, thrill, and then—an overwhelming sadness.

CHAPTER XXII

No one cared that we arrived late at the feast.

I expected everyone to be gossiping about Lorraine's arrest, yet this turned out to be only one of the many topics discussed by the guests partaking in the buffet laid out in the northern part of the gardens. Despite the scandalous nature of the incident, the scenery staged for the evening meal by and large overshadowed it, and I could almost understand why.

The magical landscape created by Louis and his *magiciens* outdid everything they'd created before. Amid the trimmed hedges of the Versailles gardens, a porphyry and marble grotto sprung from the ground, like the entrance to a mythical cave. Inside, a corridor made of interwoven green plants led to a grove that offered a riot of greenery to the eyes of the observers. Tall, entwined branches shot up toward the clear night sky, supporting giant flowers and enclosing the octagonal space with a thick wall of vegetation. Magical lanterns dotted the place, turning blooming petals into shimmering blossoms and coating every surface with a surreal glow. The smell of magic hung in the air and tickled my nose, almost nauseating.

One side of the clearing held a very large table overloaded with piles of food on gilded plates and sculpted fountains pouring colorful drinks. The other half of the grove had been turned into a vast open-air ballroom. Lully's music boomed from an orchestra in the middle while the courtiers' chatter rose amid the clinking of silverware and tinkling of glasses. A dense crowd filled the entire grass-covered ground, and the whole place reminded me of a huge aviary whose captive birds ignored they were in a cage.

The result felt both awe-inspiring and utterly wrong.

"I can't do it," Philippe said.

His fingers crushed mine, and he stood so stiff with tension that he almost shook. I pressed my lips against his white knuckles and looked up into his red-rimmed eyes. Much as I feared, Lorraine's fall had shaken him to the core, and his face bore the haunted look that betrayed feelings in turmoil. But he couldn't afford to make a scene. His association with Lorraine put him in a precarious enough position as it were; angering Louis further would render it even more dangerous. I couldn't let him be mastered by his dark emotions when I had worked so hard to secure my own place at court and when I was carrying his child.

"You can," I replied. "The party is almost over. We'll leave after the fireworks display."

I nudged him toward the buffet where a servant in livery handed us strange multicolored drinks that tasted sweet and sour. Some distance away, the king chatted with Athénaïs among the crowd, and I made a point of ignoring them and searching the throng of guests for other familiar faces to distract my husband.

"He always destroys everything," Philippe said.

He stared at his brother, his brown eyes like burning coal in his pale face. I had my task cut out for me if I wanted to keep him from pouncing on Louis like a wounded wolf turning on the hunter.

"He had to arrest Lorraine," I said, my voice soothing. "He's the king, presented with worrying evidence. You understand he had no choice."

Philippe drained his glass and handed it to the attendant for a refill. "How convenient. Look at him, all brokenhearted over the fact."

Louis laughed at a word from Athénaïs just then, in a display of cheerful behavior that really didn't help my efforts.

"He's trying to salvage his evening," I replied. "You know very well how scandals destroy monarchies. He wants people to remember tonight as a success. He'll deal with Lorraine tomorrow, away from prying eyes."

Philippe swallowed half his glass in one swig and snorted bitterly. "Exactly. He'll make everyone forget about the whole thing, and it'll be as if it never happened, with the rest of us, who aren't gullible fools, living on with the truth and our memories."

The bleakness of his statement broke my heart. It called up a vision of Fouquet, alone and forgotten in his prison. I placed a hand on his cheek to draw his gaze to me and hold it.

"Lorraine committed quite terrible deeds," I said, my tone as gentle as I could make it. "I know it's hard to face this fact now, but in time—"

He wrenched my fingers from his cheek and held them tight, with an intensity that made me jump. "You don't see it, do you?"

"See . . . what?" I stammered, taken aback by his desperate gaze.

"He didn't do it!"

His voice rose, but the din of the music and conversations covered it, leaving us wrapped in a bubble of privacy by the buffet. I pulled my fingers from his grasp.

"Philippe," I said, stern now. "Lorraine made spells disappear in order to sell them to the highest bidders. He endangered French magic and the crown for his own gain, and he threatened everyone who tried to expose him. He *isn't* innocent."

I could have mentioned I was among the people he had threatened, but I wanted to keep my list of damning evidence as unbiased as possible. Seducing my husband and trying to break up my relationship with him wasn't a crime. Plotting against the king and *magiciens* was.

Philippe's features hardened and he leaned forward to whisper in my face. "How do you know he's guilty?"

His utter refusal to see sense awoke my temper, yet I strived to keep a patient tone. "He wrote a journal where he listed all the vanished spells. He organized a silent auction to sell them tonight. He—"

"You're not answering my question," Philippe interrupted. "How do you know *he* did it? How can you be sure he wasn't told to do it? Or manipulated? Or blackmailed?"

I rolled my eyes. Now he was being ridiculous. Lorraine had everything to gain by doing all he had done. Influence. Money. The ear of the king's brother.

"By whom?" I asked.

This time, he bent down so close we were almost nose to nose. "By. My. Brother."

My first instinct was to scoff, but the sincere belief in his eyes stopped me. Philippe was always blaming Louis for everything he couldn't have or control in his life. After our wedding, it had taken me weeks to realize that far from being paranoid, my husband had a point, and the king was poisoning my mind against him. I had come to trust and listen to Philippe, but in the past few months, it struck me that I had stopped heeding him. Too focused on my own problems and longings, I had doubted again Philippe's opinion. I had assumed his antagonism with his brother and his infatuation with Lorraine clouded his mind. But what if I had been the one lacking judgment?

I blinked.

"You think Louis controlled Lorraine?" I said. "But that makes no sense."

"Doesn't it?" Philippe gave an ironic shrug.

The question made me pause. I knew for a fact the king sought control and power more than anything else, and his greatest weapon was to be underestimated. Had I fallen prey to his strategy and be made oblivious by magic spells and glamorous parties like everyone else?

Doubt nagged at me, now, so I pulled him toward the edge of the clearing, as away from the crowd as we could get. We stood beneath the low branches of a leafy oak tree, the magical lantern bathing us in a warm glow.

"What do you mean?" I asked.

Uncertainty fleeted across Philippe's expression, as if he wasn't sure whether he could speak his mind or not. As if he wasn't certain I would believe him. I squeezed his hand, self-blame washing through me. His hesitation was my fault. How had we come to this point?

"Just tell me," I said.

"I know you don't like Lorraine," he started after a moment. "And you don't know him very well. Obviously you can't be blamed for it. But *I* know him." He sighed. "I'm not fool enough to think he is a perfect man, but I can't believe he would orchestrate such a complex scheme to threaten the whole of French magic and the crown."

He warmed to his subject, and began pacing.

"Does he like power and money? Yes. Parties and fine clothes and magic? Also yes. Is he secretive and ambitious? Yes again. But would he think up such a convoluted plot with the potential to destroy the kingdom and its magical foundation just for his own gain without exterior motive? I'm sorry, but it doesn't sound like him."

Malleable. That was what Louis had called Lorraine's magic— and by extension the man himself. *His association with me is obviously very beneficial to him*, he'd said. Could this be true? Could he have manipulated Lorraine to take part in some nefarious scheme in exchange for position and wealth?

I cast my mind back to the last few months, mentally leafing through my memories of the king. How hastily he'd dismissed me as his Source and recruited a low-ranking nobleman eager to do his king's bidding to further his situation. How quick he'd been to ignore my claims about vanished spells. I had accused Lorraine at every turn, when Louis could have easily been the one behind the theft of the *grimoire*, the *magicien* making spells disappear with his Source, and the schemer orchestrating a silent auction of the spells.

Suspicion coalesced into fear in my chest. If this were true, Louis had used Lorraine as a decoy, just like he'd used Louise to hide me as his Source all those months ago. The blame would fall on the ambitious courtier, used as a smokescreen to hide the true perpetrator of the magical plot, and it would be easy for the king to rid himself of him before he could talk. My throat tightened. Lorraine was about to be called a traitor, the penalty for which was death. I had helped bring him down. What if Philippe was right and he was innocent?

I couldn't let him die. Not when I wasn't sure of the truth.

"I have to speak with Lorraine," I said.

* * *

D'Artagnan stood by the orchestra, listening to the music with a glass in his hand and a tapping foot in the grass. I navigated my way through the tipsy revelers in an approximate beeline toward him, my husband on my heels.

"But you said we couldn't leave early," Philippe said. "People will notice if we're gone."

"I'm beginning to think no one would see the difference if we weren't here," I replied. "Just make sure your brother isn't looking at us."

"He's dancing with Athénaïs. Definitely not interested in us."

We reached D'Artagnan, who greeted us with a polite bow and an inquiry after my health.

"Very well, thank you," was my automatic reply, even though

my lungs burned and cold sweat dampened my skin. Then I cut to the chase. "I need your help once again. Your men arrested the Chevalier de Lorraine half an hour ago. Where did they take him?"

The musketeer's face fell at my question. "Your Highness, I'm afraid I can't—"

"Just answer her question, man," Philippe interrupted. "Then tomorrow you can tell the king whatever you want."

D'Artagnan let out a sigh, and stared into his wineglass, pondering my request.

"You didn't get in trouble last time," I pressed him. "You won't again tonight, I'll make sure of it."

Philippe shot me a suspicious glance and mouthed, *Last time?*

I ignored him and spoke to the old soldier instead. "It's very important. You know I wouldn't ask if it wasn't."

D'Artagnan nodded to himself as he reached a silent conclusion and set down his glass onto a passing servant's tray. "He's been taken to a temporary holding cell," he said. "He'll be moved once the guests have departed. The king wants to speak with him during the fireworks, but I can arrange for you to see him for a short while."

Philippe gripped my hand, his hold tight and palm clammy. "Yes. Please."

The musketeer led the way through the swarm of chatting, drinking, and dancing courtiers. We followed him at a distance, and pretended at a nonchalance we didn't feel among the partying guests. Relief descended over me when we escaped the oppressing multitude at last and found ourselves back in the vegetation corridor leading out of the grove. Perspiration still clung to my skin, but my breathing eased as we reached the grotto marking the entrance to the party. Here the crowd was sparse, and if we crossed paths with a few nobles and attendants, they were all too intent on their own destination to give us more than a flitting glance.

No one came after us, so we hurried behind D'Artagnan down a torchlit side alley. Soon he ducked through a tall hedge and into the woods hidden by the screens of greenery within the Versailles gardens. I narrowed my eyes in the sudden darkness as twigs snapped under our feet and the undergrowth rustled at our passage, invisible night birds taking flight amid the branches that caught at our clothes. Philippe cursed under his breath, his fingers crushing mine.

Torchlight flickered ahead. A garden shed materialized amid the vegetation, with two musketeers standing guard next to a pile of gardening tools and watering cans. They exchanged a few words with their leader, giving Philippe and me a moment to emerge from the trees. By the time we reached them, the two soldiers were stepping aside and D'Artagnan pushed the green wooden door open.

My pulse spiked, the pressure constricting my chest. I paused to settle my breathing. Philippe's knuckles were white from tension. I had to keep my own emotions under control if I didn't want this illicit visit to be for nothing.

D'Artagnan lit a candle inside the shed, which was too small to fit the three of us, so he moved back to let us in.

Lorraine sat on a low stool in the otherwise-empty hut. Rope bound his wrists together, shimmering with an enchanted glow. His magically enhanced outfit sparkled in the dim candlelight, out of place in these shabby surroundings. He had his shoulders hunched and his elbows on his thighs, a sneer marring his handsome face. He didn't rise when Philippe and I stepped inside the low-ceilinged building, but a joyless laugh rumbled out of him.

"Well, I suppose my night is complete now."

D'Artagnan pulled the door closed to allow us some privacy, but I still kept my voice low when I spoke.

"We don't have much time. Will you speak to us or not?"

Lorraine's arresting blue eyes flicked between Philippe and me. My husband stood rigid at my side, my hand in his like a lifeline. They stared at each other for a heartbeat in silence, before Lorraine's gaze returned to me.

"Have you come here to gloat?" he asked.

"No," I replied. "I've come here because Philippe thinks you're innocent, and I want to hear the truth from your lips."

"Why do you care?" he shot back. "Surely everything has turned out exactly as you wanted."

"I care about Philippe," I said. "And about the truth."

Lorraine chuckled again. "He warned me, you know. De Guiche. Before I managed to get rid of him. He said underestimating you two would be my downfall."

The mention of Armand's name brought fire to my core, but I clamped down on my rising temper and kept my tone calm.

"It doesn't have to be. Tell us what happened, and we can help you."

This time he barked out a laugh. "Help me? Against the king of France? Even I'm not naive enough to believe I won't be dead by the end of the week."

"Stop it," Philippe snapped, his voice strangled. He dropped my hand to step closer to Lorraine, and knelt before him on the dirt floor. "I can't help you, but Henriette can. If you ever had any feelings for me, swallow your bloody pride and tell us everything now."

Lorraine's features softened. He brought up his bound hands to my husband's chin, and pinched him lightly. "There he is," he said, his tone tender and unlike anything I'd heard from him before. "Brave and strong-willed and passionate."

Philippe pulled away from his touch, his face stern. "Stop. Stop pushing back, and tell us what you and my brother did."

"Where do you want me to start?" Lorraine straightened on his stool and gazed from my husband to me.

"Why not from the beginning?" I suggested.

Philippe returned to my side. Lorraine nodded.

"You know the beginning," he said. "You fell ill. The king asked me to be his Source."

I narrowed my eyes at him. "So you didn't have anything to do with that?"

Surprise flickered across his face and he glanced at my stomach. "Well, no. Aren't you ill because of—"

So Philippe had told him about the pregnancy. Maybe I should have been annoyed at the thought, but I wanted answers more than starting a fight. Lorraine's reply sounded sincere enough, so I pressed on.

"Spells started to vanish," I said. "Are you going to deny you were behind it?"

Lorraine inhaled a deep breath. "The king said he had a plan. A way to control French magic and ensure someone like Fouquet would never threaten him and his family again. He wished to limit access to the most powerful spells. He taught me the enchantment, and we made the portal spell *disappear*, as you say."

I bit my lip, my heartbeat quickening again. Had it really been Louis's idea all along? Lorraine's open expression meant he was either telling the truth, or a very good liar.

"It worked perfectly," Lorraine went on. "Everyone forgot the spell even existed except us."

"And Henriette," Philippe interrupted, his jawline taut with anger.

"Then we realized there was a catch," Lorraine agreed, unperturbed. "First Her Highness, then Prince Aniaba started to ask questions. What they had in common, of course, was that they had both been the king's Source at one point. The concealing spell worked on everyone but the people who had performed magic with the *magicien* who'd cast it."

Despite our vast modern knowledge of the world around us, there was still much we didn't understand about magic. The fact a loophole had appeared in the king's scheme didn't surprise me, even if I couldn't make sense of it.

"So you lied about it all," I pointed out. "And ensured no one would believe us."

"Of course," he replied. "Secrecy was paramount, and the king wasn't ready to let this small hitch in his plan stop him. We carried on, concealing more spells every week, while using them to further the building of Versailles and the organization of the royal entertainments."

"But you kept a list of the spells," I said, thinking back to his journal.

Lorraine nodded again. "By then I had taken the measure of

the king, and I thought it wise to have a safety net and to build up a nest egg in case the weather turned."

I glanced at Philippe to gauge his reaction. Lorraine's story made sense, and his sincere expression drove me to believe him, but I didn't know him as well as my husband did. Philippe surveyed him, his features drawn into hard lines yet without suspicion.

A knock at the door made us jump.

"Your Highnesses," D'Artagnan's muffled voice came through the wooden panel. "The fireworks are about to start. The king will be here shortly."

Consternation rushed through me. Time was seeping through my fingers like grains of sand, and Lorraine wasn't done with his tale.

"So that's why you organized the auction?" I turned to him, my tone urgent. "For money?"

He cast Philippe a guilty look, and his tone turned earnest. "It was stupid, I know. But the king only saw me as a tool, and the way he treated you . . . I thought I could get back at him and get away with it. I thought I could sell the spells to the court *magiciens*, and even if he found out, he wouldn't be able to do anything without admitting his own guilt in the process."

"You didn't think he'd be ruthless enough to pin it all on you?" Philippe said, irritation darkening his features.

"I didn't think I'd get exposed in public!" Lorraine shot back. "I thought he and I would deal with this behind closed doors, and he'd give in to avoid a scandal."

"Except you were found out." Philippe growled. "And look at you now. Was it worth it?"

Lorraine held up his bound hands and stood up from his stool at last. "Listen, I'm sorry. I thought I knew him well enough to play him. I'm sorry it—"

"Forget your apologies," I interrupted, aware of the passing time. "Tell me about the unlocking spell."

He paused, confusion wiping his earlier intent expression. "What spell?"

"The one you used to practice magic alone," I replied, impatient. "To open the portal in the grove tonight and to organize the auction."

He turned his full attention to me, his eyebrows drawn into a deep frown. "What are you talking about? No one can do magic alone. I performed all of tonight's enchantments with Saint-Aignan, in exchange for some of the vanished ones."

I gaped, taken aback. He hadn't used the *Déverrouille* spell? Then why had Fouquet told me about it, if not to expose him? Loud knocking rattled the door, and prevented me from dwelling on that thought. Lorraine grabbed Philippe's hands.

"I'm sorry," he said, his words rushed. "I'm sorry I didn't listen when you warned me against your brother, and I'm sorry if I hurt you—"

The door flew open, and D'Artagnan appeared. "The fireworks are starting. The king will be here any moment."

Colorful explosions burst above the trees, startling us all into action. The musketeer pushed Lorraine back toward his stool, wrenching Philippe's hands out of his grip. I stepped out of the shed, my heartbeat frantic. In the distance, fantastical creatures made of sparks and magic chased each other across the clear skies.

"Philippe!" I called under my breath.

He still faced Lorraine inside the gardening hut. "Henriette will speak to my brother," he said to him. "Don't let him intimidate you. And don't—"

"Your Highness, I'm afraid you have to go." D'Artagnan placed a firm hand on his arm to guide him out.

Philippe walked backward, glancing over the musketeer's shoulder to catch a last glimpse of the *chevalier*. If Lorraine replied, the popping noises of the fireworks swallowed his words. The guards closed the door behind their leader, the small wooden building seemingly turned back into a shed. Philippe stood frozen before it, distress all over his features. D'Artagnan met his gaze.

"Your Highness, you have to take Madame back to the party before His Majesty arrives."

The reminder snapped my husband out of his indecision. He wrapped an arm around my waist, his expression still distracted but his demeanor more poised.

"Right, my love," he said. "Let's return."

A riot of fireworks detonated above our heads, splashing colors all over the woods as we trudged back toward the party. Our conversation with Lorraine replayed in my mind while we pushed branches out of our way in the dimness shot through with flamboyant illuminations.

"You were right," I told Philippe when the dark wall of the hedge appeared before us. "It makes sense that Louis used Lorraine to make the spells vanish. I should have guessed it."

We reached the aperture in the shrubbery, and the torchlight from the path on the other side fell on Philippe's hopeful face.

"You'll speak with Louis, then? You'll ask him to release him?"

I paused before we crossed into the alley. His hand rested against my lower back, protective and light. For a long time, I had thought I had lost him to Lorraine and his own demons. It occurred to me just then how unlikely it was that I would ever lose Philippe. He might struggle to express it, or to remember it sometimes, but his love for me was one of the main constants in his life. He needed our partnership as much as I did. And he was capable of providing strength and support as much as I was. *He adores you*, Lorraine had said once out of spite. He had been right. Philippe and I shared a bond that nothing in the madness of our lives could break. We loved each other. We never willingly hurt each other.

And right now, Philippe was hurting, and I was the only one who could help.

"I will," I replied.

I had been instrumental in Lorraine's arrest, and I wouldn't be able to live with myself if he died, now that I knew his only crime had been to sell back stolen spells to *magiciens*. I didn't know whether Louis could be swayed. But I was certainly going to try my utmost to stop him from executing someone whose death would devastate my husband.

CHAPTER XXIII

A summons from the king the next day saved me the trouble of seeking an audience with him.

He received me in his council chamber a quarter of an hour before his advisers were due to arrive. A magical clock ticked on the carved mantelpiece while candles cast off the shadows thrown by the gray morning light. Clouds hung low in the sky outside the tall windows, and a chill infused the high-ceilinged room despite the fire in the hearth.

"Henriette." The king looked up from the papers he shuffled on the large table. "I'm glad we have a chance to talk."

He remained standing, forcing me to do the same. There was something petty about making a pregnant woman stand just to show one's power. In a way, and no matter how hard he tried to make people forget it, Louis would always be the terrified little boy that his mother had ushered into a carriage during the Fronde all those years ago. She had taught him to hold onto his crown and his life by subduing and using every-one, but I wondered if teaching him to love and care for those

----
----

closest to him wouldn't have been a better lesson. Only time would tell.

"As you've heard," Louis said, pacing the room with his hands at his back in a regal stance, "I'm in need of a Source once more. Your doctors assure me you've recovered your health, and therefore I wish you to join me again in my magical works."

Straightforward as always. I surveyed him, weighing my reply in my mind, and conscious this was a negotiation, even if he didn't know it yet.

"Last time we tried a spell," I said, "you will recall you thought my magic was waning, Sire. I fear I may not be the Source I used to be."

A flick of his hand waved away my objection, and he carried on circling the room, which boasted paintings of the military victories of his youth. "I believe the decline of your magical abilities were linked to your ill health. Now that you're better, you should be able to serve me once more."

Serve me. He really couldn't help himself, could he? Once, his self-assurance had fascinated me. Now it only struck me as arrogance and narcissism, and I wondered how it had taken me so long to see it.

"I hope you're right," I replied, my demeanor meek.

He clasped his hands together. "Excellent. I'm still working on that mirror spell we've discussed in the past, and I hope you'll be able to lend me your help in finally getting it right."

"You didn't complete it with your previous Source?" I held his golden gaze, wide-eyed to feign polite interest. I wasn't certain how to mention Lorraine, and he had just given me an opening.

His face was his usual impenetrable mask as he replied, "No."

"What's going to happen to him?" I asked before he could regain control of the conversation.

His features didn't waver. "He's a traitor, Henriette, and he's been arrested. You really shouldn't worry about him anymore."

"But traitors receive the death penalty," I said. "And I do worry—about you. There are so few Sources in the kingdom, what will people think if you execute one, even for perfectly good reasons? Won't they like their king better if he shows mercy and lets a man he has every right to kill live?"

A slight frown furrowed his brow. "A king has to show strength first."

I bit my lip. I had to convince him, before he could suspect me of playing him. My thoughts churned. There had to be a way to sway him. He wanted to rid himself of the threat posed by Lorraine, but I had to show him he didn't have to kill him to do so.

"See what happened with Fouquet," I said, struck by sudden inspiration. "He's rotting in prison, forgotten by everyone. You didn't have to execute him to rid yourself of him."

He crossed his arms over his chest, pondering my words. "Do you really think it will reflect badly on me if I have him killed? What would you have me do instead? I can't put him in the same jail as Fouquet."

His questions lifted my heart with hope. He was considering an alternative to the execution. Maybe I could do this.

"I think people will forget about him much quicker if you get rid of him without killing him," I said.

I didn't suggest anything more. If this was going to work, he had to reach his own conclusions. He paced the room again, until he stopped by the fireplace and stared at the crackling fire, his golden outfit shining like a beacon in the dim room.

"The man loved life at court," he said, as if to himself. "I suppose stripping him of his wealth and sending him into exile would be a worse punishment than death."

I forced my body to remain motionless to avoid betraying my stampeding heartbeat and uplifted thoughts. Seeing Lorraine go would be hard on Philippe, but it would be far less heartbreaking than watching him die.

A knock sounded at the door, and a murmur of conversations announced the arrival of the king's council members. The noise drew Louis out of his deliberation. He turned to me and gestured toward the exit.

"I'll take your counsel under advisement, Henriette. And I shall see you very soon."

Knowing I was dismissed, I left the gilded room under the curious gazes of the council members in black robes. As my heeled shoes clacked against the parquet of the king's apartments, my heart settled again. I knew Louis well enough now to trust he would choose the path he thought most favorable to him. I was almost certain he would exile Lorraine, and I would have everything I had fought to get back: my husband, my status at court, and my position as the king's Source.

Yet my chest didn't swell at this outcome. Too much had happened in the past few months—too many boundaries crossed, too many lines blurred, too many decisions regrettable—for it to feel like a victory.

Maybe this was what I had learned from it all: that being a real player at French court meant giving up a little bit of my innocence and dreams. Nothing would ever be perfect in my life here. But at least, I would have control over it.

It would have to be enough.

* * *

A stack of letters waited on my desk when I reentered my apartment. I wrapped a shawl around my shoulders to fight off the chill, lit a couple of additional candles, and settled by the window to read with Mimi in my lap. My mother described her summer in Paris, while my brother asked after my health and moaned about his wife. A third missive was from Louise, who complained about her loneliness at the Palais-Royal. The fourth one displayed stains and a barely legible spidery handwriting that made my heart stutter.

Armand's letters had been coming at regular intervals since his departure from Versailles. Always hastily written yet unbelievably lengthy, they described in flowery prose and long-winded sentences his life at the front. All his reports of the war in Poland seemed to revolve around his own exploits, and boasted about his incredible adventures abroad in grandiloquent style. Whether these missives meant to reassure me, or were proof that his way of coping with his situation was to lie to himself about it, his words puzzled and delighted me in equal measures and made me long for his return to court. Now that the instrument of his departure was removed from the scene, I dared hope it would be soon.

His letter ended as usual with reminders of his love for me and Philippe, and well wishes for us both and the baby, whom he suggested we call Armand. I chuckled to myself and sat down at my desk to grab a quill and start on my replies.

A knock at my bedroom door made Mimi bark.

"Your Highness." A maid curtsied. "The Comtesse de Soissons is here."

I glanced at the mechanical clock on the mantelpiece. I had sent a message to Olympe before going to see Louis, never expecting her to call on me so soon. I dismissed the maid with thanks and joined Olympe in my salon, my dog on my heels.

"I thought you'd come by in the afternoon," I said, lighting a few more candles around the room to cast off the persisting gloom of the day.

Olympe removed her gloves and came to stand in front of the fireplace. "You didn't mention a time, and you had me intrigued. Also I had nothing better to do, and this dreadful weather does nothing to help my mood."

I could have slapped myself for not realizing it sooner: since the death of the Queen Mother, Olympe had lost her position at court. After years as the superintendent of the Queen Mother's household, she now found herself a courtier among others, without the favor of either the king or the queen. No wonder she sought to nurture our friendship and treated my invitation as a summon. And in a way, her reaction assuaged some of the guilt I felt as I prepared to ask her for yet another favor. Maybe I wasn't using her for her skill as a *magicienne* and she wasn't using me as a means to salvage her situation at court. Maybe we were just two women helping each other in a harsh environment.

"You know I consider you a friend, don't you?" I said. "And you're free to visit me whenever you wish."

Her features wavered with uncertainty for a heartbeat. "That's . . . very generous. I appreciate your sentiment."

"Nonsense." I shrugged and pretended to ignore her emotion. "You've proven I can trust and rely on you more than once in the past few months. I think we have far more in common than we might have expected at first, and I would hate for you to feel isolated when we can share a lasting friendship instead."

To my surprise, hesitation swam in her eyes and her mouth pressed into a thin worried line. Anxiety gripped me. Was there something she wasn't telling me? She turned away from me, her hands clasped together as if to prevent them from shaking. Suspicion rose in me.

"What is it?" I asked, my voice more strained than I wished.

She bit her lip and stared at a still-life painting on the wall with a faraway gaze. My heartbeat pounded quicker, and my breathing hitched. I sat down by the fire to settle my nerves, Mimi at my feet as if she sensed my discomfort.

"You can tell me," I said, my tone gentle and reassuring despite my rising panic.

Olympe drew in a breath before facing me again. "You're right. I've come to value what we have—our friendship—more than you can know, and I do want it to last. I do want honesty and trust between us. And if this is to be the case, there's something you need to know."

I braced myself for whatever was to come, and kept silent to avoid interrupting her. Olympe had been part of the royal family's inner circle for years. She knew all of us—all the gossip, all the secrets. What was she about to tell me? A truth about Philippe, or Louis, or one of their relations? Out of instinct, I folded my hands over my growing belly. I was about to bring a child into this world of deceit and treachery. I needed it to be safe. Knowledge and allies would help make it safe. So I faced Olympe, and waited for her to utter her revelation.

"It's about Athénaïs," she said.

Her chest deflated, as if a weight had just lifted off it, but I blinked at her, uncomprehending. Athénaïs? We had barely seen each other lately. And we hadn't had a proper conversation since our talk at the *orangerie*, when she had so brazenly admitted to having an affair with Louis.

"I know about her . . . indiscretion," I said.

"It's not what I meant," Olympe replied. "Although I'm glad she was honest with you about that."

Did she mean Athénaïs hadn't been honest with me about other things? The thought chilled me to the bone, and I tightened my shawl around my shoulders. Olympe paced the space between the fireplace and the thick carpet, her agitation increasing my nervousness.

"You know Athénaïs resented having to leave court to marry a man she didn't love," she said.

I nodded. Athénaïs had been in love with Prince Aniaba, and although it had hurt me to see her so heartbroken, there had been nothing I could do to prevent her arranged marriage to the nobleman chosen by her parents. Girls like us didn't get to choose our fates in these matters.

"When she left court to get married," Olympe went on, "I accompanied her to her carriage. She was so angry, so upset, that, for a moment, I thought she would refuse to board the vehicle. But instead, she told me a secret. She swore this would be the last time she was forced to do something she didn't want. She said she would return, and rise so high no one would ever ignore her desires or wishes ever again. And she said she wouldn't forget who had helped her, and who had refused to fight for her."

A sinking feeling settled in my stomach. Was I among the people Athénaïs blamed for her situation? I had told myself there was nothing I could have done to stop her marriage. Had I lied to myself, and to her? Louis could have intervened, and I could have convinced him to do so. Was that what she thought?

I must have paled, or stiffened, for Olympe read my thoughts and gave me a grave look of apology.

"And yes, she blamed you too." She sat in the armchair opposite mine to carry on with her tale. "She returned in the spring with a plan: to undermine everyone she saw as her enemies, and to carve her way to the top."

My thoughts churned, replaying every interaction with Athénaïs, every discussion, and trying to see a pattern of behavior when I had been too taken by my own problems and ambitions to see that my friend needed me.

"As her friend," Olympe went on, "I thought nothing of helping her, at first. I admit I never liked Louise, and I didn't mind aiding in getting rid of this provincial girl."

I recalled the Spanish letter plot that had nearly cost her position at court. No wonder Athénaïs had known every detail at the ball. She had masterminded it.

"It all ran like clockwork," Olympe added. "And Athénaïs managed to become Louis's mistress without anyone the wiser, especially not the queen. He's besotted with Athénaïs, you know."

A hint of bitterness crept into her tone, a reminder she had harbored hopes of seducing the king again not so long ago herself.

"So she has him wrapped around her finger," she said, "and I won't be surprised if once he makes her his official *favorite*, she becomes more of a queen than the queen herself."

The faces of Athénaïs and Marie-Thérèse flashed before my eyes, and I could very well believe Olympe's prediction: Marie-Thérèse would be no match for Athénaïs's beauty and wit and scheming mind.

"So she's where she wanted to be," I said. "What does this have to do with me?"

"I'm afraid she sees everyone at court as an enemy now," Olympe replied. "Even her former friends."

My heart sank again, yet part of me still refused to believe the lady-in-waiting I had most trusted had turned on me without seeking to speak with me and to ask for an explanation first. "What did she do?"

"The first thing she did was reveal a secret," Olympe replied.

I drew in a sharp breath, and waited for the revelation to hit me. A secret? About me? The only one worth telling was the fact I was a Source. Who had she told?

"She told the Duchesse de Valentinois Armand was in love with you."

I gaped, and the memory of Philippe's question surfaced in my mind. *She said Armand's in love with you.*

"But it's a lie," I said, echoing my words of months ago. "Armand isn't in love with me."

Olympe tilted her head to the side, her golden gaze frank. "Isn't he?"

"Of course not."

Anger replaced tension in my core. Of course Armand wasn't in love with me. And Athénaïs was the one behind that rumor? She'd been insistent in mentioning it at every turn, but I had thought her persistence born of her love for gossip, or of her desire to see me happy. It hadn't occurred to me to think she was spreading this story to undermine me. And she'd nearly succeeded, since Philippe had given credit to this tale and nearly lost confidence in our relationship.

"In any case," Olympe went on, "your steady denials and the popularity you benefit from meant the rumor was squashed before it could really hurt you. When even the pamphlet didn't drive you from court—"

"She was behind the pamphlet?" I stood up, too distressed to keep still anymore. I paced the room, Mimi following me with her tail wagging, as if in hope of an impending walk outside. Armand and I had blamed Lorraine for the pamphlet at the time, despite Philippe's protests. Another instance when I should have trusted him instead of being overcome by my prejudice.

"Yes, but it didn't work," Olympe said, undeterred by my interruption. "So she changed strategy and went after Armand instead."

Horror filled my chest and compressed my lungs. Athénaïs and Armand had been close friends. They'd helped me when I faced Fouquet, and shared many happy moments together. Surely she couldn't blame him for anything that had befallen her, nothing that would warrant putting his very life at risk?

"But Lorraine is the one who went to Armand's father to have him sent away from court," I pointed out. "He admitted to it himself."

"And who do you think introduced him to the Duc de Gramont and suggested this whole scheme with the army?" Olympe asked. "A scheme that had Athénaïs's husband also conveniently sent off to the front."

I resumed my seat, overwhelmed by her revelations and my lungs tightening under the pressure. A cough rattled my chest, and Olympe fetched me a glass of water from a tray by the window. The cold liquid soothed my throat, but didn't settle my thoughts.

"Why are you telling me all this?" I asked once I had recovered some of my breath.

"Because we're friends, now," Olympe replied. "And I don't want to be dishonest with you anymore. I also want you to know you can trust me."

I met her steady gaze, and read no deceit or malice there. I believed her.

"And I'll admit," she added with a slight shrug, "I value your friendship even more so because you're a Source. I'm a *magicienne*. We share a bond, an understanding that my former attachment to Athénaïs could never rival. I'd rather nurture that relationship than one with a woman who has made it clear she'll look out for only herself."

My pulse steadied at last. Olympe was right. The revelation of Athénaïs's duplicity was a blow, but I didn't have to face it alone. I had people I could trust around me, and I now knew well the dangers of the French court: I wouldn't be fooled or blindsided by them again. And there was one more thing I could do to ensure I had control over my life.

"Speaking of magic," I said, my voice calm again, "there's a spell I would like us to discuss."

Olympe's golden gaze lit up with interest, and she leaned forward in her seat. "What is it?"

"Have you ever heard of an ancient spell called *Déverrouille*?"

CHAPTER XXIV

———

Olympe pursed her lips at Madame Fouquet's handwritten note.

Outside my windows, the gathered gray clouds had finally burst and rain fell on the Versailles estate, droplets dripping down the glass panes.

"Whose handwriting is this?" Olympe still frowned at the piece of paper in her hand. "Can you trust the source of this message?"

I held out my hands in helplessness. "I trust it as much as any old *grimoire*. Louis and I spent a lot of time studying ancient enchantments. There are literally thousands of them. Some have been abandoned because they're dangerous or don't give the expected outcome. But most of them have simply been forgotten because they were written down once eons ago and haven't been used since. The person who gave me this spell is a scholar who's dedicated their life to unearthing old spells. I don't know where they found it, and I haven't been able to find it referenced anywhere myself."

"But how do you know it'll work?" Olympe asked, still unconvinced.

"I don't. You're never certain these ancient spells are genuine until you test them."

"What if it does work," Olympe went on, "and it's harmful?"

The possibility had crossed my mind, of course. It was definitely within the realm of possibility that Fouquet sought to harm me—and maybe the king too—by handing me a forbidden spell that would destroy us both when we performed it.

Yet, as ever, my instinct told me to search for the best in someone. I wanted to hope in the former Crown *Magicien*'s redemption. I wanted to trust his wife's words when she'd said the spell was a thank-you–*a peace offering, a parting gift.* I wanted to believe Fouquet meant to pass on his knowledge to a kindred spirit before he died. If the *Déverrouille* spell worked, it was a wonderful, powerful spell. I understood a lover of magic like him wouldn't want to see it sink into oblivion.

"I don't think it will hurt us," I said. "But I understand if you don't want to take the risk."

Olympe read the note again, her mouth forming the silent words I now knew by heart. *To temporarily unlock the power of a Source so they can perform another spell by themselves.*

"So it unlocks your magic," she said aloud after a pause. "Supposedly for a short time, so you can cast an enchantment alone."

I nodded. "I researched it a little, without much success, as I've said. But my theory is that it was used on battlefields centuries ago, when for whatever reason a *magicien* and his Source became separated. It allowed the Source to perform a single spell and maybe save themselves, for example."

Olympe nibbled at her lip. "A sort of last-resort spell to ensure the Source wouldn't be helpless without a *magicien*? That makes sense." She put down the paper and held out her hands, resolve settling over her features. "Well, we won't know until we've tried it, will we?"

Excitement soared in my chest, yet I had to tamp it down. If the spell worked, I didn't know how long I would have to cast a second spell alone. I already knew what that second enchantment would be, so I didn't want to waste my chance. I explained all this to Olympe, whose shoulders slumped when she realized she would have to wait to experiment with this spell.

"So you want to do this tonight instead?" she asked.

"Yes," I replied, trepidation at my own daring quickening my pulse again. "I don't want us to get caught, so it's better if we do this when everyone is asleep."

"Fine." She stood up and put her gloves back on. "Where shall we meet? Please not in the woods again—not in this weather."

A smile tugged at my lips as I appraised her. A lady magician who never refused to perform a dangerous spell, but who drew the line at ruining her shoes in the forest.

"Don't worry," I said. "You won't get wet: we'll stay in the palace. Just meet me in my antechamber at two."

She shot me a sarcastic glance. "Two in the morning? I'm already regretting this new friendship of ours."

Yet her conniving smile betrayed her intention to be there without fault.

* * *

An eerie silence permeated the palace tonight.

Heavy clouds still hid the moon and stars in the sky, which deepened the darkness inside the gilded building. Candles in sconces cast odd shadows on the decorated walls as we tiptoed our way to the first floor, and Olympe held on to my hand as if she might lose me in the succession of dark salons.

We crossed paths with two soldiers on duty, and Olympe and I both stiffened, but the concealing spell we'd cast over ourselves before leaving my rooms seemed to work: They didn't notice us, their eyes sliding over our hidden forms as if they were only two more shadows in the empty salon.

Soon the large double doors barring the way to our objective rose before us, with two armed guards standing in front of it. But we'd prepared for this moment, and Olympe slammed the open door we'd just come through. Both guards rushed to investigate while shouts rose on the other side of the ornate panel. In the confusion, Olympe and I slipped inside the gallery at the end of the line of salons.

As soon as the gilded door clicked shut behind us, I let go of Olympe to end the concealing spell. In the faint torchlight rising from the gardens below, our silhouettes emerged in the darkness, reflected by the mirrors on the walls. Magic sparkled on every surface, swathing the whole room in a warm glow.

"Oh," Olympe whispered, awe in her tone.

Louis called the gallery his Hall of Mirrors, and no one but his artist *magiciens* and Sources had been given access to it yet. Its inauguration would take place in a few days, an event for all the court to witness—once Louis and I figured out the mirror spell he so desperately sought to achieve.

Olympe took a few steps forward, the parquet floor creaking slightly under her feet. Above our heads, the high ceilings displayed dozens of Le Brun's paintings to illustrate Louis's achievements as king of France. Marble pilasters with gilded capitals lined the hall, framing arcades that held windows on one side, and looking glasses on the other.

"How many mirrors are there?" Olympe whispered.

"Over three hundred and fifty," I said in the same tone, recalling an earlier boast from Louis.

"How did he manage to get all these imported from Venice?"

"He didn't," I replied. "French *magiciens* made them."

In the semidarkness, she gaped at the gilded masterpiece surrounding us, her gaze darting from the heavy chandeliers to the statues dotting the length of the room.

"I can't believe this used to be a simple terrace," she said, wonder in her tone.

Part of me shared her amazement, but another recoiled at the purpose of this grandiose achievement. Louis meant this place to be the jewel in the crown of Versailles. His plan was to turn every one of these mirrors into a weapon to spy on his courtiers and his family. His ambition and paranoia had cost me dearly already. I intended to prevent him from causing any further damage. Even a king had to be told no every once in a while.

"Why are we here?"

Olympe's question brought me back to the present, and I turned my attention to her.

"I want to perform a spell here. I'd like us to try the unlocking spell now, so I can do it afterward."

Olympe's brows drew together in the dim magical light. "What spell do you want to cast?"

My lips pulled into an enigmatic smile. "You'll see."

The less she knew, the better. Should my spell succeed, Louis wouldn't be happy. Better she stay out of it all together.

We held hands in the middle of the gallery, and for a suspended moment my heart thumped loud and fast. What if Fouquet meant me harm after all? What if believing in the good in people did lead to my downfall? Was I being reckless, trusting a former enemy's word, when a prophecy foretold my untimely death?

Olympe squeezed my fingers, as if sensing my hesitation. "If you're unsure, we don't have to—"

"No," I interrupted her, her suggestion prompting resolve to settle over me.

Weeks ago, I had visited Fouquet with a question: Was there any way to ward off death? He hadn't been able to answer me then, but had later sent me a spell. I chose to believe this was the best solution he'd been able to think of: an enchantment that allowed a Source to take control of their magic long enough to protect themselves from harm. If I was wrong, then we'd know soon enough.

I tightened my grip on Olympe's hand. *"Déverrouille."*

What made the whole endeavor difficult was that my magic both fueled the enchantment and acted as its conduit. There was no surer way to derail a spell—as the Parisian fortune-teller and the doctor *magicien* had experienced firsthand in the past. But Olympe and I had talked this through, and I trusted she was talented enough to handle such a hurdle.

As soon as I uttered the incantation, magic rushed out of me in a swirling blast of golden sparks. Olympe gasped and startled, but we held on to each other with a fierce grasp, until she took control of the spell. The sparkling flecks danced in the dim light of the hall for a few heartbeats, then regrouped to take the shape of a glittering double door. Olympe exhaled slowly, and the door opened.

A strange sensation of release spread over my limbs, as if a weight lifting off or layers peeling away. Magic thrummed along my legs and arms to the tips of my fingers and toes, and pulsed there, waiting to be cast upon the world.

Olympe dropped my hand and stepped away, her eyes wide with wonder. "Henriette . . . your eyes." Her voice sounded distorted and distant, as if we swam underwater.

"What?" I asked.

"They're golden."

I blinked. With the glittering door before us, and the magic of our spell swirling around us, everything looked bathed in specks of gold to me.

"Do the spell now," Olympe said.

The urgency in her tone didn't match my own state of mind. An odd sort of peace had taken hold of my thoughts, and time seemed to slow as magical dots floated about, carried by a gentle breeze.

"Henriette!" Olympe snapped her fingers in front of my face. "Cast your spell now!"

Her stormy expression spurred me into action. As lovely as the moment was, I had come here with a goal in mind, hadn't I? Magic tingled at my fingertips, eager for release. I closed the distance between us and the wall of mirrors, and placed my palms against their cold surface.

"*Aveugle.*"

To every spell, there was a counterspell. An enchantment could allow you to reveal what a mirror had witnessed. Another could blind the mirror and lock it forever.

The flecks of my magic twirled out of my fingers to spread into the hundreds of looking glasses in the hall. A clicking sound echoed each time my spell sealed a mirror, like a key turning into a lock with a definite *clack*. The noise reverberated along the room in rapid succession. Then it reached the last mirror, and my spell ended. The room fell silent. The golden specks of my magic dissolved into the shadows. My skin prickled, as the golden door in the center of the hall vanished and my magic settled into my core, becoming dormant once more. A breath escaped my lungs in the sudden quiet and my hands dropped at my side.

"What . . . What did you do?" Olympe's whispered question sounded loud in my ears, like fabric had just been removed from them.

My next breath caught in my throat, sparking a cough. She handed me a handkerchief, materializing at my side before I could move away from the mirrors. Banging rattled the doors, bringing me back to the reality of the dim Hall of Mirrors. The light and noise of our spells must have alerted the guards, who now struggled to get access to the room. My pulse hammered against my temples.

"We have to get out of here," Olympe said, reading my thoughts. She led me by the elbow to the nearest window, which she opened without hesitation. "Are you up for another spell?"

My breath whizzed in and out of my lungs, and tiredness dragged at my thoughts, but the insistent battering at the doors made it clear there would be no escape through them. I didn't have a choice. I gave Olympe a slight nod.

"We're going to jump," she said. "And cast a spell to break our fall. Then we're going to cloak ourselves with magic and run back to your rooms. Ready?"

I wasn't, but the gilded doors splintered under a forceful blow, taking away any choice. We couldn't get caught in the Hall of Mirrors at night after performing magic there. Talking ourselves out of *that* situation would be too complicated, and the consequences might be dire for Olympe, if not for me. We had to leave before the guards got in and recognized us.

I leaned on Olympe to climb onto the windowsill, my skirts piling around me. The hair on my arm stood up in the chill night air, and a shiver traveled along my limbs. I gripped Olympe with one hand, and rested the other on my stomach in a protective gesture. The gravel on the ground appeared uneven and rough in the dim light, and the distance between the first-floor window and the terrace below was awfully large. At our backs, a loud crack announced the final break in the doors. I swallowed a lump in my throat.

"Ready," I said.

I spoke the spell, and we jumped.

*　*　*

The Hall of Mirrors teemed with elegantly dressed courtiers in the afternoon sunshine, a stark contrast to the empty space that had greeted Olympe and me only days earlier.

Chatter mixed with violin music under the painted ceiling as everyone mingled, observing the newly open gallery with wide eyes and approving nods. The inauguration ceremony was minutes away, and I squeezed my way through the crowd in search of a familiar face.

Strong fingers gripped my forearm and I turned, expecting Philippe. But the eyes that met mine were green, and the smirk on those full lips was unmistakable.

"Darling, you look as radiant as ever."

My heartbeat thundered, and it was all I could do not to throw myself into his arms.

"When . . . When did you get back?" I stammered, my shaking voice betraying my emotions.

"Last night," Armand replied, still smiling. He dropped his hand to take a step back amid the swarming guests, and surveyed my silhouette. "Look at you. All glowing with motherly energy."

My hands landed on my belly in a self-conscious gesture—I was only just starting to show—but such tenderness laced his words that I blushed.

"I know everyone wishes a boy," I said, "but I think it's a girl."

"Excellent." He hooked his arm with mine and led me through the throng. "You can call her Armande."

I shook my head with a smile, and watched his profile as we walked, the freckles on his high cheekbones standing out in the warm light. Eager to keep up the banter I had missed so much, I asked, "No scar, then?"

He shot me a sideways glance full of mischief. "Not that you can see here. You'll have to take off my clothes to witness the proof of my chivalrous exploits."

This time, I laughed, and his eyes sparkled with pride. Then he grew sober.

"Speaking of knights," he added, "I heard the Chevalier de Lorraine is in exile. After all he did, I was surprised to hear about such clemency."

"It was all more complicated than we thought," I replied. "But this is a story for another time, I'm afraid."

Taking the hint, he nodded, and his gaze landed on Athénaïs conferring with the king. "There's a lot that I missed, it seemed. I'm counting on you to fill me in on all the details."

I steered him away from Louis and his secret mistress. I hadn't spoken to Athénaïs since Olympe's revelations, and I intended to keep our relationship to a mere exchange of formalities from now on. It was a pity that things had reached this point, but she had broken my trust too thoroughly for me to pretend we were still friends. She had made her choices, and I had made mine. Maybe life would bring us back together in the future, maybe it wouldn't. For now, I had other allies at court, and other concerns pressing on my mind.

We crossed paths with Marie-Thérèse and her entourage, Prince Aniaba at her side. We exchanged smiles and nods, but the moving courtiers carried us away from each other before we could strike up a conversation.

We reached Lully's orchestra and found Philippe standing by a gilded statue and studying the paintings above. The silver trimmings of his burgundy outfit shimmered in the sunlight, and his bejeweled hand rested on the intricate pommel of his decorated cane. I slipped out of Armand's grasp to link arms with him.

"There you are," I teased. "I thought I'd lost you."

He deposited a distracted kiss on my temple. "Nonsense. You know me, always around." His attention landed on Armand. "I see you found the war hero."

His tone was more indifferent than bitter, and sadness tugged at me on his behalf. Because of the Fronde, Louis would never let his brother near the army. It was unlikely he would ever know the type of recognition Armand now enjoyed. A selfish part of me felt relief at the idea he would never leave me for a battlefield, but another saw in Armand everything he wished he could be: a man free to live as he pleased, to have adventures abroad, to shine as brightly as he could, and to love whom he wanted. I could see now how in many ways, Armand was the unfettered version of Philippe. And I knew which one I loved the most.

"We were looking for you." I kissed his hand, a familiar gesture I had never allowed myself in public until then.

But I was past hiding who I was. Within moments I would reveal I was a Source to the entire French court. By now most of these nobles knew I was with child, and standing here with my husband and Armand rendered any rumor about the three of us meaningless. Fouquet, Lorraine, Athénaïs, and even Louis had tried to manipulate and hurt me, and they'd failed. I was still here—still alive, still in control. An open challenge to anyone who dared come after me and the people I loved.

Hands clapped in the middle of the hall, and a hush spread over the assembled courtiers.

"Welcome!" Louis's voice rose under the gilded arcades. "Welcome to the inauguration of the Hall of Mirrors!"

I pulled out of Philippe's grasp, and for an instant he held on to me, hesitation on his handsome face. I flashed him a reassuring smile.

"Trust me," I said.

He let me go. I moved amid the guests while the king spoke, his confident speech holding the crowd in thrall. His tone hadn't been as self-possessed this morning, when I had told him the mirror spell he wished to perform was impossible.

Although he was aware of the intrusion in the Hall of Mirrors, he didn't know a spell had been performed there to prevent any nefarious use of the looking glasses. I had no wish for him to find out in front of hundreds of courtiers, and even less intention to let him know I was behind the counterspell.

Anger had darkened his features at my refusal, yet he had had no choice but to give in. In time, he might recruit another Source willing to try the mirror spell, and he might find out about the locking enchantment then. But given his arrogance, it was unlikely he would ever suspect me of the deed—he could never see me as more than a pawn in his own game.

So in the meantime, I suggested another means of distraction for his guests on this inauguration day: a simple illusion spell that was sure to awe yet wouldn't grant the king more power than he already had.

I reached Louis's side as he finished his speech, and he welcomed me with an extended hand and an inscrutable smile.

"My dear Madame," he announced, "is going to help me with today's celebrations. Some space, if you please?"

As one, the courtiers shuffled back, their expression both eager and astonished. The king grabbed my fingers and held up his free hand outward.

"*Révèle*," I said.

Louis pulled at my magic, which flew out of me in a rush of golden particles and scattered on the surface of the windows along the hall. The prophecy spell took shape in the glass, visions of the future that reflected in the mirrors opposite them.

Gasps and murmurs greeted the predictions, then silence quickly fell as silhouettes moved along the walls, sights of what was to come in the gilded gallery.

Courtiers in glittering clothes dancing to swelling music by candlelight.

Foreign dignitaries in resplendent outfits presenting gifts to Louis in the sunshine.

A small boy running at night along the parquet floor with a toy clasped against his chest.

Another crowd of twirling nobles in striking white wigs, with unfamiliar sparkling drinks in odd-shaped glasses in their hands.

The images began to move faster, figures blurring in an endless ballet of changing visions. Voices echoed and overlapped, turning unintelligible.

Servants moving furniture.

The hall empty and drenched in darkness.

New people buzzing about, dressed in strange black fashion.

Tables set for meetings.

Leaves and dust accumulating in the once-again bare gallery.

Sunset and sunrise.

Night and day.

Then shouts and noise once more.

People on ladders, people carrying buckets, people washing mirrors.

More crowds, their apparels too peculiar to describe, standing around the hall with their mouths gaping—a strange reflection of the courtiers watching the prophecy now.

An endless parade of strangers, speaking indecipherable words, their eyes bright with wonder and magic.

And on all their lips, in many languages, a word we could hear from across time.

Versailles.

Versailles.

Versailles.

EPILOGUE

"Once upon a time, a beautiful foreign princess came to live at the French court, where she met a handsome prince—"

"That's not how it starts!" Marie-Louise interrupted, her high-pitched voice loud in protestation.

I raised my eyebrows in mock surprise, and made a show of checking the leather-bound book in my hands. "Isn't it?"

Her delicate mouth pinched in a disapproving pout, my daughter pointed at the open page before us. "No, we're reading *Cinderella*."

"Are we?" I said, my tone still full of mischief.

She held my gaze, her golden eyes bright in the candlelight. "Yes, please."

Dropping my playful tone, I began again, while Marie-Louise nestled back against me on the nursery's sofa.

"Once upon a time . . ."

It had been a very hot day at Versailles, and all the windows were thrown open to let in the evening summer breeze. It played in the sheer curtains and teased my daughter's dark curls, carrying in distant noises of partying courtiers, echoing laughter, and tinkling glass. The quiet apartments reserved for the royal children and their staff offered a stark contrast to the busy salons I had left earlier. As I read, I kept my voice low to avoid disturbing Louis's children, already asleep in the bedroom next door.

Her thumb in her mouth, Marie-Louise listened to the story, her eyelids growing heavy and her breathing even. Life at court kept me away from her most of the day, but I did do my best to be the one to put her to bed every night. Tonight, heat clung to my body and fever burned my skin, yet I refused to let it affect our little ritual. Six years after my wedding to Philippe, she was our only living child, and I treasured every moment with her.

"Why are you whispering?" she mumbled, drawing me from my distracted thoughts.

"I wasn't certain you were still listening, *mon amour*," I said.

"I am," she replied. "But you have to read again the part when her godmother makes her a dress with magic, because I didn't hear it well."

I took a sip from a glass of water left by a thoughtful maid and obediently resumed my reading. Outside the open windows, the night grew darker, but the *château*'s lights turned the sprawling building into a beacon, the stars in the clear skies muted. In the story, Cinderella lost her slipper on the castle's steps, and as ever when we reached this part of the tale, Marie-Louise fidgeted.

She didn't like the hopelessness of that moment, and I kept an eye on her as I read the next paragraph, watching out for tears and already poised to skip ahead.

The nursery door creaked open. I startled, but Marie-Louise only straightened, her eyes wide and her expression intent. Philippe tiptoed in with exaggerated care.

"My ladies." He sank in a deep bow. "I apologize for disturbing you. I'm looking for two beautiful princesses, one of whom is very, very tiny."

Marie-Louise's face lit up with glee. "Father!" she squealed.

She launched herself off the sofa to throw her arms around him. Philippe lifted her with a laugh, and planted loud kisses on her cheeks. I relaxed my stance in my seat, as Marie-Louise whispered secrets in her father's ear and played with the ribbons of his lavish coat.

When she was born, and the magical glow in her eyes hadn't faded, marking her as a *magicienne*, Philippe had let out a sigh.

"Oh well," he'd said with a resigned smile.

Those two words, more than the jovial mask he'd promptly put on, had betrayed his thoughts: He'd hoped his child would be like a piece of him in the world, but his daughter was showing more similarities with his brother and his late mother. My reassurances had failed to comfort him at the time, but a few years later, Marie-Louise was already demonstrating she was her father's daughter more than anything else. Her features were mine, yes, but her personality, much like her dark hair, were very much inherited from Philippe.

"What story was *Maman* reading?" he asked, settling down

next to me with Marie-Louise in his lap. The smell of his perfume mixed with the night air, strong and soothing.

"*Cinderella*," she said. "She's lost her shoe and the prince is trying to find her."

Philippe gave me a conspiratorial look. "My favorite part! The handsome prince is coming to save the day. Sounds *oddly* familiar."

I rolled my eyes above our daughter's head. "Does it? Because I only recall the princess saving the d—"

He bent down and his lips landed on mine, his kiss silencing me. The book slipped from my hands, caught by Marie-Louise before it could land on the carpet. I drew away from Philippe with a half-hearted glare. His eyes sparkled with mischief. I turned back to our daughter.

"Shall I read the ending?"

Her expression turned eager. "Can we show Father the new trick first?"

Philippe raised an inquisitive eyebrow, which Marie-Louise took as an assent. She jumped off his lap and shot off toward the nearest vase of flowers. When her magical skills became apparent at birth, I resolved one thing: My daughter wouldn't grow up like I had, her gift kept secret and untrained. For as long as I lived, I would help her hone her skills as a *magicienne* and become a young woman unafraid of her powers and her fate.

And so even if tiredness weighed down my limbs and my breaths were shallow, I would gladly answer her call and show Philippe the latest enchantment she'd learned.

Her little feet tapping on the parquet floor, she rushed back to my side, a handful of fallen petals cradled in her cupped hands.

"Look," she told her father. "It's very easy."

"Easy for you, sweetheart," Philippe corrected her, his tone so gentle she didn't notice his comment.

Intent on her goal, she stood before me with her hands held out, her face a picture of focus. "Now, *Maman*."

I clasped my hands around hers, took in a breath, and whispered the spell. "*Apparais*."

In my mind's eye, the glittery magic left my core and coalesced into my palms, before transferring to my daughter's hands to soak the petals. Thousands of brilliant particles swirling in her cupped fingers, the enchantment shaped the remains of the flowers into a new, shiny thing devised by her. Although Marie-Louise was right—it was only an illusion spell—it wasn't the simplest one, and it delighted me that she had already mastered it.

The spell ended, and the magic dispersed into thin air as I withdrew my hands to allow my daughter to open hers. A colorful butterfly flapped its wings in her palms, before taking flight in a graceful arc above our heads. Marie-Louise let out a delightful cry.

"Look, look!"

Her gaze, bright with magic and wonder, followed the tiny creature as it fluttered about the room, its vibrant body catching the candlelight.

"It's a butterfly, Father, can you see?"

"I can see, sweetheart," Philippe said.

Although he smiled at her, there was wistfulness in his tone. Magic was something only she and I could share, and despite her efforts to include him in our enchanted experiments, he remained forever excluded from such experience, amazed by her talent yet unable to fully understand it.

I gripped his fingers, forcing his mind back to us. "It's just an illusion," I reminded him in a low tone, while our daughter chased after the butterfly she'd let loose into the world. "She's just happy to show you what she's been doing. In a couple of years it'll be her riding skills, and later her paintings, or her dance moves."

Amusement returned to Philippe's features. "Oh dear. Don't tell me we're raising a proper lady."

I patted his hand. "Don't worry. We're not raising a lady; we're raising a queen. So I'm also going to have her learn how to swim and shoot the musket. And I'm counting on you to teach her how to cheat at cards and wield a sword."

"Whoever told you I could wield a sword?" Philippe feigned surprise. "I hate weapons, everyone knows that."

This time, it was my turn to place a light kiss on his cheek. "Ah, but I know you better than *everyone*."

"Can we read the end of the story now?" Marie-Louise popped up before us with her book held out, like an actor appearing on stage with her script in hand.

Philippe grabbed her waist and lifted her onto the sofa, where she snuggled between us and placed the book back in my lap. But the spell had drawn upon my last strengths, and exhaustion now tugged at me. Reading my expression, Philippe took Perrault's book with a conniving nod.

"How about I read the end of the tale?" He leafed through the pages, until he found the correct passage. "So the prince was looking for his bride, was he?"

Marie-Louise nodded, her thumb back in her mouth. Philippe wrapped his arm around my shoulders and started reading, his low voice steady and calm in the quiet evening. Thanks to the lost slipper, Cinderella was recognized as the mysterious princess, and returned to the prince, who promptly married her. Soothed by Philippe's voice, my body unwound and my mind wandered.

Was it really six years since I walked down the aisle in the chapel at the Palais-Royal to marry him? It felt like lifetimes ago; it felt like yesterday. The events may seem like distant memories, but the emotions they'd awakened in me remained etched in my soul.

The loneliness of those first weeks at the Tuileries Palace.

The bliss of our swim in the lake at Fontainebleau.

Terror as I held his limp body in my arms at Vaux-le-Vicomte.

Elation at the news of my pregnancy at Saint-Cloud.

Joy and sadness and wonder and fear and delight and anger at Versailles.

Philippe's voice droned on, moving on to the next tale in the book. A maid glided into the nursery to close the windows, her footsteps silent. As the last panel swung shut, Marie-Louise's butterfly fluttered out, before dissolving into a burst of sparkling glitter behind the glass. Engrossed in her fairy tale, my daughter didn't notice. The maid left. Around us, the gilded walls of the palace enveloped us like a cocoon.

Six years ago, a prophecy had foretold my death, I had agreed to an arranged marriage in a foreign court and been told to forget about happiness. World-changing fates and illustrious legacies were what royals could expect instead.

Yet as I sat in the heart of the Palace of Versailles with my daughter and my husband at my side, I felt at peace with our own form of happiness. My own legacy might not be as celebrated as others', but it was right here: a girl who would be queen, a love that endured, and a spark of magic in the dark night.

HISTORICAL NOTES

———————————

This is a work of fiction, and most of this story was born of my imagination. However, it is based on historical facts, and the reader might be surprised to find that some of the most outlandish events mentioned here actually happened.

The French court of the Sun King Louis XIV was rife with intrigue: Courtiers schemed out of love, ambition, or greed. They kept diaries, exchanged letters, and gossiped endlessly. A lot went on in the salons and behind the closed doors of private apartments, and everything was recorded in one manner or another. Nothing remained secret for long.

Most of the events used in this story occurred between 1662 and 1668. The "Spanish-letter plot" occurred in 1662. Louise fled to the Chaillot convent, where she was pursued by Louis on horseback, in the spring of 1664. The Pleasures of the Enchanted Island took place a few weeks later. Anne d'Autriche died in January 1666. The Grand Royal Entertainment was staged in July 1668.

Athénaïs de Montespan usurped Louise de La Vallière sometime between November 1666 and July 1667. She remained the king's mistress for fifteen years and gave him seven children. The infamous Affair of the Poisons brought about her downfall. It also brought down Olympe de Soissons, who left court and lived an adventurous life in exile.

The Chevalier de Lorraine didn't stay banished for long. He spent a few years in Italy, then returned to court, where he lived a turbulent existence at Philippe's side for the next thirty years.

Armand, on the other hand, left court after Henriette's death to join the army again. He died in 1673, aged thirty-six. Did he and Henriette have an affair? The question divided the French court in the seventeenth century, and it still divides historians today. I choose to think that their passionate friendship remained platonic. I like to think of them as kindred spirits, too flamboyant and alive to be reduced to one narrative.

Nicolas Fouquet remained imprisoned in the Alpine fortress of Pignerol for the rest of his life. Interestingly, another famous prisoner was kept there at that time: an anonymous captive known by the nickname of "the Man in the Iron Mask."

Louis was king of France for seventy-two years, making him the longest reigning monarch in French history, and one of the most famous. The absolute monarchy he strove to build went on after his death, until the French Revolution some seventy-five years later. To this day, the Palace of Versailles still stands on the outskirts of Paris.

This is a novel, and for the sake of intelligibility, some historical figures who played critical roles at the Sun King's French court don't appear in those pages: the notorious Marquis de Vardes, whose deeds I attributed here to Lorraine; the equally infamous Mademoiselle de Montalais, and Mademoiselle de la Mothe, whom I pushed aside in favor of Athénaïs.

Including Charles Perrault's fairy tales in this book was a choice on my part as well, as it's a historical inaccuracy: they weren't published until the 1690s. However, they are so intricately linked with the story of Versailles that I thought it important to mention them.

For clarity's sake, I also chose to limit the number of settings in this story. In the 1660s, the French court was still itinerant—constantly moving between Paris (the Louvre Palace, the Palais-Royal), Saint-Germain-en-Laye, Fontainebleau, and Versailles. The latter became the permanent residence of the king and his court only in 1682, and the Hall of Mirrors wasn't opened until 1684. As a result, Henriette never saw Versailles completed, and she never lived there.

Henriette and Philippe had three children together. Marie-Louise, known as Mademoiselle, was born in 1662. She looked like her mother but had her father's dark hair. She was always Philippe's favorite child. At seventeen she became queen of Spain. Philippe-Charles was born in 1664 but died two years later. Anne-Marie was born in 1669 and later became queen of Sardinia.

Henriette died at Saint-Cloud on June 30, 1670. Late in the afternoon, she complained of acute stomach pain. From then on her symptoms worsened, and she succumbed in the middle of the night. She was twenty-six. Her sudden death shocked the whole French court, as she was widely popular and the first of the younger generation to pass away. Soon after her death, rumors of poisoning circulated, and Lorraine was blamed. As she was the king of England's sister, an inquiry and an autopsy were ordered. Although the report was inconclusive at the time, it is detailed enough to allow modern doctors to establish she died of natural causes (likely peritonitis).

At her funeral, Bishop Bossuet gave a eulogy that remains

famous in France to this day. The shocking opening sentence—
"Madame se meurt, Madame est morte . . ." (Madame is dying,
Madame is dead . . .)—still strikes the imagination, and encom-
passes the impact her unexpected death had on her contempo-
raries. Eighteen months after her death, Philippe was forced by
Louis to remarry for political reasons.

History isn't kind to women, and by many standards
Henriette is a minor historical figure. Although the daughter
of a king (England's Charles I), the sister of a king (England's
Charles II), and the sister-in-law of a king (France's Louis XIV),
she wasn't a queen herself, and she didn't give birth to any kings.
In most history books, she is a footnote, often described as a
coquette who may or may not have seduced her brother-in-law and
her husband's lover.

Despite all this, the reason we know so much about her is
because her friend, the French writer Madame de La Fayette,
wrote her biography. Titled *Histoire de Madame Henriette
d'Angleterre*, it was first published posthumously in 1720. It is
one of the best accounts of life at the Sun King's court, and it is
still in print today.

As she died young, only a few portraits of Henriette remain.
To my knowledge, two can be found at Versailles. One hangs
at Vaux-le-Vicomte. One is in the Scottish National Portrait
Gallery in Edinburgh. In the latter, a very large portrait painted
just after her wedding in 1661, she wears an incredible gown of
velvet fleur-de-lis, and her beauty radiates from the canvas. She
stares at the onlooker, a mysterious smile on her lips. She looks
like a girl with secrets.

ACKNOWLEDGMENTS

———

I am very grateful to everyone who helped bring this book to life:

My editor, Liz Szabla, and the amazing team at Feiwel & Friends—US Macmillan, for understanding the heart of this story and working unbelievably hard to get it into readers' hands.

My agent, Carrie Pestritto, and everyone at Laura Dail Literary, for supporting me and my writing every step of the way.

My friends and early readers, for your help in promoting *In the Shadow of the Sun*, and for your enthusiasm for this sequel: Rachel Fenn, Jessica Rubinkowski, Katie Bucklein, Sarah Glenn Marsh, Kalyn Josephson, Rachel O'Laughlin, Jennifer Gruenke, Kat Ellis, Erin Bledsoe, Leta R. Patton, Julie Eshbaugh, and Stacey Lee. Writing and getting this duology published has been an amazing journey, and I'm very grateful to you for helping me along the way.

My friends Séverine, Justine, and Clémentine, for letting me share my passion for Versailles with you.

Last but not least, everyone who picked up and read *In the Shadow of the Sun*: you made writing this sequel so much easier. Thank you.

Thank you for reading this Feiwel and Friends book.

The friends who made

UNDER A STARLIT SKY

possible are:

JEAN FEIWEL, *Publisher*

LIZ SZABLA, *Associate Publisher*

RICH DEAS, *Senior Creative Director*

MALLORY GRIGG, *Art Director*

HOLLY WEST, *Senior Editor*

ANNA ROBERTO, *Senior Editor*

KAT BRZOZOWSKI, *Senior Editor*

ALEXEI ESIKOFF, *Senior Managing Editor*

TAYLOR PITTS, *Production Editor*

KIM WAYMER, *Senior Production Manager*

EMILY SETTLE, *Associate Editor*

ERIN SIU, *Assistant Editor*

FOYINSI ADEGBONMIRE, *Editorial Assistant*